THE GOOD SOLDIER

THE GOOD SOLDIER

A TALE OF PASSION

Ford Madox Ford

edited by Kenneth Womack and William Baker

broadview literary texts

National Library of Canada Cataloguing in Publication

Ford, Ford Madox, 1873-1939
    The good soldier : a tale of passion/ Ford Madox Ford ; edited by Kenneth Womack and William Baker.

(Broadview literary texts)
Includes bibliographical references.
ISBN 1-55111-381-3

I. Womack, Kenneth II. Baker, William, 1944– III. Title. IV. Series.

PR6011.053G66 2002   813'.52   C2002-904904-0

Broadview Press Ltd. is an independent, international publishing house, incorporated in 1985. Broadview believes in shared ownership, both with its employees and with the general public; since the year 2000 Broadview shares have traded publicly on the Toronto Venture Exchange under the symbol BDP.

We welcome comments and suggestions regarding any aspect of our publications—please feel free to contact us at the addresses below or at broadview@broadviewpress.com.

North America
PO Box 1243, Peterborough, Ontario, Canada K9J 7H5
3576 California Road, Orchard Park, NY, USA 14127
Tel: (705) 743-8990; Fax: (705) 743-8353
email: customerservice@broadviewpress.com

UK, Ireland, and continental Europe
Thomas Lyster Ltd., Units 3 & 4a, Old Boundary Way
Burscough Road, Ormskirk
Lancashire, L39 2YW
Tel: (01695) 575112; Fax: (01695) 570120
email: books@tlyster.co.uk

Australia and New Zealand
UNIREPS, University of New South Wales
Sydney, NSW, 2052
Tel: 61 2 9664 0999; Fax: 61 2 9664 5420
email: info.press@unsw.edu.au

www.broadviewpress.com

Broadview Press Ltd. gratefully acknowledges the financial support of the Government of Canada through the Book Publishing Industry Development Program for our publishing activities.

This book is printed on acid-free paper containing 30% post-consumer fibre.

Eco-Logo Certified
30 % Post.

Series editor: Professor L.W. Conolly
Advisory editor for this volume: Michel Pharand

PRINTED IN CANADA

Contents

Acknowledgments • 6

Introduction • 7

Ford Madox Ford: A Brief Chronology • 19

The Good Soldier: A Narrative Chronology • 23

A Note on the Text • 26

The Good Soldier: A Tale of Passion • 27
   Dedicatory Letter to Stella Ford (1927) • 29

Appendix A: Ford Madox Ford, "On Heaven" • 232

Appendix B: Ford Madox Ford, excerpts from *Henry James:
       A Critical Study* • 246

Appendix C: Ford Madox Ford, "On Impressionism" • 260

Appendix D: Contemporary Reviews • 281

Appendix E: Ford Madox Ford, "Techniques" • 293

Appendix F: F.L. Cross, "Anglo-Catholicism and the Twentieth
       Century" • 309

Appendix G: H.C. Allen, from *Great Britain and the United
       States: A History of Anglo-American Relations,
       1783–1952* • 337

Appendix H: Ezra Pound, Obituary for Ford Madox
       Ford • 360

Select Bibliography • 364

Acknowledgments

We would like to thank the many friends and colleagues who assisted us in seeing this edition through its production, including Carole Bookhamer, Will Bush, Dianne L. Carson, Todd F. Davis, James M. Decker, Suzanne Kimmen, Graham Law, Thomas R. Liszka, Adam J. Locke, Matt Masucci, Amanda L. Moore, Corinda K. Moore, Candace Stitt, Michael W. Wolfe, Andrea E. Womack, and Andrew Womack. We are also indebted to the world of Ford scholarship—particularly Thomas C. Moser, Max Saunders, and Martin Stannard, and Joseph Wiesenfarth—whose erudition and fine studies of Ford Madox Ford's life and work helped make this edition possible. We are grateful to Don LePan, Barbara Conolly, Leonard Conolly, Judith Earnshaw, Julia Gaunce, Mical Moser, Michel Pharand and all of the staff at Broadview Press for their encouragement and advice throughout this project.

Kenneth Womack would like to thank Kjell Meling, Associate Dean and Director of Academic Affairs, and the Altoona College Advisory Board for their assistance in the form of a courseload reduction. William Baker would like to thank his colleagues in the Department of English and University Libraries at Northern Illinois University for granting him release time from teaching and other duties, as well as for their sympathetic understanding and appreciation of his scholarly needs.

Introduction

Ford Madox Ford claims that he began composing *The Good Soldier* on 17 December 1913, his fortieth birthday. Remarkably, he had been thinking about writing the novel "for fully another decade." In 1929, he told Allen Tate that "he had had the entire novel—every sentence—in his head before he began to write it in 1913" (Saunders, I, 400). Tate attributed this aspect of *The Good Soldier's* composition to the fact that Ford "had the most prodigious memory I have ever encountered in any man. And *The Good Soldier*," he added, "is not only his masterpiece, but in my view the masterpiece of British fiction in this century." In his 1927 dedicatory letter, Ford claimed that he intended to title the novel *The Saddest Story*, only to see that title discarded by his publisher in favor of a more commercially viable one for England's prewar climate. For Ford, *The Good Soldier* represented his "great auk's egg"—the literary masterwork into which he would put "*all* that I knew about writing." Published by John Lane and the Bodley Head in London on 17 March 1915, the novel embodied far more than the epitome of Ford's writerly knowledge—although it certainly accomplished that feat in magisterial fashion. Completed in July 1914 and partially serialized in an issue of Wyndham Lewis's *Blast*, *The Good Soldier* was a novel over which Ford "sweated real drops of sweat and shed real drops of tears" (Mizener 253). Graham Greene later wrote that "one cannot help wondering what agonies of frustration and error lay behind *The Good Soldier*" (Saunders, I, 402). Indeed, when Ford began composing the novel in 1913, his personal life lay in a shambles—his relationship with Violet Hunt was faltering, he was experiencing recurring bouts of neurasthenia, and he felt abandoned by his literary friends during a time of great public embarrassment and acrimony. For Ford, life truly was "all a darkness," to borrow a phrase from John Dowell, *The Good Soldier's* hapless narrator.

Born in Fair Lawn Villas, Merton, Surrey, on 17 December 1873, Ford was christened Ford Hermann Hueffer by his parents, Francis Hueffer and Catherine Madox Brown. A journalist and the recipient of a doctorate in philology from the University of Göttingen, his father settled in England in 1869 after emigrating from Germany. He later wrote and edited a number of books himself and was appointed as the music critic for the *Times* in 1879. As the daughter of Pre-Raphaelite painter Ford Madox Brown, Ford's mother possessed equally, if not more impressive cultural credentials. Characterized by a peculiar combination of artistic refinement and mental oppression, Ford's childhood afforded him the opportunity to grow up in a cultured circle that included the children of such luminaries as William Rossetti, the husband of his maternal Aunt Lucy, and Richard Garnett. Yet Ford would never forget his father's proclamation that he was the family's "patient but extremely stupid donkey" (Mizener 5), an epithet that would engender a lifetime's worth of feelings of inadequacy and low self-esteem. Ford later described his youth as a period of severe "moral torture" (Mizener 5). Perhaps even more significantly, the early death of Ford's father of a heart attack in January 1889 left the Hueffers in desperate financial straits and unable to fund his university education. During this era, Ford fell under the influence of his grandfather, Ford Madox Brown, whose rashness, inherent geniality, and fierce independence left an indelible mark on his grandson. The elderly painter "was the finest man I ever knew," according to Ford. "He had his irascibilities, his fits of passion when, tossing his white head, his mane of hair would fly all over his face, and when he would blaspheme impressively after the manner of our great grandfathers." Ford later lamented that "I would give much of what I possess to be able ... to live once more some of those old evenings in [his] studio." (Mizener 14) While Ford Madox Brown was notably ineffectual in his business and financial practices, he believed deeply in the power of genius and the creative significance of artistic craftsmanship—qualities that would impinge upon Ford's own commitment to the seriousness and value of the novel as a literary form.

After a brief stint at London's University College School, Ford spent much of this era carousing with the youthful intelligentsia, particularly Edward Garnett, and spending his afternoons at the British Museum. Ford's idle existence came to a sudden conclusion in 1891 with the publication of his first book, *The Brown Owl*, a collection of fairy stories. Buoyed by the volume's success, he quickly produced two more fairy narratives, *The Feather*

(1892) and *The Queen Who Flew* (1894). While Ford later wrote that "the stories are about Princes and Princesses and such twaddle" (Mizener 17), his love of children and the imaginative potential of the fairy stories motivated their composition.

During the summer of 1892, Ford began courting Elsie Martindale, whose family he visited regularly at their home in Winchelsea. After a European tour in which he visited relatives in Germany and France, Ford proposed to Elsie in October 1892. His courtship of her during the early 1890s illustrates the romantic outbursts and infatuations that would mark much of his adult life. On topics ranging from literature to religion to suicidal threats, Ford's letters to Elsie during this period demonstrate the manner in which fits of romantic passion would suddenly—and with great permanency—alter the direction of his life. "You," Ford wrote to Elsie in one instance, "are my friend because to you alone I can talk with a feeling of perfect ease and your ideas alone fit mine" (Mizener 22). When Elsie's parents refused to recognize their engagement because of Ford's literary background and his questionable future prospects, the young couple eloped and married in Gloucester on 17 May 1894. Sadly, Ford and Elsie's marriage was rarely a happy union, as the Martindales subsequently threatened legal action to dissolve it. Ford and Elsie suffered from a variety of financial difficulties, and Ford soon became depressed over his inability to establish himself as a writer.

In September 1898, Edward Garnett introduced Ford to Joseph Conrad. Their relationship would, simply put, change the course of Ford's artistic career, as well as irrevocably alter his theory of the novel as a literary genre. As a young writer, Ford approached his association with the older, established author with an understandable degree of trepidation. Ford later remembered coming upon Conrad rather unexpectedly in London, where he saw "an old, shrunken, wizened man, in an unbrushed bowler, and ancient burst-seamed overcoat, one wrist wrapped in flannel, the other hand helping him to lean on a hazel walking-stick, cut from a hedge and prepared at home" (Mizener 41–42). Conrad "had in one tortured eye a round piece of dirty window-glass." The origins of their eventual collaboration remain difficult to ascertain. Clearly, a professional relationship with Conrad provided Ford with the opportunity to work with a writer who possessed enormous creative gifts, while Conrad found in Ford a valuable source of moral and psychological support. Of Polish descent, Conrad confronted numerous linguistic and cultural obstacles during his years in England. According to Ford, "I was useful to Conrad as writer and as man in a great many subordinate ways during his early days of struggle and deep poverty" (Mizener 46). He carried out Conrad's "literary dustings and sweepings, correcting his proofs, writing from his dictation, suggesting words when he was at a loss, or bringing to his memory incidents that he had forgotten" (Mizener 46). Their decade-long collaboration produced three largely undistinguished novels, *The Inheritors* (1901), *Romance* (1903), and *The Nature of a Crime* (1909), yet their creative relationship completely altered the nature of Ford's aesthetic. Although he would later exaggerate his success in comparison to Conrad's significant place in the twentieth-century fictive canon, Ford admitted that his association with Conrad "was fortunate for me I am sure, for if I know anything of how to write almost the whole of that knowledge was acquired then" (Mizener 48).

Perhaps most importantly, Ford's collaboration allowed the two writers to develop a common theory of the novel that involves a dynamic narrative voice in collusion with concrete notions of literary character and irony of situation. While his relationship with Conrad hardly yielded the critical and commercial successes of which he dreamed, it nevertheless afforded him the ambition for embarking upon his *Fifth Queen* trilogy, which included *The Fifth Queen* (1906), *Privy Seal* (1907), and *The Fifth Queen Crowned* (1908). In addition to working at a phenomenally productive rate during this era, Ford began editing *The English Review*, which, during his tenure from December 1908 to January 1910, featured such writers as H.G. Wells, Thomas Hardy, John Galsworthy, Henry James, and D.H. Lawrence, among others. His intent had been to establish *The English Review* "with the definite design of giving imaginative literature a chance in England" (Mizener 154). To that end, the journal was a substantial success. Yet by the end of the decade, Ford's financial mismanagement left the periodical in ruin; *The English Review*'s high standards nevertheless provide convincing testimony to his commitment to the artistic excellence of his day.

Ford's troubled marriage reached its tragic nadir at this time after his disastrous affair with his wife's sister, Mary Martindale, during the early years of the new century. Following the onset of a bout with depression during this era, Ford witnessed the demise of his creative relationship with Conrad, as well as recurring instances of severe guilt and agoraphobia. In March 1907, Ford met Violet Hunt, the daughter of an Oxford fellow at Corpus Christi College and noted watercolorist. An established novelist in her own right, Hunt became Ford's lover in June 1909 after his separation from Elsie and following his threats of suicide. He subsequently thanked her for "the tenderness that has saved one's reason and one's life" (Mizener 179).

Ford could hardly have been prepared for the social and legal acrimony that accompanied his new relationship with Hunt. Refusing to grant Ford a divorce, Elsie inaugurated a series of legal actions that threw him into another bout of depression and personal turmoil. In January 1910, for example, Elsie petitioned Ford for the restitution of her conjugal rights. At one juncture, Ford spent eight days in Brixton Gaol for ignoring a court order to pay support money to Elsie. In October 1911, a false report that Ford had secured a German divorce and married Hunt appeared in the *Daily Mirror*. Elsie threatened the newspaper with legal action until they published a retraction and paid damages. Elsie later successfully sued *Throne* magazine for referring to Hunt as "Mrs. Hueffer." Elsie's legal recriminations succeeded in thwarting Ford's efforts at achieving public recognition for his relationship with Hunt. Yet despite his public and private woes, he published a number of works during this period, including such novels as *The Simple Life Limited* (1911), *The Panel* (1912), *The Desirable Alien* (1913; with Hunt), and *Mr. Fleight* (1913). He also published two works of literary criticism, including *The Critical Attitude* (1911) and *Henry James: A Critical Study* (1913) [see Appendix B]. In November 1913, Ford secured a publisher for his *Collected Poems* in exchange for a much-needed advance. During that same year, his legal and financial dilemmas finally caught up with him and he was forced into bankruptcy court.

It was in precisely such a desultory state that Ford prepared to compose the novel that would become his universally acknowledged masterpiece. Shortly before beginning to write

The Good Soldier, Ford acceded to Hunt's pleas to compose a poem about the possibility of a spiritual heaven. "You say you believe in a heaven," she reportedly told him. "I wish you'd write one for me. I want no beauty, I want no damned optimism; I want just a plain, workaday heaven that I can go to some day and enjoy it when I'm there" (Mizener 245). Soon thereafter, Ford produced "On Heaven" [see Appendix A], which he dedicated to "V.H., who asked for a working Heaven." Clearly, Ford himself—like the perpetually bewildered Dowell, the *Good Soldier's* narrator—dreamed of his own earthly nirvana where he could pursue his craft with his beloved by his side: "Is there any terrestrial paradise where, amidst the whispering of the olive-leaves, people can be with whom they like and have what they like and take their ease in shadows and in coolness?" Forty years of age and with his public and private lives in absolute disarray, Ford seemed utterly unprepared to write the novel that would make his name. Yet a knowing Ezra Pound—in a letter of August 1913 to Alice Corbin Henderson, the Associate Editor of *Poetry*—viewed Ford as a literary giant among what ultimately amounted to an unprecedented generation of literary giants. "About Hueffer, he is still playing about," Pound wrote. "But he has it in him to be the most important prose author in England, before he shuffles off, after James and Hardy have departed, etc." (Saunders, I, 401).

For many of Ford's critics, *The Good Soldier* indeed proved to be the moment when he harnessed the creative powers that he had nurtured for so long, when he finally put the theory of the novel that he had developed with Conrad into action. Many critics ascribe the genesis of the novel to *The Spirit of the People* (1907), the third volume in Ford's trilogy on the sociological nuances of Englishness. Ford devotes particular attention in *The Spirit of the People* to the manner in which Englishmen stereotypically suppress their emotions to their own—as well as to their friends' and relations'—detriment. In one instance, Ford offers an anecdote about a married couple, whom he refers to as "good people." The husband had developed a romantic attachment with their ward, a young woman who dies in Brindisi after parting company with the couple. The would-be lovers' discussion of trivial matters prior to their separation made an indelible impression on Ford. Written during the awful, foreboding years before the First World War, *The Good Soldier*, in many ways, signals the demise of the Edwardian gentleman, a good soldier of sorts whose own characteristic emotional reticence functions as a kind of silent, unrewarded virtue. Aptly described by David Gorman as a "masterpiece of concentration," *The Good Soldier* evinces Ford's theoretical approach to the novel as an "impressionistic" phenomenon. In his essay, "On Impressionism" [see Appendix C], Ford instructs his readers to remember "always [to] consider the impressions that you are making upon the mind of the reader, and always consider that the first impression with which you present him will be so strong that it will be all that you can ever do to efface it, to alter it or even quite slightly to modify it."

The Good Soldier deftly operates upon a series of impressionistic layers of its own. Ford's construction of these narrative levels in the novel is, for many critics, *The Good Soldier*'s great achievement. By depicting Dowell in the act of telling his story in all of its perplexing proportions—and then having his narrator reconsider these very same issues from varying temporal vantage points—Ford succeeds in demonstrating the ways in which a rich American Quaker finds himself utterly ill-equipped to traverse his own confounding subterranean levels of emotion because of the layers upon layers of acculturated personal reserve that shield him from the world. In *Henry James: A Critical Study*, Ford discusses the very same dilemmas that confront his baffled narrator in *The Good Soldier*. In the most complex of fictions, Ford writes, "the mind passes, as it does in real life, perpetually backwards and forwards between the apparent aspect of things and the essentials of life" (Ford 153). Clearly, for Dowell, the "apparent aspect of things" becomes distorted and impenetrable. His leisured existence and sheltered upbringing leave him entirely unequipped to comprehend the emotional rhythms of human discourse and interrelationships. As he observes in *Henry James: A Critical Study*, the novelist's mission—particularly in a highly personal and revealing work such as *The Good Soldier*—involves the creation of nuanced and realistic representations of life. "That, you know, is what life really is," Ford writes, "a series of such meaningless episodes beneath the shadow of doom—or of impending bliss, if you prefer it" (155).

In the novel, one of the more interesting subtexts of Dowell's narrative concerns the *way* in which he tells his story. Rather than having Dowell compose his narrative in simple chronological fashion, Ford replicates the peculiarly human machinery of his narrator's mind by allowing him to tell his story in a deliberately fragmented manner:

> I have, I am aware, told this story in a very rambling way so that it may be difficult for anyone to find their path through what may be a sort of maze. I cannot help it. I have stuck to my idea of being in a country cottage with a silent listener, hearing between the gusts of the wind and amidst the noises of the distant sea, the story as it comes. And, when one discusses an affair—a long, sad affair—one goes back, one goes forward. One remembers points that one has forgotten and one explains them all the more minutely since one recognizes that one has forgotten to mention them in their proper places and that one may have given, by omitting them, a false impression. I console myself with thinking that this is a real story and that, after all, real stories are probably told best in the way a person telling a story would tell them. They will then seem most real.

Self-consciously attempting to challenge the generic boundaries of the novel in *The Good Soldier*, Ford employs such passages in an effort to provide Dowell's narrative with a kind of verisimilitude that illustrates the complex meanderings of the human memory. As Graham Greene astutely remarked, "the impression which will be left most strongly on the reader is the sense of Ford's involvement. A novelist is not a vegetable absorbing nourishment mechanically from soil and air: material is not easily or painlessly gained" (Saunders, I, 402). One of *The Good Soldier*'s greatest strengths is the way in which Ford's profound emphasis upon technique in the novel never overwhelms its other, perhaps even more significant, attempts at telling Dowell's sad story. In his 1935 essay on "Techniques" (see Appendix E), Ford differentiates between traditional novels that merely make "statements," and more innovative narratives that awaken the reader's senses by building "suggestions of happenings on suggestions of happenings." Hence, Ford's realistic narrative technique affords his readers with a form of discrepant awareness that allows us to encounter the events of the novel in concert with Dowell's discoveries of the truth about his wife Florence's infidelities, the exact circumstances of her death, and Edward Ashburnham's mind-numbing duplicity, among a host of narrative cruxes. As Arthur Mizener observes in *The Saddest Story: A Biography of Ford Madox Ford* (1971), "The ironic wit of *The Good Soldier*'s style depends, not on a discrepancy between the narrator's attitude and Ford's, but on a discrepancy between Dowell's attitude as a participant in the events and Dowell's attitude as a narrator of them" (Mizener 265).

In addition to providing Ford with the means for exploring such themes as the confounding machinations of the human heart, the slippery ethical concept of "good people," and the cultural dilemmas of early twentieth-century Anglo-Catholicism (see Appendix F), the narrative of *The Good Soldier* deftly examines the peculiar relationship between Americans and their British counterparts during the Edwardian era (see Appendix G). As Henry James achieves with his much-heralded "international theme" in such works as *Daisy Miller* (1878) and *The Portrait of a Lady* (1881), Ford infuses *The Good Soldier* with an international quality when he juxtaposes the novel's four principal characters—Edward and Leonora Ashburnham, the aristocratic and seemingly cultured Europeans, and John and Florence Dowell, the ostensibly naïve, nouveau-riche Americans. The results of the two couples' international communion are telling indeed, with Dowell, the novel's decidedly unaware and often unreliable narrator, enjoying the ineffectual life of the newly rich American gentleman and his wife Florence fulfilling Ford's vision of the strange combination of bold and obtrusive attributes that often symbolize American vanity. Dowell reveals this aspect of Florence's character when he remarks upon her strange romantic pursuit of Ashburnham: "She cut out poor dear Edward from sheer vanity; she meddled between him and Leonora from a sheer, imbecile spirit of district visiting. Do you understand that, whilst she was Edward's mistress, she was perpetually trying to reunite him to his wife? She would gabble on to Leonora about forgiveness—treating the subject from the bright, American point of view. And Leonora would treat her like the whore she was." In sharp contrast with her audacious American counterpart, Leonora exemplifies stereotypically European qualities of fortitude and restraint, bravely weathering Edward's infidelities with Mrs. Basil and La Dolciquita, among numerous others. All the while, Edward represents the stereotypical landed English gentleman, a calm and sentimental good soldier.

Max Saunders, one of Ford's biographers, describes the novel as "Ford's most sustained virtuoso performance." For Saunders, none of Ford's other works "has the same pitch of technical intensity and tortuous inevitability" as *The Good Soldier* (Saunders, I, 402). The novel hardly earned for Ford any substantial critical or commercial success, however, and received mixed reviews in the popular and academic press alike upon its publication—from Rebecca West's exaltation of *The Good Soldier's* "extreme beauty and wisdom" to Theodore Dreiser's derision of the novel's "encrusting formalism" (see Appendix D). Ford's life after the novel's publication likewise continued in its tortured progress through illness, depression, and ineffectual romance. In August 1915, he escaped from the traumas of his public and private lives by enlisting in the British army. A company officer for the British Expeditionary Force in France during the war, Ford rarely saw combat, although he did engage in various verbal spats with his superiors. After receiving a concussion from an exploding shell, Ford suffered another nervous breakdown. His protracted psychological and physical recovery forced him to spend the duration of the war in England. Now estranged from Violet Hunt, Ford met Stella Bowen, an Australian painter, while on military leave. In June 1919, they moved into Red Ford cottage deep in the Sussex countryside, where they grew vegetables and raised livestock. Also in 1919, he legally changed his name to Ford Madox Ford at the urging of his current publisher, who reportedly claimed that "if you'd sign your books 'Ford' I might be able to sell the beastly things" (Peterson 114).

In November 1922, Ford and Stella relocated to Paris, where he hoped, rather ambitiously, to assume his rightful place within the French literary scene. During this period, his brief editorship of the *Transatlantic Review* resulted in the publication of experimental works by Ezra Pound and e. e. cummings. Ford also published a noteworthy fragment of James Joyce's *Finnegans Wake* as "Work in Progress," the title that the Irish novelist would adopt until the novel's publication in 1939. Ford's relationship with Stella began to falter in the mid-1920s, especially after his affairs with novelist Jean Rhys and Rene Wright. His time in Paris is most notable for the composition of his most ambitious work, the tetralogy of novels entitled *Parade's End* (1924–28). Originally published as four novels—*Some Do Not, No More Parades, A Man Could Stand Up*, and *Last Post*—*Parade's End* traces the war- and peace-time experiences of Christopher Tietjens, the hero of the tetralogy who finds his Edwardian values of duty and loyalty shattered by the awful human tragedy of the Great War. In *Parade's End*, Ford deftly explores the nuances of literary realism, while simultaneously experimenting with the technique of Impressionist "rendering" that he had contemplated with great frequency in his nonfiction. Ford imagined writing a novel "on an immense scale, a little cloudy in immediate attack, but with the salient points and the final impression extraordinarily clear. I wanted the Novelist in fact to appear in his really proud position as historian of his own time" (Bradbury vii–xxviii). Second only in importance in Ford's canon to *The Good Soldier, Parade's End* proved to be his other genuine masterpiece throughout a prodigious literary output that David Dow Harvey's *Ford Madox Ford, 1873–1939: A Bibliography of Works and Criticism* enumerates as including some 81 books, 419 periodical contributions, and 57 miscellaneous contributions to other writers' volumes.

In 1930, Ford met Polish American painter Janice Biala, with whom he moved to Villa Paul at Cape Brun, where he suffered a heart attack in December. During the early years of the 1930s, he published a series of travelogues, additional works of nonfiction, and planned to publish an American trilogy of novels about the postwar world. He would complete only two installments of the trilogy, *The Rash Act* (1933) and *Henry for Hugh* (1934). In 1937, Allen Tate arranged for Ford to assume the position of writer and critic in residence at Michigan's Olivet College, where he worked on his last published work, *The March of Literature* (1938), an intellectual analysis of literary history. In 1938, Olivet College awarded him a doctorate in literature. After suffering a heart attack and battling uremia, Ford pledged to spend the summer in the South of France. He died in Deauville on 26 June 1939 of heart failure. For some years after his death, Ford's literary reputation survived primarily because of his collaborations with Conrad, as well as for his editorships of *The English Review* and *The Transatlantic Review*. In the latter half of the century, however, Ford was recognized as a central literary figure, particularly for his contributions to the development of the novel as a literary form. As Frank MacShane remarks, "Ford has finally emerged, along with Conrad and Lawrence and Joyce, about whom there has never been much doubt, as one of the few important writers" of the twentieth century (16). Clearly, Ford's substantial contemporary reputation in letters owes much to the artistic significance of *The Good Soldier* and *Parade's End*.

Sources Cited in the Introduction

Bradbury, Malcolm. Introduction to Ford Madox Ford, *Parade's End* (New York: Knopf, 1992).

Ford, Ford Madox. *Henry James: A Critical Study* (London: Martin Secker, 1913).

Gorman, David. Lecture, Northern Illinois University, Fall 1992.

MacShane, Frank, ed. *Ford Madox Ford: The Critical Heritage* (London: Routledge and Kegan Paul, 1972).

Mizener, Arthur. *The Saddest Story: A Biography of Ford Madox Ford* (New York: World, 1971).

Peterson, Richard F. "Ford Madox Ford," *Dictionary of Literary Biography*. Volume 34. *British Novelists 1890–1929* (Detroit: Gale Research, 1984).

Saunders, Max. *Ford Madox Ford: A Dual Life* (Oxford: Oxford University Press, 1996).

Ford Madox Ford: A Brief Chronology

1873   Born Ford Hermann Hueffer on 17 December in Merton, Surrey

1881   Attends Praetorius School, Folkestone, Kent

1889   Ford's father, Dr. Francis Hueffer, dies; Ford goes to live with his grandfather, Ford Madox Brown, the Pre-Raphaelite painter; briefly attends University College School, London

1891   *The Brown Owl* (children's fairy-tale) published under the name Ford H. Madox Hueffer

1892   Converts to Roman Catholicism; *The Shifting of the Fire* (novel) published; *The Feather* (children's fairy-tale) published

1893   Ford's grandfather dies; *The Questions at the Well* (poems) published

1894   Ford marries Elsie Martindale on 17 May; takes up residence in southern Kent; *The Queen Flew* (children's fairy-tale) published

1896   *Ford Madox Brown* (biography) published

1897   Daughter Christina is born

1898   Meets Joseph Conrad

1900   Daughter Katharine is born; *Poems for Pictures* and *The Cinque Ports* (history) published

1901   *The Inheritors* (novel, with Conrad) published

1902   *Rossetti* (art criticism) published

1903   *Romance* (novel, with Conrad) published

1904   Travels to Germany to seek a cure for neurasthenia; *The Face of the Night* (poems) published.

1905   *The Soul of London* (essays), *The Benefactor* (novel), and *Hans Holbein* (art criticism) published

1906   Travels to the United States; *The Fifth Queen* (historical romance), *The Heart of the Country* (essays), and *Christina's Fairy Book* (fairy-tales) published

1907   Takes up residence in London; meets Violet Hunt; *Privy Seal* (historical romance), *From Inland* (poems),

An English Girl (novel), *The Pre-Raphaelite Brotherhood* (art criticism), and *The Spirit of the People* (essays) published

1908 Founds *The English Review*; *The Fifth Queen Crowned* (historical romance) and *Mr. Apollo* (fantasy) published

1909 Leaves Elsie Martindale for Violet Hunt; *The Nature of a Crime* (novel, with Conrad) published; *The "Half Moon"* (historical romance) published; loses editorship of *The English Review*

1910 *A Call* (novel), *Songs from London* (poems), and *The Portrait* (historical romance) published

1911 Marriage to Violet Hunt falsely reported in the *Daily Mirror* on 21 October; *The Simple Life Limited* (novel), *Ancient Lights* (reminiscences), *Ladies Whose Bright Eyes* (historical fantasy), and *The Critical Attitude* (criticism) published

1912 *High Germany* (poems), *The Panel* (novel), and *The New Humpty-Dumpty* (novel) published

1913 Ford in Bankruptcy Court; *The Desirable Alien* (novel, with Hunt), *Mr. Fleight* (novel), *The Young Lovell* (historical romance), *Collected Poems*, and *Henry James* (criticism) published

1915 Commissioned as a Second Lieutenant in the Welch Regiment on 14 August; *The Good Soldier* (novel), *When Blood Is Their Argument* (war propaganda), *Between St. Dennis and St. George* (war propaganda), and *Zeppelin Nights* (novel, with Hunt) published

1916 Participates in the Battle of the Somme with the Welch Battalion; reassigned to Wales after collapsing; later hospitalized after returning to Rouen

1917 Meets Stella Bowen in England

1918 *On Heaven* (poems) published

1919 Resigns commission in January; moves in April to Sussex, where he is joined by Stella in June; changes name to Ford Madox Ford

1920 Daughter Julia is born

1921   *A House* (long poem) and *Thus to Revisit* (reminiscences) published

1923   Begins editing *The Transatlantic Review* in December; *The Marsden Case* (novel), *Mr. Bosphorous and the Muses* (pantomime), and *Women and Men* (essays) published

1924   Begins affair with Jean Rhys; travels to the United States; *The Transatlantic Review* ceases publication in November; *Some Do Not* (novel, first installment of *Parade's End*) and *Joseph Conrad* (reminiscences and criticism) published

1925   *No More Parades* (second installment of *Parade's End*) published

1926   *A Mirror to France* (essays) and *A Man Could Stand Up* (third installment of *Parade's End*) published

1927   Separates from Stella Bowen; *New Poems, New York Is Not America* (essays), and *New York Essays* published

1928   *Last Post* (final installment in *Parade's End*) and *A Little Less Than Gods* (historical romance) published

1929   *The English Novel* (criticism) and *No Enemy* (fictionalized autobiography) published

1930   Meets Janice Biala, Polish-American painter

1931   *When the Wicked Man* (novel) and *Return to Yesterday* (reminiscences) published

1933   *The Rash Act* (novel) and *It Was the Nightingale* (reminiscences) published

1934   *Henry for Hugh* (novel) published

1935   *Provence* (travelogue) published

1936   *Vive Le Roy* (novel) and *Collected Poems* published

1937   Appointed writer and critic in residence, Olivet College, Michigan; *Great Trade Route* (travelogue) and *Portraits from Life* (reminiscences and criticism; published in England in 1938 as *Mightier than the Sword*) published

1939   Dies in Deauville, France, on 26 June; *The March of Literature* (criticism) published

FORD MADOX FORD

Ford in 1906. [This photograph is housed in the
Ford Madox Ford Collection at the Cornell University Library.]

The Good Soldier: *A Narrative Chronology*

1868	John Dowell is born
1870 or 1871	Edward Ashburnham is born
1873	Leonora Powys is born
1874	Florence Hurlbird is born
1892?	Edward marries Leonora and they take up residence in Branshaw Teleragh
1894?	Edward becomes embroiled in the Kilsyte case
1895	Edward consorts with La Dolciquita in Monte Carlo and Antibes
1896	Edward and Leonora lease out Branshaw Teleragh and move to India
1896–1904	During their lengthy stay in India, Edward engages Mrs. Basil in a love affair; the Ashburnhams meet the Maidans
1899	On her birthday, August 4th, Florence begins a world tour with her uncle and Jimmy
1900	Florence begins a love affair with Jimmy on August 4th
1901	Dowell marries Florence on August 4th, despite the objections of the Misses Hurlbird; the Dowells set sail for Europe on the *Pocahontas*; Florence continues her affair with Jimmy during her European travels with Dowell
1904	Edward and Leonora return to Branshaw Teleragh in the company of Maisie Maidan; in Bad Nauheim, Florence witnesses Leonora in the act of boxing Maisie's ears, an event that precipitates the fateful meeting between the Dowells and the Ashburnhams
1904	On August 4th, the Dowells and the Ashburnhams visit the town of M—— in order to view Luther's protest; Florence hints at her affair with Edward; Maisie dies of a heart attack later that evening in Nauheim after

eavesdropping on a conversation between
Florence and Edward

1904–13 Florence and Edward conduct a love affair for
nearly a decade, during which time Edward
dispatches with Jimmy after nearly knocking
"Mr. Jimmy's teeth down his throat"; Edward
visits the Dowells in Paris on at least three
occasions in 1905, including one instance in the
company of Leonora

1913 On August 4th, Florence eavesdrops as Edward
confesses his love to Nancy Rufford in
Nauheim; after observing Dowell with
Bagshawe, she commits suicide; Dowell assumes
that she has died of a heart attack; he later
declares his intentions to marry Nancy

1913 On September 1st, the Ashburnhams and Nancy
return to Branshaw Teleragh; Dowell travels to
the United States in order to sort out the
financial complexities of the Hurlbird estate;
in November and December, the Ashburnhams'
domestic bliss with Nancy deteriorates and
Edward decides to send Nancy to India to
live with her father; Edward and Leonora
separately cable Dowell and entreat him to
come stay with them in order to function as a
calming influence upon their household;
Dowell accompanies Edward and Nancy to the
train station to see her off on her voyage to
India; several days later, Nancy cables that she is
having a "rattling good time," and Edward
subsequently commits suicide

1913–14 After Edward's funeral, Leonora takes Dowell
into her confidence and begins sharing the
details of Edward's affair with Florence, his
various other romantic affairs, and the truth
about Florence's death; Dowell spends six
months composing all but the final two chapters
of *The Good Soldier*; in mid-1914, Dowell learns

that Nancy has gone mad after hearing about
Edward's suicide

1915–16   Dowell travels through Europe, Africa, and Asia
in order to bring Nancy back to Branshaw
Teleragh, which he has purchased from Leonora
and where he lives with Nancy in her
interminable madness; Leonora marries Rodney
Bayham and becomes pregnant; Dowell finishes
composing *The Good Soldier*

A Note on the Text

The text of this edition of *The Good Soldier* is based on the first edition of the novel published by John Lane and the Bodley Head on 17 March 1915. Originally published under the name of Ford Madox Hueffer, this text is the only edition whose production Ford is known to have overseen. Ford appended his "Dedicatory Letter to Stella Ford" to the second American edition of the novel, published by Albert and Charles Boni, on 24 February 1927. The novel's manuscript is housed at Cornell University, which also possesses the typescript of *The Good Soldier*. Some of Ford's extensive revisions are included in the footnotes to the present edition.

THE

GOOD SOLDIER

A TALE OF PASSION

BY

FORD MADOX HUEFFER

AUTHOR OF "THE FIFTH QUEEN," ETC.

"Beati Immaculati"

LONDON : JOHN LANE, THE BODLEY HEAD
NEW YORK : JOHN LANE COMPANY
MCMXV

"Beati Immaculati"[1]

---

[1] Psalm 119.1: "Blessed are the undefiled."

DEDICATORY LETTER TO STELLA FORD[1]

My dear Stella,

I have always regarded this as my best book—at any rate as the best book of mine of a pre-war period; and between its writing and the appearance of my next novel nearly ten years must have elapsed, so that whatever I may have since written may be regarded as the work of a different man—as the work of *your* man. For it is certain that without the incentive to live that you offered me I should scarcely have survived the war-period and it is more certain still that without your spurring me again to write I should never have written again. And it happens that, by a queer chance, the *Good Soldier* is almost alone amongst my books in being dedicated to no one: Fate must have elected to let it wait the ten years that it waited—for this dedication.

What I am now I owe to you: what I was when I wrote the *Good Soldier* I owed to the concatenation of circumstances of a rather purposeless and wayward life.[2] Until I sat down to write this book—on the 17th December 1913[3]—I had never attempted to extend myself, to use a phrase of race-horse training. Partly because I had always entertained very fixedly the idea that—whatever may be the case with other writers—I at least should not be able to write a novel by which I should care to stand before reaching the age of forty; partly because I very definitely did not want to come into competition with other writers whose claim or whose need for recognition and what recognitions bring were greater than my own. I had never really tried to put into any novel of mine *all* that I knew about writing. I had written rather desultorily a number of books—a great number—but they had all been in the nature of *pastiches*, of pieces of rather precious writing, or of *tours de force*. But I have always been mad about writing—about the way writing should

---

[1] Stella Bowen (1893–1947), Australian painter who lived with Ford from 1919 to 1927.
[2] In 1909, Ford separated from his wife Elsie, whom he left for Violet Hunt. Elsie refused permission for Ford's legal marriage to Hunt. Her refusal and its subsequent complications resulted in an enormous and very public social scandal.
[3] Ford turned 40 on 17 December 1913.

be done and partly alone, partly with the companionship of Conrad,[1] I had even at that date made exhaustive studies into how words should be handled and novels constructed.

So, on the day I was forty I sat down to show what I could do—and the *Good Soldier* resulted. I fully intended it to be my last book. I used to think—and I do not know that I do not think the same now—that one book was enough for any man to write, and, at the date when the *Good Soldier* was finished, London at least and possibly the world appeared to be passing under the dominion of writers newer and much more vivid. Those were the passionate days of the literary Cubists, Vorticists, Imagistes[2] and the rest of the tapageur[3] and riotous Jeunes[4] of that young decade. So I regarded myself as the Eel which, having reached the deep sea, brings forth its young and dies—or as the Great Auk[5] I considered that, having reached my allotted, I had laid my one egg and might as well die. So I took a formal farewell of Literature in the columns of a magazine called the *Thrush*—which also, poor little auk that it was, died of the effort.[6] Then I prepared to stand aside in favour of our good friends—yours and mine—Ezra, Eliot, Wyndham Lewis, H.D.,[7] and the rest of the clamorous young writers who were then knocking at the door.

But greater clamours beset London and the world which till then had seemed to lie at the proud feet of those conquerors;

---

1   Joseph Conrad (1857–1924), Polish-born novelist, Ford's collaborator and close friend.
2   Three pre-1914 avant-garde movements in the visual and literary arts. The "Cubists," developed by Pablo Picasso (1881–1973) in 1907 and continuing into the 1920s, abandoned conventions such as perspective and experimented with multidimensional viewpoints. The "Vorticists," led by Wyndham Lewis, reacted to Victorian sentimentality, focusing instead on violence, energy, and the machine. The "Imagists," led by Ezra Pound, advocated the direct presentation of an object with precision, rather than via symbolism.
3   The rowdy, noisy, and showy generation of avant-garde writers.
4   A sympathetic descriptor for the young.
5   Seabird, unable to fly and extinct since around 1844, that had a large body and smallish wings.
6   *Thrush*, a short-lived poetry magazine to which Ford contributed in December 1909, ceased operations in 1910.
7   Ezra Pound (1885–1972), American poet, founder of the Imagist movement, critic, and translator; Thomas Stearns Eliot (1888–1965), American poet, critic, editor, and dramatist; Wyndham Lewis (1884–1957), British painter, editor, critic, novelist, and leader of the Vorticist movement; H.D. [Hilda Doolittle] (1886–1961), American Imagist poet.

Cubism, Vorticism, Imagism and the rest never had their fair chance amid the voices of the cannon, and so I have come out of my hole again and beside your strong, delicate and beautiful works have taken heart to lay some work of my own.

The Good Soldier, however, remains my great auk's egg for me as being something of a race that will have no successors and as it was written so long ago I may not seem over-vain if I consider it for a moment or two. No author, I think, is deserving of much censure for vanity if, taking down one of his ten-year-old books, he exclaims: "Great Heavens, did I write as well as that then?" for the implication always is that one does not any longer write so well and few are so envious as to censure the complacencies of an extinct volcano.

Be that as it may, I was lately forced into the rather close examination of this book, for I had to translate it into French,[1] that forcing me to give it much closer attention than would be the case in any reading however minute. And I will permit myself to say that I was astounded at the work I must have put into the construction of the book, at the intricate tangle of references and cross-references. Nor is that to be wondered at for, though I wrote it with comparative rapidity, I had it hatching within myself for fully another decade. That was because the story is a true story and because I had it from Edward Ashburnham himself and I could not write it till all the others were dead.[2] So I carried it about with me all those years, thinking about it from time to time.

I had in those days an ambition: that was to do for the English novel what in *Fort comme la Mort*, Maupassant had done for the French.[3] One day I had my reward, for I happened to be in a company where a fervent young admirer exclaimed: "By Jove,

---

[1] After World War I, Ford translated *The Good Soldier* from memory "by simply rewriting the book in French without looking at in English."

[2] An example of Ford's multiple ironies: Ashburnham—a name implying English reliability and steadiness in addition to referring to a tree that lives a long time—is a composite of several figures, real, fictional, and part of Ford's actual and fantasy lives.

[3] Guy de Maupassant (1850–1893), French realist novelist and short-story writer. In *Fort Comme la Mort* [*Strong as Death*] (1889), Maupassant writes about a love triangle involving an older man doomed by his obsession with a much younger woman. The character's love for Anne, similar to Ashburnham's desire for Nancy, was as "strong as death."

The Good Soldier is the finest novel in the English language!" whereupon my friend Mr. John Rodker[1] who has always had a properly tempered admiration for my work remarked in his clear, slow drawl: "Ah yes. It is, but you have left out a word. It is the finest French novel in the English language!"

With that—which is my tribute to my masters and betters of France—I will leave the book to the reader. But I should like to say a word about the title. This book was originally called by me *The Saddest Story*, but since it did not appear till the darkest days of the war were upon us, Mr. Lane[2] importuned me with letters and telegrams—I was by that time engaged in other pursuits![3]— to change the title which he said would at that date render the book unsaleable. One day, when I was on parade, I received a final wire of appeal from Mr. Lane, and the telegraph being reply-paid I seized the reply-form and wrote in hasty irony: "Dear Lane, Why not *The Good Soldier*?" ...To my horror six months later the book appeared under that title.[4]

I have never ceased to regret it but, since the War, I have received so much evidence that the book has been read under that name that I hesitate to make a change for fear of causing confusion. Had the chance occurred during the War I should not have hesitated to make the change, for I had only two evidences that anyone had ever heard of it. On one occasion I met the adjutant of my regiment just come off leave and looking extremely sick. I said: "Great Heavens, man, what is the matter with you?" He replied: "Well, the day before yesterday I got engaged to be married and today I have been reading *The Good Soldier*."

---

1   John Rodker (1894–1955), English poet and translator.

2   John Lane (1854–1926), publisher of *The Good Soldier*.

3   During the early years of World War I, Ford worked closely with Charles Masterman, who was charged with countering German propaganda in the United States, which operatives such as Masterman and Ford were attempting to bring into the war on the British side. Ford composed two works of propaganda, *When Blood Is Their Argument: An Analysis of Prussian Culture* (1915) and *Between St. Dennis and St. George* (1915).

4   On 17 December 1914, Ford wrote to Lane, his publisher, that "'The Saddest Story'— I say it in all humility—is about the best book you every published and the title is about the best title....Why not call the book 'The Roaring Joke'? Or call it anything you like, or perhaps it would be better to call it 'A Good Soldier'—that might do. At any rate it is all I can think of."

On the other occasion I was on parade again, being examined in drill, on the Guards' Square at Chelsea. And, since I was petrified with nervousness, having to do it before a half-dozen elderly gentlemen with red hatbands, I got my men about as hopelessly boxed as it is possible to do with the gentlemen privates of H.M. Coldstream Guards. Whilst I stood stiffly at attention one of the elderly red hat-bands[1] walked close behind by back and said distinctly in my ear, "Did you say, *The Good Soldier?*" So no doubt Mr. Lane was avenged. At any rate I have learned that irony may be a two-edged sword.

You, my dear Stella, will have heard me tell these stories a great many times. But the seas now divide us and I put them in this, your letter, which you will read before you see me in the hope that they may give you some pleasure with the illusion that you are hearing familiar—and very devoted—tones. And so I subscribe myself in all truth and in the hope that you will accept at once the particular dedication of this book and the general dedication of the edition.[2] Your

F.M.F.

New York, *January 9, 1927.*

---

[1] Senior officers.

[2] I.e., for the collection of Ford's work planned in the United States.

PART I

I

This is the saddest story I have ever heard.

We had known the Ashburnhams for nine seasons of the town of Nauheim[1] with an extreme intimacy—or, rather, with an acquaintanceship as loose and easy and yet as close as a good glove's with your hand. My wife and I knew Captain and Mrs. Ashburnham as well as it was possible to know anybody, and yet, in another sense, we knew nothing at all about them. This is, I believe, a state of things only possible with English people of whom, till today, when I sit down to puzzle out what I know of this sad affair, I knew nothing whatever. Six months ago I had never been to England, and, certainly, I had never sounded the depths of an English heart. I had known the shallows.

I don't mean to say that we were not acquainted with many English people. Living, as we perforce lived, in Europe, and being, as we perforce were, leisured Americans, which is as much as to say that we were un-American, we were thrown very much into the society of the nicer English. Paris, you see, was our home. Somewhere between Nice and Bordighera[2] provided yearly winter quarters for us, and Nauheim always received us from July to September. You will gather from this statement that one of us had, as the saying is, a "heart," and, from the statement that my wife is dead, that she was the sufferer.

Captain Ashburnham also had a heart. But, whereas a yearly month or so at Nauheim tuned him up to exactly the right pitch

---

[1] Bad Nauheim, a German spa on the slopes of the Taunus Mountains near Frankfurt. Ford and Hunt visited the spa in August 1910. According to *Baedeker's Northern Germany* (1913), Nauheim's amenities included warm saline springs impregnated with carbonic acid gas. The curative properties of the waters were especially recommended for "cardiac diseases."

[2] Nice, the fashionable tourist city on the French Mediterranean coast, the French Riviera. Bordighera, a winter tourist town on the Italian northeastern coast, colonized by the English upper class during the late nineteenth century.

for the rest of the twelvemonth, the two months or so were only just enough to keep poor Florence alive from year to year. The reason for his heart was, approximately, polo, or too much hard sportsmanship in his youth. The reason for poor Florence's broken years was a storm at sea upon our first crossing to Europe, and the immediate reasons for our imprisonment in that continent were doctor's orders. They said that even the short Channel crossing might well kill the poor thing.

When we all first met, Captain Ashburnham, home on sick leave from an India to which he was never to return, was thirty-three; Mrs. Ashburnham—Leonora—was thirty-one. I was thirty-six and poor Florence thirty. Thus today Florence would have been thirty-nine and Captain Ashburnham forty-two; whereas I am forty-five and Leonora forty.[1] You will perceive, therefore, that our friendship has been a young-middle-aged affair, since we were all of us of quite quiet dispositions, the Ashburnhams being more particularly what in England it is the custom to call "quite good people."

They were descended, as you will probably expect, from the Ashburnham who accompanied Charles I to the scaffold,[2] and, as you must also expect with this class of English people, you would never have noticed it. Mrs. Ashburnham was a Powys; Florence was a Hurlbird of Stamford, Connecticut, where, as you know, they are more old-fashioned than even the inhabitants of Cranford, England,[3] could have been. I myself am a Dowell of Philadelphia, Pa., where, it is historically true, there are more old English families than you would find in any six English counties taken together. I carry about with me, indeed—as if it were the only thing that invisibly anchored me to any spot upon the globe—the title deeds of my farm, which once covered several blocks between Chestnut and Walnut Streets.[4] These title deeds

---

1   The manuscript, typed ribbon copy of the first section, and the complete typescript—all of which are housed at Cornell University—reveal significant differences in assigning ages to Ford's principal characters.

2   In *The Cinque Ports* (1900), Ford wrote about Ashburnham's loyalty to Charles I, who was executed in 1649.

3   An allusion to Elizabeth Gaskell's 1853 novel *Cranford*, which focuses on a "peaceful" country village.

4   Two streets in what was once fashionable downtown Philadelphia.

are of wampum,[1] the grant of an Indian chief to the first Dowell, who left Farnham in Surrey in company with William Penn.[2] Florence's people, as is so often the case with the inhabitants of Connecticut, came from the neighbourhood of Fordingbridge,[3] where the Ashburnhams' place is. From there, at this moment, I am actually writing.

You may well ask why I write. And yet my reasons are quite many. For it is not unusual in human beings who have witnessed the sack of a city or the falling to pieces of a people to desire to set down what they have witnessed for the benefit of unknown heirs or of generations infinitely remote; or, if you please, just to get the sight out of their heads. Someone has said that the death of a mouse from cancer is the whole sack of Rome by the Goths, and I swear to you that the breaking up of our little four-square coterie was such another unthinkable event. Supposing that you should come upon us sitting together at one of the little tables in front of the club house, let us say, at Homburg,[4] taking tea of an afternoon and watching the miniature golf, you would have said that, as human affairs go, we were an extraordinarily safe castle. We were, if you will, one of those tall ships with the white sails upon a blue sea, one of those things that seem the proudest and the safest of all the beautiful and safe things that God has permitted the mind of men to frame. Where better could one take refuge? Where better?

Permanence? Stability! I can't believe it's gone. I can't believe that that long, tranquil life, which was just stepping a minuet, vanished in four crashing days at the end of nine years and six weeks. Upon my word, yes, our intimacy was like a minuet, simply because on every possible occasion and in every possible circumstance we knew where to go, where to sit, which table we unanimously should choose; and we could rise and go, all four

---

[1]   Beads used by North American Indians as money or pledges, as well as substitutes for writing.

[2]   Penn (1644–1718), the English Quaker who founded Pennsylvania.

[3]   Fordingbridge, a small Hampshire town in southern England on the Avon River with a bridge—a "ford"—across it. Ford visited Fordingbridge in 1904 and 1910—in the latter instance, with Hunt and her mother.

[4]   Bad Homburg, German spa town in the Taunus Mountains, famous for its mineral springs and made fashionable by Edward VII.

together, without a signal from any one of us, always to the music of the Kur[1] orchestra, always in the temperate sunshine, or, if it rained, in discreet shelters. No, indeed, it can't be gone. You can't kill a minuet de la cour.[2] You may shut up the music-book, close the harpsichord; in the cupboard and presses the rats may destroy the white satin favours.[3] The mob may sack Versailles; the Trianon may fall,[4] but surely the minuet—the minuet itself is dancing itself away into the furthest stars, even as our minuet of the Hessian bathing places[5] must be stepping itself still. Isn't there any heaven where old beautiful dances, old beautiful intimacies prolong themselves? Isn't there any Nirvana[6] pervaded by the faint thrilling of instruments that have fallen into the dust of worm-wood but that yet had frail, tremulous, and everlasting souls?

No, by God, it is false! It wasn't a minuet that we stepped; it was a prison—a prison full of screaming hysterics, tied down so that they might not outsound the rolling of our carriage wheels as we went along the shaded avenues of the Taunus Wald.[7]

And yet I swear by the sacred name of my creator that it was true. It was true sunshine; the true music; the true splash of the fountains from the mouth of stone dolphins. For, if for me we were four people with the same tastes, with the same desires, acting—or, no, not acting—sitting here and there unanimously, isn't that the truth? If for nine years I have possessed a goodly apple that is rotten at the core and discover its rottenness only in nine years and six months less four days, isn't it true to say that for nine years I possessed a goodly apple? So it may well be with Edward Ashburnham, with Leonora his wife and with poor dear

---

[1] The "cure hall" or tourist's public building at German health resorts, as well as the center of a resort's social activities.

[2] A slow court dance of the *cour* (*coeur* in the typescript) or "heart."

[3] In medieval and Renaissance literary texts, the young woman presented her suitor with ribbons or a glove as a sign of favor.

[4] The "Trianon" are two small royal villas in the park at Versailles, the residence of the French monarchy for a century. Versailles was attacked by the mob during the French Revolution (1789–1793).

[5] Public health baths in spa towns in the German grand duchy of Hessen.

[6] In Buddhist philosophy, Nirvana represents the supreme state in which passions and the self are extinguished.

[7] An expanse of woodlands in the Taunus Mountains that stretches north of Wiesbaden and Bad Homburg.

Florence. And, if you come to think of it, isn't it a little odd that the physical rottenness of at least two pillars of our four-square house never presented itself to my mind as a menace to its security? It doesn't so present itself now though the two of them are actually dead. I don't know....

I know nothing—nothing in the world—of the hearts of men. I only know that I am alone—horribly alone. No hearthstone will ever again witness, for me, friendly intercourse. No smoking-room will ever be other than peopled with incalculable simulacra[1] amidst smoke wreaths. Yet, in the name of God, what should I know if I don't know the life of the hearth and of the smoking-room, since my whole life has been passed in those places? The warm hearthside!—Well, there was Florence: I believe that for the twelve years her life lasted, after the storm that seemed irretrievably to have weakened her heart—I don't believe that for one minute she was out of my sight, except when she was safely tucked up in bed and I should be downstairs, talking to some good fellow or other in some lounge or smoking-room or taking my final turn with a cigar before going to bed. I don't, you understand, blame Florence. But how can she have known what she knew? How could she have got to know it? To know it so fully. Heavens! There doesn't seem to have been the actual time. It must have been when I was taking my baths, and my Swedish exercises,[2] being manicured. Leading the life I did, of the sedulous, strained nurse, I had to do something to keep myself fit. It must have been then! Yet even that can't have been enough time to get the tremendously long conversations full of worldly wisdom that Leonora has reported to me since their deaths. And is it possible to imagine that during our prescribed walks in Nauheim and the neighbourhood she found time to carry on the protracted negotiations which she did carry on between Edward Ashburnham and his wife? And isn't it incredible that during all that time Edward and Leonora never spoke a word to each other in private? What is one to think of humanity?

For I swear to you that they were the model couple. He was as devoted as it was possible to be without appearing fatuous. So

---

[1]   Deceptive image, deceptive substitute, or shadowy likeness.
[2]   Therapeutic exercise system.

well set up, with such honest blue eyes, such a touch of stupidity, such a warm goodheartedness! And she—so tall, so splendid in the saddle, so fair! Yes, Leonora was extraordinarily fair and so extraordinarily the real thing that she seemed too good to be true. You don't, I mean, as a rule, get it all so superlatively together. To be the county family, to look the county family,[1] to be so appropriately and perfectly wealthy; to be so perfect in manner—even just to the saving touch of insolence that seems to be necessary. To have all that and to be all that! No, it was too good to be true. And yet, only this afternoon, talking over the whole matter she said to me: "Once I tried to have a lover but I was so sick at the heart, so utterly worn out that I had to send him away." That struck me as the most amazing thing I had ever heard. She said "I was actually in a man's arms. Such a nice chap! Such a dear fellow! And I was saying to myself, fiercely, hissing it between my teeth, as they say in novels—and really clenching them together: I was saying to myself: 'Now, I'm in for it and I'll really have a good time for once in my life—for once in my life!' It was in the dark, in a carriage, coming back from a hunt ball. Eleven miles we had to drive! And then suddenly the bitterness of the endless poverty, of the endless acting—it fell on me like a blight, it spoilt everything. Yes, I had to realize that I had been spoilt even for the good time when it came. And I burst out crying and I cried and I cried for the whole eleven miles. Just imagine *me* crying! And just imagine me making a fool of the poor dear chap like that. It certainly wasn't playing the game, was it now?"

I don't know; I don't know; was that last remark of hers the remark of a harlot, or is it what every decent woman, county family or not county family, thinks at the bottom of her heart? Or thinks all the time for the matter of that? Who knows?

Yet, if one doesn't know that at this hour and day, at this pitch of civilisation to which we have attained, after all the preachings of all the moralists, and all the teachings of all the mothers to all the daughters in *saecula saeculorum*[2]... but perhaps that is what all

---

[1] Important people in a county's social structure; often a family with a large amount of property in a given rural area.
[2] "For ever and ever" in the Catholic liturgy.

mothers teach all daughters, not with lips but with the eyes, or with heart whispering to heart. And, if one doesn't know as much as that about the first thing in the world, what does one know and why is one here?

I asked Mrs. Ashburnham whether she had told Florence that and what Florence had said and she answered: "Florence didn't offer any comment at all. What could she say? There wasn't anything to be said. With the grinding poverty we had to put up with to keep up appearances, and the way the poverty came about—*you* know what I mean—any woman would have been justified in taking a lover and presents too. Florence once said about a very similar position—she was a little too well-bred, too American, to talk about mine—that it was a case of perfectly open riding and the woman could just act on the spur of the moment. She said it in American of course, but that was the sense of it. I think her actual words were: 'That it was up to her to take it or leave it'"....

I don't want you to think that I am writing Teddy Ashburnham down a brute. I don't believe he was. God knows, perhaps all men are like that. For as I've said what do I know even of the smoking-room? Fellows come in and tell the most extraordinarily gross stories—so gross that they will positively give you a pain. And yet they'd be offended if you suggested that they weren't the sort of person you could trust your wife alone with. And very likely they'd be quite properly offended—that is if you can trust anybody alone with anybody. But that sort of fellow obviously takes more delight in listening to or in telling gross stories—more delight than in anything else in the world. They'll hunt languidly and dress languidly and dine languidly and work without enthusiasm and find it a bore to carry on three minutes' conversation about anything whatever and yet, when the other sort of conversation begins, they'll laugh and wake up and throw themselves about in their chairs. Then, if they so delight in the narration, how is it possible that they can be offended—and properly offended—at the suggestion that they might make attempts upon your wife's honour? Or again: Edward Ashburnham was the cleanest looking sort of chap;—an excellent magistrate, a first rate soldier, one of the best landlords, so they said, in Hampshire, England. To the poor and to hopeless drunkards, as I myself have witnessed, he was like a painstaking guardian. And he never told a story that couldn't have gone into the columns of the *Field*[1] more than once or twice in all the nine years of my knowing him. He didn't even like hearing them; he would fidget and get up and go out to buy a cigar or something of that sort. You would have said that he was just exactly the sort of chap that you could have trusted your wife with. And I trusted mine—and it was madness.

And yet again you have me. If poor Edward was dangerous because of the chastity of his expressions—and they say that is always the hall-mark of a libertine—what about myself? For I solemnly avow that not only have I never so much as hinted at an impropriety in my conversation in the whole of my days; and more than that, I will vouch for the cleanness of my thoughts and the absolute chastity of my life. At what, then, does it all work out? Is the whole thing a folly and a mockery? Am I no better than a eunuch or is the proper man—the man with the right to existence—a raging stallion forever neighing after his neighbour's womankind?

I don't know. And there is nothing to guide us. And if everything is so nebulous about a matter so elementary as the morals of sex, what is there to guide us in the more subtle morality of all other personal contacts, associations, and activities? Or are we meant to act on impulse alone? It is all a darkness.

II

I don't know how it is best to put this thing down—whether it would be better to try and tell the story from the beginning, as if it were a story; or whether to tell it from this distance of time,

---

[1] An illustrated newspaper founded in 1853 that focused on country activities. Read largely by the upper middle classes with rural interests, the *Field* reported golf tournaments, equestrian events, and other pursuits of the leisured classes in the country.

as it reached me from the lips of Leonora or from those of Edward himself.[1]

So I shall just imagine myself for a fortnight or so at one side of the fireplace of a country cottage, with a sympathetic soul opposite me. And I shall go on talking, in a low voice while the sea sounds in the distance and overhead the great black flood of wind polishes the bright stars. From time to time we shall get up and go to the door and look out at the great moon and say: "Why, it is nearly as bright as in Provence!" And then we shall come back to the fireside, with just the touch of a sigh because we are not in that Provence where even the saddest stories are gay. Consider the lamentable history of Peire Vidal.[2] Two years ago Florence and I motored from Biarritz to Las Tours, which is in the Black Mountains.[3] In the middle of a tortuous valley there rises up an immense pinnacle and on the pinnacle are four castles—Las Tours, the Towers. And the immense mistral[4] blew down that valley which was the way from France into Provence so that the silver grey olive leaves appeared like hair flying in the wind, and the tufts of rosemary crept into the iron rocks that they might not be torn up by the roots.

It was, of course, poor dear Florence who wanted to go to Las Tours. You are to imagine that, however much her bright personality came from Stamford, Connecticut, she was yet a graduate of Poughkeepsie.[5] I never could imagine how she did it—the

---

[1]   In the Cornell manuscript of the novel, the text reads: "I have asked novelists about these things, but they don't seem able to tell you much. They say it comes. I don't know that I particularly want to write a novel; but I do know that I want what I write to be read by at least one sympathetic soul, or by all souls that are in sympathy throughout the world. How many are they? A million? A hundred million? Or isn't there one? Here again one has just no means of knowing—none! But, I suppose, if I want to write something that will be read by one sympathetic soul I must want to write a novel—I don't see how to get away from that."

[2]   Piere Vidal (c. 1180–c. 1206), a Provençal Troubadour whose love poetry was noted for its strength of personal feeling and simplicity of style. Ford's father Francis Hueffer writes in *The Troubadours: A History of Provençal Life and Literature in the Middle Ages* (1878) about Vidal's suicidal passion for La Louve. Troubadours were medieval Provençal poet-musicians.

[3]   Ford undertook a similar journey with Hunt following a court case brought against him by his wife Elsie in 1913. He and Hunt traveled from the French Atlantic coast to the Mediterranean coast of France.

[4]   A violent, cold, and dry wind.

[5]   Vassar College, an exclusive women's college in Poughkeepsie, New York.

queer, chattery person that she was. With the far-away look in her eyes—which wasn't, however, in the least romantic—I mean that she didn't look as if she were seeing poetic dreams, or looking through you, for she hardly ever did look at you!—holding up one hand as if she wished to silence any objection—or any comment for the matter of that—she would talk. She would talk about William the Silent,[1] about Gustave the Loquacious,[2] about Paris frocks, about how the poor dressed in 1337, about Fantin Latour,[3] about the Paris-Lyons-Mediterranée train-de-luxe, about whether it would be worth while to get off at Tarascon and go across the windswept suspension-bridge, over the Rhone to take another look at Beaucaire.[4]

We never did take another look at Beaucaire, of course—beautiful Beaucaire, with the high, triangular white tower, that looked as thin as a needle and as tall as the Flatiron, between Fifth and Broadway[5]—Beaucaire with the grey walls on the top of the pinnacle surrounding an acre and a half of blue irises, beneath the tallness of the stone pines. What a beautiful thing the stone pine is....

No, we never did go back anywhere. Not to Heidelberg, not to Hamelin, not to Verona, not to Mont Majour—not so much as to Carcassonne itself.[6] We talked of it, of course, but I guess Florence got all she wanted out of one look at a place. She had the seeing eye.

I haven't, unfortunately, so that the world is full of places to which I want to return—towns with the blinding white sun upon them; stone pines against the blue of the sky; corners of

---

[1] William the Silent (1533–1584), Prince of Orange and the leader of the Dutch revolt against Spain. Initially a Catholic and then a Calvinist, he had four wives—the last of which was a renegade nun and a French princess.

[2] Probably Gustavus I (1496–1560), Swedish king and the founder of the Swedish state who established a national protestant church.

[3] Fantin Latour (1836–1904), French painter, illustrator, and printmaker noted for his still-lifes with flowers and group portraits of leading French artistic personalities.

[4] Tarascon and Beaucaire—which were also visited by Ford and Hunt in 1913—are near the mouth of the Rhône. They face each other across the river and are noted for their medieval architecture.

[5] Ford first visited New York City in 1906 and saw the early skyscraper, a wedge-shaped building at the junction of Fifth Avenue and Broadway.

[6] Ford and Hunt stayed at the Hôtel de la Cité in Carcassonne in February 1913.

gables, all carved and painted with stags and scarlet flowers and crowstepped[1] gables with the little saint at the top; and grey and pink palazzi and walled towns a mile or so back from the sea, on the Mediterranean, between Leghorn and Naples. Not one of them did we see more than once, so that the whole world for me is like spots of colour in an immense canvas. Perhaps if it weren't so I should have something to catch hold of now.

Is all this digression or isn't it digression? Again I don't know. You, the listener, sit opposite me. But you are so silent. You don't tell me anything. I am, at any rate, trying to get you to see what sort of life it was I led with Florence and what Florence was like. Well, she was bright; and she danced. She seemed to dance over the floors of castles and over seas and over and over the salons of modistes[2] and over the *plages*[3] of the Riviera—like a gay tremulous beam, reflected from water upon a ceiling. And my function in life was to keep that bright thing in existence. And it was almost as difficult as trying to catch with your hand that dancing reflection. And the task lasted for years.

Florence's aunts used to say that I must be the laziest man in Philadelphia. They had never been to Philadelphia and they had the New England conscience. You see, the first thing they said to me when I called in on Florence in the little ancient, colonial, wooden house beneath the high, thin-leaved elms—the first question they asked me was not how I did but what did I do. And I did nothing. I suppose I ought to have done something, but I didn't see any call to do it. Why does one do things? I just drifted in and wanted Florence. First I had drifted in on Florence at a Browning tea,[4] or something of the sort in Fourteenth Street,[5] which was then still residential. I don't know why I had gone to New York; I don't know why I had gone to the tea. I don't see why Florence should have gone to that sort of spelling bee.[6] It wasn't the place at which,

---

1   Step-like projections.
2   Dressmakers, milliners, and fashion designers.
3   Beaches.
4   A meeting of devotees, usually middle-class women with intellectual pretensions, of the poet Robert Browning (1812–1889).
5   A major street in lower Manhattan, New York.
6   Spelling competitions often attended by women slightly down the social scale from the frequent attendees of Browning teas.

even then, you expected to find a Poughkeepsie graduate. I guess Florence wanted to raise the culture of the Stuyvesant[1] crowd and did it as she might have gone in slumming. Intellectual slumming, that was what it was. She always wanted to leave the world a little more elevated than she found it. Poor dear thing, I have heard her lecture Teddy Ashburnham by the hour on the difference between a Franz Hals and a Wouwerman and why the Pre-Mycenaic statues[2] were cubical with knobs on the top. I wonder what he made of it? Perhaps he was thankful.

I know I was. For do you understand my whole attentions, my whole endeavours were to keep poor dear Florence on to topics like the finds at Gnossos and the mental spirituality of Walter Pater.[3] I had to keep her at it, you understand, or she might die. For I was solemnly informed that if she became excited over anything or if her emotions were really stirred her little heart might cease to beat. For twelve years I had to watch every word that any person uttered in any conversation and I had to head it off what the English call "things"—off love, poverty, crime, religion and the rest of it. Yes, the first doctor that we had when she was carried off the ship at Havre assured me that this must be done. Good God, are all these fellows monstrous idiots, or is there a freemasonry between all of them from end to end of the earth? ...That is what makes me think of that fellow Peire Vidal.

Because, of course, his story is culture and I had to head her towards culture and at the same time it's so funny and she hadn't got to laugh, and it's so full of love and she wasn't to think of love. Do you know the story? Las Tours of the Four Castles had for chatelaine[4] Blanche Somebody-or-other who was called as a

---

[1] A wealthy area of Manhattan, New York, named after the last Dutch governor of New York, Peter Stuyvesant (1592–1672).

[2] Franz Hals (c. 1580–1666), Dutch portrait and genre painter who spent most of his life in poverty. Philips Wouwerman (1619–1668), Dutch landscape painter and apparently Hals's student. Heinrich Schiemann and others excavated Mycenae, an ancient Greek city.

[3] Gnossos, or Knossos, a city in ancient Crete that was excavated between 1900 and 1908. It was the legendary site of the palace of King Minos. Walter Pater (1839–1894), English essayist and aesthetic critic.

[4] Mistress of a château, or country house. A chatelaine was an ornamental set of short chains that the château's mistress wore on her belt for carrying keys. As Martin Stannard notes, this key chain foreshadows the key that Leonora wears on her wrist and associates her intertextually with La Louve.

term of commendation, La Louve—the She-Wolf. And Peire Vidal the Troubadour paid his court to La Louve. And she wouldn't have anything to do with him. So, out of compliment to her—the things people do when they're in love!—he dressed himself up in wolfskins and went up into the Black Mountains. And the shepherds of the Montagne Noire and their dogs mistook him for a wolf and he was torn with the fangs and beaten with clubs. So they carried him back to Las Tours and La Louve wasn't at all impressed. They polished him up and her husband remonstrated seriously with her. Vidal was, you see, a great poet and it was not proper to treat a great poet with indifference.

So Peire Vidal declared himself Emperor of Jerusalem or somewhere and the husband had to kneel down and kiss his feet though La Louve wouldn't. And Peire set sail in a rowing boat with four companions to redeem the Holy Sepulchre.[1] And they struck on a rock somewhere, and, at great expense, the husband had to fit out an expedition to fetch him back. And Peire Vidal fell all over the Lady's bed while the husband, who was a most ferocious warrior, remonstrated some more about the courtesy that is due to great poets. But I suppose La Louve was the more ferocious of the two. Anyhow, that is all that came of it. Isn't that a story?

You haven't an idea of the queer old-fashionedness of Florence's aunts—the Misses Hurlbird,[2] nor yet of her uncle. An extraordinarily lovable man, that Uncle John. Thin, gentle, and with a "heart" that made his life very much what Florence's afterwards became. He didn't reside at Stamford; his home was in Waterbury where the watches come from.[3] He had a factory there which, in our queer American way, would change its functions almost from

[1] One of the goals of the Crusades was to rescue Jesus's burial place from the Turks. The Holy Sepulchre was subsequently built on the site thought to be where Jesus was crucified and buried.

[2] In *Return to Yesterday* (1931), Ford recalls how in November 1904 he encountered "two adorably old-maidish ladies from Stamford, Conn." called Hurlbird "in the immense, shadowed drawing room" of a Rhineland health spa. They promised him "that if I would visit them at Stamford and eat their peaches and frozen cream for breakfast I should be restored to complete health. I eventually did so [in 1906] and the promise came true."

[3] Industrial Connecticut city, then known for manufacturing clocks and watches.

year to year. For nine months or so it would manufacture buttons out of bone. Then it would suddenly produce brass buttons for coachmen's liveries. Then it would take a turn at embossed tin lids for candy boxes. The fact is that the poor old gentleman, with his weak and fluttering heart, didn't want his factory to manufacture anything at all. He wanted to retire. And he did retire when he was seventy. But he was so worried at having all the street boys in the town point after him and exclaim: "There goes the laziest man in Waterbury!" that he tried taking a tour round the world. And Florence and a young man called Jimmy went with him. It appears from what Florence told me that Jimmy's function with Mr. Hurlbird was to avoid exciting topics for him. He had to keep him, for instance, out of political discussions. For the poor old man was a violent Democrat in days when you might travel the world over without finding anything but a Republican.[1] Anyhow, they went round the world.

＼ I think an anecdote is about the best way to give you an idea of what the old gentleman was like. For it is perhaps important that you should know what the old gentleman was; he had a great deal of influence in forming the character of my poor dear wife.

Just before they set out from San Francisco for the South Seas old Mr. Hurlbird said he must take something with him to make little presents to people he met on the voyage. And it struck him that the things to take for that purpose were oranges—because California is the orange country—and comfortable folding chairs. So he bought I don't know how many cases of oranges—the great cool California oranges, and half-a-dozen folding chairs in a special case that he always kept in his cabin. There must have been half a cargo of fruit.

For, to every person on board the several steamers that they employed—to every person with whom he had so much as a nodding acquaintance, he gave an orange every morning. And they

---

[1]   The two major American political parties. The Democrats between 1860 and 1912 elected but a single President; the rest were Republicans. In the nineteenth century, the Republicans were associated with the North, anti-slavery, and protective trade tariffs. The Democrats were associated with anti-Federalism, anti-big business, opposed to cultural associations with England, and supported the tenets of the French Revolution.

lasted him right round the girdle of this mighty globe of ours. When they were at North Cape,[I] even, he saw on the horizon, poor dear thin man that he was, a lighthouse. "Hello," says he to himself, "these fellows must be very lonely. Let's take them some oranges." So he had a boatload of his fruit out and had himself rowed to the lighthouse on the horizon. The folding chairs he lent to any lady that he came across and liked or who seemed tired and invalidish on the ship. And so, guarded against his heart and, having his niece with him, he went round the world....

He wasn't obtrusive about his heart. You wouldn't have known he had one. He only left it to the physical laboratory at Waterbury for the benefit of science, since he considered it to be quite an extraordinary kind of heart. And the joke of the matter was that, when, at the age of eighty-four, just five days before poor Florence, he died of bronchitis there was found to be absolutely nothing the matter with that organ. It had certainly jumped or squeaked or something just sufficiently to take in the doctors, but it appears that that was because of an odd formation of the lungs. I don't much understand about these matters.

I inherited his money because Florence died five days after him. I wish I hadn't. It was a great worry. I had to go out to Waterbury just after Florence's death because the poor dear old fellow had left a good many charitable bequests and I had to appoint trustees. I didn't like the idea of their not being properly handled.

Yes, it was a great worry. And just as I had got things roughly settled I received the extraordinary cable from Ashburnham begging me to come back and have a talk with him. And immediately afterwards came one from Leonora saying, "Yes, please do come. You could be so helpful." It was as if he had sent the cable without consulting her and had afterwards told her. Indeed, that was pretty much what had happened, except that he had told the girl and the girl told the wife. I arrived, however, too late to be of any good if I could have been of any good. And then I had my first taste of English life. It was amazing. It was overwhelming. I never shall forget the polished cob that Edward, beside me, drove; the animal's action, its highstepping, its skin that was like

---

[I]   The northernmost tip of Europe, where tourist steamers regularly stopped.

satin. And the peace! And the red cheeks! And the beautiful, beautiful old house.

Just near Branshaw Teleragh it was and we descended on it from the high, clear, windswept waste of the New Forest.[1] I tell you it was amazing to arrive there from Waterbury. And it came into my head—for Teddy Ashburnham, you remember, had cabled to me to "come and have a talk" with him—that it was unbelievable that anything essentially calamitous could happen to that place and those people. I tell you it was the very spirit of peace. And Leonora, beautiful and smiling, with her coils of yellow hair, stood on the top doorstep, with a butler and footman and a maid or so behind her. And she just said: "So glad you've come," as if I'd run down to lunch from a town ten miles away, instead of having come half the world over at the call of two urgent telegrams.

The girl was out with the hounds, I think.

And that poor devil beside me was in an agony. Absolute, hopeless, dumb agony such as passes the mind of man to imagine.[2]

III

It was a very hot summer, in August 1904; and Florence had already been taking the baths for a month. I don't know how it feels to be a patient at one of those places. I never was a patient anywhere. I daresay the patients get a home feeling and some sort of anchorage in the spot. They seem to like the bath attendants, with their cheerful faces, their air of authority, their white linen. But, for myself, to be at Nauheim gave me a sense—what shall

---

[1] After finishing *The Soul of London* (1905), Ford toured this wooded part of Hampshire in southwest England in the spring of 1904 in an attempt to recuperate from a nervous breakdown. He was accompanied by the writer W. H. Hudson (1841–1922).

[2] In the Cornell manuscript of the novel, the text reads: "But all this is rather wandering round sort of stuff. Only it's the way it comes into my head. I must try to be more direct. I will put down very shortly the essential facts about Florence and myself and then we can get on to the first meeting of all us four at Nauheim. Or no, I will go straight on to Nauheim. I don't know how to tell this story."

I say?—a sense almost of nakedness—the nakedness that one feels on the sea-shore or in any great open space. I had no attachments, no accumulations. In one's own home it is as if little, innate sympathies draw one to particular chairs that seem to enfold one in an embrace, or take one along particular streets that seem friendly when others may be hostile. And, believe me, that feeling is a very important part of life. I know it well, that have been for so long a wanderer upon the face of public resorts. And one is too polished up. Heaven knows I was never an untidy man. But the feeling that I had when, whilst poor Florence was taking her morning bath, I stood upon the carefully swept steps of the Englischer Hof,[1] looking at the carefully arranged trees in tubs upon the carefully arranged gravel whilst carefully arranged people walked past in carefully calculated gaiety, at the carefully calculated hour, the tall trees of the public gardens, going up to the right; the reddish stone of the baths—or were they white half-timber chalets? Upon my word I have forgotten, I who was there so often. That will give you the measure of how much I was in the landscape. I could find my way blindfolded to the hot rooms, to the douche rooms, to the fountain in the centre of the quadrangle where the rusty water gushes out. Yes, I could find my way blindfolded. I know the exact distances. From the Hotel Regina[2] you took one hundred and eighty-seven paces, then, turning sharp, lefthanded, four hundred and twenty took you straight down to the fountain. From the Englischer Hof, starting on the sidewalk, it was ninety-seven paces and the same four hundred and twenty, but turning left-handed this time.[3]

And now you understand that, having nothing in the world to do—but nothing whatever! I fell into the habit of counting

---

[1] Today the "Deutsches Hof." The private hotel in Bad Nauheim is on a tree-lined street, 1 Kuchlerstrasse, walking distance from the health spa and *kärpark*.

[2] Near the "Englischer Hof" at 8 Kuchlerstrasse.

[3] In the Cornell manuscript of the novel, the text reads: "From the end of the tennis courts to Florence's seat after she had been at Nauheim a week was exactly five hundred steps; from the same place to a seat higher up the hill—she was allowed so much to extend her walk during the second week—was just seven hundred and fifty. From the same place to the steps of the Casino, by the path Dr. Bittelman told us to take during the fourth week was exactly seven hundred and fifty. And so on...."

my footsteps. I would walk with Florence to the baths. And, of course, she entertained me with her conversation. It was, as I have said, wonderful what she could make conversation out of. She walked very lightly, and her hair was very nicely done, and she dressed beautifully and very expensively. Of course she had money of her own, but I shouldn't have minded. And yet you know I can't remember a single one of her dresses. Or I can remember just one, a very simple one of blue figured silk—a Chinese pattern—very full in the skirts and broadening out over the shoulders. And her hair was copper-coloured, and the heels of her shoes were exceedingly high, so that she tripped upon the points of her toes. And when she came to the door of the bathing place, and when it opened to receive her, she would look back at me with a little coquettish smile, so that her cheek appeared to be caressing her shoulder.

I seem to remember that, with that dress, she wore an immensely broad Leghorn hat—like the Chapeau de Paille of Rubens,[1] only very white. The hat would be tied with a lightly knotted scarf of the same stuff as her dress. She knew how to give value to her blue eyes. And round her neck would be some simple pink, coral beads. And her complexion had a perfect clearness, a perfect smoothness ...

Yes, that is how I most exactly remember her, in that dress, in that hat, looking over her shoulder at me so that the eyes flashed very blue—dark pebble blue ...

And, what the devil! For whose benefit did she do it? For that of the bath attendant? of the passers-by? I don't know. Anyhow, it can't have been for me, for never, in all the years of her life, never on any possible occasion, or in any other place did she so smile to me, mockingly, invitingly. Ah, she was a riddle; but then, all other women are riddles. And it occurs to me that some way back I began a sentence that I have never finished ... It was about the feeling that I had when I stood on the steps of my hotel every morning before starting out to fetch Florence back from the bath. Natty, precise, well-brushed, conscious of being rather small amongst the long English, the lank Americans, the rotund

---

[1] A Leghorn hat, a straw hat painted by the Flemish painter Peter Paul Rubens (1577–1640) in *Chapeau de Paille: The Straw Hat*. This portrait depicts the sister of the artist's second wife wearing a prominent Leghorn hat.

Germans, and the obese Russian Jewesses, I should stand there, tapping a cigarette on the outside of my case, surveying for a moment the world in the sunlight. But a day was to come when I was never to do it again alone. You can imagine, therefore, what the coming of the Ashburnhams meant to me.

I have forgotten the aspect of many things but I shall never forget the aspect of the dining-room of the Hotel Excelsior[1] on that evening—and on so many other evenings. Whole castles have vanished from my memory, whole cities that I have never visited again, but that white room, festooned with papier-mâché fruits and flowers; the tall windows; the many tables; the black screen round the door with three golden cranes flying upward on each panel; the palm-tree in the centre of the room; the swish of the waiter's feet; the cold expensive elegance; the mien of the diners as they came in every evening—their air of earnestness as if they must go through a meal prescribed by the Kur authorities and their air of sobriety as if they must seek not by any means to enjoy their meals—those things I shall not easily forget. And then, one evening, in the twilight, I saw Edward Ashburnham lounge round the screen into the room. The head waiter, a man with a face all grey—in what subterranean nooks or corners do people cultivate those absolutely grey complexions?—went with the timorous patronage of these creatures towards him and held out a grey ear to be whispered into. It was generally a disagreeable ordeal for newcomers but Edward Ashburnham bore it like an Englishman and a gentleman. I could see his lips form a word of three syllables—remember I had nothing in the world to do but to notice these niceties—and immediately I knew that he must be Edward Ashburnham, Captain, Fourteenth Hussars,[2] of Branshaw House, Branshaw Teleragh. I knew it because every evening just before dinner, whilst I waited in the hall, I used, by the courtesy of Monsieur Schontz, the proprietor, to inspect the little police reports that each guest was expected to sign upon taking a room.

---

[1] A more exclusive hotel than either the Englischer Hof or Hotel Regina and within easy walking distance of both of them. As Martin Stannard observes, "Ford places characters in establishments exactly reflecting their social status rather than their wealth."

[2] A "snobby," light-calvary regiment.

The head waiter piloted him immediately to a vacant table, three away from my own—the table that the Grenfalls of Falls River, N.J., had just vacated. It struck me that that was not a very nice table for the newcomers, since the sunlight, low though it was, shone straight down upon it, and the same idea seemed to come at the same moment into Captain Ashburnham's head. His face hitherto had, in the wonderful English fashion, expressed nothing whatever. Nothing. There was in it neither joy nor despair; neither hope nor fear; neither boredom nor satisfaction. He seemed to perceive no soul in that crowded room; he might have been walking in a jungle. I never came across such a perfect expression before and I never shall again. It was insolence and not insolence; it was modesty and not modesty. His hair was fair, extraordinarily, ordered in a wave, running from the left temple to the right; his face was a light brick-red, perfectly uniform in tint up to the roots of the hair itself; his yellow moustache was as stiff as a toothbrush and I verily believe that he had his black smoking jacket thickened a little over the shoulder-blades so as to give himself the air of the slightest possible stoop. It would be like him to do that; that was the sort of thing he thought about. Martingales, Chiffney bits, boots; where you got the best soap, the best brandy, the name of the chap who rode a plater[1] down the Khyber cliffs;[2] the spreading power of number three shot before a charge of number four powder ... by heavens, I hardly ever heard him talk of anything else. Not in all the years that I knew him did I hear him talk of anything but these subjects. Oh, yes, once he told me that I could buy my special shade of blue ties cheaper from a firm in Burlington Arcade[3] than from my own people in New York. And I have bought my ties from that firm ever since. Otherwise I should not remember the name of the Burlington Arcade. I wonder what it looks like. I have never seen it. I imagine it to be two immense rows of pillars, like those of the Forum at Rome, with Edward Ashburnham striding down

---

[1]   Martingales are straps for controlling the upward movement of a horse's head; "Chiffney bits" are horse's bits that were invented by the jockey Samuel Chiffney (c. 1753–1807). A "plater" refers to a second-rate racehorse competing in plate and prize races.

[2]   Khyber cliffs in the Khyber Pass, then in India, now Pakistan.

[3]   A fashionable central London covered passageway consisting of small shops.

between them. But it probably isn't—the least like that. Once also he advised me to buy Caledonian Deferred,[1] since they were due to rise. And I did buy them and they did rise. But of how he got the knowledge I haven't the faintest idea. It seemed to drop out of the blue sky.

And that was absolutely all that I knew of him until a month ago—that and the profusion of his cases, all of pigskin and stamped with his initials, E.F.A. There were gun cases, and collar cases, and shirt cases, and letter cases and cases each containing four bottles of medicine; and hat cases and helmet cases. It must have needed a whole herd of the Gadarene swine[2] to make up his outfit. And, if I ever penetrated into his private room it would be to see him standing, with his coat and waistcoat off and the immensely long line of his perfectly elegant trousers from waist to boot heel. And he would have a slightly reflective air and he would be just opening one kind of case and just closing another.

Good God, what did they all see in him; for I swear there was all there was of him, inside and out; though they said he was a good soldier. Yet Leonora adored him with a passion that was like an agony, and hated him with an agony that was as bitter as the sea. How could he arouse anything like a sentiment, in anybody?

What did he even talk to them about—when they were under four eyes?—Ah, well, suddenly, as if by a flash of inspiration, I know. For all good soldiers are sentimentalists—all good soldiers of that type. Their profession, for one thing, is full of the big words, courage, loyalty, honour, constancy. And I have given a wrong impression of Edward Ashburnham if I have made you think that literally never in the course of our nine years of intimacy did he discuss what he would have called "the graver things." Even before his final outburst to me, at times, very late at night, say, he has blurted out something that gave an insight into the sentimental view of the cosmos that was his. He would say how much the society of a good woman could do towards redeeming you, and he would say that constancy was the finest

---

[1]   I.e., stock.

[2]   See Matthew 8.28–32, Mark 5.1–13, and Luke 8.26–33. Jesus visits the country of the Gadarenes, where he encounters violent, unclothed madmen. He casts out these devils into a herd of pigs, who then rush headlong into a lake, where they drown.

of the virtues. He said it very stiffly, of course, but still as if the statement admitted of no doubt.

Constancy! Isn't that the queer thought? And yet, I must add that poor dear Edward was a great reader—he would pass hours lost in novels of a sentimental type—novels in which typewriter girls married Marquises and governesses Earls. And in his books, as a rule, the course of true love ran as smooth as buttered honey. And he was fond of poetry, of a certain type—and he could even read a perfectly sad love story. I have seen his eyes filled with tears at reading of a hopeless parting. And he loved, with a sentimental yearning, all children, puppies, and the feeble generally....

So, you see, he would have plenty to gurgle about to a woman—with that and his sound common sense about martingales and his—still sentimental—experiences as a county magistrate; and with his intense, optimistic belief that the woman he was making love to at the moment was the one he was destined, at last, to be eternally constant to.... Well, I fancy he could put up a pretty good deal of talk when there was no man around to make him feel shy. And I was quite astonished, during his final burst-out to me—at the very end of things, when the poor girl was on her way to that fatal Brindisi[1] and he was trying to persuade himself and me that he had never really cared for her— I was quite astonished to observe how literary and how just his expressions were. He talked like quite a good book—a book not in the least cheaply sentimental. You see, I suppose he regarded me not so much as a man. I had to be regarded as a woman or a solicitor.[2] Anyhow, it burst out of him on that horrible night. And then, next morning, he took me over to the Assizes[3] and I saw how, in a perfectly calm and business-like way he set to work to secure a verdict of not guilty for a poor girl, the daughter of one of his tenants, who had been accused of murdering her baby. He spent two hundred pounds on her defence.... Well, that was Edward Ashburnham.

---

[1] An Italian Adriatic coastal port.
[2] In the English legal system, a solicitor, or lawyer, gives confidential legal advice to a client and rarely appears in court, which is frequented by barristers.
[3] The county court where trials are conducted.

I had forgotten about his eyes. They were as blue as the sides of a certain type of box of matches. When you looked at them carefully you saw that they were perfectly honest, perfectly straightforward, perfectly, perfectly stupid. But the brick pink of his complexion, running perfectly level to the brick pink of his inner eyelids, gave them a curious, sinister expression—like a mosaic of blue porcelain set in pink china. And that chap, coming into a room, snapped up the gaze of every woman in it, as dexterously as a conjurer pockets billiard balls. It was most amazing. You know the man on the stage who throws up sixteen balls at once and they all drop into pockets all over his person, on his shoulders, on his heels, on the inner side of his sleeves; and he stands perfectly still and does nothing. Well, it was like that. He had rather a rough, hoarse voice.

And, there he was, standing by the table. I was looking at him, with my back to the screen. And suddenly, I saw two distinct expressions flicker across his immobile eyes. How the deuce did they do it, those unflinching blue eyes with the direct gaze? For the eyes themselves never moved, gazing over my shoulder towards the screen. And the gaze was perfectly level and perfectly direct and perfectly unchanging. I suppose that the lids really must have rounded themselves a little and perhaps the lips moved a little too, as if he should be saying: "There you are, my dear." At any rate, the expression was that of pride, of satisfaction, of the possessor. I saw him once afterwards, for a moment, gaze upon the sunny fields of Branshaw and say: "All this is my land!"

And then again, the gaze was perhaps more direct, harder if possible—hardy too. It was a measuring look; a challenging look. Once when we were at Wiesbaden[1] watching him play in a polo match against the Bonner Hussaren I saw the same look come into his eyes, balancing the possibilities, looking over the ground. The German Captain, Count Baron Idigon von Lelöffel,[2] was right up by their goal posts, coming with the ball in an easy canter in that tricky German fashion. The rest of the field were just

---

[1] An elegant, highly fashionable spa town near Frankfurt, much more fashionable and cosmopolitan than nearby Bad Nauheim.

[2] The Bonner Hussaren were the Hussars of Bonn, Germany. Ford and Hunt met a polo-playing Hussar, Count Lelöffel, during their 1910 visit to Bad Nauheim.

anywhere. It was only a scratch sort of affair. Ashburnham was quite close to the rails not five yards from us and I heard him saying to himself: "Might just be done!" And he did it. Goodness! he swung that pony round with all its four legs spread out, like a cat dropping off a roof....

Well, it was just that look that I noticed in his eyes: "It might," I seem even now to hear him muttering to himself, "just be done."

I looked round over my shoulder and saw, tall, smiling brilliantly and buoyant—Leonora. And, little and fair, and as radiant as the track of sunlight along the sea—my wife.

That poor wretch! to think that he was at that moment in a perfect devil of a fix, and there he was, saying at the back of his mind: "It might just be done." It was like a chap in the middle of the eruption of a volcano, saying that he might just manage to bolt into the tumult and set fire to a haystack. Madness? Predestination? Who the devil knows?

Mrs. Ashburnham exhibited at that moment more gaiety than I have ever since known her to show. There are certain classes of English people—the nicer ones when they have been to many spas, who seem to make a point of becoming much more than usually animated when they are introduced to my compatriots. I have noticed this often. Of course, they must first have accepted the Americans. But that once done, they seem to say to themselves: "Hallo, these women are so bright. We aren't going to be outdone in brightness." And for the time being they certainly aren't. But it wears off. So it was with Leonora—at least until she noticed me. She began, Leonora did—and perhaps it was that that gave me the idea of a touch of insolence in her character, for she never afterwards did any one single thing like it—she began by saying in quite a loud voice and from quite a distance:

"Don't stop over by that stuffy old table, Teddy. Come and sit by these nice people!"

And that was an extraordinary thing to say. Quite extraordinary. I couldn't for the life of me refer to total strangers as nice people. But, of course, she was taking a line of her own in which I at any rate—and no one else in the room, for she too had taken the trouble to read through the list of guests—counted any more than so many clean, bull terriers. And she sat down rather brilliantly at a vacant table, beside ours—one that was reserved for the Guggenheimers. And she just sat absolutely deaf to the remonstrances of the head waiter with his face like a grey ram's. That poor chap was doing his steadfast duty too. He knew that the Guggenheimers of Chicago, after they had stayed there a month and had worried the poor life out of him, would give him two dollars fifty and grumble at the tipping system. And he knew that Teddy Ashburnham and his wife would give him no trouble whatever except what the smiles of Leonora might cause in his apparently unimpressionable bosom—though you never can tell what may go on behind even a not quite spotless plastron![1]— And every week Edward Ashburnham would give him a solid, sound, golden English sovereign. Yet this stout fellow was intent on saving that table for the Guggenheimers of Chicago. It ended in Florence saying:

"Why shouldn't we all eat out of the same trough?—that's a nasty New York saying. But I'm sure we're all nice quiet people and there can be four seats at our table. It's round."

Then came, as it were, an appreciative gurgle from the Captain and I was perfectly aware of a slight hesitation—a quick sharp motion in Mrs. Ashburnham, as if her horse had checked. But she put it at the fence all right, rising from the seat she had taken and sitting down opposite me, as it were, all in one motion.

I never thought that Leonora looked her best in evening dress. She seemed to get it too clearly cut, there was no ruffling. She always affected black and her shoulders were too classical. She seemed to stand out of her corsage as a white marble bust might out of a black Wedgwood vase.[2] I don't know.

I loved Leonora always and, today, I would very cheerfully lay down my life, what is left of it, in her service. But I am sure I never had the beginnings of a trace of what is called the sex instinct towards her. And I suppose—no I am certain that she never had it towards me. As far as I am concerned I think it was

---

[1]   A man's starched shirt-front or a steel breastplate.

[2]   Corsage: the bodice of a woman's dress; expensive Wedgwood vases were made in Sheffordshire in central England. On such vases, white figures stand out against a generally blue background; hence, black backgrounds are unusual.

those white shoulders that did it. I seemed to feel when I looked at them that, if ever I should press my lips upon them they would be slightly cold—not icily, not without a touch of human heat, but, as they say of baths, with the chill off. I seemed to feel chilled at the end of my lips when I looked at her ...

No, Leonora always appeared to me at her best in a blue tailor-made.[1] Then her glorious hair wasn't deadened by her white shoulders. Certain women's lines guide your eyes to their necks, their eyelashes, their lips, their breasts. But Leonora's seemed to conduct your gaze always to her wrist. And the wrist was at its best in a black or a dog-skin glove and there was always a gold circlet with a little chain supporting a very small golden key to a dispatch box. Perhaps it was that in which she locked up her heart and her feelings.

Anyhow, she sat down opposite me and then, for the first time, she paid any attention to my existence. She gave me, suddenly, yet deliberately, one long stare. Her eyes too were blue and dark and the eyelids were so arched that they gave you the whole round of the irises. And it was a most remarkable, a most moving glance, as if for a moment a lighthouse had looked at me. I seemed to perceive the swift questions chasing each other through the brain that was behind them. I seemed to hear the brain ask and the eyes answer with all the simpleness of a woman who was a good hand at taking in qualities of a horse—as indeed she was. "Stands well; has plenty of room for his oats behind the girth. Not so much in the way of shoulders," and so on. And so her eyes asked: "Is this man trustworthy in money matters; is he likely to try to play the lover; is he likely to let his women be troublesome? Is he, above all, likely to babble about my affairs?"

And, suddenly, into those cold, slightly defiant, almost defensive china blue orbs, there came a warmth, a tenderness, a friendly recognition ... oh, it was very charming and very touching—and quite mortifying. It was the look of a mother to her son, of a sister to her brother. It implied trust; it implied the want of any necessity for barriers. By God, she looked at me as if I

---

[1] A seemingly non-sexually provocative, tightly fitting woman's suit made by a tailor as opposed to a dressmaker.

were an invalid—as any kind woman may look at a poor chap in a bath chair. And, yes, from that day forward she always treated me and not Florence as if I were the invalid. Why, she would run after me with a rug upon chilly days. I suppose, therefore, that her eyes had made a favourable answer. Or, perhaps, it wasn't a favourable answer. And then Florence said: "And so the whole round table is begun."[1] Again Edward Ashburnham gurgled slightly in his throat; but Leonora shivered a little, as if a goose had walked over her grave. And I was passing her the nickel-silver basket of rolls. Avanti![2] ...

IV

So began those nine years of uninterrupted tranquillity. They were characterized by an extraordinary want of any communicativeness on the part of the Ashburnhams to which, we on our part replied by leaving out quite as extraordinarily, and nearly as completely, the personal note. Indeed, you may take it that what characterized our relationship was an atmosphere of taking everything for granted. The given proposition was, that we were all "good people." We took for granted that we all liked beef underdone but not too underdone; that both men preferred a good liqueur brandy after lunch; that both women drank a very light Rhine wine qualified with Fachingen water[3]—that sort of thing. It was also taken for granted that we were both sufficiently well off to afford anything that we could reasonably want in the way of amusements fitting to our station—that we could take motor cars and carriages by the day; that we could give each

---

[1] This allusion refers to the Pre-Raphaelite Brotherhood, who were influenced by perceptions of the chivalric traditions of King Arthur and the Knights of the Round Table. In *Rossetti: A Critical Essay on His Art* (1902), Ford cites Dante Gabriel Rossetti's comment on the demise of the Pre-Raphaelite Brotherhood: "So the whole round table is dissolved."

[2] "Forward!"

[3] A German mineral spring water containing reputedly curative and digestive properties.

other dinners and dine our friends and we could indulge if we liked in economy. Thus, Florence was in the habit of having the *Daily Telegraph*[1] sent to her every day from London. She was always an Anglo-maniac, was Florence; the Paris edition of the *New York Herald* was always good enough for me. But when we discovered that the Ashburnhams' copy of the London paper followed them from England, Leonora and Florence decided between them to suppress one subscription one year and the other the next. Similarly it was the habit of the Grand Duke of Nassau Schwerin,[2] who came yearly to the baths, to dine once with about eighteen families of regular Kur guests. In return he would give a dinner of all the eighteen at once. And, since these dinners were rather expensive (you had to take the Grand Duke and a good many of his suite and any members of the diplomatic bodies that might be there)—Florence and Leonora, putting their heads together, didn't see why we shouldn't give the Grand Duke his dinner together. And so we did. I don't suppose the Serenity minded that economy, or even noticed it. At any rate, our joint dinner to the Royal Personage gradually assumed the aspect of a yearly function. Indeed, it grew larger and larger, until it became a sort of closing function for the season, at any rate as far as we were concerned.

I don't in the least mean to say that we were the sort of persons who aspired to mix "with royalty." We didn't; we hadn't any claims; we were just "good people." But the Grand Duke was a pleasant, affable sort of royalty, like the late King Edward VII, and it was pleasant to hear him talk about the races and, very occasionally, as a bonne bouche,[3] about his nephew, the Emperor; or to have him pause for a moment in his walk to ask after the progress of our cures or to be benignantly interested in the amount of money we had put on Lelöffel's hunter for the Frankfurt Welter Stakes.

But upon my word, I don't know how we put in our time. How does one put in one's time? How is it possible to have

---

[1]   A fashionable London morning daily newspaper.

[2]   During their visit to Nauheim, Ford and Hunt met the grand duke of Hesse— Darmstadt, who bore a physical resemblance to Edward VII, the English monarch who reigned from 1901–1910.

[3]   Literally in French "a pleasant taste in the mouth."

achieved nine years and to have nothing whatever to show for it? Nothing whatever, you understand. Not so much as a bone penholder, carved to resemble a chessman and with a hole in the top through which you could see four views of Nauheim. And, as for experience, as for knowledge of one's fellow beings— nothing either. Upon my word, I couldn't tell you offhand whether the lady who sold the so expensive violets at the bottom of the road that leads to the station, was cheating me or no; I can't say whether the porter who carried our traps[1] across the station at Leghorn was a thief or no when he said that the regular tariff was a lira a parcel. The instances of honesty that one comes across in this world are just as amazing as the instances of dishonesty. After forty-five years of mixing with one's kind, one ought to have acquired the habit of being able to know something about one's fellow beings. But one doesn't.

I think the modern civilised habit—the modern English habit of taking every one for granted is a good deal to blame for this. I have observed this matter long enough to know the queer, subtle thing that it is; to know how the faculty, for what it is worth, never lets you down.

Mind, I am not saying that this is not the most desirable type of life in the world; that it is not an almost unreasonably high standard. For it is really nauseating, when you detest it, to have to eat every day several slices of thin, tepid, pink india rubber, and it is disagreeable to have to drink brandy when you would prefer to be cheered up by warm, sweet Kümmel.[2] And it is nasty to have to take a cold bath in the morning when what you want is really a hot one at night. And it stirs a little of the faith of your fathers that is deep down within you to have to have it taken for granted that you are an Episcopalian[3] when really you are an old-fashioned Philadelphia Quaker.

But these things have to be done; it is the cock that the whole of this society owes to Æsculapius.[4]

---

[1] Luggage.

[2] Sweet, cumin-flavored German liqueur.

[3] American equivalent of the English Anglican religious denomination.

[4] Greek God of Medicine to whom cocks were sacrificed. According to Plato's *Phaedo*, these are the final reflections of Socrates, i.e., death as the ultimate cure for life.

And the odd, queer thing is that the whole collection of rules applies to anybody—to the anybodies that you meet in hotels, in railway trains, to a less degree, perhaps, in steamers, but even, in the end, upon steamers. You meet a man or a woman and,[1] from tiny and intimate sounds, from the slightest of movements, you know at once whether you are concerned with good people or with those who won't do. You know, this is to say, whether they will go rigidly through with the whole programme from the underdone beef to the Anglicanism. It won't matter whether they be short or tall; whether the voice squeak like a marionette or rumble like a town bull's; it won't matter whether they are Germans, Austrians, French, Spanish, or even Brazilians—they will be the Germans or Brazilians who take a cold bath every morning and who move, roughly speaking, in diplomatic circles.

But the inconvenient—well, hang it all, I will say it—the damnable nuisance of the whole thing is, that with all the taking for granted, you never really get an inch deeper than the things I have catalogued.

I can give you a rather extraordinary instance of this. I can't remember whether it was in our first year—the first year of us four at Nauheim, because, of course, it would have been the fourth year of Florence and myself—but it must have been in the first or second year. And that gives the measure at once of the extraordinariness of our discussion and of the swiftness with which intimacy had grown up between us. On the one hand we seemed to start out on the expedition so naturally and with so little preparation, that it was as if we must have made many such excursions before; and our intimacy seemed so deep....

Yet the place to which we went was obviously one to which Florence at least would have wanted to take us quite early, so that you would almost think we should have gone there together at the beginning of our intimacy. Florence was singularly expert as a guide to archæological exceptions and there was nothing she liked so much as taking people round ruins and showing you the window

---

[1] In the Cornell manuscript of the novel, the text reads: "from the look in his eyes, from the part of the throat from which his voice comes; from her method of sitting down in a deck-chair; from the fact that she offers you a certain type of novel which she has done reading when you are sitting with nothing in your lap after lunch."

from which someone looked down upon the murder of someone else. She only did it once; but she did it quite magnificently. She could find her way, with the sole help of Baedeker,[1] as easily about any old monument as she could about any American city where the blocks are all square and the streets all numbered, so that you can go perfectly easily from Twenty-fourth to Thirtieth.

Now it happens that fifty minutes away from Nauheim, by a good train, is the ancient city of M——,[2] upon a great pinnacle of basalt, girt with a triple road running sideways up its shoulder like a scarf. And at the top there is a castle—not a square castle like Windsor,[3] but a castle all slate gables and high peaks with gilt weathercocks flashing bravely—the castle of St. Elizabeth of Hungary.[4] It has the disadvantage of being in Prussia; and it is always disagreeable to go into that country;[5] but it is very old and there are many double-spired churches and it stands up like a pyramid out of the green valley of the Lahn.[6] I don't suppose the Ashburnhams wanted especially to go there and I didn't especially want to go there myself. But, you understand, there was no objection. It was part of the cure to make an excursion three or four times a week. So that we were all quite unanimous in being grateful to Florence for providing the motive power. Florence, of course, had a motive of her own. She was at that time engaged in educating Captain Ashburnham—oh, of course, quite pour le bon motif![7] She used to say to Leonora: "I simply can't understand how you can let him live by your side and be so ignorant!" Leonora

---

1 Popular tourist guide with detailed maps.

2 Marburg, an old university town in the Prussian province of Hesse-Nassau. Ford stayed with Hunt at the Hotel Zum Ritter in Marburg for a fortnight in the autumn of 1910.

3 Ancient castle west of London and the residence of the British royal family.

4 Elizabeth of Hungary (1207–1231), Hungarian princess canonized for her care of the sick and the poor. She came to Marburg in 1228 after the death of her husband Ludwig IV, gave up her wealth, and became a Franciscan nun.

5 Prior to the 1914–1918 war, two-thirds of Germany consisted of the Prussian kingdom. Until 1915, Ford was pro-German, associating the nation with the Arts. He associated Prussia with militarism and dictatorship. In the manuscript, Dowell expresses a strong dislike of Belgium as a rapacious imperialist country (a sentiment revealed by Ford's friend Joseph Conrad in *Heart of Darkness* [1902]). The Kaiser's invasion of Belgium provoked the First World War and Dowell's anti-Belgium remarks were omitted from Ford's text.

6 A tributary of the Rhine.

7 "With the best intentions."

herself always struck me as being remarkably well educated. At any rate, she knew beforehand all that Florence had to tell her. Perhaps she got it up out of Baedeker before Florence was up in the morning. I don't mean to say that you would ever have known that Leonora knew anything, but if Florence started to tell us how Ludwig the Courageous[1] wanted to have three wives at once—in which he differed from Henry VIII,[2] who wanted them one after the other, and this caused a good deal of trouble—if Florence started to tell us this, Leonora would just nod her head in a way that quite pleasantly rattled my poor wife.

She used to exclaim: "Well, if you knew it, why haven't you told it all already to Captain Ashburnham? I'm sure he finds it interesting!" And Leonora would look reflectively at her husband and say: "I have an idea that it might injure his hand—the hand, you know, used in connection with horses' mouths...." And poor Ashburnham would blush and mutter and would say: "That's all right. Don't you bother about me."

I fancy his wife's irony did quite alarm poor Teddy; because one evening he asked me seriously in the smoking-room if I thought that having too much in one's head would really interfere with one's quickness in polo. It struck him, he said, that brainy Johnnies generally were rather muffs[3] when they got on to four legs. I reassured him as best I could. I told him that he wasn't likely to take in enough to upset his balance. At that time the Captain was quite evidently enjoying being educated by Florence. She used to do it about three or four times a week under the approving eyes of Leonora and myself. It wasn't, you understand, systematic. It came in bursts. It was Florence clearing up one of the dark places of the earth,[4] leaving the world a little lighter than she had found it. She would tell him the story of Hamlet; explain the form of a symphony, humming the first

---

1 Dowell actually means Philip the Magnanimous. In 1527, Philip the Magnanimous (1504–1567) abolished the pilgrimage center of St. Elizabeth of Hungary and created instead the University of Marburg, the first protestant university.

2 Henry VIII (1491–1547) established the Anglican Church when Pope Clement VII (1478–1534) refused to grant him a divorce.

3 Not adept at sports.

4 An allusion to Marlow's words in Conrad's *Heart of Darkness*: "And this also ... has been one of the dark places of the earth" (in this instance, ancient Britain).

and second subjects to him, and so on; she would explain to him the difference between Armenians and Erastians;[1] or she would give him a short lecture on the early history of the United States. And it was done in a way well calculated to arrest a young attention. Did you ever read Mrs. Markham?[2] Well, it was like that....

But our excursion to M—— was a much larger, a much more full dress affair. You see, in the archives of the Schloss[3] in that city there was a document which Florence thought would finally give her the chance to educate the whole lot of us together. It really worried poor Florence that she couldn't, in matters of culture, ever get the better of Leonora. I don't know what Leonora knew or what she didn't know, but certainly she was always there whenever Florence brought out any information. And she gave, somehow, the impression of really knowing what poor Florence gave the impression of having only picked up. I can't exactly define it. It was almost something physical. Have you ever seen a retriever dashing in play after a greyhound? You see the two running over a green field, almost side by side, and suddenly the retriever makes a friendly snap at the other. And the greyhound simply isn't there. You haven't observed it quicken its speed or strain a limb; but there it is, just two yards in front of the retriever's outstretched muzzle. So it was with Florence and Leonora in matters of culture.

But on this occasion I knew that something was up. I found Florence some days before, reading books like Ranke's *History of the Popes*, Symonds' *Renaissance*, Motley's *Rise of the Dutch Republic*, and Luther's *Table Talk*.[4]

---

1 The Armenians were followers of James Arminius of the Netherlands (1560–1609), a Dutch protestant theologian opposed to Calvin's doctrines concerning predestination. The Erastians followed Swiss theologian Thomas Erastus (1524–1583), a staunch defender of the supremacy of the state in ecclesiastical matters.

2 Pseudonym of Mrs. Elizabeth Penrose (1730–1837), who wrote popular histories for schoolchildren.

3 German castle.

4 Leopold van Ranke's *History of the Popes During the Sixteenth and Seventeenth Centuries* (1840); John Addington Symonds's *The Renaissance in Italy* (1875–1876), John Lothrop Motley's *The Rise of the Dutch Republic* (1856), and Martin Luther's *Table Talk* (1566). It was in the castle of Marburg that Luther lodged his famous Protest against indulgences. Ford and Hunt visited the castle to see the Protest, probably during the spring of 1911. From these classic volumes, Florence glimpsed perspectives of Marburg, the origins of Protestantism, and the glories and abuses of Roman Catholicism.

I must say that, until the astonishment came, I got nothing but pleasure out of the little expedition. I like catching the two-forty; I like the slow, smooth roll of the great big trains—and they are the best trains in the world! I like being drawn through the green country and looking at it through the clear glass of the great windows. Though, of course, the country isn't really green. The sun shines, the earth is blood red and purple and red and green and red. And the oxen in the ploughlands are bright varnished brown and black and blackish purple; and the peasants are dressed in the black and white of magpies; and there are great flocks of magpies too. Or the peasants' dresses in another field where there are little mounds of hay that will be grey-green on the sunny side and purple in the shadows—the peasants' dresses are vermilion with emerald green ribbons and purple skirts and white shirts and black velvet stomachers.[1] Still, the impression is that you are drawn through brilliant green meadows that run away on each side to the dark purple fir-woods; the basalt pinnacles; the immense forests. And there is meadow-sweet[2] at the edge of the streams, and cattle. Why, I remember on that afternoon I saw a brown cow hitch its horns under the stomach of a black and white animal and the black and white one was thrown right into the middle of a narrow stream. I burst out laughing. But Florence was imparting information so hard and Leonora was listening so intently that no one noticed me. As for me, I was pleased to be off duty; I was pleased to think that Florence for the moment was indubitably out of mischief—because she was talking about Ludwig the Courageous (I think it was Ludwig the Courageous but I am not an historian) about Ludwig the Courageous of Hessen who wanted to have three wives at once and patronized Luther—something like that!—I was so relieved to be off duty, because she couldn't possibly be doing anything to excite herself or set her poor heart a-fluttering—that the incident of the cow was a real joy to me. I chuckled over it from time to time for the whole rest of the day. Because it does look very funny, you know, to see a black and white cow land on its back in the middle of a

---

[1] Women's ornamental chest-coverings worn underneath their bodice lacings.

[2] White, highly fragrant wildflower.

stream. It is so just exactly what one doesn't expect of a cow.

I suppose I ought to have pitied the poor animal; but I just didn't. I was out for enjoyment. And I just enjoyed myself. It is so pleasant to be drawn along in front of the spectacular towns with the peaked castles and the many double spires. In the sunlight gleams come from the city—gleams from the glass of windows; from the gilt signs of apothecaries; from the ensigns of the student corps[1] high up in the mountains; from the helmets of the funny little soldiers moving their stiff little legs in white linen trousers. And it was pleasant to get out in the great big spectacular Prussian station with the hammered bronze ornaments and the paintings of peasants and flowers and cows; and to hear Florence bargain energetically with the driver of an ancient droschka[2] drawn by two lean horses. Of course, I spoke German much more correctly than Florence, though I never could rid myself quite of the accent of the Pennsylvania Duitsch[3] of my childhood. Anyhow, we were drawn in a sort of triumph, for five marks without any trinkgeld,[4] right up to the castle. And we were taken through the museum and saw the firebacks,[5] the old glass, the old swords and the antique contraptions. And we went up winding corkscrew staircases and through the Rittersaal, the great painted hall where the Reformer and his friends met for the first time[6] under the protection of the gentleman that had three wives at once and formed an alliance with the gentleman that had six wives, one after the other (I'm not really interested in these facts but they have a bearing on my

---

1   Fraternity houses, largely occupied by wealthy students.
2   A four-wheeled open carriage for hire as a taxi. Earlier, Dowell confused Marburg's modest railway station (erected in 1910) with Wiesbaden's "spectacular" one.
3   A community, centered largely in eastern Pennsylvania, that retained the traditions and ways of life of their eighteenth-century ancestors. In *Ford Madox Ford* (1972), Grover Smith observes that "Ford could not have been guilty of this howler, for he of all people would have known that Pennsylvania *Deutsch* is not Holland *Dutch*. Dowell is [thus] marked as ignorant and pretentious."
4   Gratuities.
5   Usually cast-iron ornamental metallic plates at the back of open fireplaces.
6   Ford and Hunt visited the Rittersaal in 1910. "The great painted hall" and its murals were in fact late-nineteenth-century forgeries. The Rittersaal was, by legend, purported to be the place where Martin Luther (1483–1546) held his meeting with his fellow protestors after nailing his 95 theses to the Wittenberg Schlosskirche doors on 31 October 1517.

story). And we went through chapels, and music rooms, right up immensely high in the air to a large old chamber, full of presses, with heavily-shuttered windows all round. And Florence became positively electric. She told the tired, bored custodian what shutters to open; so that the bright sunlight streamed in palpable shafts into the dim old chamber. She explained that this was Luther's bedroom and that just where the sunlight fell had stood his bed. As a matter of fact, I believe that she was wrong and that Luther only stopped, as it were, for lunch, in order to evade pursuit. But, no doubt, it would have been his bedroom if he could have been persuaded to stop the night. And then, in spite of the protest of the custodian, she threw open another shutter and came tripping back to a large glass case.

"And there," she exclaimed with an accent of gaiety, of triumph, and of audacity. She was pointing at a piece of paper, like the half-sheet of a letter with some faint pencil scrawls that might have been a jotting of the amounts we were spending during the day. And I was extremely happy at her gaiety, in her triumph, in her audacity. Captain Ashburnham had his hands upon the glass case. "There it is—the Protest."[1] And then, as we all properly stage-managed our bewilderment, she continued: "Don't you know that is why we were all called Protestants? That is the pencil draft of the Protest they drew up. You can see the signatures of Martin Luther, and Martin Bucer, and Zwingli, and Ludwig the Courageous...."[2]

I may have got some of the names wrong, but I know that Luther and Bucer were there. And her animation continued and I was glad. She was better and she was out of mischief. She continued, looking up into Captain Ashburnham's eyes: "It's because of that piece of paper that you're honest, sober, industrious, provident, and clean-lived. If it weren't for that piece of paper you'd be like the Irish or the Italians or the Poles, but

---

[1] Ford showed Hunt the document in 1910. This was not the actual "Protest," but another document signed by Luther, Bucer, Zwingli, and others that enumerated 15 points of specific doctrinal differences between Protestantism and Catholicism.

[2] Martin Bucer (1491–1551), the German protestant reformer who negotiated between Luther and Huldrych Zwingli (1484–1531), a Swiss religious reformer. Ludwig the Courageous died some 300 years earlier.

particularly the Irish...."

And she laid one finger upon Captain Ashburnham's wrist.

I was aware of something treacherous, something frightful, something evil in the day. I can't define it and can't find a simile for it. It wasn't as if a snake had looked out of a hole. No, it was as if my heart had missed a beat. It was as if we were going to run and cry out; all four of us in separate directions, averting our heads. In Ashburnham's face I know that there was absolute panic. I was horribly frightened and then I discovered that the pain in my left wrist was caused by Leonora's clutching it:

"I can't stand this," she said with a most extraordinary passion; "I must get out of this."

I was horribly frightened. It came to me for a moment, though I hadn't time to think it, that she must be a madly jealous woman—jealous of Florence and Captain Ashburnham, of all people in the world! And it was a panic in which we fled! We went right down the winding stairs, across the immense Rittersaal to a little terrace that overlooks the Lahn, the broad valley and the immense plain into which it opens out.

"Don't you see?" she said, "don't you see what's going on?" The panic again stopped my heart. I muttered, I stuttered—I don't know how I got the words out:

"No! What's the matter? Whatever's the matter?"

She looked me straight in the eyes; and for a moment I had the feeling that those two blue discs were immense, were overwhelming, were like a wall of blue that shut me off from the rest of the world. I know it sounds absurd; but that is what it did feel like.

"Don't you see," she said, with a really horrible bitterness, with a really horrible lamentation in her voice. "Don't you see that that's the cause of the whole miserable affair; of the whole sorrow of the world? And of the eternal damnation of you and me and them...."

I don't remember how she went on; I was too frightened; I was too amazed. I think I was thinking of running to fetch assistance—a doctor, perhaps, or Captain Ashburnham. Or possibly she needed Florence's tender care, though, of course, it would have been very bad for Florence's heart. But I know that when I came out of it she was saying: "Oh, where are all the bright, happy, innocent beings in the world? Where's happiness? One reads of it in books!"

She ran her hand with a singular clawing motion upwards over her forehead. Her eyes were enormously distended; her face was exactly that of a person looking into the pit of hell and seeing horrors there. And then suddenly she stopped. She was, most amazingly, just Mrs. Ashburnham again. Her face was perfectly clear, sharp and defined; her hair was glorious in its golden coils. Her nostrils twitched with a sort of contempt. She appeared to look with interest at a gypsy caravan that was coming over a little bridge far below us.

"Don't you know," she said, in her clear hard voice, "don't you know that I'm an Irish Catholic?"

x • She trying to cover the truth up for him?
• • she using this particular to express the bigger issue of infidelity?

V

Those words gave me the greatest relief that I have ever had in my life. They told me, I think, almost more than I have ever gathered at any one moment—about myself. I don't think that before that day I had ever wanted anything very much except Florence. I have, of course, had appetites, impatiences ... Why, sometimes at a table d'hôte, when there would be, say, caviare handed round, I have been absolutely full of impatience for fear that when the dish came to me there should not be a satisfying portion left over by the other guests. I have been exceedingly impatient at missing trains. The Belgian State Railway has a trick of letting the French trains miss their connections at Brussels. That has always infuriated me. I have written about it letters to *The Times* that *The Times* never printed; those that I wrote to the Paris edition of the *New York Herald* were always printed, but they never seemed to satisfy me when I saw them. Well, that was a sort of frenzy with me.

It was a frenzy that now I can hardly realize. I can understand it intellectually. You see, in those days I was interested in people with "hearts." There was Florence, there was Edward Ashburnham—or, perhaps, it was Leonora that I was more interested in. I don't mean in the way of love. But, you see, we were both of the same profession—at any rate as I saw it. And the profession was that of keeping heart patients alive.

You have no idea how engrossing such a profession may become. Just as the blacksmith says: "By hammer and hand all Art doth stand," just as the baker thinks that all the solar system revolves around his morning delivery of rolls; as the postmaster-general believes that he alone is the preserver of society—and surely, surely, these delusions are necessary to keep us going—so did I and, as I believed, Leonora, imagine that the whole world ought to be arranged so as to ensure the keeping alive of heart patients. You have no idea how engrossing such a profession may become—how imbecile, in view of that engrossment, appear the ways of princes, of republics, of municipalities. A rough bit of road beneath the motor tyres, a couple of succeeding "thank'ee-marms"[1] with their quick jolts would be enough to set me grumbling to Leonora against the Prince or the Grand Duke or the Free City[2] through whose territory we might be passing. I would grumble like a stockbroker whose conversations over the telephone are incommoded by the ringing of bells from a city church. I would talk about mediæval survivals, about the taxes being surely high enough. The point, by the way, about the missing of the connections of the Calais boat trains at Brussels was that the shortest possible sea journey is frequently of great importance to sufferers from the heart. Now, on the Continent, there are two special heart cure places, Nauheim and Spa,[3] and to reach both of these baths from England if in order to ensure a short sea passage, you come by Calais—you have to make the connection at Brussels. And the Belgian train never waits by so much the shade of a second for the one coming from Calais or from Paris. And even if the French trains are just on time, you have to run—imagine a heart patient running!—along the

---

1   Bumps in the road.

2   Bremen, Hamburg, and Lübeck were three independent city-states within Germany. Their princes were leading figures in the Protestant Reformation.

3   Northeast Belgium resort noted for its medicinal mineral springs. Ford and Hunt visited Spa in 1910–1911. It was there, according to British newspapers, that they were rumored to have been married.

unfamiliar ways of the Brussels station and to scramble up the high steps of the moving train. Or, if you miss the connection, you have to wait five or six hours.... I used to keep awake whole nights cursing that abuse.

My wife used to run—she never, in whatever else she may have misled me, tried to give me the impression that she was not a gallant soul. But, once in the German Express, she would lean back, with one hand to her side and her eyes closed. Well, she was a good actress. And I would be in hell. In hell, I tell you. For in Florence I had at once a wife and an unattained mistress—that is what it comes to—and in the retaining of her in this world I had my occupation, my career, my ambition. It is not often that these things are united in one body. Leonora was a good actress too. By Jove she was good! I tell you, she would listen to me by the hour, evolving my plans for a shock-proof world. It is true that, at times I used to notice about her face an air of inattention as if she were listening, a mother, to the child at her knee, or as if, precisely, I were myself the patient.

You understand that there was nothing the matter with Edward Ashburnham's heart—that he had thrown up his commission and had left India and come half the world over in order to follow a woman who had really had a "heart" to Nauheim. That was the sort of sentimental ass he was. For, you understand, too, that they really needed to live in India, to econ-omize, to let the house at Branshaw Teleragh.

Of course, at that date, I had never heard of the Kilsyte case. Ashburnham had, you know, kissed a servant girl in a railway train and it was only the grace of God, the prompt functioning of the communication cord and the ready sympathy of what I believe you call the Hampshire bench,[I] that kept the poor devil out of Winchester Gaol for years and years. I never heard of that case until the final stages of Leonora's revelations....

But just think of that poor wretch.... I, who have surely the right, beg you to think of that poor wretch. Is it possible that such a luckless devil should be so tormented by blind and inscrutable destiny? For there is no other way to think of it.

[I]   The Hampshire County Court of Assizes.

None. I have the right to say it, since for years he was my wife's lover, since he killed her, since he broke up all the pleasantnesses that there were in my life. There is no priest that has the right to tell me that I must not ask pity for him, from you, silent listener beyond the hearthstone, from the world, or from the God who created in him those desires, those madnesses....

Of course, I should not hear of the Kilsyte case. I knew none of their friends; they were for me just good people—fortunate people with broad and sunny acres in a southern county. Just good people! By heavens, I sometimes think that it would have been better for him, poor dear, if the case had been such a one that I must needs have heard of it—such a one as maids and couriers and other Kur guests whisper about for years after, until gradually it dies away in the pity that there is knocking about here and there in the world. Supposing he had spent his seven years in Winchester Gaol or whatever it is that inscrutable and blind justice allots to you for following your natural but ill-timed inclinations—there would have arrived a stage when nodding gossips on the Kursaal terrace would have said "Poor fellow," thinking of his ruined career. He would have been the fine soldier with his back now bent.... Better for him, poor devil, if his back had been prematurely bent.

Why, it would have been a thousand times better....[1] For, of course, the Kilsyte case, which came at the very beginning of his finding Leonora cold and unsympathetic, gave him a nasty jar. He left servants alone after that.

It turned him, naturally, all the more loose amongst women of his own class. Why, Leonora told me that Mrs. Maidan—the woman he followed from Burma to Nauheim—assured her he awakened her attention by swearing that when he kissed the servant in the train he was driven to it. I daresay he was driven to it, by the mad passion to find an ultimately satisfying woman. I daresay he was sincere enough. Heaven help me, I daresay he was sincere enough in his love for Mrs. Maidan. She was a nice

---

[1]   In the Cornell manuscript of the novel, the text reads: "He could have put his fingers to his nose to the scoundrels that blackmailed him till the end of his days. For of course the Kilsyte case, if it were the only one that came to light, that 'got into the papers,' as they say, wasn't the only occurrence in his life."

little thing, a dear little dark woman with long lashes, of whom Florence grew quite fond. She had a lisp and a happy smile. We saw plenty of her for the first month of our acquaintance, then she died, quite quietly—of heart trouble.

But you know, poor little Mrs. Maidan—she was so gentle, so young. She cannot have been more than twenty-three and she had a boy husband out in Chitral[1] not more than twenty-four, I believe. Such young things ought to have been left alone. Of course Ashburnham could not leave her alone. I do not believe that he could. Why, even I, at this distance of time am aware that I am a little in love with her memory. I can't help smiling when I think suddenly of her—as you might at the thought of something wrapped carefully away in lavender, in some drawer, in some old house that you have long left. She was so—so submissive. Why, even to me she had the air of being submissive—to me that not the youngest child will ever pay heed to. Yes, this is the saddest story ...

No, I cannot help wishing that Florence had left her alone—with her playing with adultery. I suppose it was; though she was such a child that one has the impression that she would hardly have known how to spell such a word. No, it was just submissiveness—to the importunities, to the tempestuous forces that pushed that miserable fellow on to ruin. And I do not suppose that Florence really made much difference. If it had not been for her that Ashburnham left his allegiance for Mrs. Maidan, then it would have been some other woman. But still, I do not know. Perhaps the poor young thing would have died—she was bound to die, anyhow, quite soon—but she would have died without having to soak her noonday pillow with tears whilst Florence, below the window, talked to Captain Ashburnham about the Constitution of the United States....Yes, it would have left a better taste in the mouth if Florence had let her die in peace....

Leonora behaved better in a sense. She just boxed Mrs. Maidan's ears—yes, she hit her, in an uncontrollable access of rage, a hard blow on the side of the cheek, in the corridor of the hotel, outside Edward's rooms. It was that, you know, that

---

[1]   Distant British colonial outpost on the northwest frontier of British India, now Pakistan.

accounted for the sudden, odd intimacy that sprang up between Florence and Mrs. Ashburnham.

Because it was, of course, an odd intimacy. If you look at it from the outside nothing could have been more unlikely than that Leonora, who is the proudest creature on God's earth, would have struck up an acquaintanceship with two casual Yankees whom she could not really have regarded as being much more than a carpet beneath her feet. You may ask what she had to be proud of. Well, she was a Powys[1] married to an Ashburnham— I suppose that gave her the right to despise casual Americans as long as she did it unostentatiously. I don't know what anyone has to be proud of. She might have taken pride in her patience, in her keeping her husband out of the bankruptcy court. Perhaps she did.

At any rate that was how Florence got to know her. She came round a screen at the corner of the hotel corridor and found Leonora with the gold key that hung from her wrist caught in Mrs. Maidan's hair just before dinner. There was not a single word spoken. Little Mrs. Maidan was very pale, with a red mark down her left cheek, and the key would not come out of her black hair. It was Florence who had to disentangle it, for Leonora was in such a state that she could not have brought herself to touch Mrs. Maidan without growing sick.

And there was not a word spoken. You see, under those four eyes—her own and Mrs. Maidan's—Leonora could just let herself go as far as to box Mrs. Maidan's ears. But the moment a stranger came along she pulled herself wonderfully up. She was at first silent and then, the moment the key was disengaged by Florence she was in a state to say: "So awkward of me ... I was just trying to put the comb straight in Mrs. Maidan's hair...."

Mrs. Maidan, however, was not a Powys married to an Ashburnham; she was a poor little O'Flaherty whose husband was a boy of country parsonage origin. So there was no mistaking the sob she let go as she went desolately away along the corridor. But Leonora was still going to play up. She opened the door of Ashburnham's room quite ostentatiously, so that Florence

---

[1] A distinctly Welsh name.

should hear her address Edward in terms of intimacy and liking. "Edward," she called. But there was no Edward there.

You understand that there was no Edward there. It was then, for the only time of her career, that Leonora really compromised herself—She exclaimed ... "How frightful! ... Poor little Maisie! ..."[1]

She caught herself up at that, but of course it was too late. It was a queer sort of affair....

I want to do Leonora every justice. I love her very dearly for one thing and in this matter, which was certainly the ruin of my small household cockleshell, she certainly tripped up. I do not believe—and Leonora herself does not believe—that poor little Maisie Maidan was ever Edward's mistress. Her heart was really so bad that she would have succumbed to anything like an impassioned embrace. That is the plain English of it, and I suppose plain English is best. She was really what the other two, for reasons of their own, just pretended to be. Queer, isn't it? Like one of those sinister jokes that Providence plays upon one. Add to this that I do not suppose that Leonora would much have minded, at any other moment, if Mrs. Maidan had been her husband's mistress. It might have been a relief from Edward's sentimental gurglings over the lady and from the lady's submissive acceptance of those sounds. No, she would not have minded.

But, in boxing Mrs. Maidan's ears Leonora was just striking the face of an intolerable universe. For, that afternoon she had had a frightfully painful scene with Edward.

As far as his letters went, she claimed the right to open them when she chose. She arrogated to herself the right because Edward's affairs were in such a frightful state and he lied so about them that she claimed the privilege of having his secrets at her disposal. There was not, indeed, any other way, for the poor fool was too ashamed of his lapses ever to make a clean breast of anything. She had to drag these things out of him.

It must have been a pretty elevating job for her. But that afternoon, Edward being on his bed for the hour and a half prescribed by the Kur authorities, she had opened a letter that she took to

---

[1] Ford originally wrote "Poor little mouse!"

come from a Colonel Hervey. They were going to stay with him in Linlithgowshire[1] for the month of September and she did not know whether the date fixed would be the eleventh or the eighteenth. The address on this letter was, in handwriting, as like Colonel Hervey's as one blade of corn is like another. So she had at the moment no idea of spying on him.

But she certainly was. For she discovered that Edward Ashburnham was paying a blackmailer of whom she had never heard something like three hundred pounds a year ... It was a devil of a blow; it was like death; for she imagined that by that time she had really got to the bottom of her husband's liabilities. You see, they were pretty heavy. What had really smashed them up had been a perfectly common-place affair at Monte Carlo—an affair with a cosmopolitan harpy who passed for the mistress of a Russian Grand Duke. She exacted a twenty thousand pound pearl tiara from him as the price of her favours for a week or so. It would have pipped[2] him a good deal to have found so much, and he was not in the ordinary way a gambler. He might, indeed, just have found the twenty thousand and the not slight charges of a week at an hotel with the fair creature. He must have been worth at that date five hundred thousand dollars[3] and a little over.

Well, he must needs go to the tables and lose forty thousand pounds....[4] Forty thousand solid pounds, borrowed from sharks! And even after that he must—it was an imperative passion—enjoy the favours of the lady. He got them, of course, when it was a matter of solid bargaining, for far less than twenty thousand, as he might, no doubt, have done from the first. I daresay ten thousand dollars covered the bill.

Anyhow, there was a pretty solid hole in a fortune of a hundred thousand pounds or so. And Leonora had to fix things up; he would have run from money-lender to money-lender. And that was quite in the early days of her discovery of his infidelities—if you like to call them infidelities. And she discovered that one from public sources. God knows what would have

---

1   A Scottish county.
2   Annoyed, hurt financially.
3   About £100,000 in 1915. Today, about $7,500,000 or £5,000,000.
4   About $200,000 in 1915. Today, about $3,000,000 or £2,000,000.

happened if she had not discovered it from public sources. I suppose he would have concealed it from her until they were penniless. But she was able, by the grace of God, to get hold of the actual lenders of the money, to learn the exact sums that were needed. And she went off to England.

Yes, she went right off to England to her attorney and his while he was still in the arms of his Circe[1]—at Antibes,[2] to which place they had retired. He got sick of the lady quite quickly, but not before Leonora had had such lessons in the art of business from her attorney that she had her plan as clearly drawn up as was ever that of General Trochu[3] for keeping the Prussians out of Paris in 1870. It was about as effectual at first, or it seemed so.

That would have been, you know, in 1895, about nine years before the date of which I am talking—the date of Florence's getting her hold over Leonora; for that was what it amounted to.... Well, Mrs. Ashburnham had simply forced Edward to settle all his property upon her. She could force him to do anything; in his clumsy, good-natured, inarticulate way he was as frightened of her as of the devil. And he admired her enormously, and he was as fond of her as any man could be of any woman. She took advantage of it to treat him as if he had been a person whose estates are being managed by the Court of Bankruptcy. I suppose it was the best thing for him.

Anyhow, she had no end of a job for the first three years or so. Unexpected liabilities kept on cropping up—and that afflicted fool did not make it any easier. You see, along with the passion of the chase went a frame of mind that made him be extraordinarily ashamed of himself. You may not believe it, but he really had such a sort of respect for the chastity of Leonora's imagination that he hated—he was positively revolted at the thought that she should know that the sort of thing that he did existed in the world. So he would stick out in an agitated way against the accusation of ever having done anything. He wanted to preserve the virginity of his

---

1   In Homer's *Odyssey*, the sorceress Circe transformed men into animals. Odysseus resisted her spells and, after living with her for a year, returned to Penelope.
2   A fashionable Mediterranean resort between Nice and Cannes.
3   General Louis Jules Trochu (1815–1896), the governor of Paris during the Prussian occupation of the city in the Franco-Prussian War.

wife's thoughts. He told me that himself during the long walks we had at the last—while the girl was on the way to Brindisi.

So, of course, for those three years or so, Leonora had many agitations. And it was then that they really quarrelled.

Yes, they quarrelled bitterly.[1] That seems rather extravagant. You might have thought that Leonora would be just calmly loathing and he lachrymosely contrite. But that was not it a bit … Along with Edward's passions and his shame for them went the violent conviction of the duties of his station—a conviction that was quite unreasonably expensive. I trust I have not, in talking of his liabilities, given the impression that poor Edward was a promiscuous libertine. He was not; he was a sentimentalist. The servant girl in the Kilsyte case had been pretty, but mournful of appearance. I think that, when he had kissed her, he had desired rather to comfort her. And, if she had succumbed to his blandishments I daresay he would have set her up in a little house in Portsmouth or Winchester and would have been faithful to her for four or five years. He was quite capable of that.

No, the only two of his affairs of the heart that cost him money were that of the Grand Duke's mistress and that which was the subject of the blackmailing letter that Leonora opened. That had been a quite passionate affair with quite a nice woman. It had succeeded the one with the Grand Ducal lady. The lady was the wife of a brother officer and Leonora had known all about the passion, which had been quite a real passion and had lasted for several years. You see, poor Edward's passions were quite logical in their progression upwards. They began with a servant, went on to a courtesan and then to a quite nice woman, very unsuitably mated. For she had a quite nasty husband who, by means of letters and things, went on blackmailing poor Edward to the tune of three or four hundred a year—with threats of the divorce court. And after this lady came Maisie Maidan, and after poor Maisie only one more affair and then—the real passion of his life. His marriage with Leonora had been arranged by his

---

[1]   The Cornell manuscript of the novel includes the additional phrase, "You see, she was childless herself," which appears several paragraphs later in the Bodley Head edition of *The Good Soldier*.

parents and, though he always admired her immensely, he had hardly ever pretended to be much more than tender to her, though he desperately needed her moral support, too....

But his really trying liabilities were mostly in the nature of generosities proper to his station. He was, according to Leonora, always remitting his tenants' rents and giving the tenants to understand that the reduction would be permanent; he was always redeeming drunkards who came before his magisterial bench; he was always trying to put prostitutes into respectable places—and he was a perfect maniac about children. I don't know how many ill-used people he did not pick up and provide with careers— Leonora has told me, but I daresay she exaggerated and the figure seems so preposterous that I will not put it down. All these things, and the continuance of them seemed to him to be his duty—along with impossible subscriptions to hospitals and boy scouts and to provide prizes at cattle shows and antivivisection societies....

Well, Leonora saw to it that most of these things were not continued. They could not possibly keep up Branshaw Manor at that rate after the money had gone to the Grand Duke's mistress. She put the rents back at their old figures; discharged the drunkards from their homes, and sent all the societies notice that they were to expect no more subscriptions. To the children she was more tender; nearly all of them she supported till the age of apprenticeship or domestic service. You see, she was childless herself.[1]

She was childless herself, and she considered herself to be to blame. She had come of a penniless branch of the Powys family, and they had forced upon her poor dear Edward without making the stipulation that the children should be brought up as Catholics. And that, of course, was spiritual death to Leonora. I have given you a wrong impression if I have not made you see that Leonora was a woman of a strong, cold conscience, like all English Catholics. (I cannot, myself, help disliking this religion; there is always, at the bottom of my mind, in spite of Leonora,

---

[1] The Cornell manuscript contains a lengthy, cancelled passage detailing Ashburnham's "illegitimate offspring [who] must be sent to Eton or to the convent at Roehampton." Moreover, "every one of the girls that he ruined must be provided for as if she were at least the wife, say, of a bank manager.... It could not be done of course. And Leonora sees to it that it was not done."

the feeling of shuddering at the Scarlet Woman,[1] that filtered in upon me in the tranquillity of the little old Friends' Meeting House in Arch Street, Philadelphia.)[2] So I do set down a good deal of Leonora's mismanagement of poor dear Edward's case to the peculiarly English form of her religion. Because, of course, the only thing to have done for Edward would have been to let him sink down until he became a tramp of gentlemanly address, having, maybe, chance love affairs upon the highways.[3] He would have done so much less harm; he would have been much less agonized too. At any rate, he would have had fewer chances of ruining and of remorse. For Edward was great at remorse.

But Leonora's English Catholic conscience, her rigid principles, her coldness, even her very patience, were, I cannot help thinking, all wrong in this special case. She quite seriously and naïvely imagined that the Church of Rome disapproves of divorce; she quite seriously and naïvely believed that her church could be such a monstrous and imbecile institution as to expect her to take on the impossible job of making Edward Ashburnham a faithful husband. She had, as the English would say, the Nonconformist temperament.[4] In the United States of North America we call it the New England conscience. For, of course, that frame of mind has been driven in on the English Catholics. The centuries that they have gone through—centuries of blind and malignant oppression, of ostracism from public employment, of being, as it were, a small beleaguered garrison in a hostile country, and therefore having to act with great formality—all these things have combined to perform that conjuring trick. And I suppose that Papists in England are even technically Nonconformists.

Continental Papists are a dirty, jovial and unscrupulous crew. But that, at least, lets them be opportunists. They would have fixed poor

---

[1] A pejorative term for a woman who has had an affair.

[2] The oldest and largest Quaker meeting house, which is still in use.

[3] The Cornell manuscript contains an intriguing cancelled passage regarding Edward having committed "rapes," among his other sexual proclivities. Martin Stannard astutely suggests that this correction "shifts the image of Ashburnham from that of libertine to that of hopeless sentimentalist."

[4] On a literal level, she was a Protestant dissenter from the official Church of England. At the beginning of the twentieth century, the Nonconformists were critical of prevailing social manners and traits.

dear Edward up all right. (Forgive my writing of these monstrous things in this frivolous manner. If I did not I should break down and cry.) In Milan, say, or in Paris, Leonora would have had her marriage dissolved in six months for two hundred dollars paid in the right quarter. And Edward would have drifted about until he became a tramp of the kind I have suggested. Or he would have married a barmaid who would have made him such frightful scenes in public places and would so have torn out his moustache and left visible signs upon his face that he would have been faithful to her for the rest of his days. That was what he wanted to redeem him....

For, along with his passions and his shames there went the dread of scenes in public places, of outcry, of excited physical violence; of publicity, in short. Yes, the barmaid would have cured him. And it would have been all the better if she drank; he would have been kept busy looking after her.

I know that I am right in this. I know it because of the Kilsyte case. You see, the servant girl that he then kissed was nurse in the family of the Nonconformist head of the county—whatever that post may be called. And that gentleman was so determined to ruin Edward, who was the chairman of the Tory caucus,[1] or whatever it is—that the poor dear sufferer had the very devil of a time. They asked questions about it in the House of Commons; they tried to get the Hampshire magistrates degraded;[2] they suggested to the War Ministry that Edward was not the proper person to hold the King's commission. Yes, he got it hot and strong.

The result you have heard. He was completely cured of philandering amongst the lower classes. And that seemed a real blessing to Leonora. It did not revolt her so much to be connected—it is a sort of connection—with people like Mrs. Maidan, instead of with a little kitchenmaid.

In a dim sort of way, Leonora was almost contented when she arrived at Nauheim, that evening....

She had got things nearly straight by the long years of scraping in little stations in Chitral and Burma[3]—stations where living is

---

1 A political grouping of local members from one of the leading parties in the country.
2 Reduced in rank or social status.
3 Then part of British India.

cheap in comparison with the life of a county magnate, and where, moreover, liaisons of one sort or another are normal and inexpensive too. So that, when Mrs. Maidan came along—and the Maidan affair might have caused trouble out there because of the youth of the husband—Leonora had just resigned herself to coming home. With pushing and scraping and with letting Branshaw Teleragh, and with selling a picture and a relic of Charles I or so, she had got—and, poor dear, she had never had a really decent dress to her back in all those years and years—she had got, as she imagined, her poor dear husband back into much the same financial position as had been his before the mistress of the Grand Duke had happened along. And, of course, Edward himself had helped her a little on the financial side. He was a fellow that many men liked. He was so presentable and quite ready to lend you his cigar puncher—that sort of thing. So, every now and then some financier whom he met about would give him a good, sound, profitable tip. And Leonora was never afraid of a bit of a gamble—English Papists seldom are, I do not know why.

So nearly all her investments turned up trumps, and Edward was really in fit case to reopen Branshaw Manor and once more to assume his position in the county. Thus Leonora had accepted Maisie Maidan almost with resignation—almost with a sigh of relief. She really liked the poor child—she had to like somebody. And, at any rate, she felt she could trust Maisie—she could trust her not to rook[1] Edward for several thousands a week, for Maisie had refused to accept so much as a trinket ring from him. It is true that Edward gurgled and raved about the girl in a way that she had never yet experienced. But that, too, was almost a relief. I think she would really have welcomed it if he could have come across the love of his life. It would have given her a rest.

And there could not have been anyone better than poor little Mrs. Maidan; she was so ill she could not want to be taken on expensive jaunts…. It was Leonora herself who paid Maisie's expenses to Nauheim. She handed over the money to the boy husband, for Maisie would never have allowed it; but the husband was in agonies of fear. Poor devil!

---

[1]   Cheat, swindle.

I fancy that, on the voyage from India, Leonora was as happy as ever she had been in her life. Edward was wrapped up, completely, in his girl—he was almost like a father with a child, trotting about with rugs and physic and things, from deck to deck. He behaved, however, with great circumspection, so that nothing leaked through to the other passengers. And Leonora had almost attained to the attitude of a mother towards Mrs. Maidan. So it had looked very well—the benevolent, wealthy couple of good people, acting as saviours to the poor, dark-eyed, dying young thing. And that attitude of Leonora's towards Mrs. Maidan no doubt partly accounted for the smack in the face. She was hitting a naughty child who had been stealing chocolates at an inopportune moment.

It was certainly an inopportune moment. For, with the opening of that blackmailing letter from that injured brother officer, all the old terrors had redescended upon Leonora. Her road had again seemed to stretch out endless; she imagined that there might be hundreds and hundreds of such things that Edward was concealing from her—that they might necessitate more mortgagings, more pawnings of bracelets, more and always more horrors. She had spent an excruciating afternoon. The matter was one of a divorce case, of course, and she wanted to avoid publicity as much as Edward did, so that she saw the necessity of continuing the payments. And she did not so much mind that. They could find three hundred a year. But it was the horror of there being more such obligations.

She had had no conversation with Edward for many years—none that went beyond the mere arrangements for taking trains or engaging servants. But that afternoon she had to let him have it. And he had been just the same as ever. It was like opening a book after a decade to find the words the same. He had the same motives. He had not wished to tell her about the case because he had not wished her to sully her mind with the idea that there was such a thing as a brother officer who could be a blackmailer—and he had wanted to protect the credit of his old light of love. That lady was certainly not concerned with her husband. And he swore, and swore, and swore, that there was nothing else in the world against him. She did not believe him.

He had done it once too often—and she was wrong for the first time, so that he acted a rather creditable part in the matter. For he went right straight out to the post-office and spent several hours in coding a telegram to his solicitor, bidding that hard-headed man to threaten to take out at once a warrant against the fellow who was on his track. He said afterwards that it was a bit too thick on poor old Leonora to be ballyragged[1] any more. That was really the last of his outstanding accounts, and he was ready to take his personal chance of the divorce court if the blackmailer turned nasty. He would face it out—the publicity, the papers, the whole bally show. Those were his simple words....

He had made, however, the mistake of not telling Leonora where he was going, so that, having seen him go to his room to fetch the code for the telegram, and seeing, two hours later, Maisie Maidan come out of his room, Leonora imagined that the two hours she had spent in silent agony Edward had spent with Maisie Maidan in his arms. That seemed to her to be too much.

As a matter of fact Maisie's being in Edward's room had been the result partly of poverty, partly of pride, partly of sheer inno-cence. She could not, in the first place, afford a maid; she refrained as much as possible from sending the hotel servants on errands, since every penny was of importance to her, and she feared to have to pay high tips at the end of her stay. Edward had lent her one of his fascinating cases containing fifteen different sizes of scissors, and, having seen, from her window, his depar-ture for the post-office, she had taken the opportunity of return-ing the case. She could not see why she should not, though she felt a certain remorse at the thought that she had kissed the pillows of his bed. That was the way it took her.

But Leonora could see that, without the shadow of a doubt, the incident gave Florence a hold over her. It let Florence into things and Florence was the only created being who had any idea that the Ashburnhams were not just good people with nothing to their tails. She determined at once, not so much to give Florence the privilege of her intimacy—which would have been the payment of a kind of blackmail—as to keep Florence under observation until she could

---

[1] Mucked about, played tricks upon.

have demonstrated to Florence that she was not in the least jealous of poor Maisie. So that was why she had entered the dining-room arm in arm with my wife, and why she had so markedly planted herself at our table. She never left us, indeed, for a minute that night, except just to run up to Mrs. Maidan's room to beg her pardon and to beg her also to let Edward take her very markedly out into the gardens that night. She said herself, when Mrs. Maidan came rather wistfully down into the lounge where we were all sitting: "Now, Edward, get up and take Maisie to the Casino. I want Mrs. Dowell to tell me all about the families in Connecticut who came from Fordingbridge." For it had been discovered that Florence came of a line that had actually owned Branshaw Teleragh for two centuries before the Ashburnhams came there. And there she sat with me in that hall, long after Florence had gone to bed, so that I might witness her gay reception of that pair. She could play up.

And that enables me to fix exactly the day of our going to the town of M——. For it was the very day poor Mrs. Maidan died. We found her dead when we got back—pretty awful, that, when you come to figure out what it all means....

At any rate the measure of my relief when Leonora said that she was an Irish Catholic gives you the measure of my affection for that couple. It was an affection so intense that even to this day I cannot think of Edward without sighing. I do not believe that I could have gone on any more with them. I was getting too tired. And I verily believe, too, if my suspicion that Leonora was jealous of Florence had been the reason she gave for her outburst I should have turned upon Florence with the maddest kind of rage. Jealousy would have been incurable. But Florence's mere silly gibes at the Irish and at the Catholics could be apologized out of existence. And that I appeared to fix up in two minutes or so.

She looked at me for a long time rather fixedly and queerly while I was doing it. And at last I worked myself up to saying:

"Do accept the situation. I confess that I do not like your religion. But I like you so intensely. I don't mind saying that I have never had anyone to be really fond of, and I do not believe that anyone has ever been fond of me, as I believe you really to be."

"Oh, I'm fond enough of you," she said. "Fond enough to say that I wish every man was like you. But there are others to be considered." She was thinking, as a matter of fact, of poor Maisie. She picked a little piece of pellitory[1] out of the breast-high wall in front of us. She chafed it for a long minute between her finger and thumb, then she threw it over the coping.

"Oh, I accept the situation," she said at last, "if you can."

VI

I remember laughing at the phrase, "accept the situation," which she seemed to repeat with a gravity too intense. I said to her something like:

"It's hardly as much as that. I mean, that I must claim the liberty of a free American citizen to think what I please about your co-religionists. And I suppose that Florence must have liberty to think what she pleases and to say what politeness allows her to say."

"She had better," Leonora answered, "not say one single word against my people or my faith."

It struck me at the time, that there was an unusual, an almost threatening, hardness in her voice. It was almost as if she were trying to convey to Florence, through me, that she would seriously harm my wife if Florence went to something that was an extreme. Yes, I remember thinking at the time that it was almost as if Leonora were saying, through me to Florence:

"You may outrage me as you will; you may take all that I personally possess, but do not you care to say one single thing in view of the situation that that will set up—against the faith that makes me become the doormat for your feet."

But obviously, as I saw it, that could not be her meaning. Good people, be they ever so diverse in creed, do not threaten each other. So that I read Leonora's words to mean just no more than:

"It would be better if Florence said nothing at all against my co-religionists, because it is a point that I am touchy about."

---

[1]   A wall plant whose roots have a pungent flavor. Pellitory was used as a cure for toothaches.

That was the hint that, accordingly, I conveyed to Florence when, shortly afterwards, she and Edward came down from the tower. And I want you to understand that, from that moment until after Edward and the girl and Florence were all dead together, I had never the remotest glimpse, not the shadow of a suspicion, that there was anything wrong, as the saying is. For five minutes, then, I entertained the possibility that Leonora might be jealous; but there was never another flicker in that flame-like personality. How in the world should I get it?

For, all that time, I was just a male sick nurse. And what chance had I against those three hardened gamblers, who were all in league to conceal their hands from me? What earthly chance? They were three to one—and they made me happy. Oh God, they made me so happy that I doubt if even paradise, that shall smooth out all temporal wrongs, shall ever give me the like. And what could they have done better, or what could they have done that could have been worse? I don't know....

I suppose that, during all that time I was a deceived husband and that Leonora was pimping for Edward. That was the cross that she had to take up during her long Calvary of a life....

You ask how it feels to be a deceived husband. Just Heavens, I do not know. It feels just nothing at all. It is not Hell, certainly it is not necessarily Heaven. So I suppose it is the intermediate stage. What do they call it? Limbo. No, I feel nothing at all about that. They are dead; they have gone before their Judge who, I hope, will open to them the springs of His compassion. It is not my business to think about it. It is simply my business to say, as Leonora's people say: "*Requiem aeternam dona eis, domine, et lux perpetua luceat eis. In memoria aeterna erit....*"[1] But what were they? The just? The unjust? God knows! I think that the pair of them were only poor wretches, creeping over this earth in the shadow of an eternal wrath. It is very terrible....

It is almost too terrible, the picture of that judgement, as it appears to me sometimes, at nights. It is probably the suggestion of

---

[1] From the Mass for the dead: "Eternal rest give to them, O Lord; and let perpetual light shine upon them. The just shall be in everlasting remembrance." As Thomas C. Moser notes, Dowell pointedly ends the quotation before *justus*, its concluding phrase.

some picture that I have seen somewhere. But upon an immense plain, suspended in mid-air, I seem to see three figures, two of them clasped close in an intense embrace, and one intolerably solitary. It is in black and white, my picture of that judgement, an etching, perhaps; only I cannot tell an etching from a photographic reproduction. And the immense plain is the hand of God, stretching out for miles and miles, with great spaces above it and below it. And they are in the sight of God, and it is Florence that is alone....

And, do you know, at the thought of that intense solitude I feel an overwhelming desire to rush forward and comfort her. You cannot, you see, have acted as nurse to a person for twelve years without wishing to go on nursing them, even though you hate them with the hatred of the adder, and even in the palm of God. But, in the nights, with that vision of judgement before me, I know that I hold myself back. For I hate Florence. I hate Florence with such a hatred that I would not spare her an eternity of loneliness. She need not have done what she did. She was an American, a New Englander. She had not the hot passions of these Europeans. She cut out that poor imbecile of an Edward—and I pray God that he is really at peace, clasped close in the arms of that poor, poor girl! And, no doubt, Maisie Maidan will find her young husband again, and Leonora will burn, clear and serene, a northern light[1] and one of the archangels of God. And me.... Well, perhaps, they will find me an elevator to run.... But Florence....

She should not have done it. She should not have done it. It was playing it too low down. She cut out poor dear Edward from sheer vanity; she meddled between him and Leonora from a sheer, imbecile spirit of district visiting.[2] Do you understand that, whilst she was Edward's mistress, she was perpetually trying to reunite him to his wife? She would gabble on to Leonora about forgiveness—treating the subject from the bright, American point of view. And Leonora would treat her like the whore she was. Once she said to Florence in the early morning:

"You come to me straight out of his bed to tell me that that is my proper place. I know it, thank you."

---

1   A bright set of stars most favorably viewed in the Arctic regions.
2   A pejorative rendering of a charitable visit to the poor.

But even that could not stop Florence. She went on saying that it was her ambition to leave this world a little brighter by the passage of her brief life, and how thankfully she would leave Edward, whom she thought she had brought to a right frame of mind, if Leonora would only give him a chance. He needed, she said, tenderness beyond anything.

And Leonora would answer—for she put up with this outrage for years—Leonora, as I understand, would answer something like:

"Yes, you would give him up. And you would go on writing to each other in secret, and committing adultery in hired rooms. I know the pair of you, you know. No. I prefer the situation as it is."

Half the time Florence would ignore Leonora's remarks. She would think they were not quite ladylike. The other half of the time she would try to persuade Leonora that her love for Edward was quite spiritual—on account of her heart. Once she said:

"If you can believe that of Maisie Maidan, as you say you do, why cannot you believe it of me?"

Leonora was, I understand, doing her hair at that time in front of the mirror in her bedroom. And she looked round at Florence, to whom she did not usually vouchsafe a glance—she looked round coolly and calmly, and said:

"Never do you dare to mention Mrs. Maidan's name again. You murdered her. You and I murdered her between us. I am as much a scoundrel as you. I don't like to be reminded of it."

Florence went off at once into a babble of how could she have hurt a person whom she hardly knew, a person whom, with the best intentions, in pursuance of her efforts to leave the world a little brighter, she had tried to save from Edward. That was how she figured it out to herself. She really thought that.... So Leonora said patiently:

"Very well, just put it that I killed her and that it's a painful subject. One does not like to think that one had killed someone. Naturally not. I ought never to have brought her from India."

And that, indeed, is exactly how Leonora looked at it. It is stated a little baldly, but Leonora was always a great one for bald statements.

What had happened on the day of our jaunt to the ancient city of M—— had been this:

Leonora, who had been even then filled with pity and contrition for the poor child, on returning to our hotel had gone straight to Mrs. Maidan's room. She had wanted just to pet her. And she had perceived at first only, on the clear, round table covered with red velvet, a letter addressed to her. It ran something like:

"Oh, Mrs. Ashburnham, how could you have done it? I trusted you so. You never talked to me about me and Edward, but I trusted you. How could you buy me from my husband? I have just heard how you have—in the hall they were talking about it, Edward and the American lady. You paid the money for me to come here. Oh, how could you? How could you? I am going straight back to Bunny...."

Bunny was Mrs. Maidan's husband.

And Leonora said that, as she went on reading the letter, she had, without looking round her, a sense that that hotel room was cleared, that there were no papers on the table, that there were no clothes on the hooks, and that there was a strained silence— a silence, she said, as if there were something in the room that drank up such sounds as there were. She had to fight against that feeling, whilst she read the postscript of the letter.

"I did not know you wanted me for an adulteress," the postscript began. The poor child was hardly literate. "It was surely not right of you and I never wanted to be one. And I heard Edward call me a poor little rat to the American lady. He always called me a little rat in private, and I did not mind. But if he called me it to her, I think he does not love me any more. Oh, Mrs. Ashburnham, you knew the world and I knew nothing. I thought it would be all right if you thought it could, and I thought you would not have brought me if you did not, too. You should not have done it, and we out of the same convent...."

Leonora said that she screamed when she read that.

And then she saw that Maisie's boxes were all packed, and she began a search for Mrs. Maidan herself—all over the hotel. The manager said that Mrs. Maidan had paid her bill, and had gone up to the station to ask the Reiseverkehrsbureau[1] to make her out a plan for her immediate return to Chitral. He imagined that

---

[1] Tourist office.

he had seen her come back, but he was not quite certain. No one in the large hotel had bothered his head about the child. And she, wandering solitarily in the hall, had no doubt sat down beside a screen that had Edward and Florence on the other side. I never heard then or after what had passed between that precious couple. I fancy Florence was just about beginning her cutting out of poor dear Edward by addressing to him some words of friendly warning as to the ravages he might be making in the girl's heart. That would be the sort of way she would begin. And Edward would have sentimentally assured her that there was nothing in it; that Maisie was just a poor little rat whose passage to Nauheim his wife had paid out of her own pocket. That would have been enough to do the trick.

For the trick was pretty efficiently done. Leonora, with panic growing and with contrition very large in her heart, visited every one of the public rooms of the hotel—the dining-room, the lounge, the *Schreibzimmer*,[1] the winter garden. God knows what they wanted with a winter garden in an hotel that is only open from May till October. But there it was. And then Leonora ran—yes, she ran up the stairs—to see if Maisie had not returned to her rooms. She had determined to take that child right away from that hideous place. It seemed to her to be all unspeakable. I do not mean to say that she was not quite cool about it. Leonora was always Leonora. But the cold justice of the thing demanded that she should play the part of mother to this child who had come from the same convent. She figured it out to amount to that. She would leave Edward to Florence—and to me—and she would devote all her time to providing that child with an atmosphere of love until she could be returned to her poor young husband. It was naturally too late.

She had not cared to look round Maisie's rooms at first. Now, as soon as she came in, she perceived, sticking out beyond the bed, a small pair of feet in high-heeled shoes. Maisie had died in the effort to strap up a great portmanteau. She had died so grotesquely that her little body had fallen forward into the trunk, and it had closed upon her, like the jaws of a gigantic alligator.

---

[1] Writing room.

The key was in her hand. Her dark hair, like the hair of a Japanese, had come down and covered her body and her face.

Leonora lifted her up—she was the merest featherweight— and laid her on the bed with her hair about her. She was smiling, as if she had just scored a goal in a hockey match. You understand she had not committed suicide. Her heart had just stopped. I saw her, with the long lashes on the cheeks, with the smile about the lips, with the flowers all about her. The stem of a white lily rested in her hand so that the spike of flowers was upon her shoulder. She looked like a bride in the sunlight of the mortuary candles that were all about her, and the white coifs of the two nuns that knelt at her feet with their faces hidden might have been two swans that were to bear her away to kissing-kindness land, or wherever it is. Leonora showed her to me. She would not let either of the others see her. She wanted, you know, to spare poor dear Edward's feelings. He never could bear the sight of a corpse. And, since she never gave him an idea that Maisie had written to her, he imagined that the death had been the most natural thing in the world. He soon got over it. Indeed, it was the one affair of his about which he never felt much remorse.

PART II

I

The death of Mrs. Maidan occurred on the 4th of August 1904. And then nothing happened until the 4th of August 1913. There is the curious coincidence of dates, but I do not know whether that is one of those sinister, as if half-jocular and altogether merciless proceedings on the part of a cruel Providence that we call a coincidence. Because it may just as well have been the superstitious mind of Florence that forced her to certain acts, as if she had been hypnotized. It is, however, certain that the 4th of August always proved a significant date for her. To begin with, she was born on the 4th of August. Then, on that date in the year 1899, she set out with her uncle for the tour round the world in company with a young man called Jimmy. But that was not merely a coincidence. Her kindly old uncle, with the supposedly damaged heart, was, in his delicate way, offering her, in this trip, a birthday present to celebrate her coming of age. Then, on the 4th of August 1900, she yielded to an action that certainly coloured her whole life—as well as mine. She had no luck. She was probably offering herself a birthday present that morning....

On the 4th of August 1901, she married me, and set sail for Europe in a great gale of wind—the gale that affected her heart. And no doubt there, again, she was offering herself a birthday gift—the birthday gift of my miserable life. It occurs to me that I have never told you anything about my marriage. That was like this: I have told you, as I think, that I first met Florence at the Stuyvesants', in Fourteenth Street. And, from that moment, I determined with all the obstinacy of a possibly weak nature, if not to make her mine, at least to marry her. I had no occupation—I had no business affairs. I simply camped down there in Stamford, in a vile hotel, and just passed my days in the house, or on the verandah of the Misses Hurlbird. The Misses Hurlbird, in an odd, obstinate way, did not like my presence. But they were hampered by the national manners of these occasions. Florence had her own sitting-room. She could ask to it whom she liked, and I simply walked into that apartment. I was as timid as you will, but in that matter I was like a chicken that is determined to get across the road in front of an automobile. I would walk into Florence's pretty, little, old-fashioned room, take off my hat, and sit down.

Florence had, of course, several other fellows, too—strapping young New Englanders, who worked during the day in New York and spent only the evenings in the village of their birth. And, in the evenings, they would march in on Florence with almost as much determination as I myself showed. And I am bound to say that they were received with as much disfavour as was my portion—from the Misses Hurlbird....

They were curious old creatures, those two. It was almost as if they were members of an ancient family under some curse—they were so gentlewomanly, so proper, and they sighed so. Sometimes I would see tears in their eyes. I do not know that my courtship of Florence made much progress at first. Perhaps that was because it took place almost entirely during the daytime, on hot afternoons, when the clouds of dust hung like fog, right up as high as the tops of the thin-leaved elms. The night, I believe, is the proper season for the gentle feats of love, not a Connecticut July afternoon, when any sort of proximity is an almost appalling thought. But, if I never so much as kissed Florence, she let me discover very easily, in the course of a fortnight, her simple wants. And I could supply those wants....

She wanted to marry a gentleman of leisure; she wanted a European establishment. She wanted her husband to have an English accent, an income of fifty thousand dollars a year[1] from real estate and no ambitions to increase that income. And—she faintly hinted—she did not want much physical passion in the affair. Americans, you know, can envisage such unions without blinking.

She gave out this information in floods of bright talk—she would pop a little bit of it into comments over a view of the Rialto,[2] Venice, and, whilst she was brightly describing Balmoral Castle,[3] she would say that her ideal husband would be one who

---

[1]   About £10,000 in 1915. Today, about $750,000 or £500,000.
[2]   Venetian bridge over the Grand Canal.
[3]   Seat of the British royal family in the Scottish countryside.

could get her received at the British Court. She had spent, it seemed, two months in Great Britain—seven weeks in touring from Stratford to Strathpeffer,[1] and one as paying guest in an old English family near Ledbury,[2] an impoverished, but still stately family, called Bagshawe. They were to have spent two months more in that tranquil bosom, but inopportune events, apparently in her uncle's business, had caused their rather hurried return to Stamford. The young man called Jimmy had remained in Europe to perfect his knowledge of that continent. He certainly did: he was most useful to us afterwards.

But the point that came out—that there was no mistaking— was that Florence was coldly and calmly determined to take no look at any man who could not give her a European settlement. Her glimpse of English home life had effected this. She meant, on her marriage, to have a year in Paris, and then to have her husband buy some real estate in the neighbourhood of Fordingbridge, from which place the Hurlbirds had come in the year 1688.[3] On the strength of that she was going to take her place in the ranks of English county society. That was fixed.

I used to feel mightily elevated when I considered these details, for I could not figure out that, amongst her acquaintances in Stamford there was any fellow that would fill the bill. The most of them were not as wealthy as I, and those that were were not the type to give up the fascinations of Wall Street even for the protracted companionship of Florence. But nothing really happened during the month of July. On the 1st of August Florence apparently told her aunts that she intended to marry me.

She had not told me so, but there was no doubt about the aunts, for, on that afternoon, Miss Florence Hurlbird, Senior, stopped me on my way to Florence's sitting-room and took me, agitatedly, into the parlour. It was a singular interview, in that old-fashioned colonial room, with the spindle-legged furniture, the

---

[1] A village and spa in Scotland with health springs.

[2] Market town in Herefordshire in the Anglo-Welsh border region.

[3] In 1688, the Catholic monarch James II was deposed. The protestant monarchs William III and Mary II of Orange ascended to the English throne. In 1689, a Bill of Rights prohibited a future Catholic monarchy.

silhouettes, the miniatures, the portrait of General Braddock,[1] and the smell of lavender. You see, the two poor maiden ladies were in agonies—and they could not say one single thing direct. They would almost wring their hands and ask if I had considered such a thing as different temperaments. I assure you they were almost affectionate, concerned for me even, as if Florence were too bright for my solid and serious virtues.

For they had discovered in me solid and serious virtues. That might have been because I had once dropped the remark that I preferred General Braddock to General Washington.[2] For the Hurlbirds had backed the losing side in the War of Independence, and had been seriously impoverished and quite efficiently oppressed for that reason. The Misses Hurlbird could never forget it.

Nevertheless they shuddered at the thought of a European career for myself and Florence. Each of them really wailed when they heard that that was what I hoped to give their niece. That may have been partly because they regarded Europe as a sink of iniquity, where strange laxities prevailed. They thought the Mother Country as Erastian as any other. And they carried their protests to extraordinary lengths, for them....

They even, almost, said that marriage was a sacrament; but neither Miss Florence nor Miss Emily could quite bring herself to utter the word. And they almost brought themselves to say that Florence's early life had been characterized by flirtations—something of that sort.

I know I ended the interview by saying:

"I don't care. If Florence has robbed a bank I am going to marry her and take her to Europe."

And at that Miss Emily wailed and fainted. But Miss Florence, in spite of the state of her sister, threw herself on my neck and cried out:

"Don't do it, John. Don't do it. You're a good young man,"

---

[1]   Edward Braddock (1695–1755), Chief of Staff of British forces in North America. Fought with George Washington against the French. Attempting to take Fort Dusquesne, he led his troops into a massacre and was mortally wounded.

[2]   George Washington (1732–1799) survived the Dusquesne assault, became head of the American Revolutionary forces, and was the first elected President of the United States.

and she added, whilst I was getting out of the room to send Florence to her aunt's rescue:

"We ought to tell you more. But she's our dear sister's child."

Florence, I remember, received me with a chalk-pale face and the exclamation:

"Have those old cats been saying anything against me?" But I assured her that they had not and hurried her into the room of her strangely afflicted relatives. I had really forgotten all about that exclamation of Florence's until this moment. She treated me so very well—with such tact—that, if I ever thought of it afterwards I put it down to her deep affection for me.

And that evening, when I went to fetch her for a buggy-ride, she had disappeared. I did not lose any time. I went into New York and engaged berths on the "Pocahontas,"[1] that was to sail on the evening of the fourth of the month, and then, returning to Stamford, I tracked out,[2] in the course of the day, that Florence had been driven to Rye Station.[3] And there I found that she had taken the cars to Waterbury. She had, of course, gone to her uncle's. The old man received me with a stony, husky face. I was not to see Florence; she was ill; she was keeping her room. And, from something that he let drop—an odd Biblical phrase that I have forgotten—I gathered that all that family simply did not intend her to marry ever in her life.

I procured at once the name of the nearest minister and a rope ladder—you have no idea how primitively these matters were arranged in those days in the United States. I daresay that may be so still. And at one o'clock in the morning of the 4th of August I was standing in Florence's bedroom. I was so one-minded in my purpose that it never struck me there was anything improper in being, at one o'clock in the morning, in Florence's bedroom. I just wanted to wake her up. She was not, however, asleep. She

---

[1] A Native American princess, Pocahontas (1595–1617) was taken from Virginia to London to be baptized and married to an Englishman. She died in England. Ford and his wife sailed from New York to England in 1906 on the *Minnetonka*, named after the mythical Native American princess Minnehaha.

[2] Ascertained by looking at "tracks."

[3] Rye is a suburb of New York City with a trolley car station. It is 40 miles from Waterbury, Connecticut.

expected me, and her relatives had only just left her. She received me with an embrace of a warmth.... Well, it was the first time I had ever been embraced by a woman—and it was the last when a woman's embrace has had in it any warmth for me....

I suppose it was my own fault, what followed. At any rate, I was in such a hurry to get the wedding over, and was so afraid of her relatives finding me there, that I must have received her advances with a certain amount of absence of mind. I was out of that room and down the ladder in under half a minute. She kept me waiting at the foot an unconscionable time—it was certainly three in the morning before we knocked up that minister. And I think that that wait was the only sign Florence ever showed of having a conscience as far as I was concerned, unless her lying for some moments in my arms was also a sign of conscience. I fancy that, if I had shown warmth then, she would have acted the proper wife to me, or would have put me back again. But, because I acted like a Philadelphia gentleman, she made me, I suppose, go through with the part of a male nurse. Perhaps she thought that I should not mind.

After that, as I gather, she had not any more remorse. She was only anxious to carry out her plans. For, just before she came down the ladder, she called me to the top of that grotesque implement that I went up and down like a tranquil jumping-jack. I was perfectly collected. She said to me with a certain fierceness:

"It is determined that we sail at four this afternoon? You are not lying about having taken berths?"

I understood that she would naturally be anxious to get away from the neighbourhood of her apparently insane relatives, so that I readily excused her for thinking that I should be capable of lying about such a thing. I made it, therefore, plain to her that it was my fixed determination to sail by the "Pocahontas." She said then—it was a moonlit morning, and she was whispering in my ear whilst I stood on the ladder. The hills that surround Waterbury showed, extraordinarily tranquil, around the villa. She said, almost coldly:

"I wanted to know, so as to pack my trunks." And she added: "I may be ill, you know. I guess my heart is a little like Uncle Hurlbird's. It runs in families."

I whispered that the "Pocahontas" was an extraordinarily steady boat....

Now I wonder what had passed through Florence's mind during the two hours that she had kept me waiting at the foot of the ladder.[1] I would give not a little to know. Till then, I fancy she had had no settled plan in her mind. She certainly never mentioned her heart till that time. Perhaps the renewed sight of her Uncle Hurlbird had given her the idea. Certainly her Aunt Emily, who had come over with her to Waterbury, would have rubbed into her, for hours and hours, the idea that any accentuated discussions would kill the old gentleman. That would recall to her mind all the safeguards against excitement with which the poor silly old gentleman had been hedged in during their trip round the world. That, perhaps, put it into her head. Still, I believe there was some remorse on my account, too. Leonora told me that Florence said there was—for Leonora knew all about it, and once went so far as to ask her how she could do a thing so infamous. She excused herself on the score of an overmastering passion. Well, I always say that an overmastering passion is a good excuse for feelings. You cannot help them. And it is a good excuse for straight actions—she might have bolted with the fellow, before or after she married me. And, if they had not enough money to get along with, they might have cut their throats, or sponged on her family, though, of course, Florence wanted such a lot that it would have suited her very badly to have for a husband a clerk in a dry-goods store, which was what old Hurlbird would have made of that fellow. He hated him. No, I do not think that there is much excuse for Florence.

God knows. She was a frightened fool, and she was fantastic, and I suppose that, at that time, she really cared for that imbecile. He certainly didn't care for her. Poor thing.... At any rate, after I had assured her that the "Pocahontas" was a steady ship, she just said:

---

[1] In the Cornell manuscript of the novel, the text reads: "Well, anyhow, I daresay she did feel remorse whilst she kept me waiting. I do not see how else she can have put in her time.... She had been lying in her bed practically dressed, and she did not do any packing until late that forenoon. So, as I figure it out still, from the moment I came into her room until the time she came to me at the top of the ladder she was wrestling with herself."

"You'll have to look after me in certain ways—like Uncle Hurlbird is looked after. I will tell you how to do it." And then she stepped over the sill, as if she were stepping on board a boat. I suppose she had burnt hers!

I had no doubt eye-openers enough. When we reentered the Hurlbird mansion at eight o'clock the Hurlbirds were just exhausted. Florence had a hard, triumphant air. We had got married about four in the morning and had sat about in the woods above the town till then, listening to a mocking-bird imitate an old tom-cat. So I guess Florence had not found getting married to me a very stimulating process. I had not found anything much more inspiring to say than how glad I was, with variations. I think I was too dazed. Well, the Hurlbirds were too dazed to say much. We had breakfast together, and then Florence went to pack her grips and things. Old Hurlbird took the opportunity to read me a full-blooded lecture, in the style of an American oration, as to the perils for young American girlhood lurking in the European jungle. He said that Paris was full of snakes in the grass, of which he had had bitter experience. He concluded, as they always do, poor, dear old things, with the aspiration that all American women should one day be sexless—though that is not the way they put it....

Well, we made the ship all right by one-thirty—and there was a tempest blowing. That helped Florence a good deal. For we were not ten minutes out from Sandy Hook[1] before Florence went down into her cabin and her heart took her. An agitated stewardess came running up to me, and I went running down. I got my directions how to behave to my wife. Most of them came from her, though it was the ship doctor who discreetly suggested to me that I had better refrain from manifestations of affection. I was ready enough.

I was, of course, full of remorse. It occurred to me that her heart was the reason for the Hurlbirds' mysterious desire to keep their youngest and dearest unmarried. Of course, they would be too refined to put the motive into words. They were old stock

---

[1]   The final American landmark that ships encounter as they move into the Atlantic Ocean.

New Englanders. They would not want to have to suggest that a husband must not kiss the back of his wife's neck. They would not like to suggest that he might, for the matter of that. I wonder, though, how Florence got the doctor to enter the conspiracy— the several doctors.

Of course her heart squeaked a bit—she had the same configuration of the lungs as her Uncle Hurlbird. And, in his company, she must have heard a great deal of heart talk from specialists. Anyhow, she and they tied me pretty well down—and Jimmy, of course, that dreary boy—what in the world did she see in him? He was lugubrious, silent, morose. He had no talent as a painter. He was very sallow and dark, and he never shaved sufficiently. He met us at Havre, and he proceeded to make himself useful for the next two years, during which he lived in our flat in Paris, whether we were there or not. He studied painting at Julien's,[1] or some such place....

That fellow had his hands always in the pockets of his odious, square-shouldered, broad-hipped, American coats, and his dark eyes were always full of ominous appearances. He was, besides, too fat. Why, I was much the better man....

And I daresay Florence would have given me the better. She showed signs of it. I think, perhaps, the enigmatic smile with which she used to look back at me over her shoulder when she went into the bathing place was a sort of invitation. I have mentioned that. It was as if she were saying: "I am going in here. I am going to stand so stripped and white and straight—and you are a man...." Perhaps it was that....

No, she cannot have liked that fellow long. He looked like sallow putty. I understand that he had been slim and dark and very graceful at the time of her first disgrace. But, loafing about in Paris, on her pocket money and on the allowance that old Hurlbird made him to keep out of the United States, had given him a stomach like a man of forty, and dyspeptic irritation on top of it.

God, how they worked me! It was those two between them who really elaborated the rules. I have told you something about

---

[1] Founded in 1873 by Rudolphe Julien, it was a private art studio in Paris that was fashionable with English and Americans wishing to learn drawing and painting.

them—how I had to head conversations, for all those eleven years, off such topics as love, poverty, crime, and so on. But, looking over what I have written, I see that I have unintentionally misled you when I said that Florence was never out of my sight. Yet that was the impression that I really had until just now. When I come to think of it she was out of my sight most of the time.

You see, that fellow impressed upon me that what Florence needed most of all were sleep and privacy. I must never enter her room without knocking, or her poor little heart might flutter away to its doom. He said these things with his lugubrious croak, and his black eyes like a crow's, so that I seemed to see poor Florence die ten times a day—a little, pale, frail corpse. Why, I would as soon have thought of entering her room without her permission as of burgling a church. I would sooner have committed that crime. I would certainly have done it if I had thought the state of her heart demanded the sacrilege. So at ten o'clock at night the door closed upon Florence, who had gently, and, as if reluctantly, backed up that fellow's recommendations; and she would wish me good night as if she were a *cinque cento*[1] Italian lady saying good-bye to her lover. And at ten o'clock of the next morning there she would come out the door of her room as fresh as Venus[2] rising from any of the couches that are mentioned in Greek legends.

Her room door was locked because she was nervous about thieves; but an electric contrivance on a cord was understood to be attached to her little wrist. She had only to press a bulb to raise the house. And I was provided with an axe—an axe!—great gods, with which to break down her door in case she ever failed to answer my knock, after I knocked really loud several times. It was pretty well thought out, you see.

What wasn't so well thought out were the ultimate consequences—our being tied to Europe. For that young man rubbed it so well into me that Florence would die if she crossed the Channel—he impressed it so fully on my mind that, when later Florence wanted to go to Fordingbridge, I cut the proposal

---

[1] Sixteenth century.
[2] The Roman Goddess of Beauty (the Greek Aphrodite) associated with love and sensuality.

short—absolutely short, with a curt no. It fixed her and it frightened her. I was even backed up by all the doctors. I seemed to have
had endless interviews with doctor after doctor, cool, quiet men,
who would ask, in reasonable tones, whether there was any reason
for our going to England—any special reason. And since I could
not see any special reason, they would give the verdict:"Better not,
then." I daresay they were honest enough, as things go. They probably imagined that the mere associations of the steamer might have
effects on Florence's nerves. That would be enough, that and a
conscientious desire to keep our money on the Continent.

It must have rattled poor Florence pretty considerably, for you
see, the main idea—the only main idea of her heart, that was
otherwise cold—was to get to Fordingbridge and be a county
lady in the home of her ancestors. But Jimmy got her, there: he
shut on her the door of the Channel; even on the fairest day of
blue sky, with the cliffs of England shining like mother of pearl
in full view of Calais, I would not have let her cross the steamer
gangway to save her life. I tell you it fixed her.

It fixed her beautifully, because she could not announce herself
as cured, since that would have put an end to the locked bedroom
arrangements. And, by the time she was sick of Jimmy—which
happened in the year 1903—she had taken on Edward Ashburnham.
Yes, it was a bad fix for her, because Edward could have taken her
to Fordingbridge and, though he could not give her Branshaw
Manor, that home of her ancestors being settled on his wife, she
could at least have pretty considerably queened it there or thereabouts, what with our money and the support of the Ashburnhams.
Her uncle, as soon as he considered that she had really settled down
with me—and I sent him only the most glowing accounts of her
virtue and constancy—made over to her a very considerable part
of his fortune for which he had no use. I suppose that we had,
between us, fifteen thousand a year in English money, though I
never quite knew how much of hers went to Jimmy. At any rate,
we could have shone in Fordingbridge.

I never quite knew, either, how she and Edward got rid of
Jimmy. I fancy that fat and disreputable raven must have had his six
golden front teeth knocked down his throat by Edward one morning whilst I had gone out to buy some flowers in the Rue de la

Paix, leaving Florence and the flat in charge of those two. And serve him very right, is all that I can say. He was a bad sort of blackmailer; I hope Florence does not have his company in the next world.

As God is my Judge, I do not believe that I would have separated those two if I had known that they really and passionately loved each other. I do not know where the public morality of the case comes in, and, of course, no man really knows what he would have done in any given case. But I truly believe that I would have united them, observing ways and means as decent as I could. I believe that I should have given them money to live upon and that I should have consoled myself somehow. At that date I might have found some young thing, like Maisie Maidan, or the poor girl, and I might have had some peace. For peace I never had with Florence, and hardly believe that I cared for her in the way of love after a year or two of it. She became for me a rare and fragile object, something burdensome, but very frail. Why, it was as if I had been given a thin-shelled pullet's egg to carry on my palm from Equatorial Africa to Hoboken.[1] Yes, she became for me, as it were, the subject of a bet—the trophy of an athlete's achievement, a parsley crown[2] that is the symbol of his chastity, his soberness, his abstentions, and of his inflexible will. Of intrinsic value as a wife, I think she had none at all for me. I fancy I was not even proud of the way she dressed.

But her passion for Jimmy was not even a passion, and, mad as the suggestion may appear, she was frightened for her life. Yes, she was afraid of me. I will tell you how that happened.

I had, in the old days, a darky servant, called Julius, who valeted me, and waited on me, and loved me, like the crown of his head. Now, when we left Waterbury to go to the "Pocahontas," Florence entrusted to me one very special and very precious leather grip. She told me that her life might depend on that grip, which contained her drugs against heart attacks. And, since I was never much of a hand at carrying things, I entrusted this, in turn, to Julius, who was a grey-haired chap of sixty or so, and very picturesque at that. He made so much impression on Florence that she

---

[1]   Port town in northeast New Jersey. It faces New York City on the Hudson River.
[2]   In classical legend, parsley was intertwined to form a chaplet to mark the virtues. It was also used at funerals.

regarded him as a sort of father, and absolutely refused to let me take him to Paris. He would have inconvenienced her.

Well, Julius was so overcome with grief at being left behind that he must needs go and drop the precious grip. I saw red, I saw purple. I flew at Julius. On the ferry, it was, I filled up one of his eyes; I threatened to strangle him. And, since an unresisting negro can make a deplorable noise and a deplorable spectacle, and, since that was Florence's first adventure in the married state, she got a pretty idea of my character. It affirmed in her the desperate resolve to conceal from me the fact that she was not what she would have called "a pure woman."[1] For that was really the mainspring of her fantastic actions. She was afraid that I should murder her....

So she got up the heart attack, at the earliest possible opportunity, on board the liner. Perhaps she was not so very much to be blamed. You must remember that she was a New Englander, and that New England had not yet come to loathe darkies as it does now. Whereas, if she had come from even so little south as Philadelphia, and had been an oldish family, she would have seen that for me to kick Julius was not so outrageous an act as for her cousin, Reggie Hurlbird, to say—as I have heard him say to his English butler—that for two cents he would bat him on the pants. Besides, the medicine-grip did not bulk as largely in her eyes as it did in mine, where it was the symbol of the existence of an adored wife of a day. To her it was just a useful lie....

Well, there you have the position, as clear as I can make it— the husband an ignorant fool, the wife a cold sensualist with imbecile fears—for I was such a fool that I should never have known what she was or was not—and the blackmailing lover. And then the other lover came along....

Well, Edward Ashburnham was worth having. Have I conveyed to you the splendid fellow that he was—the fine soldier, the excellent landlord, the extraordinarily kind, careful and industrious magistrate, the upright, honest, fair-dealing, fair-thinking, public character? I suppose I have not conveyed it to you. The truth is

---

[1]   *Tess of the D'Urbervilles* (1891), Thomas Hardy's tale of the tragedy of an innocent woman, is subtitled "A Pure Woman."

that I never knew it until the poor girl came along—the poor girl who was just as straight, as splendid and as upright as he. I swear she was. I suppose I ought to have known. I suppose that was, really, why I liked him so much—so infinitely much. Come to think of it, I can remember a thousand little acts of kindliness, of thoughtfulness for his inferiors, even on the Continent. Look here, I know of two families of dirty, unpicturesque, Hessian paupers[1] that that fellow, with an infinite patience, rooted up, got their police reports, set on their feet, or exported to my patient land. And he would do it quite inarticulately, set in motion by seeing a child crying in the street. He would wrestle with dictionaries, in that unfamiliar tongue....Well, he could not bear to see a child cry. Perhaps he could not bear to see a woman and not give her the comfort of his physical attractions.

But, although I liked him so intensely, I was rather apt to take these things for granted. They made me feel comfortable with him, good towards him; they made me trust him. But I guess I thought it was part of the character of any English gentleman. Why, one day he got it into his head that the head waiter at the Excelsior had been crying—the fellow with the grey face and grey whiskers. And then he spent the best part of a week, in correspondence and up at the British consul's, in getting the fellow's wife to come back from London and bring back his girl baby. She had bolted with a Swiss scullion.[2] If she had not come inside the week he would have gone to London himself to fetch her. He was like that.

Edward Ashburnham was like that, and I thought it was only the duty of his rank and station. Perhaps that was all that it was— but I pray God to make me discharge mine as well. And, but for the poor girl, I daresay that I should never have seen it, however much the feeling might have been over me. She had for him such enthusiasm that, although even now I do not understand the technicalities of English life, I can gather enough. She was with them during the whole of our last stay at Nauheim.

Nancy Rufford was her name; she was Leonora's only friend's only child, and Leonora was her guardian, if that is the correct

---

[1] People from Hessen, Germany, of which Marburg was the capital.
[2] The lowest rank of servants.

term. She had lived with the Ashburnhams ever since she had been of the age of thirteen, when her mother was said to have committed suicide owing to the brutalities of her father. Yes, it is a cheerful story....

Edward always called her "the girl," and it was very pretty, the evident affection he had for her and she for him. And Leonora's feet she would have kissed—those two were for her the best man and the best woman on earth—and in heaven. I think that she had not a thought of evil in her head—the poor girl....

Well, anyhow, she chanted Edward's praises to me for the hour together, but, as I have said, I could not make much of it. It appeared that he had the D.S.O.,[1] and that his troop loved him beyond the love of men. You never saw such a troop as his. And he had the Royal Humane Society's medal with a clasp. That meant, apparently, that he had twice jumped off the deck of a troopship to rescue what the girl called "Tommies" who had fallen overboard in the Red Sea and such places. He had been twice recommended for the V.C.,[2] whatever that might mean, and, although owing to some technicalities he had never received that apparently coveted order, he had some special place about his sovereign at the coronation. Or perhaps it was some post in the Beefeaters'.[3] She made him out like a cross between Lohengrin and the Chevalier Bayard.[4] Perhaps he was.... But he was too silent a fellow to make that side of him really decorative. I remember going to him at about that time and asking him what the D.S.O. was, and he grunted out:

"It's a sort of a thing they give grocers who've honourably supplied the troops with adulterated coffee in war-time"—something of that sort. He did not quite carry conviction to me, so, in the end, I put it directly to Leonora. I asked her fully and squarely—prefacing the question with some remarks, such as

---

[1] Distinguished Service Order, granted to officers for meritorious wartime service.

[2] Victoria Cross, the highest British military award for conspicuous bravery in action.

[3] The Yeomen of the Guard who protect the British monarch.

[4] According to German legend, Lohengrin aided a lady in distress. He leaves her when she breaks her promise not to inquire about his origins. The Chevalier Bayard refers to Pierre Terrail (1473–1524), a French soldier whose contemporaries called him "the fearless and blameless knight."

those that I have already given you, as to the difficulty one has in really getting to know people when one's intimacy is conducted as an English acquaintanceship—I asked her whether her husband was not really a splendid fellow—along at least the lines of his public functions. She looked at me with a slightly awakened air—with an air that would have been almost startled if Leonora could ever have been startled.

"Didn't you know?" she asked. "If I come to think of it there is not a more splendid fellow in any three counties, pick them where you will—along those lines." And she added, after she had looked at me reflectively for what seemed a long time:

"To do my husband justice there could not be a better man on the earth. There would not be room for it—along those lines."

"Well," I said, "then he must really be Lohengrin and the Cid[1] in one body. For there are not any other lines that count."

Again she looked at me for a long time.

"It's your opinion that there are no other lines that count?" she asked slowly.

"Well," I answered gaily, "you're not going to accuse him of not being a good husband, or of not being a good guardian to your ward?"

She spoke then slowly, like a person who is listening to the sounds in a sea-shell held to her ear—and, would you believe it?—she told me afterwards that, at that speech of mine, for the first time she had a vague inkling of the tragedy that was to follow so soon—although the girl had lived with them for eight years or so:

"Oh, I'm not thinking of saying that he is not the best of husbands, or that he is not very fond of the girl."

And then I said something like:

"Well, Leonora, a man sees more of these things than even a wife. And, let me tell you, that in all the years I've known Edward he has never, in your absence, paid a moment's attention to any other woman—not by the quivering of an eyelash. I should have noticed. And he talks of you as if you were one of the angels of God."

---

[1] Nickname of Rodrigo, Dias de Bivar (1043–1099), Spanish war hero and national leader.

"Oh," she came up to the scratch, as you could be sure Leonora would always come up to the scratch, "I am perfectly sure that he always speaks nicely of me."

I daresay she had practice in that sort of scene—people must have been always complimenting her on her husband's fidelity and adoration. For half the world—the whole of the world that knew Edward and Leonora believed that his conviction in the Kilsyte affair had been a miscarriage of justice—a conspiracy of false evidence, got together by Nonconformist adversaries. But think of the fool that I was....

II

Let me think where we were. Oh, yes ... that conversation took place on the 4th of August 1913. I remember saying to her that, on that day, exactly nine years before, I had made their acquaintance, so that it had seemed quite appropriate and like a birthday speech to utter my little testimonial to my friend Edward. I could quite confidently say that, though we four had been about together in all sorts of places, for all that length of time, I had not, for my part, one single complaint to make of either of them. And I added, that that was an unusual record for people who had been so much together. You are not to imagine that it was only at Nauheim that we met. That would not have suited Florence.

I find, on looking at my diaries, that on September the fourth, 1904, Edward accompanied Florence and myself to Paris, where we put him up till the twenty-first of that month. He made another short visit to us in December of that year—the first year of our acquaintance. It must have been during this visit that he knocked Mr. Jimmy's teeth down his throat. I daresay Florence had asked him to come over for that purpose. In 1905 he was in Paris three times—once with Leonora, who wanted some frocks. In 1906 we spent the best part of six weeks together at Mentone, and Edward stayed with us in Paris on his way back to London. That was how it went.

The fact was that in Florence the poor wretch had got hold of a Tartar,[1] compared with whom Leonora was a sucking kid. He must have had a hell of a time. Leonora wanted to keep him for— what shall I say—for the good of her church, as it were, to show that Catholic women do not lose their men. Let it go at that, for the moment. I will write more about her motives later, perhaps. But Florence was sticking on to the proprietor of the home of her ancestors. No doubt he was also a very passionate lover. But I am convinced that he was sick of Florence within three years of even interrupted companionship and the life that she led him....

If ever Leonora so much as mentioned in a letter that they had had a woman staying with them—or, if she so much as mentioned a woman's name in a letter to me—off would go a desperate cable in cipher to that poor wretch at Branshaw, commanding him on pain of an instant and horrible disclosure to come over and assure her of his fidelity. I daresay he would have faced it out; I daresay he would have thrown over Florence and taken the risk of exposure. But there he had Leonora to deal with. And Leonora assured him that, if the minutest fragment of the real situation ever got through to my senses, she would wreak upon him the most terrible vengeance that she could think of. And he did not have a very easy job. Florence called for more and more attentions from him as the time went on. She would make him kiss her at any moment of the day; and it was only by his making it plain that a divorced lady could never assume a position in the county of Hampshire that he could prevent her from making a bolt of it with him in her train. Oh, yes, it was a difficult job for him.

For Florence, if you please, gaining in time a more composed view of nature, and overcome by her habits of garrulity, arrived at a frame of mind in which she found it almost necessary to tell me all about it—nothing less than that. She said that her situation was too unbearable with regard to me.

She proposed to tell me all, secure a divorce from me, and go with Edward and settle in California.... I do not suppose that she was really serious in this. It would have meant the extinction of all hopes of Branshaw Manor for her. Besides she had got it into

---

[1] A violent-tempered woman.

her head that Leonora, who was as sound as a roach, was consumptive. She was always begging Leonora, before me, to go and see a doctor. But, none the less, poor Edward seems to have believed in her determination to carry him off. He would not have gone; he cared for his wife too much. But, if Florence had put him at it, [1] that would have meant my getting to know of it, and his incurring Leonora's vengeance. And she could have made it pretty hot for him in ten or a dozen different ways. And she assured me that she would have used every one of them. She was determined to spare my feelings. And she was quite aware that, at that date, the hottest she could have made it for him would have been to refuse, herself, ever to see him again....

Well, I think I have made it pretty clear. Let me come to the fourth of August 1913, the last day of my absolute ignorance— and, I assure you, of my perfect happiness. For the coming of that dear girl only added to it all.

On that fourth of August I was sitting in the lounge with a rather odious Englishman called Bagshawe, who had arrived that night, too late for dinner. Leonora had just gone to bed and I was waiting for Florence and Edward and the girl to come back from a concert at the Casino. They had not gone there all together. Florence, I remember, had said at first that she would remain with Leonora and me and Edward and the girl had gone off alone. And then Leonora had said to Florence with perfect calmness:

"I wish you would go with those two. I think the girl ought to have the appearance of being chaperoned with Edward in these places. I think the time has come." So Florence, with her light step, had slipped out after them. She was all in black for some cousin or other. Americans are particular in those matters.

We had gone on sitting in the lounge till towards ten, when Leonora had gone up to bed. It had been a very hot day, but there it was cool. The man called Bagshawe had been reading *The Times* on the other side of the room, but then he moved over to me with some trifling question as a prelude to suggesting an acquaintance. I fancy he asked me something about the poll-tax

---

[1] A metaphor for hunting, as a horse might be placed before a fence in order to jump over it. In other words, she forced her will upon him.

on Kur-guests, and whether it could not be sneaked out of. He was that sort of person.

Well, he was an unmistakable man, with a military figure, rather exaggerated, with bulbous eyes that avoided your own, and a pallid complexion that suggested vices practised in secret along with an uneasy desire for making acquaintance at whatever cost....The filthy toad....

He began by telling me that he came from Ludlow Manor, near Ledbury. The name had a slightly familiar sound, though I could not fix it in my mind. Then he began to talk about a duty on hops, about Californian hops, about Los Angeles, where he had been. He was fencing for a topic with which he might gain my affection.

And then, quite suddenly, in the bright light of the street, I saw Florence running. It was like that—Florence running with a face whiter than paper and her hand on the black stuff over her heart. I tell you, my own heart stood still; I tell you I could not move. She rushed in at the swing doors. She looked round that place of rush chairs, cane tables and newspapers. She saw me and opened her lips. She saw the man who was talking to me. She stuck her hands over her face as if she wished to push her eyes out. And she was not there any more.

I could not move; I could not stir a finger. And then that man said:

"By Jove: Florry Hurlbird." He turned upon me with an oily and uneasy sound meant for a laugh. He was really going to ingratiate himself with me.

"Do you know who that is?" he asked. "The last time I saw that girl she was coming out of the bedroom of a young man called Jimmy at five o'clock in the morning. In my house at Ledbury. You saw her recognize me." He was standing on his feet, looking down at me. I don't know what I looked like. At any rate, he gave a sort of gurgle and then stuttered:

"Oh, I say...." Those were the last words I ever heard of Mr. Bagshawe's. A long time afterwards I pulled myself out of the lounge and went up to Florence's room. She had not locked the door—for the first time of our married life. She was lying, quite respectably arranged, unlike Mrs. Maidan, on her bed. She had a little phial that rightly should have contained nitrate of amyl,[1] in her right hand. That was on the fourth of August 1913.

---

[1]   A clear, yellow-colored inflammable liquid inhaled in order to dilate the blood vessels and to ease pain in the lower part of the chest. Also used to relieve the symptoms of cyanide poisoning.

PART III

I

The odd thing is that what sticks out in my recollection of the rest of that evening was Leonora's saying:

"Of course you might marry her," and, when I asked whom, she answered:

"The girl."

Now that is to me a very amazing thing—amazing for the light of possibilities that it casts into the human heart. For I had never had the slightest conscious idea of marrying the girl; I never had the slightest idea even of caring for her. I must have talked in an odd way, as people do who are recovering from an anæsthetic. It is as if one had a dual personality, the one I being entirely unconscious of the other. I had thought nothing; I had said such an extraordinary thing.

I don't know that analysis of my own psychology matters at all to this story. I should say that it didn't or, at any rate, that I had given enough of it. But that odd remark of mine had a strong influence upon what came after. I mean, that Leonora would probably never have spoken to me at all about Florence's relations with Edward if I hadn't said, two hours after my wife's death:

"Now I can marry the girl."

She had, then, taken it for granted that I had been suffering all that she had been suffering, or, at least, that I had permitted all that she had permitted. So that, a month ago, about a week after the funeral of poor Edward, she could say to me in the most natural way in the world—I had been talking about the duration of my stay at Branshaw—she said with her clear, reflective intonation:

"Oh, stop here for ever and ever if you can." And then she added, "You couldn't be more of a brother to me, or more of a counsellor, or more of a support. You are all the consolation I have in the world. And isn't it odd to think that if your wife hadn't been my husband's mistress, you would probably never have been here at all?"

That was how I got the news—full in the face, like that. I didn't say anything and I don't suppose I felt anything, unless maybe it was with that mysterious and unconscious self that underlies most people. Perhaps one day when I am unconscious or walking in my sleep I may go and spit upon poor Edward's grave. It seems about the most unlikely thing I could do; but there it is.

No, I remember no emotion of any sort, but just the clear feeling that one has from time to time when one hears that some Mrs. So-and-So is *au mieux*[1] with a certain gentleman. It made things plainer, suddenly, to my curiosity. It was as if I thought, at that moment, of a windy November evening, that, when I came to think it over afterwards, a dozen unexplained things would fit themselves into place. But I wasn't thinking things over then. I remember that distinctly. I was just sitting back, rather stiffly, in a deep armchair. That is what I remember. It was twilight.

Branshaw Manor lies in a little hollow with lawns across it and pine-woods on the fringe of the dip. The immense wind, coming from across the forest, roared overhead. But the view from the window was perfectly quiet and grey. Not a thing stirred, except a couple of rabbits on the extreme edge of the lawn. It was Leonora's own little study that we were in and we were waiting for the tea to be brought. I, as I have said, was sitting in the deep chair, Leonora was standing in the window twirling the wooden acorn at the end of the window-blind cord desultorily round and round. She looked across the lawn and said, as far as I can remember:

"Edward has been dead only ten days and yet there are rabbits on the lawn."

I understand that rabbits do a great deal of harm to the short grass in England. And then she turned round to me and said without any adornment at all, for I remember her exact words:

"I think it was stupid of Florence to commit suicide."

I cannot tell you the extraordinary sense of leisure that we two seemed to have at that moment. It wasn't as if we were waiting for a train, it wasn't as if we were waiting for a meal—it was just that there was nothing to wait for. Nothing.

---

[1] Intimate, on very good terms.

There was an extreme stillness with the remote and intermittent sound of the wind. There was the grey light in that brown, small room. And there appeared to be nothing else in the world.

I knew then that Leonora was about to let me into her full confidence. It was as if—or no, it was the actual fact that—Leonora with an odd English sense of decency had determined to wait until Edward had been in his grave for a full week before she spoke. And with some vague motive of giving her an idea of the extent to which she must permit herself to make confidences, I said slowly—and these words too I remember with exactitude—

"Did Florence commit suicide? I didn't know."

I was just, you understand, trying to let her know that, if she were going to speak she would have to talk about a much wider range of things than she had before thought necessary.

So that that was the first knowledge I had that Florence had committed suicide. It had never entered my head. You may think that I had been singularly lacking in suspiciousness; you may consider me even to have been an imbecile. But consider the position.

In such circumstances of clamour, of outcry, of the crash of many people running together, of the professional reticence of such people as hotel-keepers, the traditional reticence of such "good people" as the Ashburnhams—in such circumstances it is some little material object, always, that catches the eye and that appeals to the imagination. I had no possible guide to the idea of suicide and the sight of the little flask of nitrate of amyl in Florence's hand suggested instantly to my mind the idea of the failure of her heart. Nitrate of amyl, you understand, is the drug that is given to relieve sufferers from angina pectoris.

Seeing Florence, as I had seen her, running with a white face and with one hand held over her heart, and seeing her, as I immediately afterwards saw her, lying upon her bed with the so familiar little brown flask clenched in her fingers, it was natural enough for my mind to frame the idea. As happened now and again, I thought, she had gone out without her remedy and, having felt an attack coming on whilst she was in the gardens, she had run in to get the nitrate in order, as quickly as possible, to obtain relief. And it was equally inevitable my mind should frame the thought that her heart, unable to stand the strain of the running, should have broken in her side. How could I have known that, during all the years of our married life, that little brown flask had contained, not nitrate of amyl, but prussic acid?[1] It was inconceivable.

Why, not even Edward Ashburnham, who was, after all more intimate with her than I was, had an inkling of the truth. He just thought that she had dropped dead of heart disease. Indeed, I fancy that the only people who ever knew that Florence had committed suicide were Leonora, the Grand Duke, the head of the police and the hotel-keeper. I mention these last three because my recollection of that night is only the sort of pinkish effulgence from the electric-lamps in the hotel lounge. There seemed to bob into my consciousness, like floating globes, the faces of those three. Now it would be the bearded, monarchical, benevolent head of the Grand Duke; then the sharp-featured, brown, cavalry-moustached features of the chief of police; then the globular, polished and high-collared vacuousness that represented Monsieur Schontz, the proprietor of the hotel. At times one head would be there alone, at another the spiked helmet of the official would be close to the healthy baldness of the prince; then M. Schontz's oiled locks would push in between the two. The sovereign's soft, exquisitely trained voice would say, "Ja, ja, ja!", each word dropping out like so many soft pellets of suet; the subdued rasp of the official would come: "Zum Befehl Durchlaucht,"[2] like five revolver-shots; the voice of Mr. Schontz would go on and on under its breath like that of an unclean priest reciting from his breviary in the corner of a railway-carriage. That was how it presented itself to me.

They seemed to take no notice of me; I don't suppose that I was even addressed by one of them. But, as long as one or the other, or all three of them were there, they stood between me as if, I being the titular possessor of the corpse, had a right to be present at their conferences. Then they all went away and I was left alone for a long time.

---

[1]   Very poisonous mixture of water with hydrocyanic acid. Apparently, Florence substituted an antidote for cyanide poisoning with cyanide itself.

[2]   "Very good, Serene Highness."

And I thought nothing; absolutely nothing. I had no ideas; I had no strength. I felt no sorrow, no desire for action, no inclination to go upstairs and fall upon the body of my wife. I just saw the pink effulgence, the cane tables, the palms, the globular match-holders, the indented ash-trays. And then Leonora came to me and it appears that I addressed to her that singular remark:

"Now I can marry the girl."

But I have given you absolutely the whole of my recollection of that evening, as it is the whole of my recollection of the succeeding three or four days. I was in a state just simply cataleptic. They put me to bed and I stayed there; they brought me my clothes and I dressed; they led me to an open grave and I stood beside it. If they had taken me to the edge of a river, or if they had flung me beneath a railway train, I should have been drowned or mangled in the same spirit. I was the walking dead.

Well, those are my impressions.

What had actually happened had been this. I pieced it together afterwards. You will remember I said that Edward Ashburnham and the girl had gone off, that night, to a concert at the Casino[1] and that Leonora had asked Florence, almost immediately after their departure, to follow them and to perform the office of chaperone. Florence, you may also remember, was all in black, being the mourning that she wore for a deceased cousin, Jean Hurlbird. It was a very black night and the girl was dressed in cream-coloured muslin, that must have glimmered under the tall trees of the dark park like a phosphorescent fish in a cupboard. You couldn't have had a better beacon.

And it appears that Edward Ashburnham led the girl not up the straight allée that leads to the Casino, but in under the dark trees of the park. Edward Ashburnham told me all this in his final outburst. I have told you that, upon that occasion, he became deucedly vocal. I didn't pump him. I hadn't any motive. At that time I didn't in the least connect him with my wife. But the fellow talked like a cheap novelist.—Or like a very good novelist for the matter of that, if it's the business of a novelist to make

---

[1]   Bad Nauheim's Kurhaus casino closed in 1872. The mirrored room was known in the early years of the twentieth century as "the Casino."

you see things clearly.[1] And I tell you I see that thing as clearly as if it were a dream that never left me. It appears that, not very far from the Casino, he and the girl sat down in the darkness upon a public bench. The lights from that place of entertainment must have reached them through the tree-trunks, since, Edward said, he could quite plainly see the girl's face—that beloved face with the high forehead, the queer mouth, the tortured eyebrows, and the direct eyes. And to Florence, creeping up behind them, they must have presented the appearance of silhouettes. For I take it that Florence came creeping up behind them over the short grass to a tree that, I quite well remember, was immediately behind that public seat. It was not a very difficult feat for a woman instinct with jealousy. The Casino orchestra was, as Edward remembered to tell me, playing the Rakocsy march,[2] and although it was not loud enough, at that distance, to drown the voice of Edward Ashburnham it was certainly sufficiently audible to efface, amongst the noises of the night, the slight brushings and rustlings that might have been made by the feet of Florence or by her gown in coming over the short grass. And that miserable woman must have got it in the face, good and strong. It must have been horrible for her. Horrible! Well, I suppose she deserved all that she got.

Anyhow, there you have the picture, the immensely tall trees, elms most of them, towering and feathering away up into the black mistiness that trees seem to gather about them at night; the silhouettes of those two upon the seat; the beams of light coming from the Casino, the woman all in black peeping with fear behind the tree-trunk. It is melodrama; but I can't help it.

And then, it appears, something happened to Edward Ashburnham.[3] He assured me—and I see no reason for disbelieving

---

[1] Ford was very friendly with his collaborator Joseph Conrad and greatly admired his work. Ford's *Joseph Conrad: A Personal Remembrance* was published in 1924. Conrad wrote in his 1897 Preface to *The Nigger of the "Narcissus"* that "my task ... is, by the power of the written word, ... to make you *see*."

[2] Austro-Hungarian march celebrating a military victory. Arranged for orchestra by Hector Berlioz (1803–1869) in 1846 and composed by János Bihári (1764–1827) in 1809.

[3] In the Cornell manuscript of the novel, the text reads: "Something very similar happened to me [a little later] in the same evening. As far as I can make ... it out the other half of his dual personality spoke—to the girl."

him—that until that moment he had had no idea whatever of caring for the girl. He said that he had regarded her exactly as he would have regarded a daughter. He certainly loved her, but with a very deep, very tender and very tranquil love. He had missed her when she went away to her convent-school; he had been glad when she had returned. But of more than that he had been totally unconscious. Had he been conscious of it, he assured me, he would have fled from it as from a thing accursed. He realized that it was the last outrage upon Leonora. But the real point was his entire unconsciousness. He had gone with her into that dark park with no quickening of the pulse, with no desire for the intimacy of solitude. He had gone, intending to talk about polo-ponies, and tennis-racquets; about the temperament of the reverend Mother at the convent she had left and about whether her frock for a party when they got home should be white or blue. It hadn't come into his head that they would talk about a single thing that they hadn't always talked about; it had not even come into his head that the tabu which extended around her was not inviolable. And then, suddenly, that—

He was very careful to assure me that at that time there was no physical motive about his declaration. It did not appear to him to be a matter of a dark night and a propinquity and so on. No, it was simply of her effect on the moral side of his life that he appears to have talked. He said that he never had the slightest notion to enfold her in his arms or so much as to touch her hand. He swore that he did not touch her hand. He said that they sat, she at one end of the bench, he at the other; he leaning slightly towards her and she looking straight towards the light of the Casino, her face illuminated by the lamps. The expression upon her face he could only describe as "queer."

At another time, indeed, he made it appear that he thought she was glad. It is easy to imagine that she was glad, since at that time she could have had no idea of what was really happening. Frankly, she adored Edward Ashburnham. He was for her, in everything that she said at that time, the model of humanity, the hero, the athlete, the father of his country, the law-giver. So that for her, to be suddenly, intimately and overwhelmingly praised must have been a matter for mere gladness, however overwhelming it were.

It must have been as if a god had approved her handiwork or a king her loyalty. She just sat still and listened, smiling.

And it seemed to her that all the bitterness of her childhood, the terrors of her tempestuous father, the bewailings of her cruel-tongued mother were suddenly atoned for. She had her recompense at last. Because, of course, if you come to figure it out, a sudden pouring forth of passion by a man whom you regard as a cross between a pastor and a father might, to a woman, have the aspect of mere praise for good conduct. It wouldn't, I mean, appear at all in the light of an attempt to gain possession. The girl, at least, regarded him as firmly anchored to his Leonora. She had not the slightest inkling of any infidelities. He had always spoken to her of his wife in terms of reverence and deep affection. He had given her the idea that he regarded Leonora as absolutely impeccable[1] and as absolutely satisfying. Their union had appeared to her to be one of those blessed things that are spoken of and contemplated with reverence by her church.

So that, when he spoke of her as being the person he cared most for in the world, she naturally thought that he meant to except Leonora and she was just glad. It was like a father saying that he approved of a marriageable daughter ... And Edward, when he realized what he was doing, curbed his tongue at once.[2] She was just glad and she went on being just glad.

I suppose that that was the most monstrously wicked thing that Edward Ashburnham ever did in his life. And yet I am so near to all these people that I cannot think any of them wicked. It is impossible of me to think of Edward Ashburnham as anything but straight, upright and honourable. That, I mean, is, in spite of everything, my permanent view of him. I try at times by dwelling on some of the things that he did to push that image of him away, as you might try to push aside a large pendulum. But it always comes back—the memory of his innumerable acts of kindness, of his efficiency, of his unspiteful tongue. He was such a fine fellow.

---

[1] Above sinful behavior.

[2] In the Cornell manuscript of the novel, the text reads: "And when he spoke of her as the only woman he had ever loved—and, upon my soul, I believe that she was the only woman that he had ever loved!—she simply took it, making allowances for the odd phraseology, as the kindliness of a father loving his young daughter."

So I feel myself forced to attempt to excuse him in this as in so many other things. It is, I have no doubt, a most monstrous thing to attempt to corrupt a young girl just out of a convent. But I think Edward had no idea at all of corrupting her. I believe that he simply loved her. He said that that was the way of it and I, at least, believe him and I believe too that she was the only woman he ever really loved. He said that that was so; and he did enough to prove it. And Leonora said that it was so and Leonora knew him to the bottom of his heart.

I have come to be very much of a cynic in these matters; I mean that it is impossible to believe in the permanence of man's or woman's love. Or, at any rate, it is impossible to believe in the permanence of any early passion. As I see it, at least, with regard to man, a love affair, a love for any definite woman—is something in the nature of a widening of the experience. With each new woman that a man is attracted to there appears to come a broadening of the outlook, or, if you like, an acquiring of new territory. A turn of the eyebrow, a tone of the voice, a queer characteristic gesture—all these things, and it is these things that cause to arise the passion of love—all these things are like so many objects on the horizon of the landscape that tempt a man to walk beyond the horizon, to explore. He wants to get, as it were, behind those eyebrows with the peculiar turn, as if he desired to see the world with the eyes that they overshadow. He wants to hear that voice applying itself to every possible proposition, to every possible topic; he wants to see those characteristic gestures against every possible background. Of the question of the sex-instinct I know very little and I do not think that it counts for very much in a really great passion. It can be aroused by such nothings—by an untied shoelace, by a glance of the eye in passing—that I think it might be left out of the calculation. I don't mean to say that any great passion can exist without a desire for consummation. That seems to me to be a commonplace and to be therefore a matter needing no comment at all. It is a thing, with all its accidents, that must be taken for granted, as, in a novel, or a biography, you take it for granted that the characters have their meals with some regularity. But the real fierceness of desire, the real heat of a passion long continued and withering up the soul of a man is the craving for identity with the woman that he loves. He desires to see with the same eyes, to touch with the same sense of touch, to hear with the same ears, to lose his identity, to be enveloped, to be supported. For, whatever may be said of the relation of the sexes, there is no man who loves a woman that does not desire to come to her for the renewal of his courage, for the cutting asunder of his difficulties. And that will be the mainspring of his desire for her. We are all so afraid, we are all so alone, we all so need from the outside the assurance of our own worthiness to exist.[1]

So, for a time, if such a passion come to fruition, the man will get what he wants. He will get the moral support, the encouragement, the relief from the sense of loneliness, the assurance of his own worth. But these things pass away; inevitably they pass away as the shadows pass across sun-dials. It is sad, but it is so. The pages of the book will become familiar; the beautiful corner of the road will have been turned too many times. Well, this is the saddest story.

And yet I do believe that for every man there comes at last a woman—or no, that is the wrong way of formulating it. For every man there comes at last a time of life when the woman who then sets her seal upon his imagination has set her seal for good. He will travel over no more horizons; he will never again set the knapsack over his shoulders; he will retire from those scenes. He will have gone out of the business.

That at any rate was the case with Edward and the poor girl. It was quite literally the case. It was quite literally the case that his passions—for the mistress of the Grand Duke, for Mrs. Basil, for little Mrs. Maidan, for Florence, for whom you will—these passions were merely preliminary canters compared to his final race with death for her. I am certain of that. I am not going to be so American as to say that all true love demands some sacrifice. It doesn't. But I think that love will be truer and more permanent in which self-sacrifice has been exacted. And, in the case of the other women, Edward just cut in and cut them out as he did with the polo-ball from under the nose of Count Baron von Lelöffel. I don't mean to

---

[1]   According to Martin Stannard, "Ford presumably saw the passage regarding the 'real fierceness of desire ... worthiness to exist' as an important statement on heterosexual love since he once transcribed it as the dedication of a copy of the novel."

say that he didn't wear himself as thin as a lath in the endeavour to capture the other women; but over her he wore himself to rags and tatters and death—in the effort to leave her alone.

And, in speaking to her on that night, he wasn't, I am convinced, committing a baseness. It was as if his passion for her hadn't existed; as if the very words that he spoke, without knowing that he spoke them, created the passion as they went along. Before he spoke, there was nothing; afterwards, it was the integral fact of his life. Well, I must get back to my story.

And my story was concerning itself with Florence—with Florence, who heard those words from behind the tree. That of course is only conjecture, but I think the conjecture is pretty well justified. You have the fact that those two went out, that she followed them almost immediately afterwards through the darkness and, a little later, she came running back to the hotel with that pallid face and the hand clutching her dress over her heart. It can't have been only Bagshawe. Her face was contorted with agony before ever her eyes fell upon me or upon him beside me. But I dare say Bagshawe may have been the determining influence in her suicide. Leonora says that she had that flask, apparently of nitrate of amyl, but actually of prussic acid, for many years and that she was determined to use it if ever I discovered the nature of her relationship with that fellow Jimmy. You see, the mainspring of her nature must have been vanity. There is no reason why it shouldn't have been; I guess it is vanity that makes most of us keep straight, if we do keep straight, in this world.

If it had been merely a matter of Edward's relations with the girl I dare say Florence would have faced it out. She would no doubt have made him scenes, have threatened him, have appealed to his sense of honour, to his promises. But Mr. Bagshawe and the fact that the date was the 4th of August must have been too much for her superstitious mind. You see, she had two things that she wanted. She wanted to be a great lady, installed in Branshaw Teleragh. She wanted also to retain my respect.

She wanted, that is to say, to retain my respect for as long as she lived with me. I suppose, if she had persuaded Edward Ashburnham to bolt with her she would have let the whole thing go with a run. Or perhaps she would have tried to exact from me a new respect for the greatness of her passion on the lines of all for love and the world well lost. That would be just like Florence.

In all matrimonial associations there is, I believe, one constant factor—a desire to deceive the person with whom one lives as to some weak spot in one's character or in one's career. For it is intolerable to live constantly with one human being who perceives one's small meannesses. It is really death to do so—that is why so many marriages turn out unhappily.

I, for instance, am a rather greedy man; I have a taste for good cookery and a watering tooth at the mere sound of the names of certain comestibles. If Florence had discovered this secret of mine I should have found her knowledge of it so unbearable that I never could have supported all the other privations of the régime that she extracted from me. I am bound to say that Florence never discovered this secret.

Certainly she never alluded to it; I dare say she never took sufficient interest in me.

And the secret weakness of Florence—the weakness that she could not bear to have me discover was just that early escapade with the fellow called Jimmy. Let me, as this is in all probability the last time I shall mention Florence's name, dwell a little upon the change that had taken place in her psychology. She would not, I mean, have minded if I had discovered that she was the mistress of Edward Ashburnham. She would rather have liked it. Indeed, the chief trouble of poor Leonora in those days was to keep Florence from making, before me, theatrical displays, on one line or another, of that very fact. She wanted, in one mood, to come rushing to me, to cast herself on her knees at my feet and to declaim a carefully arranged, frightfully emotional, outpouring as to her passion. That was to show that she was like one of the great erotic women of whom history tells us. In another mood she would desire to come to me disdainfully and to tell me that I was considerably less than a man and that what had happened was what must happen when a real male came along. She wanted to say that in cool, balanced and sarcastic sentences. That was when she wished to appear like the heroine of a French comedy. Because of course she was always play-acting.

But what she didn't want me to know was the fact of her first escapade with the fellow called Jimmy. She had arrived at figuring out the sort of low-down Bowery[1] tough that that fellow was. Do you know what it is to shudder, in later life, for some small, stupid action—usually for some small, quite genuine piece of emotionalism—of your early life? Well, it was that sort of shuddering that came over Florence at the thought that she had surrendered to such a low fellow. I don't know that she need have shuddered. It was her fooling old uncle's work; he ought never to have taken those two round the world together and shut himself up in his cabin for the greater part of the time. Anyhow, I am convinced that the sight of Mr. Bagshawe and the thought that Mr. Bagshawe—for she knew that unpleasant and toad-like personality—the thought that Mr. Bagshawe would almost certainly reveal to me that he had caught her coming out of Jimmy's bedroom at five o'clock in the morning on the 4th of August 1900[2]—that was the determining influence in her suicide. And no doubt the effect of the date was too much for her superstitious personality. She had been born on the 4th of August; she had started to go round the world on the 4th of August; she had become a low fellow's mistress on the 4th of August. On the same day of the year she had married me; on that 4th she had lost Edward's love and Bagshawe had appeared like a sinister omen—like a grin on the face of Fate. It was the last straw. She ran upstairs, arranged herself decoratively upon her bed—she was a sweetly pretty woman with smooth pink and white cheeks, long hair, the eyelashes falling like a tiny curtain on her cheeks. She drank the little phial of prussic acid and there she lay—Oh, extremely charming and clear-cut—looking with a puzzled expression at the electric-light bulb that hung from the ceiling, or perhaps through it, to the stars above. Who knows? Anyhow, there was an end of Florence.

You have no idea how quite extraordinarily for me that was the end of Florence. From that day to this I have never given her another thought; I have not bestowed upon her so much as a sigh. Of course, when it has been necessary to talk about her to Leonora or when for the purpose of these writings I have tried

---

[1] A tough area in working-class lower Manhattan.
[2] Britain declared war on Germany on 4 August 1914. The date provides a key to the chronology of the events related in Ford's narrative.

to figure her out, I have thought about her as I might do about a problem in Algebra. But it has always been as a matter for study, not for remembrance. She just went completely out of existence, like yesterday's paper.

I was so deadly tired. And I dare say that my week or ten days of affaissement[1]—of what was practically catalepsy—was just the repose that my exhausted nature claimed after twelve years of the repression of my instincts, after twelve years of playing the trained poodle. For that was all that I had been. I suppose that it was the shock that did it—the several shocks. But I am unwilling to attribute my feelings at that time to anything so concrete as a shock. It was a feeling so tranquil. It was as if an immensely heavy—an unbearably heavy knapsack, supported upon my shoulders by straps, had fallen off and left my shoulders themselves that the straps had cut into, numb and without sensation of life. I tell you, I had no regret. What had I to regret? I suppose that my inner soul— my dual personality—had realized long before that Florence was a personality of paper—that she represented a real human being with a heart, with feelings, with sympathies and with emotions only as a bank-note represents a certain quantity of gold. I know that that sort of feeling came to the surface in me the moment the man Bagshawe told me that he had seen her coming out of that fellow's bedroom. I thought suddenly that she wasn't real; she was just a mass of talk out of guidebooks, of drawings out of fashion-plates. It is even possible that, if that feeling had not possessed me, I should have run up sooner to her room and might have prevented her drinking the prussic acid. But I just couldn't do it; it would have been like chasing a scrap of paper—an occupation ignoble for a grown man.

And, as it began, so that matter has remained. I didn't care whether she had come out of that bedroom or whether she hadn't. It simply didn't interest me. Florence didn't matter.

I suppose you will retort that I was in love with Nancy Rufford and that my indifference was therefore discreditable. Well, I am not seeking to avoid discredit. I was in love with Nancy Rufford as I am in love with the poor child's memory,

---

[1] Nervous collapse or breakdown.

quietly and quite tenderly in my American sort of way. I had never thought about it until I heard Leonora state that I might now marry her. But, from that moment until her worse than death, I do not suppose that I much thought about anything else. I don't mean to say that I sighed about her or groaned; I just wanted to marry her as some people want to go to Carcassonne.

Do you understand the feeling—the sort of feeling that you must get certain matters out of the way, smooth out certain fairly negligible complications before you can go to a place that has, during all your life, been a sort of dream city? I didn't attach much importance to my superior years. I was forty-five and she, poor thing, was only just rising twenty-two. But she was older than her years and quieter. She seemed to have an odd quality of sainthood, as if she must inevitably end in a convent with a white coif framing her face. But she had frequently told me that she had no vocation; it just simply wasn't there—the desire to become a nun. Well, I guess that I was a sort of convent myself; it seemed fairly proper that she should make her vows to me.

No, I didn't see any impediment on the score of age. I dare say no man does, and I was pretty confident that, with a little preparation, I could make a young girl happy. I could spoil her as few young girls have ever been spoiled; and I couldn't regard myself as personally repulsive. No man can, or if he ever comes to do so, that is the end of him. But, as soon as I came out of my catalepsy, I seemed to perceive that my problem—that what I had to do to prepare myself for getting into contact with her, was just to get back into contact with life. I had been kept for twelve years in a rarefied atmosphere; what I then had to do was a little fighting with real life, some wrestling with men of business, some travelling amongst larger cities, something harsh, something masculine. I didn't want to present myself to Nancy Rufford as a sort of an old maid. That was why, just a fortnight after Florence's suicide, I set off for the United States.

Immediately after Florence's death Leonora began to put the leash upon Nancy Rufford and Edward. She had guessed what had happened under the trees near the Casino. They stayed at Nauheim some weeks after I went, and Leonora has told me that that was the most deadly time of her existence. It seemed like a long, silent duel with invisible weapons, so she said. And it was rendered all the more difficult by the girl's entire innocence. For Nancy was always trying to go off alone with Edward—as she had been doing all her life, whenever she was home for holidays. She just wanted him to say nice things to her again.

You see, the position was extremely complicated. It was as complicated as it well could be, along delicate lines. There was the complication caused by the fact that Edward and Leonora never spoke to each other except when other people were present. Then, as I have said, their demeanours were quite perfect. There was the complication caused by the girl's entire innocence; there was the further complication that both Edward and Leonora really regarded the girl as their daughter. Or it might be more precise to say that they regarded her as being Leonora's daughter. And Nancy was a queer girl; it is very difficult to describe her to you.

She was tall and strikingly thin; she had a tortured mouth, agonized eyes, and a quite extraordinary sense of fun. You, might put it that at times she was exceedingly grotesque and at times extraordinarily beautiful. Why, she had the heaviest head of black hair that I have ever come across; I used to wonder how she could bear the weight of it. She was just over twenty-one and at times she seemed as old as the hills, at times not much more than sixteen. At one moment she would be talking of the lives of the saints and at the next she would be tumbling all over the lawn with the St. Bernard puppy. She could ride to hounds like a Mænad[1] and she could sit for hours perfectly still, steeping hand-kerchief after handkerchief in vinegar when Leonora had one of

---

[1] A female disciple of Dionysus, according to classical Greek legend. The Mænads indulged in orgiastic discharges of irrational feelings through controlled rituals.

her headaches. She was, in short, a miracle of patience who could be almost miraculously impatient. It was no doubt the convent training that effected that. I remember that one of her letters to me, when she was about sixteen, ran something like:

"On Corpus Christi"[1]—or it may have been some other saint's day, I cannot keep these things in my head—"our school played Roehampton[2] at Hockey. And, seeing that our side was losing, being three goals to one against us at half-time, we retired into the chapel and prayed for victory. We won by five goals to three." And I remember that she seemed to describe afterwards a sort of saturnalia.[3] Apparently, when the victorious fifteen, or eleven, came into the refectory for supper, the whole school jumped upon the tables and cheered and broke the chairs on the floor and smashed the crockery—for a given time, until the Reverend Mother rang a hand-bell. That is of course the Catholic tradition—saturnalia that can end in a moment, like the crack of a whip. I don't of course like the tradition, but I am bound to say that it gave Nancy—or at any rate Nancy had—a sense of rectitude that I have never seen surpassed. It was a thing like a knife that looked out of her eyes and that spoke with her voice, just now and then. It positively frightened me. I suppose that I was almost afraid to be in a world where there could be so fine a standard. I remember when she was about fifteen or sixteen on going back to the convent I once gave her a couple of English sovereigns as a tip. She thanked me in a peculiarly heartfelt way, saying that it would come in extremely handy. I asked her why and she explained. There was a rule at the school that the pupils were not to speak when they walked through the garden from the chapel to the refectory. And, since this rule appeared to be idiotic and arbitrary, she broke it on purpose day after day. In the evening the children were all asked if they had committed any faults during the day, and every evening Nancy confessed that she had broken this particular rule. It cost her sixpence a time, that being the fine

---

[1] Catholic festival held on the Thursday of the week following Whitsun; it honors the Eucharist.

[2] An elite Catholic boarding school for girls in west London.

[3] Scenes of wild revelry. In *Provence* (1938), Ford describes convent schools in Tarascon where saturnalia were permitted.

attached to the offence. Just for the information I asked her why she always confessed, and she answered in these exact words: "Oh, well, the girls of the Holy Child have always been noted for their truthfulness. It's a beastly bore, but I've got to do it."

I dare say that the miserable nature of her childhood, coming before the mixture of saturnalia and discipline that was her convent life, added something to her queernesses. Her father was a violent madman of a fellow, a major of one of what I believe are called the Highland regiments. He didn't drink, but he had an ungovernable temper, and the first thing that Nancy could remember was seeing her father strike her mother with his clenched fist so that her mother fell over sideways from the breakfast table and lay motionless. The mother was no doubt an irritating woman and the privates of that regiment appear to have been irritating, too, so that the house was a place of outcries and perpetual disturbances. Mrs. Rufford was Leonora's dearest friend and Leonora could be cutting enough at times. But I fancy she was as nothing to Mrs. Rufford. The Major would come in to lunch harassed and already spitting out oaths after an unsatisfactory morning's drilling of his stubborn men beneath a hot sun. And then Mrs. Rufford would make some cutting remark and pandemonium would break loose. Once, when she had been about twelve, Nancy had tried to intervene between the pair of them. Her father had struck her full upon the forehead a blow so terrible that she had lain unconscious for three days. Nevertheless Nancy seemed to prefer her father to her mother. She remembered rough kindnesses from him. Once or twice when she had been quite small he had dressed her in a clumsy, impatient, but very tender way. It was nearly always impossible to get a servant to stay in the family and, for days at a time, apparently, Mrs. Rufford would be incapable. I fancy she drank. At any rate she had so cutting a tongue that even Nancy was afraid of her—she so made fun of any tenderness, she so sneered at all emotional displays. Nancy must have been a very emotional child....

Then one day, quite suddenly, on her return from a ride at Fort William,[1] Nancy had been sent, with her governess, who

---

[1] Town in west Scotland with a well-known Benedictine monastery.

had a white face, right down South to that convent school. She had been expecting to go there in two months' time. Her mother disappeared from her life at that time. A fortnight later Leonora came to the convent and told her that her mother was dead. Perhaps she was. At any rate I never heard until the very end what became of Mrs. Rufford. Leonora never spoke of her.

And then Major Rufford went to India, from which he returned very seldom and only for very short visits; and Nancy lived herself gradually into the life at Branshaw Teleragh. I think that, from that time onwards, she led a very happy life, till the end. There were dogs and horses and old servants and the Forest.[1] And there were Edward and Leonora, who loved her.

I had known her all the time—I mean that she always came to the Ashburnhams' at Nauheim for the last fortnight of their stay, and I watched her gradually growing. She was very cheerful with me. She always even kissed me, night and morning, until she was about eighteen. And she would skip about and fetch me things and laugh at my tales of life in Philadelphia. But, beneath her gaiety, I fancy that there lurked some terrors. I remember one day, when she was just eighteen, during one of her father's rare visits to Europe, we were sitting in the gardens, near the iron-stained fountain. Leonora had one of her headaches and we were waiting for Florence and Edward to come from their baths. You have no idea how beautiful Nancy looked that morning.

We were talking about the desirability of taking tickets in lotteries—of the moral side of it, I mean. She was all in white, and so tall and fragile; and she had only just put her hair up, so that the carriage of her neck had that charming touch of youth and of unfamiliarity. Over her throat there played the reflection from a little pool of water, left by a thunderstorm of the night before, and all the rest of her features were in the diffused and luminous shade of her white parasol. Her dark hair just showed beneath her broad, white hat of pierced, chip straw; her throat was very long and leaned forward, and her eyebrows, arching a little as she laughed at some old-fashionedness in my phraseology, had abandoned their tense line. And there was a little colour

---

[1] The New Forest.

in her cheeks and light in her deep blue eyes. And to think that that vivid white thing, that saintly and swanlike being—to think that ... Why, she was like the sail of a ship, so white and so definite in her movements. And to think that she will never ... Why, she will never do anything again. I can't believe it ...

Anyhow we were chattering away about the morality of lotteries. And then, suddenly, there came from the arcades behind us the overtones of her father's unmistakable voice; it was as if a modified foghorn had boomed with a reed inside it. I looked round to catch sight of him. A tall, fair, stiffly upright man of fifty, he was walking away with an Italian baron who had had much to do with the Belgian Congo. They must have been talking about the proper treatment of natives, for I heard him say:

"Oh, hang humanity!"

When I looked again at Nancy her eyes were closed and her face was more pallid than her dress, which had at least some pinkish reflections from the gravel. It was dreadful to see her with her eyes closed like that.

"Oh" she exclaimed, and her hand that had appeared to be groping, settled for a moment on my arm. "Never speak of it. Promise never to tell my father of it. It brings back those dreadful dreams ..." And, when she opened her eyes she looked straight into mine. "The blessed saints," she said, "you would think they would spare you such things. I don't believe all the sinning in the world could make one deserve them."

They say the poor thing was always allowed a light at night, even in her bedroom.... And yet, no young girl could more archly and lovingly have played with an adored father. She was always holding him by both coat lapels; cross-questioning him as to how he spent his time; kissing the top of his head. Ah, she was well-bred, if ever anyone was.

The poor, wretched man cringed before her—but she could not have done more to put him at his ease. Perhaps she had had lessons in it at her convent. It was only that peculiar note of his voice, used when he was overbearing or dogmatic, that could unman her—and that was only visible when it came unexpectedly. That was because the bad dreams that the blessed saints allowed her to have for her sins always seemed to her to herald themselves by the booming sound of her father's voice. It was that sound that had always preceded his entrance for the terrible lunches of her childhood....

I have reported, earlier in this chapter, that Leonora said, during that remainder of their stay at Nauheim, after I had left, it had seemed to her that she was fighting a long duel with unseen weapons against silent adversaries. Nancy, as I have also said, was always trying to go off with Edward alone. That had been her habit for years. And Leonora found it to be her duty to stop that. It was very difficult. Nancy was used to having her own way, and for years she had been used to going off with Edward, ratting, rabbiting, catching salmon down at Fordingbridge, district-visiting of the sort that Edward indulged in, or calling on the tenants. And at Nauheim she and Edward had always gone up to the Casino alone in the evenings—at any rate whenever Florence did not call for his attendance. It shows the obviously innocent nature of the regard of those two that even Florence had never had any idea of jealousy. Leonora had cultivated the habit of going to bed at ten o'clock.

I don't know how she managed it, but, for all the time they were at Nauheim, she contrived never to let those two be alone together, except in broad daylight, in very crowded places. If a Protestant had done that it would no doubt have awakened a self-consciousness in the girl. But Catholics, who have always reservations and queer spots of secrecy, can manage these things better. And I dare say that two things made this easier—the death of Florence and the fact that Edward was obviously sickening. He appeared, indeed, to be very ill; his shoulders began to be bowed; there were pockets under his eyes; he had extraordinary moments of inattention.

And Leonora describes herself as watching him as a fierce cat watches an unconscious pigeon in a roadway. In that silent watching, again, I think she was a Catholic—of a people that can think thoughts alien to ours and keep them to themselves. And the thoughts passed through her mind; some of them even got through to Edward with never a word spoken. At first she thought that it might be remorse, or grief, for the death of Florence that was oppressing him. But she watched and watched, and uttered apparently random sentences about Florence before the girl, and she perceived that he had no grief and no remorse. He had not any idea that Florence could have committed suicide without writing at least a tirade to him. The absence of that made him certain that it had been heart disease. For Florence had never undeceived him on that point. She thought it made her seem more romantic.

No, Edward had no remorse. He was able to say to himself that he had treated Florence with gallant attentiveness of the kind that she desired until two hours before her death. Leonora gathered that from the look in his eyes, and from the way he straightened his shoulders over her as she lay in her coffin—from that and a thousand other little things. She would speak suddenly about Florence to the girl and he would not start in the least; he would not even pay attention, but would sit with bloodshot eyes gazing at the tablecloth. He drank a good deal, at that time—a steady soaking of drink every evening till long after they had gone to bed.

For Leonora made the girl go to bed at ten, unreasonable though that seemed to Nancy. She would understand that, whilst they were in a sort of half mourning for Florence, she ought not to be seen at public places, like the Casino; but she could not see why she should not accompany her uncle upon his evening strolls though the park. I don't know what Leonora put up as an excuse—something, I fancy, in the nature of a nightly orison[1] that she made the girl and herself perform for the soul of Florence. And then, one evening, about a fortnight later, when the girl, growing restive at even devotional exercises, clamoured once more to be allowed to go for a walk with Edward, and when Leonora was really at her wits' end, Edward gave himself into her hands. He was just standing up from dinner and had his face averted.

But he turned his heavy head and his bloodshot eyes upon his wife and looked full at her.

"Doctor von Hauptmann," he said, "has ordered me to go to bed immediately after dinner. My heart's much worse."

---

[1] Prayer.

He continued to look at Leonora for a long minute—with a sort of heavy contempt. And Leonora understood that, with his speech, he was giving her the excuse that she needed for separating him from the girl, and with his eyes he was reproaching her for thinking that he would try to corrupt Nancy.

He went silently up to his room and sat there for a long time—until the girl was well in bed—reading in the Anglican prayer-book. And about half-past ten she heard his footsteps pass her door, going outwards. Two and a half hours later they came back, stumbling heavily.

She remained, reflecting upon this position until the last night of their stay at Nauheim. Then she suddenly acted. For, just in the same way, suddenly after dinner, she looked at him and said:

"Teddy, don't you think you could take a night off from your doctor's orders and go with Nancy to the Casino. The poor child has had her visit so spoiled."

He looked at her in turn for a long, balancing minute.

"Why, yes," he said at last. Nancy jumped out of her chair and kissed him.

Those two words, Leonora said, gave her the greatest relief of any two syllables she had ever heard in her life. For she realized that Edward was breaking up, not under the desire for possession, but from the dogged determination to hold his hand. She could relax some of her vigilance.

Nevertheless, she sat in the darkness behind her half-closed jalousies,[1] looking over the street and the night and the trees until, very late, she could hear Nancy's clear voice coming closer and saying:

"You did look an old guy[2] with that false nose."

There had been some sort of celebration of a local holiday up in the Kursaal. And Edward replied with his sort of sulky good nature:

"As for you, you looked like old Mother Sideacher."[3]

---

[1] Blinds or shutters with adjustable slats.

[2] A strangely dressed man.

[3] Various possibilities of meaning, including a reference to a game involving a Witch or a nickname for Nancy's former headmistress, "the old beggar woman who always amused them."

The girl came swinging along, a silhouette beneath a gas-lamp; Edward, another, slouched at her side. They were talking just as they had talked any time since the girl had been seventeen; with the same tones, the same joke about an old beggar woman who always amused them at Branshaw. The girl, a little later, opened Leonora's door whilst she was still kissing Edward on the forehead as she had done every night.

"We've had a most glorious time," she said. "He's ever so much better. He raced me for twenty yards home. Why are you all in the dark?"

Leonora could hear Edward going about in his room, but, owing to the girl's chatter, she could not tell whether he went out again or not. And then, very much later, because she thought that if he were drinking again something must be done to stop it, she opened for the first time, and very softly, the never-opened door between their rooms. She wanted to see if he had gone out again. Edward was kneeling beside his bed with his head hidden in the counterpane. His arms, outstretched, held out before him a little image of the blessed virgin—a tawdry, scarlet and Prussian blue affair that the girl had given him on her first return from the convent. His shoulders heaved convulsively three times, and heavy sobs came from him before she could close the door. He was not a Catholic; but that was the way it took him.

Leonora slept for the first time that night with a sleep from which she never once started.

III

And then Leonora completely broke down—on the day that they returned to Branshaw Teleragh. It is the infliction of our miserable minds—it is the scourge of atrocious but probably just destiny that no grief comes by itself. No, any great grief, though the grief itself may have gone, leaves in its place a train of horrors, of misery, and despair. For Leonora was, in herself, relieved. She felt that she could trust Edward with the girl and she knew that

Nancy could be absolutely trusted. And then, with the slackening of her vigilance, came the slackening of her entire mind. This is perhaps the most miserable part of the entire story. For it is miserable to see a clear intelligence waver; and Leonora wavered.

You are to understand that Leonora loved Edward with a passion that was yet like an agony of hatred. And she had lived with him for years and years without addressing to him one word of tenderness. I don't know how she could do it. At the beginning of that relationship she had been just married off to him. She had been one of seven daughters in a bare, untidy Irish manor-house to which she had returned from the convent I have so often spoken of. She had left it just a year and she was just nineteen. It is impossible to imagine such inexperience as was hers. You might almost say that she had never spoken to a man except a priest. Coming straight from the convent, she had gone in behind the high walls of the manor-house that was almost more cloistral than any convent could have been. There were the seven girls, there was the strained mother, there was the worried father at whom, three times in the course of that year, the tenants took pot-shots from behind a hedge. The women-folk, upon the whole, the tenants respected. Once a week each of the girls, since there were seven of them, took a drive with the mother in the old basketwork chaise[1] drawn by a very fat, very lumbering pony. They paid occasionally a call, but even these were so rare that, Leonora has assured me, only three times in the year that succeeded her coming home from the convent did she enter another person's house. For the rest of the time the seven sisters ran about in the neglected gardens between the unpruned espaliers.[2] Or they played lawn-tennis or fives[3] in an angle of a great wall that surrounded the garden—an angle from which the fruit trees had long died away. They painted in water-colour; they embroidered; they copied verses into albums. Once a week they went to Mass; once a week to the confessional, accompanied by an old nurse. They were happy since they had known no other life.

It appeared to them a singular extravagance when, one day, a

---

[1] Light open carriage, usually carrying two people.
[2] Fruit trees trained to grow around a framework.
[3] A game played at public schools in which a ball is hit by hand against the wall of a three-sided court.

photographer was brought over from the county town and photographed them standing, all seven, in the shadow of an old apple tree with the grey lichen on the raddled trunk.

But it wasn't an extravagance.

Three weeks before Colonel Powys had written to Colonel Ashburnham:

"I say, Harry, couldn't your Edward marry one of my girls? It would be a god-send to me, for I'm at the end of my tether and, once one girl begins to go off the rest of them will follow."

He went on to say that all his daughters were tall, upstanding, clean-limbed and absolutely pure, and he reminded Colonel Ashburnham that, they having been married on the same day, though in different churches, since the one was a Catholic and the other an Anglican—they had said to each other, the night before, that, when the time came, one of their sons should marry one of their daughters. Mrs. Ashburnham had been a Powys and remained Mrs. Powys' dearest friend. They had drifted about the world as English soldiers do, seldom meeting, but their women always in correspondence one with another. They wrote about minute things such as the teething of Edward and of the earlier daughters or the best way to repair a Jacob's ladder in a stocking. And, if they met seldom, yet it was often enough to keep each other's personalities fresh in their minds, gradually growing a little stiff in the joints, but always with enough to talk about and with a store of reminiscences. Then, as his girls began to come of age when they must leave the convent in which they were regularly interned during his years of active service, Colonel Powys retired from the army with the necessity of making a home for them. It happened that the Ashburnhams had never seen any of the Powys girls, though, whenever the four parents met in London, Edward Ashburnham was always of the party. He was at that time twenty-two and, I believe, almost as pure in mind as Leonora herself. It is odd how a boy can have his virgin intelligence untouched in this world.

That was partly due to the careful handling of his mother, partly to the fact that the house to which he went at Winchester[1]

---

[1] Winchester College, an elite English public school.

had a particularly pure tone and partly to Edward's own peculiar aversion from anything like coarse language or gross stories. At Sandhurst[1] he had just kept out of the way of that sort of thing. He was keen on soldiering, keen on mathematics, on land-surveying, on politics and, by a queer warp of his mind, on literature. Even when he was twenty-two he would pass hours reading one of Scott's novels[2] or the Chronicles of Froissart.[3]

Mrs. Ashburnham considered that she was to be congratulated, and almost every week she wrote to Mrs. Powys, dilating upon her satisfaction.

Then, one day, taking a walk down Bond Street with her son, after having been at Lord's,[4] she noticed Edward suddenly turn his head round to take a second look at a well-dressed girl who had passed them. She wrote about that, too, to Mrs. Powys, and expressed some alarm. It had been, on Edward's part, the merest reflex action. He was so very abstracted at that time owing to the pressure his crammer[5] was putting upon him that he certainly hadn't known what he was doing.

It was this letter of Mrs. Ashburnham's to Mrs. Powys that had caused the letter from Colonel Powys to Colonel Ashburnham— a letter that was half-humorous, half longing. Mrs. Ashburnham caused her husband to reply, with a letter a little more jocular— something to the effect that Colonel Powys ought to give them some idea of the goods that he was marketing. That was the cause of the photograph. I have seen it, the seven girls, all in white dresses, all very much alike in feature—all, except Leonora, a little heavy about the chins and a little stupid about the eyes. I dare say it would have made Leonora, too, look a little heavy and a little stupid, for it was not a good photograph. But the black shadow

---

1   The foremost army officer training school in England.

2   Ford read Scott's *Ivanhoe* (1819) with rapt attention as a child.

3   Jean Froissart's (c. 1333–1400) *Chronicles* provide a record of France, Spain, and Britain from 1325 to 1400.

4   Lord's Cricket Ground in St. John's Wood, London. Home of the sport's governing body, Lord's was also a social center where fashionable citizens gathered to watch a day's match. Ford was quite fond of the sport.

5   Private tutor who packs (or "crams") information into his pupils in order for them to pass their examinations.

from one of the branches of the apple tree cut right across her face, which is all but invisible.

There followed an extremely harassing time for Colonel and Mrs. Powys. Mrs. Ashburnham had written to say that, quite sincerely, nothing would give greater ease to her maternal anxieties than to have her son marry one of Mrs. Powys' daughters if only he showed some inclination to do so. For, she added, nothing but a love-match was to be thought of in her Edward's case. But the poor Powys couple had to run things so very fine[1] that even the bringing together of the young people was a desperate hazard.

The mere expenditure upon sending one of the girls over from Ireland to Branshaw was terrifying to them; and whichever girl they selected might not be the one to ring Edward's bell. On the other hand, the expenditure upon mere food and extra sheets for a visit from the Ashburnhams to them was terrifying, too. It would mean, mathematically, going short in so many meals themselves, afterwards. Nevertheless they chanced it, and all the three Ashburnhams came on a visit to the lonely manor-house. They could give Edward some rough shooting, some rough fishing and a whirl of femininity; but I should say the girls made really more impression upon Mrs. Ashburnham than upon Edward himself. They appeared to her to be so clean run and so safe. They were indeed so clean run that, in a faint sort of way, Edward seems to have regarded them rather as boys than as girls. And then, one evening, Mrs. Ashburnham had with her boy one of those conversations that English mothers have with English sons. It seems to have been a criminal sort of proceeding, though I don't know what took place at it. Anyhow, next morning Colonel Ashburnham asked on behalf of his son for the hand of Leonora. This caused some consternation to the Powys couple, since Leonora was the third daughter and Edward ought to have married the eldest. Mrs. Powys, with her rigid sense of the proprieties, almost wished to reject the proposal. But the Colonel, her husband, pointed out that the visit would have cost them sixty pounds, what with the hire of an extra servant, of a

---

[1]   I.e., maintain a very careful and exacting budget.

horse and car, and with the purchase of beds and bedding and extra tablecloths. There was nothing else for it but the marriage. In that way Edward and Leonora became man and wife.

I don't know that a very minute study of their progress towards complete disunion is necessary. Perhaps it is. But there are many things that I cannot well make out, about which I cannot well question Leonora, or about which Edward did not tell me. I do not know that there was ever any question of love from Edward to her. He regarded her, certainly, as desirable amongst her sisters. He was obstinate to the extent of saying that if he could not have her he would not have any of them. And, no doubt, before the marriage, he made her pretty speeches out of books that he had read. But, as far as he could describe his feelings at all, later, it seems that, calmly and without any quickening of the pulse, he just carried the girl off, there being no opposition. It had, however, been all so long ago that it seemed to him, at the end of his poor life, a dim and misty affair. He had the greatest admiration for Leonora.

He had the very greatest admiration. He admired her for her truthfulness, for her cleanness of mind, and the clean-run-ness of her limbs, for her efficiency, for the fairness of her skin, for the gold of her hair, for her religion, for her sense of duty. It was a satisfaction to take her about with him.

But she had not for him a touch of magnetism. I suppose, really, he did not love her because she was never mournful; what really made him feel good in life was to comfort somebody who would be darkly and mysteriously mournful. That he had never had to do for Leonora. Perhaps, also, she was at first too obedient. I do not mean to say that she was submissive—that she deferred, in her judgements, to his. She did not. But she had been handed over to him, like some patient mediæval virgin; she had been taught all her life that the first duty of a woman is to obey. And there she was.

In her, at least, admiration for his qualities very soon became love of the deepest description. If his pulses never quickened she, so I have been told, became what is called an altered being when he approached her from the other side of a dancing floor. Her eyes followed him about full of trustfulness, of admiration, of gratitude, and of love. He was also, in a great sense, her pastor and guide—and he guided her into what, for a girl straight out of a convent, was almost heaven. I have not the least idea of what an English officer's wife's existence may be like. At any rate, there were feasts, and chatterings, and nice men who gave her the right sort of admiration, and nice women who treated her as if she had been a baby. And her confessor approved of her life, and Edward let her give little treats to the girls of the convent she had left, and the Reverend Mother approved of him. There could not have been a happier girl for five or six years.

For it was only at the end of that time that clouds began, as the saying is, to arise. She was then about twenty-three, and her purposeful efficiency made her perhaps have a desire for mastery. She began to perceive that Edward was extravagant in his largesses.[1] His parents died just about that time, and Edward, though they both decided that he should continue his soldiering, gave a great deal of attention to the management of Branshaw through a steward. Aldershot[2] was not very far away, and they spent all his leaves there.

And, suddenly, she seemed to begin to perceive that his generosities were almost fantastic. He subscribed much too much to things connected with his mess, he pensioned off his father's servants, old or new, much too generously. They had a large income, but every now and then they would find themselves hard up. He began to talk of mortgaging a farm or two, though it never actually came to that.

She made tentative efforts at remonstrating with him. Her father, whom she saw now and then, said that Edward was much too generous to his tenants; the wives of his brother officers remonstrated with her in private; his large subscriptions made it difficult for their husbands to keep up with them. Ironically enough, the first real trouble between them came from his desire to build a Roman Catholic chapel at Branshaw. He wanted to do it to honour Leonora, and he proposed to do it very expensively. Leonora did not want it; she could perfectly well drive from Branshaw to the

---

[1] Gifts, presents.
[2] Military town near Sandhurst in Hampshire.

nearest Catholic Church as often as she liked. There were no Roman Catholic tenants and no Roman Catholic servants except her old nurse who could always drive with her. She had as many priests to stay with her as could be needed—and even the priests did not want a gorgeous chapel in that place where it would have merely seemed an invidious instance of ostentation. They were perfectly ready to celebrate mass for Leonora and her nurse, when they stayed at Branshaw, in a cleaned-up outhouse. But Edward was as obstinate as a hog about it.

He was truly grieved at his wife's want of sentiment—at her refusal to receive that amount of public homage from him. She appeared to him to be wanting in imagination—to be cold and hard. I don't exactly know what part her priests played in the tragedy that it all became; I dare say they behaved quite creditably but mistakenly. But then, who would not have been mistaken with Edward? I believe he was even hurt that Leonora's confessor did not make strenuous efforts to convert him. There was a period when he was quite ready to become an emotional Catholic.

I don't know why they did not take him on the hop; but they have queer sorts of wisdoms, those people, and queer sorts of tact. Perhaps they thought that Edward's too early conversion would frighten off other Protestant desirables from marrying Catholic girls. Perhaps they saw deeper into Edward than he saw himself and thought that he would make a not very creditable convert. At any rate they—and Leonora—left him very much alone. It mortified him very considerably. He has told me that if Leonora had then taken his aspirations seriously everything would have been different. But I dare say that was nonsense.

At any rate it was over the question of the chapel that they had their first and really disastrous quarrel. Edward at that time was not well; he supposed himself to be overworked with his regimental affairs—he was managing the mess at the time. And Leonora was not well—she was beginning to fear that their union might be sterile. And then her father came over from Glasmoyle to stay with them.

Those were troublesome times in Ireland, I understand. At any rate Colonel Powys had tenants on the brain—his own tenants having shot at him with shot-guns. And, in conversation with

Edward's land-steward, he got it into his head that Edward managed his estates with a mad generosity towards his tenants. I understand also that those years—the nineties—were very bad for farming. Wheat was fetching only a few shillings the hundred; the price of meat was so low that cattle hardly paid for raising; whole English counties were ruined. And Edward allowed his tenants very high rebates.

To do both justice Leonora has since acknowledged that she was in the wrong at that time and that Edward was following out a more far-seeing policy in nursing his really very good tenants over a bad period. It was not as if the whole of his money came from the land; a good deal of it was in rails. But old Colonel Powys had that bee in his bonnet and, if he never directly approached Edward himself on the subject, he preached unceasingly, whenever he had the opportunity, to Leonora. His pet idea was that Edward ought to sack all his own tenants and import a set of farmers from Scotland. That was what they were doing in Essex. He was of opinion that Edward was riding hotfoot to ruin.

That worried Leonora very much—it worried her dreadfully; she lay awake nights; she had an anxious line round her mouth. And that, again, worried Edward. I do not mean to say that Leonora actually spoke to Edward about his tenants—but he got to know that someone, probably her father, had been talking to her about the matter. He got to know it because it was the habit of his steward to look in on them every morning about breakfast time to report any little happenings. And there was a farmer called Mumford who had only paid half his rent for the last three years. One morning the land-steward reported that Mumford would be unable to pay his rent at all that year. Edward reflected for a moment and then he said something like:

"Oh well, he's an old fellow and his family have been our tenants for over two hundred years. Let him off altogether."

And then Leonora—you must remember that she had reason for being very nervous and unhappy at that time—let out a sound that was very like a groan. It startled Edward, who more than suspected what was passing in her mind—it startled him into a state of anger. He said sharply:

"You wouldn't have me turn out people who've been earning money for us for centuries—people to whom we have responsibilities—and let in a pack of Scotch farmers?"

He looked at her, Leonora said, with what was practically a glance of hatred and then, precipitately, he left the breakfast-table. Leonora knew that it probably made it all the worse that he had been betrayed into a manifestation of anger before a third party. It was the first and last time that he ever was betrayed into such a manifestation of anger. The land-steward, a moderate and well-balanced man whose family also had been with the Ashburnhams for over a century, took it upon himself to explain that he considered Edward was pursuing a perfectly proper course with his tenants. He erred perhaps a little on the side of generosity, but hard times were hard times, and every one had to feel the pinch, landlord as well as tenants. The great thing was not to let the land get into a poor state of cultivation. Scotch farmers just skinned your fields and let them go down and down. But Edward had a very good set of tenants who did their best for him and for themselves. These arguments at that time carried very little conviction to Leonora. She was nevertheless much concerned by Edward's outburst of anger.

The fact is that Leonora had been practising economies in her department. Two of the under-housemaids had gone and she had not replaced them; she had spent much less that year upon dress. The fare she had provided at the dinners they gave had been much less bountiful and not nearly so costly as had been the case in preceding years, and Edward began to perceive a hardness and determination in his wife's character. He seemed to see a net closing round him—a net in which they would be forced to live like one of the comparatively poor county families of the neighbourhood. And, in the mysterious way in which two people, living together, get to know each other's thoughts without a word spoken, he had known, even before his outbreak, that Leonora was worrying about his managing of the estates. This appeared to him to be intolerable. He had, too, a great feeling of self-contempt because he had been betrayed into speaking harshly to Leonora before that land-steward. She imagined that his nerve must be deserting him, and there can have been few men more miserable than Edward was at that period.

You see, he was really a very simple soul—very simple. He imagined that no man can satisfactorily accomplish his life's work without loyal and whole-hearted coöperation of the woman he lives with. And he was beginning to perceive dimly that, whereas his own traditions were entirely collective, his wife was a sheer individualist. His own theory—the feudal theory of an over-lord doing his best by his dependents, the dependents meanwhile doing their best for the over-lord—this theory was entirely foreign to Leonora's nature. She came of a family of small Irish landlords—that hostile garrison in a plundered country. And she was thinking unceasingly of the children she wished to have.

I don't know why they never had any children—not that I really believe that children would have made any difference. The dissimilarity of Edward and Leonora was too profound. It will give you some idea of the extraordinary naïveté of Edward Ashburnham that, at the time of his marriage and for perhaps a couple of years after, he did not really know how children are produced. Neither did Leonora. I don't mean to say that this state of things continued, but there it was. I dare say it had a good deal of influence on their mentalities. At any rate they never had a child. It was the Will of God.

It certainly presented itself to Leonora as being the Will of God—as being a mysterious and awful chastisement of the Almighty. For she had discovered shortly before this period that her parents had not exacted from Edward's family the promise that any children she should bear should be brought up as Catholics. She herself had never talked of the matter with either her father, her mother, or her husband. When at last her father had let drop some words leading her to believe that that was the fact she tried desperately to extort the promise from Edward. She encountered an unexpected obstinacy. Edward was perfectly willing that the girls should be Catholic; the boys must be Anglican. I don't understand the bearings of these things in English society. Indeed, Englishmen seem to me to be a little mad in matters of politics or of religion. In Edward it was particularly queer because he himself was perfectly ready to become a Romanist.[1] He

---

[1] I.e., a Roman Catholic. The term has pejorative connotations.

seemed, however, to contemplate going over to Rome himself and yet letting his boys be educated in the religion of their immediate ancestors. This may appear illogical, but I dare say it is not so illogical as it looks. Edward, that is to say, regarded himself as having his own body and soul at his own disposal. But his loyalty to the traditions of his family would not permit him to bind any future inheritors of his name or beneficiaries by the death of his ancestors. About the girls it did not so much matter. They would know other homes and other circumstances. Besides, it was the usual thing. But the boys must be given the opportunity of choosing—and they must have first of all the Anglican teaching. He was perfectly unshakable about this.

Leonora was in an agony during all this time. You will have to remember she seriously believed that children who might be born to her went in danger, if not absolutely of damnation at any rate of receiving false doctrine. It was an agony more terrible than she could describe. She didn't indeed attempt to describe it, but I could tell from her voice when she said, almost negligently, "I used to lie awake whole nights. It was no good my spiritual advisers trying to console me." I knew from her voice how terrible and how long those nights must have seemed and of how little avail were the consolations of her spiritual advisers. Her spiritual advisers seemed to have taken the matter a little more calmly. They certainly told her that she must not consider herself in any way to have sinned. Nay, they seem even to have extorted, to have threatened her, with a view to getting her out of what they considered to be a morbid frame of mind. She would just have to make the best of things, to influence the children when they came, not by propaganda, but by personality. And they warned her that she would be committing a sin if she continued to think that she had sinned. Nevertheless, she continued to think that she had sinned.

Leonora could not be aware that the man whom she loved passionately and whom, nevertheless, she was beginning to try to rule with a rod of iron—that this man was becoming more and more estranged from her. He seemed to regard her as being not only physically and mentally cold, but even as being actually wicked and mean. There were times when he would almost shudder if she spoke to him. And she could not understand how he could consider her wicked or mean. It only seemed to her a sort of madness in him that he should try to take upon his own shoulders the burden of his troop, of his regiment, of his estate and of half of his country. She could not see that in trying to curb what she regarded as megalomania she was doing anything wicked. She was just trying to keep things together for the sake of the children who did not come. And, little by little, the whole of their intercourse became simply one of agonized discussion as to whether Edward should subscribe to this or that institution or should try to reclaim this or that drunkard. She simply could not see it.

Into this really terrible position of strain, from which there appeared to be no issue, the Kilsyte case came almost as a relief. It is part of the peculiar irony of things that Edward would certainly never have kissed that nurse-maid if he had not been trying to please Leonora. Nurse-maids do not travel first-class and, that day, Edward travelled in a third-class carriage in order to prove to Leonora that he was capable of economies. I have said that the Kilsyte case came almost as a relief to the strained situation that then existed between them. It gave Leonora an opportunity of backing him up in a whole-hearted and absolutely loyal manner. It gave her the opportunity of behaving to him as he considered a wife should behave to her husband.

You see, Edward found himself in a railway carriage with a quite pretty girl of about nineteen. And the quite pretty girl of about nineteen, with dark hair and red cheeks and blue eyes, was quietly weeping. Edward had been sitting in his corner thinking about nothing at all. He had chanced to look at the nurse-maid; two large, pretty tears came out of her eyes and dropped into her lap. He immediately felt that he had got to do something to comfort her. That was his job in life. He was desperately unhappy himself and it seemed to him the most natural thing in the world that they should pool their sorrows. He was quite democratic; the idea of the difference in their station never seems to have occurred to him. He began to talk to her. He discovered that her young man had been seen walking out with Annie of Number 54. He moved over to her side of the carriage. He told her that the report probably wasn't true; that, after all, a young man might take a walk with Annie from Number 54 without its denoting anything very serious. And he assured me that he felt at least quite half-fatherly when he put his arm around her waist and kissed her. The girl, however, had not forgotten the difference of her station.

All her life, by her mother, by other girls, by schoolteachers, by the whole tradition of her class she had been warned against gentlemen. She was being kissed by a gentleman. She screamed, tore herself away; sprang up and pulled a communication cord.

Edward came fairly well out of the affair in the public estimation; but it did him, mentally, a good deal of harm.

IV

It is very difficult to give an all-round impression of any man. I wonder how far I have succeeded with Edward Ashburnham. I dare say I haven't succeeded at all. It is even very difficult to see how such things matter. Was it the important point about poor Edward that he was very well built, carried himself well, was moderate at the table and led a regular life—that he had, in fact, all the virtues that are usually accounted English? Or have I in the least succeeded in conveying that he was all those things and had all those virtues? He certainly was them and had them up to the last months of his life. They were the things that one would set upon his tombstone. They will, indeed, be set upon his tombstone by his widow.

And have I, I wonder, given the due impression of how his life was portioned and his time laid out? Because, until the very last, the amount of time taken up by his various passions was relatively small. I have been forced to write very much about his passions, but you have to consider—I should like to be able to make you consider—that he rose every morning at seven, took a cold bath, breakfasted at eight, was occupied with his regiment from nine until one; played polo or cricket with the men when it was the season for cricket, till tea-time. Afterwards he would occupy himself with the letters from his land-steward or with the affairs of his mess, till dinner time. He would dine and pass the evening playing cards, or playing billiards with Leonora or at social functions of one kind or another. And the greater part of his life was taken up by that—by far the greater part of his life. His love-affairs, until the very end, were sandwiched in at odd moments or took place during the social evenings, the dances and dinners. But I guess I have made it hard for you, O silent listener, to get that impression. Anyhow, I hope I have not given you the idea that Edward Ashburnham was a pathological case. He wasn't. He was just a normal man and very much of a sentimentalist. I dare say the quality of his youth, the nature of his mother's influence, his ignorances, the crammings that he received at the hands of army coaches—I dare say that all these excellent influences upon his adolescence were very bad for him. But we all have to put up with that sort of thing and no doubt it is very bad for all of us. Nevertheless, the outline of Edward's life was an outline perfectly normal of the life of a hard-working, sentimental and efficient professional man.

That question of first impressions has always bothered me a good deal—but quite academically. I mean that, from time to time I have wondered whether it were or were not best to trust to one's first impressions in dealing with people. But I never had anybody to deal with except waiters and chambermaids and the Ashburnhams, with whom I didn't know that I was having any dealings. And, as far as waiters and chambermaids were concerned, I have generally found that my first impressions were correct enough. If my first idea of a man was that he was civil, obliging, and attentive, he generally seemed to go on being all those things. Once, however, at our Paris flat we had a maid who appeared to be charming and transparently honest. She stole, nevertheless, one of Florence's diamond rings. She did it, however, to save her young man from going to prison. So here, as somebody says somewhere, was a special case.

And, even in my short incursion into American business life—an incursion that lasted during part of August and nearly the whole of September—I found that to rely upon first impressions was the best thing I could do. I found myself automatically docketing and labelling each man as he was introduced to me, by the run of his features and by the first words that he spoke. I can't, however, be regarded as really doing business during the time that I spent in the United States. I was just winding things up. If it hadn't been for my idea of marrying the girl I might possibly have looked for something to do in my own country. For my experiences there were vivid and amusing. It was exactly as if I had come out of a museum into a riotous fancy-dress ball. During my life with Florence I had almost come to forget that there were such things as fashions or occupations or the greed of gain. I had, in fact, forgotten that there was such a thing as a dollar and that a dollar can be extremely desirable if you don't happen to possess one. And I had forgotten, too, that there was such a thing as gossip that mattered. In that particular, Philadelphia was the most amazing place I have ever been in in my life. I was not in that city for more than a week or ten days and I didn't there transact anything much in the way of business, nevertheless the number of times that I was warned by everybody against everybody else was simply amazing. A man I didn't know would come up behind my lounge chair in the hotel, and, whispering cautiously beside my ear, would warn me against some other man that I equally didn't know but who would be standing by the bar. I don't know what they thought I was there to do—perhaps to buy out the city's debt or get a controlling hold of some railway interest. Or, perhaps, they imagined that I wanted to buy a newspaper, for they were either politicians or reporters, which, of course, comes to the same thing. As a matter of fact, my property in Philadelphia was mostly real estate in the old-fashioned part of the city and all I wanted to do there was just to satisfy myself that the houses were in good repair and the doors kept properly painted. I wanted also to see my relations, of whom I had a few. These were mostly professional people and they were mostly rather hard up because of the big bank failure in 1907 or thereabouts.[1] Still, they were very nice. They would have been nicer still if they hadn't, all of them, had what appeared to me to be the mania that what they called influences were working against them. At any rate, the impression of that city was one of old-fashioned rooms, rather

---

[1] In October 1907, stock market speculation was followed by the panicked selling of shares. Many bank failures ensued as a consequence of the panic.

English than American in type, in which handsome but careworn ladies, cousins of my own, talked principally about mysterious movements that were going on against them. I never got to know what it was all about; perhaps they thought I knew or perhaps there weren't any movements at all. It was all very secret and subtle and subterranean. But there was a nice young fellow called Carter who was a sort of second-nephew of mine, twice removed. He was handsome and dark and gentle and tall and modest. I understand also that he was a good cricketer. He was employed by the real-estate agents who collected my rents. It was he, therefore, who took me over my own property and I saw a good deal of him and of a nice girl called Mary, to whom he was engaged. At that time I did, what I certainly shouldn't do now— I made some careful inquiries as to his character. I discovered from his employers that he was just all that he appeared, honest, industrious, high-spirited, friendly and ready to do anyone a good turn. His relatives, however—they were mine too—seemed to have something darkly mysterious against him. I imagined that he must have been mixed up in some case of graft or that he had at least betrayed several innocent and trusting maidens. I pushed, however, that particular mystery home and discovered it was only that he was a Democrat. My own people were mostly Republicans. It seemed to make it worse and more darkly mysterious to them that young Carter was what they called a sort of a Vermont Democrat, which was the whole ticket[1] and no mistake. But I don't know what it means. Anyhow, I suppose that my money will go to him when I die—I like the recollection of his friendly image and of the nice girl he was engaged to. May Fate deal very kindly with them.

I have said just now that, in my present frame of mind, nothing would ever make me make inquiries as to the character of any man that I liked at first sight. (The little digression as to my Philadelphia experiences was really meant to lead around to this.) For who in this world can give anyone a character? Who in this world knows anything of any other heart—or of his own? I don't

---

[1] The normal party nomination as opposed to a divided nomination that represents a faction or wing of the party.

mean to say that one cannot form an average estimate of the way a person will behave. But one cannot be certain of the way any man will behave in every case—and until one can do that a "character" is of no use to anyone. That, for instance, was the way with Florence's maid in Paris. We used to trust that girl with blank cheques for the payment of the tradesmen. For quite a time she was so trusted by us. Then, suddenly, she stole a ring. We should not have believed her capable of it; she would not have believed herself capable of it. It was nothing in her character. So, perhaps, it was with Edward Ashburnham.

Or, perhaps, it wasn't. No, I rather think it wasn't. It is diffi-cult to figure out. I have said that the Kilsyte case eased the immediate tension for him and Leonora. It let him see that she was capable of loyalty to him; it gave her her chance to show that she believed in him. She accepted without question his statement that, in kissing the girl, he wasn't trying to do more than administer fatherly comfort to a weeping child. And, indeed, his own world—including the magistrates—took that view of the case. Whatever people say, one's world can be perfectly charitable at times ... But, again, as I have said, it did Edward a great deal of harm.

That, at least, was his view of it. He assured me that, before that case came on and was wrangled about by counsel with all sorts of dirty-mindedness that counsel in that sort of case can impute, he had not had the least idea that he was capable of being unfaithful to Leonora. But, in the midst of that tumult—he says that it came suddenly into his head whilst he was in the witness-box—in the midst of those august ceremonies of the law there came suddenly into his mind the recollection of the softness of the girl's body as he had pressed her to him. And, from that moment, that girl appeared desirable to him—and Leonora completely unattractive.

He began to indulge in day-dreams in which he approached the nurse-maid more tactfully and carried the matter much further. Occasionally he thought of other women in terms of wary courtship—or, perhaps, it would be more exact to say that he thought of them in terms of tactful comforting, ending in absorption. That was his own view of the case. He saw himself as the victim of the law. I don't mean to say that he saw himself as a kind of Dreyfus.[1] The law, practically, was quite kind to him. It stated that in its view Captain Ashburnham had been misled by an ill-placed desire to comfort a member of the opposite sex and it fined him five shillings for his want of tact, or of knowledge of the world. But Edward maintained that it had put ideas into his head.

I don't believe it, though he certainly did. He was twenty-seven then, and his wife was out of sympathy with him—some crash was inevitable. There was between them a momentary rapprochement;[2] but it could not last. It made it, probably, all the worse that, in that particular matter Leonora had come so very well up to the scratch.[3] For, whilst Edward respected her more and was grateful to her, it made her seem by so much the more cold in other matters that were near his heart—his responsibilities, his career, his tradition. It brought his despair of her up to a point of exasperation—and it riveted on him the idea that he might find some other woman who would give him the moral support that he needed. He wanted to be looked upon as a sort of Lohengrin.

At that time, he says, he went about deliberately looking for some woman who could help him. He found several—for there were quite a number of ladies in his set who were capable of agreeing with this handsome and fine fellow that the duties of a feudal gentleman were feudal. He would have liked to pass his days talking to one or other of these ladies. But there was always an obstacle—if the lady were married there would be a husband who claimed the greater part of her time and attention. If, on the other hand, it were an unmarried girl he could not see very much of her for fear of compromising her. At that date, you understand, he had not the least idea of seducing any one of these

---

[1] Alfred Dreyfus (1859–1935), an innocent victim of a grave injustice. A French army officer of Jewish origin, he was wrongly convicted in 1894 and deported for life to Devil's Island. In 1906, he was released following the revelation that forged evidence was used against him. A major French political scandal ensued when right-wing and Catholic politicized elements refused to admit a miscarriage of justice.

[2] Establishment of cordial relations.

[3] The "scratch" refers to the beginning of a horse race; literally, responding well to a challenge.

ladies. He wanted only moral support at the hands of some female, because he found men difficult to talk to about ideals. Indeed, I do not believe that he had, at any time, any idea of making any one his mistress. That sounds queer; but I believe it is quite true as a statement of character.

It was, I believe, one of Leonora's priests—a man of the world—who suggested that she should take him to Monte Carlo. He had the idea that what Edward needed, in order to fit him for the society of Leonora, was a touch of irresponsibility. For Edward, at that date, had much the aspect of a prig. I mean that, if he played polo and was an excellent dancer he did the one for the sake of keeping himself fit and the other because it was a social duty to show himself at dances, and, when there, to dance well. He did nothing for fun except what he considered to be his work in life. As the priest saw it, this must for ever estrange him from Leonora—not because Leonora set much store by the joy of life, but because she was out of sympathy with Edward's work. On the other hand, Leonora did like to have a good time, now and then, and, as the priest saw it, if Edward could be got to like having a good time now and then too, there would be a bond of sympathy between them. It was a good idea, but it worked out wrongly.

It worked out, in fact, in the mistress of the Grand Duke. In anyone less sentimental than Edward that would not have mattered. With Edward it was fatal. For, such was his honourable nature, that for him, to enjoy a woman's favours, made him feel that she had a bond on him for life. That was the way it worked out in practice. Psychologically it meant that he could not have a mistress without falling violently in love with her. He was a serious person—and in this particular case it was very expensive. The mistress of the Grand Duke—a Spanish dancer of passionate appearance—singled out Edward for her glances at a ball that was held in their common hotel. Edward was tall, handsome, blond and very wealthy as she understood—and Leonora went up to bed early. She did not care for public dances, but she was relieved to see that Edward appeared to be having a good time with several amiable girls. And that was the end of Edward—for the Spanish dancer of passionate appearance wanted one night of him for his beaux yeux.[1] He took her into the dark gardens and, remembering suddenly the girl of the Kilsyte case, he kissed her. He kissed her passionately, violently, with a sudden explosion of the passion that had been bridled all his life—for Leonora was cold, or, at any rate well behaved. La Dolciquita liked this reversion, and he passed the night in her bed.

When the palpitating creature was at last asleep in his arms he discovered that he was madly, was passionately, was overwhelmingly in love with her. It was a passion that had arisen like fire in dry corn. He could think of nothing else; he could live for nothing else. But La Dolciquita was a reasonable creature without an ounce of passion in her. She wanted a certain satisfaction of her appetites and Edward had appealed to her the night before. Now that was done with and, quite coldly, she said that she wanted money if he was to have any more of her. It was a perfectly reasonable commercial transaction. She did not care two buttons for Edward or for any man and he was asking her to risk a very good situation with the Grand Duke. If Edward could put up sufficient money to serve as a kind of insurance against accident she was ready to like Edward for a time that would be covered, as it were, by the policy. She was getting fifty thousand dollars a year from her Grand Duke; Edward would have to pay a premium of two years' hire for a month of her society. There would not be much risk of the Grand Duke's finding it out and it was not certain that he would give her the keys of the street[2] if he did find out. But there was the risk—a twenty per cent risk, as she figured it out. She talked to Edward as if she had been a solicitor with an estate to sell—perfectly quietly and perfectly coldly without any inflections in her voice. She did not want to be unkind to him; but she could see no reason for being kind to him. She was a virtuous business woman with a mother and two sisters and her own old age to be provided comfortably for. She did not expect more than a five years' further run. She was twenty-four and, as she said: "We Spanish women are horrors at thirty." Edward swore that he would provide for her for life if she would come to him and leave off

[1] Literally, his "pretty eyes."
[2] I.e., he would throw her out.

talking so horribly; but she only shrugged one shoulder slowly and contemptuously. He tried to convince this woman, who, as he saw it, had surrendered to him her virtue, that he regarded it as in any case his duty to provide for her, and to cherish her and even to love her—for life. In return for her sacrifice he would do that. In return, again, for his honourable love she would listen for ever to the accounts of his estate. That was how he figured it out.

She shrugged the same shoulder with the same gesture and held out her left hand with the elbow at her side:

"Enfin, mon ami,"[1] she said, "put in this hand the price of that tiara at Forli's[2] or ..." And she turned her back on him.

Edward went mad; his world stood on its head; the palms in front of the blue sea danced grotesque dances. You see, he believed in the virtue, tenderness and moral support of women. He wanted more than anything to argue with La Dolciquita; to retire with her to an island and point out to her the damnation of her point of view and how salvation can only be found in true love and the feudal system. She had once been his mistress, he reflected, and, by all the moral laws she ought to have gone on being his mistress or at the very least his sympathetic confidante. But her rooms were closed to him; she did not appear in the hotel. Nothing: blank silence. To break that down he had to have twenty thousand pounds. You have heard what happened.

He spent a week of madness; he hungered; his eyes sank in; he shuddered at Leonora's touch. I dare say that nine-tenths of what he took to be his passion for La Dolciquita was really discomfort at the thought that he had been unfaithful to Leonora. He felt uncommonly bad, that is to say—oh, unbearably bad, and he took it all to be love. Poor devil, he was incredibly naïve. He drank like a fish after Leonora was in bed and he spread himself over the tables, and this went on for about a fortnight. Heaven knows what would have happened; he would have thrown away every penny that he possessed.

On the night after he had lost about forty thousand pounds and whilst the whole hotel was whispering about it, La Dolciquita

---

[1] "Look here, my friend."
[2] Apparently, a jewelry shop in Monte Carlo.

walked composedly into his bedroom. He was too drunk to recognize her, and she sat in his armchair, knitting and holding smelling salts to his nose—for he was pretty far gone with alcoholic poisoning—and, as soon as he was able to understand her, she said:

"Look here, mon ami, do not go to the tables again. Take a good sleep now and come and see me this afternoon."

He slept till the lunch hour. By that time Leonora had heard the news. A Mrs. Colonel Whelen had told her. Mrs. Colonel Whelen seems to have been the only sensible person who was ever connected with the Ashburnhams. She had argued it out that there must be a woman of the harpy variety connected with Edward's incredible behaviour and mien; and she advised Leonora to go straight off to Town[1]—which might have the effect of bringing Edward to his senses—and to consult her solicitor and her spiritual adviser. She had better go that very morning; it was no good arguing with a man in Edward's condition.

Edward, indeed, did not know that she had gone. As soon as he woke he went straight to La Dolciquita's room and she stood him his lunch in her own apartments. He fell on her neck and wept, and she put up with it for a time. She was quite a good-natured woman. And, when she had calmed him down with Eau de Mélisse,[2] she said:

"Look here, my friend, how much money have you left? Five thousand dollars? Ten?" For the rumour went that Edward had lost two kings' ransoms a night for fourteen nights and she imagined that he must be near the end of his resources.

The Eau de Mélisse had calmed Edward to such an extent that, for the moment, he really had a head on his shoulders. He did nothing more than grunt:

"And then?"

"Why," she answered, "I may just as well have the ten thousand dollars[3] as the tables. I will go with you to Antibes for a week for that sum."

---

[1] To London.
[2] Medicinal cordial; melissa is an herb.
[3] Today, about $150,000 or £100,000.

Edward grunted: "Five." She tried to get seven thousand five hundred; but he stuck to his five thousand and the hotel expenses at Antibes. The sedative carried him just as far as that and then he collapsed again. He had to leave for Antibes at three; he could not do without it. He left a note for Leonora saying that he had gone off for a week with the Clinton Morleys, yachting.

He did not enjoy himself very much at Antibes. La Dolciquita could talk of nothing with any enthusiasm except money, and she tired him unceasingly, during every waking hour for presents of the most expensive description. And, at the end of a week, she just quietly kicked him out. He hung about in Antibes for three days. He was cured of the idea that he had any duties towards La Dolciquita—feudal or otherwise. But his sentimentalism required of him an attitude of Byronic gloom—as if his court had gone into half-mourning. Then his appetite suddenly returned, and he remembered Leonora. He found at his hotel at Monte Carlo a telegram from Leonora, dispatched from London, saying; "Please return as soon as convenient." He could not understand why Leonora should have abandoned him so precipitately when she only thought that he had gone yachting with the Clinton Morleys. Then he discovered that she had left the hotel before he had written the note. He had a pretty rocky journey back to town; he was frightened out of his life—and Leonora had never seemed so desirable to him.

V

I call this the Saddest Story, rather than "The Ashburnham Tragedy," just because it is so sad, just because there was no current to draw things along to a swift and inevitable end. There is about it none of the elevation that accompanies tragedy; there is about it no nemesis, no destiny. Here were two noble people— for I am convinced that both Edward and Leonora had noble natures—here then, were two noble natures, drifting down life, like fireships[1] afloat on a lagoon and causing miseries, heart-aches, agony of the mind and death. And they themselves steadily deteriorated? And why? For what purpose? To point what lesson? It is all a darkness.

There is not even any villain in the story—for even Major Basil, the husband of the lady who next, and really, comforted the unfor-tunate Edward—even Major Basil was not a villain in this piece. He was a slack, loose, shiftless sort of fellow—but he did not do anything to Edward. Whilst they were in the same station in Burma he borrowed a good deal of money—though, really, since Major Basil had no particular vices, it was difficult to know why he wanted it. He collected—different types of horses' bits from the earliest times to the present day—but, since he did not prosecute even this occupation with any vigour, he cannot have needed much money for the acquirement, say, of the bit of Genghis Khan's charger—if Genghis Khan had a charger. And when I say that he borrowed a good deal of money from Edward I do not mean to say that he had more than a thousand pounds[2] from him during the five years that the connection lasted. Edward, of course, did not have a great deal of money; Leonora was seeing to that. Still he may have had five hundred pounds a year English, for his menus plaisirs[3]—for his regimental subscriptions and for keeping his men smart. Leonora hated that; she would have preferred to buy dresses for herself or to have devoted the money to paying off a mort-gage. Still, with her sense of justice, she saw that, since she was managing a property bringing in three thousand a year with a view to re-establishing it as a property of five thousand a year and since the property really, if not legally, belonged to Edward, it was reasonable and just that Edward should get a slice of his own. Of course she had the devil of a job.

I don't know that I have got the financial details exactly right. I am a pretty good head at figures, but my mind, still, sometimes mixes up pounds with dollars and I get a figure wrong. Anyhow, the proposition was something like this: Properly worked and

---

[1]   Ships carrying combustibles sent amongst the enemy's fleet to set them afire. Also, slang for a person suffering from a sexual disease.

[2]   Today, about $75,000 or £50,000.

[3]   Pocket money, spending money.

without rebates to the tenants and keeping up schools and things, the Branshaw estate should have brought in about five thousand a year when Edward had it. It brought in actually about four. (I am talking in pounds, not dollars.) Edward's excesses with the Spanish Lady had reduced its value to about three—as the maximum figure, without reductions. Leonora wanted to get it back to five.

She was, of course, very young to be faced with such a proposition—twenty-four is not a very advanced age. So she did things with a youthful vigour that she would, very likely, have made more merciful, if she had known more about life. She got Edward remarkably on the hop. He had to face her in a London hotel, when he crept back from Monte Carlo with his poor tail between his poor legs. As far as I can make out she cut short his first mumblings and his first attempts at affectionate speech with words something like:

"We're on the verge of ruin. Do you intend to let me pull things together? If not I shall retire to Hendon on my jointure."[1] (Hendon represented a convent to which she occasionally went for what is called a "retreat" in Catholic circles.)

And poor dear Edward knew nothing—absolutely nothing. He did not know how much money he had, as he put it, "blued"[2] at the tables. It might have been a quarter of a million for all he remembered. He did not know whether she knew about La Dolciquita or whether she imagined that he had gone off yachting or had stayed at Monte Carlo. He was just dumb and he just wanted to get into a hole and not have to talk. Leonora did not make him talk and she said nothing herself.

I do not know much about English legal procedure—I cannot, I mean, give technical details of how they tied him up. But I know that, two days later, without her having said more than I have reported to you, Leonora and her attorney had become the trustees, as I believe it is called, of all Edward's property and there was an end of Edward as the good landlord and father of his people. He went out.

---

[1] Part of an estate belonging to the wife. Hendon is a suburb in north London. In 1905, Ford's impressions of London and its environs, *The Soul of London*, was published.

[2] Squandered, gambled, or thrown away.

Leonora then had three thousand a year at her disposal. She occupied Edward with getting himself transferred to a part of his regiment that was in Burma—if that is the right way to put it. She herself had an interview, lasting a week or so—with Edward's land-steward. She made him understand that the estate would have to yield up to its last penny. Before they left for India she had let Branshaw for seven years at a thousand a year. She sold two Vandykes[1] and a little silver for eleven thousand pounds and she raised, on mortgage, twenty-nine thousand. That went to Edward's money-lending friends in Monte Carlo. So she had to get the twenty-nine thousand back, for she did not regard the Vandykes and the silver as things she would have to replace. They were just frills to the Ashburnham vanity. Edward cried for two days over the disappearance of his ancestors and then she wished she had not done it; but it did not teach her anything and it lessened such esteem as she had for him. She did not also understand that to let Branshaw affected him with a feeling of physical soiling—that it was almost as bad for him as if a woman belonging to him had become a prostitute. That was how it did affect him; but I dare say she felt just as bad about the Spanish dancer.

So she went at it. They were eight years in India, and during the whole of that time she insisted that they must be self-supporting—they had to live on his Captain's pay, plus the extra allowance for being at the front. She gave him the five hundred a year for Ashburnham frills as she called it to herself—and she considered she was doing him very well.

Indeed, in a way, she did him very well—but it was not his way. She was always buying him expensive things which, as it were, she took off her own back. I have, for instance, spoken of Edward's leather cases. Well, they were not Edward's at all; they were Leonora's manifestations. He liked to be clean, but he preferred, as it were, to be threadbare. She never understood that, and all that pigskin was her idea of a reward to him for putting her up to a little speculation by which she made eleven hundred pounds. She did, herself, the threadbare business. When they went

---

[1]   Refers to the paintings of English artist Sir Anthony Vandyke (1787–1855).

up to a place called Simla,[1] where, as I understand, it is cool in the summer and very social—when they went up to Simla for their healths it was she who had him prancing around, as we should say in the United States, on a thousand-dollar horse with the gladdest of glad rags all over him. She herself used to go into "retreat." I believe that was very good for her health and it was also very inexpensive.

It was probably also very good for Edward's health, because he pranced about mostly with Mrs. Basil, who was a nice woman and very, very kind to him. I suppose she was his mistress, but I never heard it from Edward, of course. I seem to gather that they carried it on in a high romantic fashion, very proper to both of them—or, at any rate, for Edward; she seems to have been a tender and gentle soul who did what he wanted. I do not mean to say that she was without character; that was her job, to do what Edward wanted. So I figured it out that for those five years, Edward wanted long passages of deep affection kept up in long, long talks and that every now and then they "fell," which would give Edward an opportunity for remorse and an excuse to lend the Major another fifty. I don't think that Mrs. Basil considered it to be "falling"; she just pitied him and loved him.

You see, Leonora and Edward had to talk about something during all these years. You cannot be absolutely dumb when you live with a person unless you are an inhabitant of the North of England or the State of Maine. So Leonora imagined the cheerful device of letting him see the accounts of his estate and discussing them with him. He did not discuss them much; he was trying to behave prettily. But it was old Mr. Mumford—the farmer who did not pay his rent—that threw Edward into Mrs. Basil's arms. Mrs. Basil came upon Edward in the dusk, in the Burmese garden, with all sorts of flowers and things. And he was cutting up that crop—with his sword, not a walking-stick. He was also carrying on and cursing in a way you would not believe.

She ascertained that an old gentleman called Mumford had been ejected from his farm and had been given a little cottage

---

[1]   Simla, a town in the Punjab. During the British colonial period, it served as the viceroy's summer home and as a social center.

rent-free, where he lived on ten shillings a week from a farmers' benevolent society, supplemented by seven that was being allowed him by the Ashburnham trustees. Edward had just discovered that fact from the estate accounts. Leonora had left them in his dressing-room and he had begun to read them before taking off his marching-kit. That was how he came to have a sword. Leonora considered that she had been unusually generous to old Mr. Mumford in allowing him to inhabit a cottage, rent-free, and in giving him seven shillings a week. Anyhow, Mrs. Basil had never seen a man in such a state as Edward was. She had been passionately in love with him for quite a time, and he had been longing for her sympathy and admiration with a passion as deep. That was how they came to speak about it, in the Burmese garden, under the pale sky, with sheafs of severed vegetation, misty and odorous, in the night around their feet. I think they behaved themselves with decorum for quite a time after that, though Mrs. Basil spent so many hours over the accounts of the Ashburnham estate that she got the name of every field by heart. Edward had a huge map of his lands in his harness room and Major Basil did not seem to mind. I believe that people do not mind much in lonely stations.

It might have lasted for ever if the Major had not been made what is called a brevet-colonel[1] during the shuffling of troops that went on just before the South African War.[2] He was sent off somewhere else and, of course, Mrs. Basil could not stay with Edward. Edward ought, I suppose, to have gone to the Transvaal. It would have done him a great deal of good to get killed. But Leonora would not let him; she had heard awful stories of the extravagance of the hussar regiment in war-time—how they left hundred-bottle cases of champagne at five guineas a bottle, on the veldt[3] and so on. Besides, she preferred to see how Edward was spending his five hundred a year. I don't mean to say that Edward had any grievance in that. He was never a man of the

---

[1] Military commission that affords an officer with a higher rank than the one for which he is paid.

[2] The Boer War (1899–1902), fought between the Transvaal and the Orange Free State—the two Boer republics and the British, respectively.

[3] South African grassland.

deeds of heroism sort and it was just as good for him to be sniped at up in the hills of the North Western frontier, as to be shot at by an old gentleman in a top hat at the bottom of some spruit.[1] Those are more or less his words about it. I believe he quite distinguished himself over there. At any rate, he had his D.S.O. and was made a brevet-major.

Leonora, however, was not in the least keen on his soldiering. She hated also his deeds of heroism. One of their bitterest quarrels came after he had, for the second time, in the Red Sea, jumped overboard from the troop-ship and rescued a private soldier. She stood it the first time and even complimented him. But the Red Sea was awful, that trip, and the private soldiers seemed to develop a suicidal craze. It got on Leonora's nerves; she figured Edward, for the rest of that trip, jumping overboard every ten minutes. And the mere cry of "Man overboard" is a disagreeable, alarming and disturbing thing. The ship gets stopped and there are all sorts of shouts. And Edward would not promise not to do it again, though, fortunately they struck a streak of cooler weather when they were in the Persian Gulf. Leonora had got it into her head that Edward was trying to commit suicide, so I guess it was pretty awful for her when he would not give the promise. Leonora ought never to have been on that troopship; but she got there somehow, as an economy.

Major Basil discovered his wife's relation with Edward just before he was sent to his other station. I don't know whether that was a blackmailer's adroitness or just a trick of destiny. He may have known of it all the time or he may not. At any rate, he got hold of, just about then, some letters and things. It cost Edward three hundred pounds immediately. I do not know how it was arranged; I cannot imagine how even a blackmailer can make his demands. I suppose there is some sort of way of saving your face. I figure the Major as disclosing the letters to Edward with furious oaths, then accepting his explanations that the letters were perfectly innocent if the wrong construction were not put upon them. Then the Major would say: "I say, old chap, I'm deuced hard up. Couldn't you lend me three hundred or so?" I

---

[1]   Dry tributary or stream in South Africa.

fancy that was how it was. And, year by year, after that there would come a letter from the Major, saying that he was deuced hard up and couldn't Edward lend him three hundred or so.

Edward was pretty hard hit when Mrs. Basil had to go away. He really had been very fond of her, and he remained faithful to her memory for quite a long time. And Mrs. Basil had loved him very much and continued to cherish a hope of reunion with him. Three days ago there came a quite proper but very lamentable letter from her to Leonora, asking to be given particulars as to Edward's death. She had read the advertisement of it in an Indian paper. I think she must have been a very nice woman....

And then the Ashburnhams were moved somewhere up towards a place or a district called Chitral. I am no good at geography of the Indian Empire. By that time they had settled down into a model couple and they never spoke in private to each other. Leonora had given up even showing the accounts of the Ashburnham estate to Edward. He thought that that was because she had piled up such a lot of money that she did not want him to know how she was getting on any more. But, as a matter of fact, after five or six years it had penetrated to her mind that it was painful to Edward to have to look on at the accounts of his estate and have no hand in the management of it. She was trying to do him a kindness. And, up in Chitral, poor dear little Maisie Maidan came along....

That was the most unsettling to Edward of all his affairs. It made him suspect that he was inconstant. The affair with the Dolciquita he had sized up as a short attack of madness like hydrophobia. His relations with Mrs. Basil had not seemed to him to imply moral turpitude of a gross kind. The husband had been complaisant; they had really loved each other; his wife was very cruel to him and had long ceased to be a wife to him. He thought that Mrs. Basil had been his soul-mate, separated from him by an unkind fate—something sentimental of that sort.

But he discovered that, whilst he was still writing long weekly letters to Mrs. Basil, he was beginning to be furiously impatient if he missed seeing Maisie Maidan during the course of the day. He discovered himself watching the doorways with impatience; he discovered that he disliked her boy husband very much for hours at a time. He discovered that he was getting up at unearthly hours in order to have time, later in the morning, to go for a walk with Maisie Maidan. He discovered himself using little slang words that she used and attaching a sentimental value to those words. These, you understand, were discoveries that came so late that he could do nothing but drift. He was losing weight; his eyes were beginning to fall in; he had touches of bad fever. He was, as he described it, pipped.[1]

And, one ghastly hot day, he suddenly heard himself say to Leonora:

"I say, couldn't we take little Mrs. Maidan with us to Europe and drop her at Nauheim?"

He hadn't had the least idea of saying that to Leonora. He had merely been standing, looking at an illustrated paper, waiting for dinner. Dinner was twenty minutes late or the Ashburnhams would not have been alone together. No, he hadn't had the least idea of framing that speech. He had just been standing in a silent agony of fear, of longing, of heat, of fever. He was thinking that they were going back to Branshaw in a month and that Maisie Maidan was going to remain behind and die. And then, that had come out.

The punkah[2] swished in the darkened room; Leonora lay exhausted and motionless in her cane lounge;[3] neither of them stirred. They were both at that time very ill in indefinite ways.

And then Leonora said:

"Yes. I promised it to Charlie Maidan this afternoon. I have offered to pay her ex's[4] myself."

Edward just saved himself from saying: "Good God!" You see, he had not the least idea of what Leonora knew—about Maisie, about Mrs. Basil, even about La Dolciquita. It was a pretty enigmatic situation for him. It struck him that Leonora must be intending to manage his loves as she managed his money affairs and it made her more hateful to him—and more worthy of respect.

Leonora, at any rate, had managed his money to some purpose. She had spoken to him, a week before, for the first time in several

---

[1]   Exhausted.
[2]   Anglo-Indian expression for a large ceiling fan.
[3]   A day-bed made of cane.
[4]   Expenses.

years—about money. She had made twenty-two thousand pounds[1] out of the Branshaw land and seven by the letting of Branshaw furnished. By fortunate investments—in which Edward had helped her—she had made another six or seven thousand that might well become more. The mortgages were all paid off, so that, except for the departure of the two Vandykes and the silver, they were as well off as they had been before the Dolciquita had acted the locust. It was Leonora's great achievement. She laid the figures before Edward, who maintained an unbroken silence.

"I propose," she said, "that you should resign from the Army and that we should go back to Branshaw. We are both too ill to stay here any longer."

Edward said nothing at all.

"This," Leonora continued passionlessly, "is the great day of my life."

Edward said:

"You have managed the job amazingly. You are a wonderful woman." He was thinking that if they went back to Branshaw they would leave Maisie Maidan behind. That thought occupied him exclusively. They must, undoubtedly, return to Branshaw; there could be no doubt that Leonora was too ill to stay in that place. She said:

"You understand that the management of the whole of the expenditure of the income will be in your hands. There will be five thousand a year."

She thought that he cared very much about the expenditure of an income of five thousand a year and that the fact that she had done so much for him would rouse in him some affection for her. But he was thinking exclusively of Maisie Maidan—of Maisie, thousands of miles away from him. He was seeing the mountains between them—blue mountains and the sea and sunlit plains. He said:

"That is very generous of you." And she did not know whether that were praise or a sneer. That had been a week before. And all that week he had passed in an increasing agony at the thought that those mountains, that sea and those sunlit plains

---

[1] Today, about $1,500,000 or £1,000,000.

would be between him and Maisie Maidan. That thought shook him in the burning nights: the sweat poured from him and he trembled with cold, in the burning noons—at that thought. He had no minute's rest; his bowels turned round and round within him: his tongue was perpetually dry and it seemed to him that the breath between his teeth was like air from a pest-house.[1]

He gave no thought to Leonora at all; he had sent in his papers.[2] They were to leave in a month. It seemed to him to be his duty to leave that place and to go away, to support Leonora. He did his duty.

It was horrible, in their relationship at that time, that whatever she did caused him to hate her. He hated her when he found that she proposed to set him up as the Lord of Branshaw again—as a sort of dummy lord, in swaddling clothes. He imagined that she had done this in order to separate him from Maisie Maidan. Hatred hung in all the heavy nights and filled the shadowy corners of the room. So when he heard that she had offered to the Maidan boy to take his wife to Europe with him, automatically he hated her since he hated all that she did. It seemed to him, at that time, that she could never be other than cruel even if, by accident, an act of hers were kind.... Yes, it was a horrible situation.

But the cool breezes of the ocean seemed to clear up that hatred as if it had been a curtain. They seemed to give him back admiration for her, and respect. The agreeableness of having money lavishly at command, the fact that it had bought for him the companionship of Maisie Maidan—these things began to make him see that his wife might have been right in the starving and scraping upon which she had insisted. He was at ease; he was even radiantly happy when he carried cups of bouillon[3] for Maisie Maidan along the deck. One night, when he was leaning beside Leonora, over the ship's side, he said suddenly:

"By Jove, you're the finest woman in the world. I wish we could be better friends."

---

1   Hospital for people suffering from the plague and other highly contagious diseases.
2   I.e., he had formally requested to resign from his military duties.
3   Soup, broth.

She just turned away, without a word and went to her cabin. Still, she was very much better in health.

And, now, I suppose I must give you Leonora's side of the case....

That is very difficult. For Leonora, if she preserved an unchanged front, changed very frequently her point of view. She had been drilled—in her tradition, in her upbringing—to keep her mouth shut. But there were times, she said, when she was so near yielding to the temptation of speaking that afterwards she shuddered to think of those times. You must postulate that what she desired above all things was to keep a shut mouth to the world, to Edward and to the women that he loved. If she spoke she would despise herself.

From the moment of his unfaithfulness with La Dolciquita she never acted the part of wife to Edward. It was not that she intended to keep herself from him as a principle, for ever. Her spiritual advisers, I believe, forbade that. But she stipulated that he must, in some way, perhaps symbolical, come back to her. She was not very clear as to what she meant; probably she did not know herself. Or perhaps she did.

There were moments when he seemed to be coming back to her; there were moments when she was within a hair of yielding to her physical passion for him. In just the same way, at moments, she almost yielded to the temptation to denounce Mrs. Basil to her husband or Maisie Maidan to hers. She desired then to cause the horrors and pains of public scandals. For, watching Edward more intently and with more straining of ears than that which a cat bestows upon a bird overhead, she was aware of the progress of his passion for each of these ladies. She was aware of it from the way in which his eyes returned to doors and gateways; she knew from his tranquillities when he had received satisfactions.

At times she imagined herself to see more than was warranted. She imagined that Edward was carrying on intrigues with other women—with two at once; with three. For whole periods she imagined him to be a monster of libertinage and she could not see that he could have anything against her. She left him his liberty; she was starving herself to build up his fortunes; she allowed herself none of the joys of femininity—no dresses, no jewels—hardly even friendships, for fear they should cost money.

And yet, oddly, she could not but be aware that both Mrs. Basil and Maisie Maidan were nice women. The curious, discounting eye which one woman can turn on another did not prevent her seeing that Mrs. Basil was very good to Edward and Mrs. Maidan very good for him. That seemed her to be a monstrous and incomprehensible working of Fate's. Incomprehensible! Why, she asked herself again and again, did none of the good deeds that she did for her husband ever come through to him, or appear to him as good deeds? By what trick of mania could not he let her be as good to him as Mrs. Basil was? Mrs. Basil was not so extraordinarily dissimilar to herself. She was, it was true, tall, dark, with a soft mournful voice and a great kindness of manner for every created thing, from punkah men to flowers on the trees. But she was not so well read as Lenora, at any rate in learned books. Leonora could not stand novels. But, even with all her differences Mrs. Basil did not appear to Leonora to differ so very much from herself. She was truthful, honest and, for the rest, just a woman. And Leonora had a vague sort of idea that, to a man, all women are the same after three weeks of close intercourse. She thought that the kindness should no longer appeal, the soft and mournful voice no longer thrill, the tall darkness no longer give a man the illusion that he was going into the depths of an unexplored wood. She could not understand how Edward could go on and on maundering[1] over Mrs. Basil. She could not see why he should continue to write her long letters after their separation. After that, indeed, she had a very bad time.

She had at that period what I will call the "monstrous" theory of Edward. She was always imagining him ogling at every woman that he came across. She did not, that year, go into "retreat" at Simla because she was afraid that he would corrupt her maid in her absence. She imagined him carrying on intrigues with native women or Eurasians.[2] At dances she was in a fever of watchfulness.

---

[1] Obsessing, doting.

[2] People of mixed European—in this instance, British—and Indian/Asian parentage.

She persuaded herself that this was because she had a dread of scandals. Edward might get himself mixed up with a marriageable daughter of some man who would make a row or some husband who would matter. But, really, she acknowledged afterwards to herself, she was hoping that, Mrs. Basil being out of the way, the time might have come when Edward should return to her. All that period she passed in an agony of jealousy and fear—the fear that Edward might really become promiscuous in his habits.

So that, in an odd way, she was glad when Maisie Maidan came along—and she realized that she had not, before, been afraid of husbands and of scandals, since, then, she did her best to keep Maisie's husband unsuspicious. She wished to appear so trustful of Edward that Maidan could not possibly have any suspicions. It was an evil position for her. But Edward was very ill and she wanted to see him smile again. She thought that if he could smile again through her agency he might return, through gratitude and satisfied love—to her. At that time she thought that Edward was a person of light and fleeting passions. And she could understand Edward's passion for Maisie, since Maisie was one of those women to whom other women will allow magnetism.

She was very pretty; she was very young; in spite of her heart she was very gay and light on her feet. And Leonora was really very fond of Maisie, who was fond enough of Leonora. Leonora, indeed, imagined that she could manage this affair all right. She had no thought of Maisie's being led into adultery; she imagined that if she could take Maisie and Edward to Nauheim, Edward would see enough of her to get tired of her pretty little chatterings, and of the pretty little motions of her hands and feet. And she thought she could trust Edward. For there was not any doubt of Maisie's passion for Edward. She raved about him to Leonora as Leonora had heard girls rave about drawing masters in schools. She was perpetually asking her boy husband why he could not dress, ride, shoot, play polo, or even recite sentimental poems, like their major. And young Maidan had the greatest admiration for Edward and he adored, was bewildered by and entirely trusted his wife. It appeared to him that Edward was devoted to Leonora. And Leonora imagined that when poor Maisie was cured of her heart and Edward had seen enough of her, he would return to her. She had the vague, passionate idea that, when Edward had exhausted a number of other types of women he must turn to her. Why should not her type have its turn in his heart? She imagined that, by now, she understood him better, that she understood better his vanities and that, by making him happier, she could arouse his love.

Florence knocked all that on the head....

PART IV

I

I have, I am aware, told this story in a very rambling way so that it may be difficult for anyone to find their path through what may be a sort of maze. I cannot help it. I have stuck to my idea of being in a country cottage with a silent listener, hearing between the gusts of the wind and amidst the noises of the distant sea, the story as it comes. And, when one discusses an affair—a long, sad affair—one goes back, one goes forward. One remembers points that one has forgotten and one explains them all the more minutely since one recognizes that one has forgotten to mention them in their proper places and that one may have given, by omitting them, a false impression. I console myself with thinking that this is a real story and that, after all, real stories are probably told best in the way a person telling a story would tell them. They will then seem most real.

At any rate I think I have brought my story up to the date of Maisie Maidan's death. I mean that I have explained everything that went before it from the several points of view that were necessary—from Leonora's, from Edward's and, to some extent, from my own. You have the facts for the trouble of finding them; you have the points of view as far as I could ascertain or put them. Let me imagine myself back, then, at the day of Maisie's death—or rather at the moment of Florence's dissertation on the Protest, up in the old Castle of the town of M——. Let us consider Leonora's point of view with regard to Florence; Edward's, of course, I cannot give you for Edward naturally never spoke of his affair with my wife. (I may, in what follows, be a little hard on Florence; but you must remember that I have been writing away at this story now for six months and reflecting longer and longer upon these affairs.)

And the longer I think about them the more certain I become that Florence was a contaminating influence—she depressed and deteriorated poor Edward; she deteriorated, hopelessly, the miserable Leonora. There is no doubt that she caused Leonora's character to deteriorate. If there was a fine point about Leonora it was that she was proud and that she was silent. But that pride and that silence broke when she made that extraordinary outburst, in the shadowy room that contained the Protest, and in the little terrace looking over the river. I don't mean to say that she was doing a wrong thing. She was certainly doing right in trying to warn me that Florence was making eyes at her husband. But, if she did the right thing, she was doing it in the wrong way. Perhaps she should have reflected longer; she should have spoken, if she wanted to speak, only after reflection. Or it would have been better if she had acted—if, for instance, she had so chaperoned Florence that private communication between her and Edward became impossible. She should have gone eavesdropping; she should have watched outside bedroom doors. It is odious; but that is the way the job is done. She should have taken Edward away the moment Maisie was dead. No, she acted wrongly....

And yet, poor thing, is it for me to condemn her—and what did it matter in the end? If it had not been Florence, it would have been some other ... Still, it might have been a better woman than my wife. For Florence was vulgar; Florence was a common flirt who would not, at the last, *lâcher prise*;[1] and Florence was an unstoppable talker. You could not stop her; nothing would stop her. Edward and Leonora were at least proud and reserved people. Pride and reserve are not the only things in life; perhaps they are not even the best things. But if they happen to be your particular virtues you will go all to pieces if you let them go. And Leonora let them go. She let them go before poor Edward did even. Consider her position when she burst out over the Luther-Protest.... Consider her agonies....

You are to remember that the main passion of her life was to get Edward back; she had never, till that moment, despaired of getting him back. That may seem ignoble; but you have also to remember that her getting him back represented to her not only a victory for herself. It would, as it appeared to her, have been a victory for all wives and a victory for her Church. That was how it presented itself to her. These things are a little inscrutable. I

[1]   "Let go."

don't know why the getting back of Edward should have represented to her a victory for all wives, for Society and for her Church. Or, maybe, I have a glimmering of it.

She saw life as a perpetual sex-battle between husbands who desire to be unfaithful to their wives, and wives who desire to recapture their husbands in the end. That was her sad and modest view of matrimony. Man, for her, was a sort of brute who must have his divagations,[1] his moments of excess, his nights out, his, let us say, rutting seasons. She had read few novels, so that the idea of a pure and constant love succeeding the sound of wedding bells had never been very much presented to her. She went, numbed and terrified, to the Mother Superior of her childhood's convent with the tale of Edward's infidelities with the Spanish dancer, and all that the old nun, who appeared to her to be infinitely wise, mystic and reverend, had done had been to shake her head sadly and to say:

"Men are like that. By the blessing of God it will all come right in the end."

That was what was put before her by her spiritual advisers as her programme in life. Or, at any rate, that was how their teachings came through to her—that was the lesson she told me she had learned of them. I don't know exactly what they taught her. The lot of women was patience and patience and again patience—*ad majorem Dei gloriam*[2]—until upon the appointed day, if God saw fit, she should have her reward. If then, in the end, she should have succeeded in getting Edward back she would have kept her man within the limits that are all that wifehood has to expect. She was even taught that such excesses in men are natural, excusable—as if they had been children.

And the great thing was that there should be no scandal before the congregation. So she had clung to the idea of getting Edward back with a fierce passion that was like an agony. She had looked the other way; she had occupied herself solely with one idea. That was the idea of having Edward appear, when she did get him back, wealthy, glorious as it were, on account of his lands, and upright. She would show, in fact, that in an unfaithful world one

---

[1] Digressions.
[2] "For the greater glory of God," the official motto of the Jesuits (the Society of Jesus).

Catholic woman had succeeded in retaining the fidelity of her husband. And she thought she had come near her desires.

Her plan with regard to Maisie had appeared to be working admirably. Edward had seemed to be cooling off towards the girl. He did not hunger to pass every minute of the time at Nauheim beside the child's recumbent form; he went out to polo matches; he played auction bridge in the evenings; he was cheerful and bright. She was certain that he was not trying to seduce that poor child; she was beginning to think that he had never tried to do so. He seemed in fact to be dropping back into what he had been for Maisie in the beginning—a kind, attentive, superior officer in the regiment, paying gallant attentions to a bride. They were as open in their little flirtations as the dayspring from on high.[1] And Maisie had not appeared to fret when he went off on excursions with us; she had to lie down for so many hours on her bed every afternoon, and she had not appeared to crave for the attentions of Edward at those times.

And Edward was beginning to make little advances to Leonora. Once or twice, in private—for he often did it before people—he had said: "How nice you look!" or "What a pretty dress!" She had gone with Florence to Frankfurt, where they dress as well as in Paris, and had got herself a gown or two. She could afford it, and Florence was an excellent adviser as to dress. She seemed to have got hold of the clue to the riddle.

Yes, Leonora seemed to have got hold of the clue to the riddle. She imagined herself to have been in the wrong to some extent in the past. She should not have kept Edward on such a tight rein with regard to money. She thought she was on the right tack in letting him—as she had done only with fear and irresolution—have again the control of his income. He came even a step towards her and acknowledged, spontaneously, that she had been right in husbanding, for all those years, their resources. He said to her one day:

"You've done right, old girl. There's nothing I like so much as to have a little to chuck away. And I can do it, thanks to you."

---

[1]   According to Martin Stannard, "the 'dayspring' is a metaphor both for the Grace of God and for the Messiah as its (future) terrestrial manifestation."

That was really, she said, the happiest moment of her life. And he, seeming to realize it, had ventured to pat her on the shoulder. He had, ostensibly, come in to borrow a safety pin of her.

And the occasion of her boxing Maisie's ears, had, after it was over, riveted in her mind the idea that there was no intrigue between Edward and Mrs. Maidan. She imagined that, from henceforward, all that she had to do was to keep him well supplied with money and his mind amused with pretty girls. She was convinced that he was coming back to her. For that month she no longer repelled his timid advances that never went very far. For he certainly made timid advances. He patted her on the shoulder; he whispered into her ear little jokes about the odd figures that they saw up at the Casino. It was not much to make a little joke—but the whispering of it was a precious intimacy....

And then—smash—it all went. It went to pieces at the moment when Florence laid her hand upon Edward's wrist, as it lay on the glass sheltering the manuscript of the Protest, up in the high tower with the shutters where the sunlight here and there streamed in. Or, rather, it went when she noticed the look in Edward's eyes as he gazed back into Florence's. She knew that look.

She had known—since the first moment of their meeting, since the moment of our all sitting down to dinner together— that Florence was making eyes at Edward. But she had seen so many women make eyes at Edward—hundreds and hundreds of women, in railway trains, in hotels, aboard liners, at street corners. And she had arrived at thinking that Edward took little stock in women that made eyes at him. She had formed what was, at that time, a fairly correct estimate of the methods of, the reasons for, Edward's loves. She was certain that hitherto they had consisted of the short passion for the Dolciquita, the real sort of love for Mrs. Basil, and what she deemed the pretty courtship of Maisie Maidan. Besides she despised Florence so haughtily that she could not imagine Edward's being attracted by her. And she and Maisie were a sort of bulwark round him.

She wanted, besides, to keep her eyes on Florence—for Florence knew that she had boxed Maisie's ears. And Leonora desperately desired that her union with Edward should appear to be flawless. But all that went....

With the answering gaze of Edward into Florence's blue and uplifted eyes, she knew that it had all gone. She knew that that gaze meant that those two had had long conversations of an intimate kind—about their likes and dislikes, about their natures, about their views of marriage. She knew what it meant that she, when we all four walked out together, had always been with me ten yards ahead of Florence and Edward. She did not imagine that it had gone further than talks about their likes and dislikes, about their natures or about marriage as an institution. But, having watched Edward all her life, she knew that that laying on of hands, that answering of gaze with gaze, meant that the thing was unavoidable. Edward was such a serious person.

She knew that any attempt on her part to separate those two would be to rivet on Edward an irrevocable passion; that, as I have before told you, it was a trick of Edward's nature to believe that the seducing of a woman gave her an irrevocable hold over him for life. And that touching of hands, she knew, would give that woman an irrevocable claim—to be seduced. And she so despised Florence that she would have preferred it to be a parlour-maid. There are very decent parlour-maids.

And suddenly, there came into her mind the conviction that Maisie Maidan had a real passion for Edward; that this would break her heart—and that she, Leonora, would be responsible for that. She went, for the moment, mad. She clutched me by the wrist; she dragged me down those stairs and across that whispering Rittersaal with the high painted pillars, the high painted chimney piece. I guess she did not go mad enough.

She ought to have said:

"Your wife is a harlot who is going to be my husband's mistress ..." That might have done the trick. But, even in her madness she was afraid to go as far as that. She was afraid that, if she did, Edward and Florence would make a bolt of it and that, if they did that, she would lose forever all chance of getting him back in the end. She acted very badly to me.

Well, she was a tortured soul who put her Church before the interests of a Philadelphia Quaker. That is all right—I daresay the Church of Rome is the more important of the two.

A week after Maisie Maidan's death she was aware that

Florence had become Edward's mistress. She waited outside Florence's door and met Edward as he came away. She said nothing and he only grunted. But I guess he had a bad time.

Yes, the mental deterioration that Florence worked in Leonora was extraordinary; it smashed up her whole life and all her chances. It made her, in the first place, hopeless—for she could not see how, after that, Edward could return to her—after a vulgar intrigue with a vulgar woman. His affair with Mrs. Basil, which was now all that she had to bring, in her heart, against him, she could not find it in her to call an intrigue. It was a love affair—a pure enough thing in its way. But this seemed to her to be a horror—a wantonness, all the more detestable to her, because she so detested Florence. And Florence talked....

That was what was terrible, because Florence forced Leonora herself to abandon her high reserve—Florence and the situation. It appears that Florence was in two minds whether to confess to me or to Leonora. Confess she had to. And she pitched at last on Leonora, because if it had been me she would have had to confess a great deal more. Or, at least, I might have guessed a great deal more, about her "heart," and about Jimmy. So she went to Leonora one day and began hinting and hinting. And she enraged Leonora to such an extent that at last Leonora said:

"You want to tell me that you are Edward's mistress. You can be. I have no use for him."

That was really a calamity for Leonora, because, once started, there was no stopping the talking. She tried to stop—but it was not to be done. She found it necessary to send Edward messages through Florence; for she would not speak to him. She had to give him, for instance, to understand that if I ever came to know of his intrigue she would ruin him beyond repair. And it complicated matters a good deal that Edward, at about this time, was really a little in love with her. He thought that he had treated her so badly; that she was so fine. She was so mournful that he longed to comfort her, and he thought himself such a blackguard that there was nothing he would not have done to make amends. And Florence communicated these items of information to Leonora.

I don't in the least blame Leonora for her coarseness to Florence; it must have done Florence a world of good. But I do blame her for giving way to what was in the end a desire for communicativeness. You see that business cut her off from her Church. She did not want to confess what she was doing because she was afraid that her spiritual advisers would blame her for deceiving me. I rather imagine that she would have preferred damnation to breaking my heart. That is what it works out at. She need not have troubled.

But, having no priests to talk to she had to talk to someone and, as Florence insisted on talking to her, she talked back, in short, explosive sentences, like one of the damned. Precisely like one of the damned. Well, if a pretty period in hell on this earth can spare her any period of pain in Eternity—where there are not any periods—I guess Leonora will escape hell fire.

Her conversations with Florence would be like this. Florence would happen in on her, whilst she was doing her wonderful hair, with a proposition from Edward, who seems about that time to have conceived the naïve idea that he might become a polygamist. I daresay it was Florence who put it into his head. Anyhow, I am not responsible for the oddities of the human psychology. But it certainly appears that at about that date Edward cared more for Leonora than he had ever done before—or, at any rate, for a long time. And, if Leonora had been a person to play cards and if she had played her cards well, and if she had had no sense of shame and so on, she might then have shared Edward with Florence until the time came for jerking that poor cuckoo out of the nest.

Well, Florence would come to Leonora with some such proposition. I do not mean to say that she put it baldly, like that. She stood out that she was not Edward's mistress until Leonora said that she had seen Edward coming out of her room at an advanced hour of the night. That checked Florence a bit; but she fell back upon her "heart" and stuck out that she had merely been conversing with Edward in order to bring him to a better frame of mind. Florence had, of course, to stick to that story; for even Florence would not have had the face to implore Leonora to grant her favours to Edward if she had admitted that she was Edward's mistress. That could not be done. At the same time

Florence had such a pressing desire to talk about something. There would have been nothing else to talk about but a rapprochement between that estranged pair. So Florence would go on babbling and Leonora would go on brushing her hair. And then Leonora would say suddenly something like:

"I should think myself defiled if Edward touched me now that he has touched you."

That would discourage Florence a bit; but after a week or so, on another morning she would have another try.

And even in other things Leonora deteriorated. She had promised Edward to leave the spending of his own income in his own hands. And she had fully meant to do that. I daresay she would have done it too; though, no doubt, she would have spied upon his banking account in secret. She was not a Roman Catholic for nothing. But she took so serious a view of Edward's unfaithfulness to the memory of poor little Maisie that she could not trust him any more at all.

So when she got back to Branshaw she started, after less than a month, to worry him about the minutest items of his expenditure. She allowed him to draw his own cheques, but there was hardly a cheque that she did not scrutinize—except for a private account of about five hundred a year which, tacitly, she allowed him to keep for expenditure on his mistress or mistresses. He had to have his jaunts to Paris; he had to send expensive cables in cipher to Florence about twice a week. But she worried him about his expenditure on wines, on fruit trees, on harness, on gates, on the account at his blacksmith's for work done to a new patent army stirrup that he was trying to invent. She could not see why he should bother to invent a new Army stirrup and she was really enraged when, after the invention was mature, he made a present to the War Office of the designs and the patent rights. It was a remarkably good stirrup.

I have told you, I think, that Edward spent a great deal of time, and about two hundred pounds for law fees on getting a poor girl, the daughter of one of his gardeners, acquitted of a charge of murdering her baby. That was positively the last act of Edward's life. It came at a time when Nancy Rufford was on her way to India; when the most horrible gloom was over the household; when

Edward, himself, was in an agony and behaving as prettily as he knew how. Yet even then Leonora made him a terrible scene about this expenditure of time and trouble. She sort of had the vague idea that what had passed with the girl and the rest of it ought to have taught Edward a lesson—the lesson of economy. She threatened to take his banking account away from him again. I guess that made him cut his throat. He might have stuck it out otherwise—but the thought that he had lost Nancy and that, in addition, there was nothing left for him but a dreary, dreary succession of days in which he could be of no public service ... Well, it finished him.

It was during those years that Leonora tried to get up a love affair of her own with a fellow called Bayham—a decent sort of fellow. A really nice man. But the affair was no sort of success. I have told you about it already....

II

Well, that about brings me up to the date of my receiving, in Waterbury, the laconic cable from Edward to the effect that he wanted me to go to Branshaw and have a chat. I was pretty busy at the time and I was half minded to send him a reply cable to the effect that I would start in a fortnight. But I was having a long interview with old Mr. Hurlbird's attorneys and immediately afterwards I had to have a long interview with the Misses Hurlbird, so I delayed cabling.

I had expected to find the Misses Hurlbird excessively old—in the nineties or thereabouts. The time had passed so slowly that I had the impression that it must have been thirty years since I had been in the United States. It was only twelve years. Actually Miss Hurlbird was just sixty-one and Miss Florence Hurlbird fifty-nine and they were both, mentally and physically, as vigorous as could be desired. They were, indeed, more vigorous, mentally, than suited my purpose, which was to get away from the United States as quickly as I could. The Hurlbirds were an exceedingly united family—exceedingly united except on one set of points. Each of the three of them had a separate doctor, whom they trusted implicitly—and each had a separate attorney. And each of them distrusted the other's doctor and the other's attorney. And, naturally, the doctors and the attorneys warned one all the time—against each other. You cannot imagine how complicated it all became for me. Of course I had an attorney of my own—recommended to me by young Carter, my Philadelphia nephew.

I do not mean to say that there was any unpleasantness of a grasping kind. The problem was quite another one—a moral dilemma. You see, old Mr. Hurlbird had left all his property to Florence with the mere request that she would have erected to him in the city of Waterbury, Conn., a memorial that should take the form of some sort of institution for the relief of sufferers from the heart. Florence's money had all come to me—and with it old Mr. Hurlbird's. He had died just five days before Florence.

Well, I was quite ready to spend a round million dollars on the relief of sufferers from the heart. The old gentleman had left about a million and a half; Florence had been worth about eight hundred thousand—and as I figured it out, I should cut up at about a million myself. Anyhow, there was ample money. But I naturally wanted to consult the wishes of his surviving relatives and then the trouble really began. You see, it had been discovered that Mr. Hurlbird had had nothing whatever the matter with his heart. His lungs had been a little affected all through his life and he had died of bronchitis.

It struck Miss Florence Hurlbird that, since her brother had died of lungs and not of heart, his money ought to go to lung patients. That, she considered, was what her brother would have wished. On the other hand, by a kink, that I could not at the time understand, Miss Hurlbird insisted that I ought to keep the money all to myself. She said that she did not wish for any monuments to the Hurlbird family.

At the time I thought that that was because of a New England dislike for necrological[1] ostentation. But I can figure out now, when I remember certain insistent and continued questions that she put to me, about Edward Ashburnham, that there was

---

[1] Worship of the dead.

another idea in her mind. And Leonora has told me that, on Florence's dressing-table, beside her dead body there had lain a letter to Miss Hurlbird—a letter which Leonora posted without telling me. I don't know how Florence had time to write to her aunt; but I can quite understand that she would not like to go out of the world without making some comments. So I guess Florence had told Miss Hurlbird a good bit about Edward Ashburnham in a few scrawled words—and that that was why the old lady did not wish the name of Hurlbird perpetuated. Perhaps also she thought that I had earned the Hurlbird money.

It meant a pretty tidy lot of discussing, what with the doctors warning each other about the bad effects of discussions, on the health of the old ladies, and warning me covertly against each other, and saying that old Mr. Hurlbird might have died of heart, after all, in spite of the diagnosis of *his* doctor. And the solicitors all had separate methods of arranging about how the money should be invested and entrusted and bound.

Personally, I wanted to invest the money so that the interest could be used for the relief of sufferers from the heart. If old Mr. Hurlbird had not died of any defects in that organ he had considered that it was defective. Moreover, Florence had certainly died of her heart, as I saw it. And when Miss Florence Hurlbird stood out that the money ought to go to chest sufferers I was brought to thinking that there ought to be a chest institution too, and I advanced the sum that I was ready to provide to a million and a half of dollars. That would have given seven hundred and fifty thousand to each class of invalid. I did not want money at all badly. All I wanted it for was to be able to give Nancy Rufford a good time. I did not know much about housekeeping expenses in England where, I presumed, she would wish to live. I knew that her needs at that time were limited to good chocolates, and a good horse or two, and simple, pretty frocks. Probably she would want more than that later on. But even if I gave a million and a half dollars to these institutions I should still have the equivalent of about twenty thousand a year English, and I considered that Nancy could have a pretty good time on that or less.

Anyhow, we had a stiff set of arguments up at the Hurlbird

mansion, which stands on a bluff over the town. It may strike you, silent listener, as being funny if you happen to be European. But moral problems of that description and the giving of millions to institutions are immensely serious matters in my country. Indeed, they are the staple topics for consideration amongst the wealthy classes. We haven't got peerages and social climbing to occupy us much, and decent people do not take interest in politics or elderly people in sport. So that there were real tears shed by both Miss Hurlbird and Miss Florence before I left that city.

I left it quite abruptly. Four hours after Edward's telegram came another from Leonora, saying: "Yes, do come. You could be so helpful." I simply told my attorney that there was the million and a half; that he could invest it as he liked, and that the purposes must be decided by the Misses Hurlbird. I was, anyhow, pretty well worn out by all the discussions. And, as I have never heard yet from the Misses Hurlbird, I rather think that Miss Hurlbird, either by revelations or by moral force, has persuaded Miss Florence that no memorial to their names shall be erected in the city of Waterbury, Conn. Miss Hurlbird wept dreadfully when she heard that I was going to stay with the Ashburnhams, but she did not make any comments. I was aware, at that date, that her niece had been seduced by that fellow Jimmy before I had married her—but I contrived to produce on her the impression that I thought Florence had been a model wife. Why, at that date I still believed that Florence had been perfectly virtuous after her marriage to me. I had not figured it out that she could have played it so low down as to continue her intrigue with that fellow under my roof. Well, I was a fool. But I did not think much about Florence at that date. My mind was occupied with what was happening at Branshaw.

I had got it into my head that the telegrams had something to do with Nancy. It struck me that she might have shown signs of forming an attachment for some undesirable fellow and that Leonora wanted me to come back and marry her out of harm's way. That was what was pretty firmly in my mind. And it remained in my mind for nearly ten days after my arrival at that beautiful old place. Neither Edward nor Leonora made any motion to talk to me about anything other than the weather and the crops. Yet, although there were several young fellows about, I could not see that any one in particular was distinguished by the girl's preference. She certainly appeared illish and nervous, except when she woke up to talk gay nonsense to me. Oh, the pretty thing that she was....

I imagined that what must have happened was that the undesirable young man had been forbidden the place and that Nancy was fretting a little.

What had happened was just Hell. Leonora had spoken to Nancy; Nancy had spoken to Edward; Edward had spoken to Leonora—and they had talked and talked. And talked. You have to imagine horrible pictures of gloom and half lights, and emotions running through silent nights—through whole nights. You have to imagine my beautiful Nancy appearing suddenly to Edward, rising up at the foot of his bed, with her long hair falling, like a split cone of shadow, in the glimmer of a night-light that burned beside him. You have to imagine her, a silent, a no doubt agonized figure, like a spectre, suddenly offering herself to him—to save his reason! And you have to imagine his frantic refusal—and talk. And talk! My God!

And yet, to me, living in the house, enveloped with the charm of the quiet and ordered living, with the silent, skilled servants whose mere laying out of my dress clothes was like a caress—to me who was hourly with them they appeared like tender, ordered and devoted people, smiling, absenting themselves at the proper intervals; driving me to meets—just good people! How the devil—how the devil do they do it?

At dinner one evening Leonora said—she had just opened a telegram:

"Nancy will be going to India, tomorrow, to be with her father."

No one spoke. Nancy looked at her plate; Edward went on eating his pheasant. I felt very bad; I imagined that it would be up to me to propose to Nancy that evening. It appeared to me to be queer that they had not given me any warning of Nancy's departure. But I thought that that was only English manners—some sort of delicacy that I had not got the hang of. You must remember that at that moment I trusted in Edward and Leonora and in Nancy Rufford, and in the tranquility of ancient haunts of peace, as I had trusted in my mother's love. And that evening Edward spoke to me.

What in the interval had happened had been this:
Upon her return from Nauheim Leonora had completely broken down—because she knew she could trust Edward. That seems odd but, if you know anything about breakdowns, you will know that, by the ingenious torments that fate prepares for us, these things come as soon as, a strain having relaxed, there is nothing more to be done. It is after a husband's long illness and death that a widow goes to pieces; it is at the end of a long rowing contest that a crew collapses and lies forward upon its oars. And that was what happened to Leonora.

From certain tones in Edward's voice; from the long, steady stare that he had given her from his bloodshot eyes on rising from the dinner table in the Nauheim hotel, she knew that, in the affair of the poor girl, this was a case in which Edward's moral scruples, or his social code, or his idea that it would be playing it *too* low down, rendered Nancy perfectly safe. The girl, she felt sure, was in no danger at all from Edward. And in that she was perfectly right. The smash was to come from herself.

She relaxed; she broke; she drifted, at first quickly, then with an increasing momentum, down the stream of destiny. You may put it that, having been cut off from the restraints[1] of her religion, for the first time in her life, she acted along the lines of her instinctive desires. I do not know whether to think that, in that she was no longer herself; or that, having let loose the bonds of her standards, her conventions and her traditions, she was being, for the first time, her own natural self. She was torn between her intense, maternal love for the girl and an intense jealousy of the woman who realizes that the man she loves has met what appears to be the final passion of his life. She was divided between an intense disgust for Edward's weakness in conceiving this passion, an intense pity for the miseries that he was enduring, and a feeling equally intense,

---

[1]   Martin Stannard suggests that this may be yet another allusion to Conrad's *Heart of Darkness*, in which the native helmsman had "no restraint—just like Kurtz—a tree swayed by the wind."

but one that she hid from herself—a feeling of respect for Edward's determination to keep himself, in this particular affair, unspotted.

And the human heart is a very mysterious thing. It is impossible to say that Leonora, in acting as she then did, was not filled with a sort of hatred of Edward's final virtue. She wanted, I think, to despise him. He was, she realized, gone from her for good. Then let him suffer, let him agonize; let him, if possible, break and go to that Hell that is the abode of broken resolves. She might have taken a different line. It would have been so easy to send the girl away to stay with some friends; to have taken her away herself upon some pretext or other. That would not have cured things but it would have been the decent line.... But, at that date, poor Leonora was incapable of taking any line whatever.

She pitied Edward frightfully at one time—and then she acted along the lines of pity; she loathed him at another and then she acted as her loathing dictated. She gasped, as a person dying of tuberculosis gasps for air. She craved madly for communication with some other human soul. And the human soul that she selected was that of the girl.

Perhaps Nancy was the only person that she could have talked to. With her necessity for reticences, with her coldness of manner, Leonora had singularly few intimates. She had none at all, with the exception of the Mrs. Colonel Whelen, who had advised her about the affair with La Dolciquita, and the one or two religious, who had guided her through life. The Colonel's wife was at that time in Madeira;[1] the religious she now avoided. Her visitors' book had seven hundred names in it; there was not a soul that she could speak to. She was Mrs. Ashburnham of Branshaw Teleragh.

She was the great Mrs. Ashburnham of Branshaw and she lay all day upon her bed in her marvellous, light, airy bedroom with the chintzes and the Chippendale and the portraits of deceased Ashburnhams by Zoffany and Zucchero.[2] When there was a meet

---

[1] Island in the Atlantic Ocean and a Portuguese possession, fashionable amongst upper-class British tourists.

[2] Johann Zoffany (1753–1810), British portrait artist and one of the founders of the Royal Academy. Frederigo Zucchero (1543–1609), Italian painter who composed a portrait of Elizabeth I in 1576.

she would struggle up—supposing it were within driving distance—and let Edward drive her and the girl to the cross-roads or the country house. She would drive herself back alone; Edward would ride off with the girl. Ride Leonora could not, that season—her head was too bad. Each pace of her mare was an anguish.

But she drove with efficiency and precision; she smiled at the Gimmers and Ffoulkes and the Hedley Seatons. She threw with exactitude pennies to the boys who opened gates for her; she sat upright on the seat of the high dog-cart;[1] she waved her hands to Edward and Nancy as they rode off with the hounds, and everyone could hear her clear, high voice, in the chilly weather, saying:

"Have a good time!"

Poor forlorn woman! ...

There was however one spark of consolation. It came from the fact that Rodney Bayham, of Bayham, followed her always with his eyes. It had been three years since she had tried her abortive love-affair with him. Yet still, on the winter mornings he would ride up to her shafts and just say: "Good day," and look at her with eyes that were not imploring, but seemed to say: "You see, I am still, as the Germans say, A.D.—at disposition."

It was a great consolation, not because she proposed ever to take him up again but because it showed her that there was in the world one faithful soul in riding-breeches. And it showed her that she was not losing her looks.

And, indeed, she was not losing her looks. She was forty, but she was as clean run as on the day she had left the convent—as clear in outline, as clear coloured in the hair, as dark blue in the eyes. She thought that her looking-glass told her this; but there are always the doubts.... Rodney Bayham's eyes took them away.

It is very singular that Leonora should not have aged at all. I suppose that there are some types of beauty and even of youth made for the embellishments that come with enduring sorrow. That is too elaborately put. I mean that Leonora, if everything had prospered, might have become too hard and, maybe, overbearing. As it was she was tuned down to appearing efficient—and yet sympathetic. That is the rarest of all blends. And yet I

---

[1]   Two-wheeled carriage pulled by a single horse.

swear that Leonora, in her restrained way, gave the impression of being intensely sympathetic. When she listened to you she appeared also to be listening to some sound that was going on in the distance. But still, she listened to you and took in what you said, which, since the record of humanity is a record of sorrows, was, as a rule, something sad.

I think that she must have taken Nancy through many terrors of the night and many bad places of the day. And that would account for the girl's passionate love for the elder woman. For Nancy's love for Leonora was an admiration that is awakened in Catholics by their feeling for the Virgin Mary and for various of the saints. It is too little to say that the girl would have laid her life at Leonora's feet. Well, she laid there the offer of her virtue— and her reason. Those were sufficient installments of her life. It would today be much better for Nancy Rufford if she were dead.

Perhaps all these reflections are a nuisance; but they crowd on me. I will try to tell the story.

You see—when she came back from Nauheim Leonora began to have her headaches—headaches lasting through whole days, during which she could speak no word and could bear to hear no sound. And, day after day, Nancy would sit with her, silent and motionless for hours, steeping handkerchiefs in vinegar and water, and thinking her own thoughts. It must have been very bad for her—and her meals alone with Edward must have been bad for her too—and beastly bad for Edward. Edward, of course, wavered in his demeanour. What else could he do? At times he would sit silent and dejected over his untouched food. He would utter nothing but monosyllables when Nancy spoke to him. Then he was simply afraid of the girl falling in love with him. At other times he would take a little wine; pull himself together; attempt to chaff Nancy about a stake and binder hedge[1] that her mare had checked at or talk about the habits of the Chitralis. That was when he was thinking that it was rough on the poor girl that he should have become a dull companion. He realized that his talking to her in the park at Nauheim had done her no harm.

---

[1] Another metaphor relating to horses and racing; literally, an artificial fence for horses to jump over.

But all that was doing a great deal of harm to Nancy. It gradually opened her eyes to the fact that Edward was a man with his ups and downs and not an invariably gay uncle like a nice dog, a trustworthy horse or a girl friend. She would find him in attitudes of frightful dejection, sunk into his armchair in the study that was half a gun-room. She would notice through the open door that his face was the face of an old, dead man, when he had no one to talk to. Gradually it forced itself upon her attention that there were profound differences between the pair that she regarded as her uncle and her aunt. It was a conviction that came very slowly.

It began with Edward's giving an oldish horse to a young fellow called Selmes. Selmes' father had been ruined by a fraudulent solicitor and the Selmes family had had to sell their hunters. It was a case that had excited a good deal of sympathy in that part of the county. And Edward, meeting the young man one day, unmounted, and seeing him to be very unhappy had offered to give him an old Irish cob upon which he was riding. It was a silly sort of thing to do, really. The horse was worth from thirty to forty pounds and Edward might have known that the gift would upset his wife. But Edward just had to comfort that unhappy young man whose father he had known all his life. And what made it all the worse was that young Selmes could not afford to keep the horse even. Edward recollected this, immediately after he had made the offer, and said quickly:

"Of course I mean that you should stable the horse at Branshaw until you have time to turn round or want to sell him and get a better."

Nancy went straight home and told all this to Leonora who was lying down. She regarded it as a splendid instance of Edward's quick consideration for the feelings and the circumstances of the distressed. She thought it would cheer Leonora up—because it ought to cheer any woman up to know that she had such a splendid husband. That was the last girlish thought she ever had. For Leonora, whose headache had left her collected but miserably weak, turned upon her bed and uttered words that were amazing to the girl:

"I wish to God," she said, "that he was your husband, and not mine. We shall be ruined. We shall be ruined. Am I *never* to have a chance?" And suddenly Leonora burst into a passion of tears. She pushed herself up from the pillows with one elbow and sat there—crying, crying, crying, with her face hidden in her hands and the tears falling through her fingers.

The girl flushed, stammered and whimpered as if she had been personally insulted.

"But if Uncle Edward ..." she began.

"That man," said Leonora, with an extraordinary bitterness, "would give the shirt off his back and off mine—and off yours to any ..." She could not finish the sentence.

At that moment she had been feeling an extraordinary hatred and contempt for her husband. All the morning and all the afternoon she had been lying there thinking that Edward and the girl were together—in the field and hacking it home at dusk. She had been digging her sharp nails into her palms.

The house had been very silent in the drooping winter weather. And then, after an eternity of torture, there had invaded it the sound of opening doors, of the girl's gay voice saying:

"Well, it was only under the mistletoe." ... And there was Edward's gruff undertone. Then Nancy had come in, with feet that had hastened up the stairs and that tiptoed as they approached the open door of Leonora's room. Branshaw had a great big hall with oak floors and tiger skins. Round this hall there ran a gallery upon which Leonora's doorway gave. And even when she had the worst of her headaches she liked to have her door open—I suppose so that she might hear the approaching footsteps of ruin and disaster. At any rate she hated to be in a room with a shut door.

At that moment Leonora hated Edward with a hatred that was like hell, and she would have liked to bring her riding-whip down across the girl's face. What right had Nancy to be young and slender and dark, and gay at times, at times mournful? What right had she to be exactly the woman to make Leonora's husband happy? For Leonora knew that Nancy would have made Edward happy.

Yes, Leonora wished to bring her riding-whip down on Nancy's young face. She imagined the pleasure she would feel when the lash fell across those queer features; the pleasure she would feel at drawing the handle at the same moment toward her, so as to cut deep into the flesh and to leave a lasting wheal.

Well, she left a lasting wheal, and her words cut deeply into the girl's mind....

They neither of them spoke about that again. A fortnight went by—a fortnight of deep rains, of heavy fields, of bad scent.[1] Leonora's headaches seemed to have gone for good. She hunted once or twice, letting herself be piloted by Bayham, whilst Edward looked after the girl. Then, one evening, when those three were dining alone, Edward said, in the queer, deliberate, heavy tones that came out of him in those days (he was looking at the table):

"I have been thinking that Nancy ought to do more for her father. He is getting an old man. I have written to Colonel Rufford, suggesting that she should go to him."

Leonora called out:

"How dare you? How dare you?"

The girl put her hand over her heart and cried out: "Oh, my sweet Saviour, help me!" That was the queer way she thought within her mind, and the words forced themselves to her lips. Edward said nothing.

And that night, by a merciless trick of the devil that pays attention to this sweltering hell of ours, Nancy Rufford had a letter from her mother. It came whilst Leonora was talking to Edward, or Leonora would have intercepted it as she had intercepted others. It was an amazing and a horrible letter....

I don't know what it contained. I just average out from its effects on Nancy that her mother, having eloped with some worthless sort of fellow, had done what is called "sinking lower and lower." Whether she was actually on the streets I do not know, but I rather think that she eked out a small allowance that she had from her husband by that means of livelihood. And I think that she stated as much in her letter to Nancy and upbraided the girl with living in luxury whilst her mother starved. And it must have been horrible in tone, for Mrs. Rufford was a cruel sort of woman at the best of times. It must have seemed to that poor girl, opening her letter, for distraction from another grief, up in her bedroom, like the laughter of a devil.

---

[1]   False trail for horses when hunting.

I just cannot bear to think of my poor dear girl at that moment....

And, at the same time, Leonora was lashing, like a cold fiend, into the unfortunate Edward. Or, perhaps, he was not so unfortunate; because he had done what he knew to be the right thing, he may be deemed happy. I leave it to you. At any rate, he was sitting in his deep chair, and Leonora came into his room—for the first time in nine years. She said:

"This is the most atrocious thing you have done in your atrocious life." He never moved and he never looked at her. God knows what was in Leonora's mind exactly.

I like to think that, uppermost in it was concern and horror at the thought of the poor girl's going back to a father whose voice made her shriek in the night. And, indeed, that motive was very strong with Leonora. But I think there was also present the thought that she wanted to go on torturing Edward with the girl's presence. She was, at that time, capable of that.

Edward was sunk in his chair; there were in the room two candles, hidden by green glass shades. The green shades were reflected in the glasses of the book-cases that contained not books but guns with gleaming brown barrels and fishing-rods in green baize over-covers. There was dimly to be seen, above a mantelpiece encumbered with spurs, hooves and bronze models of horses, a dark-brown picture of a white horse.

"If you think," Leonora said, "that I do not know that you are in love with the girl ..." She began spiritedly, but she could not find any ending for the sentence. Edward did not stir; he never spoke. And then Leonora said:

"If you want me to divorce you, I will. You can marry her then. She's in love with you."

He groaned at that, a little, Leonora said. Then she went away.

Heaven knows what happened in Leonora after that. She certainly does not herself know. She probably said a good deal more to Edward than I have been able to report; but that is all that she has told me and I am not going to make up speeches. To follow her psychological development of that moment I think we must allow that she upbraided him for a great deal of their past life, whilst Edward sat absolutely silent. And, indeed, in speaking of it afterwards, she has said several times: "I said a great deal more to him than I wanted to, just because he was so silent." She talked, in fact, in the endeavour to sting him into speech.

She must have said so much that, with the expression of her grievance, her mood changed. She went back to her own room in the gallery, and sat there for a long time thinking. And she thought herself into a mood of absolute unselfishness, of absolute self-contempt, too. She said to herself that she was no good; that she had failed in all her efforts—in her efforts to get Edward back as in her efforts to make him curb his expenditure. She imagined herself to be exhausted; she imagined herself to be done. Then a great fear came over her.

She thought that Edward, after what she had said to him, must have committed suicide. She went out on to the gallery and listened; there was no sound in all the house except the regular beat of the great clock in the hall. But, even in her debased condition, she was not the person to hang about. She acted. She went straight to Edward's room, opened the door, and looked in.

He was oiling the breech action of a gun. It was an unusual thing for him to do, at that time of night, in his evening clothes. It never occurred to her, nevertheless, that he was going to shoot himself with that implement. She knew that he was doing it just for occupation—to keep himself from thinking. He looked up when she opened the door, his face illuminated by the light cast upwards from the round orifices in the green candle shades.

She said:

"I didn't imagine that I should find Nancy here." She thought that she owed that to him. He answered then:

"I don't imagine that you did imagine it." Those were the only words he spoke that night. She went, like a lame duck, back through the long corridors; she stumbled over the familiar tiger skins in the dark hall. She could hardly drag one limb after the other. In the gallery she perceived that Nancy's door was half open and that there was a light in the girl's room. A sudden madness possessed her, a desire for action, a thirst for self-explanation.

Their rooms all gave on to the gallery; Leonora's to the east, the girl's next, then Edward's. The sight of those three open doors, side by side, gaping to receive whom the chances of the black night might bring, made Leonora shudder all over her body. She went into Nancy's room.

The girl was sitting perfectly still in an armchair, very upright, as she had been taught to sit at the convent. She appeared to be as calm as a church; her hair fell, black and like a pall, down over both her shoulders. The fire beside her was burning brightly; she must have just put coals on. She was in a white silk kimono that covered her to the feet. The clothes that she had taken off were exactly folded upon the proper seats. Her long hands were one upon each arm of the chair that had a pink and white chintz back.

Leonora told me these things. She seemed to think it extraordinary that the girl could have done such orderly things as fold up the clothes she had taken off upon such a night—when Edward had announced that he was going to send her to her father, and when, from her mother, she had received that letter. The letter, in its envelope, was in her right hand.

Leonora did not at first perceive it. She said:

"What are you doing so late?" The girl answered:

"Just thinking." They seemed to think in whispers and to speak below their breaths. Then Leonora's eyes fell on the envelope, and she recognized Mrs. Rufford's handwriting.

It was one of those moments when thinking was impossible, Leonora said. It was as if stones were being thrown at her from every direction and she could only run. She heard herself exclaim:

"Edward's dying—because of you. He's dying. He's worth more than either of us...."

The girl looked past her at the panels of the half-closed door.

"My poor father," she said, "my poor father."

"You must stay here," Leonora answered fiercely. "You must stay here. I tell you you must stay here."

"I am going to Glasgow," Nancy answered. "I shall go to Glasgow tomorrow morning. My mother is in Glasgow."

It appears that it was in Glasgow that Mrs. Rufford pursued her disorderly life. She had selected that city, not because it was more profitable, but because it was the natal home of her husband to whom she desired to cause as much pain as possible.

"You must stay here," Leonora began, "to save Edward. He's dying for love of you."

The girl turned her calm eyes upon Leonora.

"I know it," she said. "And I am dying for love of him."

Leonora uttered an "Ah," that, in spite of herself, was an "Ah" of horror and of grief.

"That is why," the girl continued, "I am going to Glasgow— to take my mother away from there." She added: "To the ends of the earth," for, if the last months had made her nature that of a woman, her phrases were still romantically those of a school-girl. It was as if she had grown up so quickly that there had not been time to put her hair up. But she added: "We're no good—my mother and I."

Leonora said, with her fierce calmness:

"No. No. You're not no good. It's I that am no good. You can't let that man go on to ruin for want of you. You must belong to him."

The girl, she said, smiled at her with a queer, far-away smile— as if she were a thousand years old, as if Leonora were a tiny child.

"I knew you would come to that," she said, very slowly. "But we are not worth it—Edward and I."

III

Nancy had, in fact, been thinking ever since Leonora had made that comment over the giving of the horse to young Selmes. She had been thinking and thinking, because she had had to sit for many days silent beside her aunt's bed. (She had always thought of Leonora as her aunt.) And she had had to sit thinking during many silent meals with Edward. And then, at times, with his bloodshot eyes and creased, heavy mouth, he would smile at her. And gradually the knowledge had come to her that Edward did not love Leonora and that Leonora hated Edward. Several things contributed to form and to harden this conviction.

She was allowed to read the papers in those days—or, rather, since Leonora was always on her bed and Edward breakfasted alone and went out early, over the estate, she was left alone with the papers. One day, in the paper, she saw the portrait of a woman she knew very well. Beneath it she read the words: "The Hon. Mrs. Brand, plaintiff in the remarkable divorce case reported on p. 8." Nancy hardly knew what a divorce case was. She had been so remarkably well brought up, and Roman Catholics do not practise divorce. I don't know how Leonora had done it exactly. I suppose she had always impressed it on Nancy's mind that nice women did not read these things, and that would have been enough to make Nancy skip those pages.

She read, at any rate, the account of the Brand divorce case—principally because she wanted to tell Leonora about it. She imagined that Leonora, when her headache left her, would like to know what was happening to Mrs. Brand, who lived at Christchurch,[1] and whom they both liked very well. The case occupied three days, and the report that Nancy first came upon was that of the third day. Edward, however, kept the papers of the week, after his methodical fashion, in a rack in his gun-room, and when she had finished her breakfast Nancy went to that quiet apartment and had what she would have called a good read. It seemed to her to be a queer affair. She could not understand why one counsel should be so anxious to know all about the movements of Mr. Brand upon a certain day; she could not understand why a chart of the bedroom accommodation at Christchurch Old Hall should be produced in court. She did not even see why they should want to know that, upon a certain occasion, the drawing-room door was locked. It made her laugh; it appeared to be all so senseless that grown people should occupy themselves with such matters. It struck her, nevertheless, as odd that one of the counsel should cross-question Mr. Brand so insistently and so impertinently as to his feelings for Miss Lupton. Nancy knew Miss Lupton of Ringwood[2] very well—a jolly girl, who rode a horse with two white fetlocks. Mr. Brand persisted that he did not love Miss Lupton.... Well, of course he did not love Miss Lupton; he was a married man. You might as well think of Uncle Edward loving ... loving anybody but Leonora. When people were married there was an end of loving. There were,

[1] Hampshire coastal resort in southwest England, about 20 miles south of Fordingbridge.
[2] Hampshire town between Fordingbridge and Christchurch, near the New Forest.

no doubt, people who misbehaved—but they were poor people— or people not like those she knew.

So these matters presented themselves to Nancy's mind.

But later on in the case she found that Mr. Brand had to confess to a "guilty intimacy" with someone or other. Nancy imagined that he must have been telling someone his wife's secrets; she could not understand why that was a serious offence. Of course it was not very gentlemanly—it lessened her opinion of Mrs. Brand. But, since she found that Mrs. Brand had condoned that offence, she imagined that they could not have been very serious secrets that Mr. Brand had told. And then, suddenly, it was forced on her conviction that Mr. Brand—the mild Mr. Brand that she had seen a month or two before their departure to Nauheim, playing "Blind Man's Buff" with his children and kissing his wife when he caught her—Mr. Brand and Mrs. Brand had been on the worst possible terms. That was incredible.

Yet there it was—in black and white. Mr. Brand drank; Mr. Brand had struck Mrs. Brand to the ground when he was drunk. Mr. Brand was adjudged, in two or three abrupt words, at the end of columns and columns of paper, to have been guilty of cruelty to his wife and to have committed adultery with Miss Lupton. The last words conveyed nothing to Nancy—nothing real, that is to say. She knew that one was commanded not to commit adultery— but why, she thought, should one? It was probably something like catching salmon out of season—a thing one did not do. She gathered it had something to do with kissing, or holding someone in your arms....

And yet the whole effect of that reading upon Nancy was mysterious, terrifying and evil. She felt a sickness—a sickness that grew as she read. Her heart beat painfully; she began to cry. She asked God how He could permit such things to be. And she was more certain that Edward did not love Leonora and that Leonora hated Edward. Perhaps, then, Edward loved someone else. It was unthinkable.

If he could love someone else than Leonora, her fierce, unknown heart suddenly spoke in her side, why could it not be herself? And he did not love her.... This had occurred about a month before she got the letter from her mother. She let the matter rest until the sick feeling went off; it did that in a day or two. Then, finding that Leonora's headaches had gone, she suddenly told Leonora that Mrs. Brand had divorced her husband. She asked what, exactly, it all meant.

Leonora was lying on the sofa in the hall; she was feeling so weak that she could hardly find any words. She answered just:

"It means that Mr. Brand will be able to marry again."

Nancy said:

"But ... but ..." and then: "He will be able to marry Miss Lupton." Leonora just moved a hand in assent. Her eyes were shut.

"Then ..." Nancy began. Her blue eyes were full of horror: her brows were tight above them; the lines of pain about her mouth were very distinct. In her eyes the whole of that familiar, great hall had a changed aspect. The andirons[1] with the brass flowers at the ends appeared unreal; the burning logs were just logs that were burning and not the comfortable symbols of an indestructible mode of life. The flame fluttered before the high fireback; the St. Bernard sighed in his sleep. Outside the winter rain fell and fell. And suddenly she thought that Edward might marry someone else; and she nearly screamed.

Leonora opened her eyes, lying sideways, with her face upon the black and gold pillow of the sofa that was drawn half across the great fireplace.

"I thought," Nancy said, "I never imagined....Aren't marriages sacraments? Aren't they indissoluble? I thought you were married ... and ..." She was sobbing. "I thought you were married or not married as you are alive or dead."

"That," Leonora said, "is the law of the church. It is not the law of the land...."

"Oh yes," Nancy said, "the Brands are Protestants."

She felt a sudden safeness descend upon her, and for an hour or so her mind was at rest. It seemed to her idiotic not to have remembered Henry VIII and the basis upon which Protestantism rests. She almost laughed at herself.

The long afternoon wore on; the flames still fluttered when

---

[1] Horizontal pair of bars on short feet, placed on each side of a fireplace to support burning wood.

the maid made up the fire; the St. Bernard awoke and lolloped away towards the kitchen. And then Leonora opened her eyes and said almost coldly:

"And you? Don't you think you will get married?"

It was so unlike Leonora that, for the moment, the girl was frightened in the dusk. But then, again, it seemed a perfectly reasonable question.

"I don't know," she answered. "I don't know that anyone wants to marry me."

"Several people want to marry you," Leonora said.

"But I don't want to marry," Nancy answered. "I should like to go on living with you and Edward. I don't think I am in the way or that I am really an expense. If I went you would have to have a companion. Or, perhaps, I ought to earn my living...."

"I wasn't thinking of that," Leonora answered in the same dull tone. "You will have money enough from your father. But most people want to be married."

I believe that she then asked the girl if she would not like to marry me, and that Nancy answered that she would marry me if she were told to; but that she wanted to go on living there. She added:

"If I married anyone I should want him to be like Edward."

She was frightened out of her life. Leonora writhed on her couch and called out: "Oh, God! ..."

Nancy ran for the maid; for tablets of aspirin; for wet handkerchiefs. It never occurred to her that Leonora's expression of agony was for anything else than physical pain.

You are to remember that all this happened a month before Leonora went into the girl's room at night. I have been casting back again; but I cannot help it. It is so difficult to keep all these people going. I tell you about Leonora and bring her up to date; then about Edward, who has fallen behind. And then the girl gets hopelessly left behind. I wish I could put it down in diary form. Thus: On the 1st of September they returned from Nauheim. Leonora at once took to her bed. By the 1st of October they were all going to meets together. Nancy had already observed very fully that Edward was strange in his manner. About the 6th of that month Edward gave the horse to young Selmes, and

Nancy had cause to believe that her aunt did not love her uncle. On the 20th she read the account of the divorce case, which is reported in the papers of the 18th and the two following days. On the 23rd she had the conversation with her aunt in the hall—about marriage in general and about her own possible marriage. Her aunt's coming to her bedroom did not occur until the 12th of November....

Thus she had three weeks for introspection—for introspection beneath gloomy skies, in that old house, rendered darker by the fact that it lay in a hollow crowned by fir trees with their black shadows. It was not a good situation for a girl. She began thinking about love, she who had never before considered it as anything other than a rather humorous, rather nonsensical matter. She remembered chance passages in chance books—things that had not really affected her at all at the time. She remembered someone's love for the Princess Badrulbadour;[1] she remembered to have heard that love was a flame, a thirst, a withering up of the vitals—though she did not know what the vitals were. She had a vague recollection that love was said to render a hopeless lover's eyes hopeless; she remembered a character in a book who was said to have taken to drink through love; she remembered that lovers' existences were said to be punctuated with heavy sighs. Once she went to the little cottage piano that was in the corner of the hall and began to play. It was a tinkly, reedy instrument, for none of that household had any turn for music. Nancy herself could play a few simple songs, and she found herself playing. She had been sitting on the window seat, looking out on the fading day. Leonora had gone to pay some calls; Edward was looking after some planting up in the new spinney.[2] Thus she found herself playing on the old piano. She did not know how she came to be doing it. A silly lilting wavering tune came from before her in the dusk—a tune in which major notes with their cheerful insistence wavered and melted into minor sounds, as, beneath a bridge the high lights on dark waters melt and waver and disappear into black depths. Well, it was a silly old tune....

It goes with the words—they are about a willow tree, I think:

---

[1]   The beloved of the hero of the Arabian Nights tale of Aladdin and the magical lamp.
[2]   A small forest created to preserve or protect game birds.

Thou art to all lost loves the best
The only true plant found.

—That sort of thing. It is Herrick,[1] I believe, and the music with the reedy, irregular, lilting sound that goes with Herrick. And it was dusk; the heavy, hewn, dark pillars that supported the gallery were like mourning presences; the fire had sunk to nothing—a mere glow amongst white ashes, ... It was a sentimental sort of place and light and hour....

And suddenly Nancy found that she was crying. She was crying quietly; she went on to cry with long convulsive sobs. It seemed to her that everything gay, everything charming, all light, all sweetness, had gone out of life. Unhappiness; unhappiness; unhappiness was all around her. She seemed to know no happy being and she herself was agonizing....

She remembered that Edward's eyes were hopeless; she was certain that he was drinking too much; at times he sighed deeply. He appeared as a man who was burning with inward flame; drying up in the soul with thirst; withering up in the vitals. Then, the torturing conviction came to her—the conviction that had visited her again and again—that Edward must love someone other than Leonora. With her little, pedagogic sectarianism she remembered that Catholics do not do this thing. But Edward was a Protestant. Then Edward loved somebody....

And, after that thought, her eyes grew hopeless; she sighed as the old St. Bernard beside her did. At meals she would feel an intolerable desire to drink a glass of wine, and then another and then a third. Then she would find herself grow gay.... But in half an hour the gaiety went; she felt like a person who is burning up with an inward flame; desiccating at the soul with thirst; withering up in the vitals. One evening she went into Edward's gunroom—he had gone to a meeting of the National Reserve Committee.[2] On the table beside his chair was a decanter of whisky. She poured out a wine-glassful and drank it off.

---

1 The opening lines of "The Willow Tree," by English poet Robert Herrick (1591–1674).

2 Apparently, a committee of Ford's invention.

Flame then really seemed to fill her body; her legs swelled; her face grew feverish. She dragged her tall height up to her room and lay in the dark. The bed reeled beneath her; she gave way to the thought that she was in Edward's arms; that he was kissing her on her face that burned; on her shoulders that burned and on her neck that was on fire.

She never touched alcohol again. Not once after that did she have such thoughts. They died out of her mind; they left only a feeling of shame so insupportable that her brain could not take it in and they vanished. She imagined that her anguish at the thought of Edward's love for another person was solely sympathy for Leonora; she determined that the rest of her life must be spent in acting as Leonora's handmaiden—sweeping, tending, embroidering, like some Deborah,[1] some mediæval saint—I am not, unfortunately, up in the Catholic hagiology.[2] But I know that she pictured herself as some personage with a depressed, earnest face and tightly closed lips, in a clear white room, watering flowers or tending an embroidery frame. Or, she desired to go with Edward to Africa and to throw herself in the path of a charging lion so that Edward might be saved for Leonora at the cost of her life. Well, along with her sad thoughts she had her childish ones.

She knew nothing—nothing of life, except that one must live sadly. That she now knew. What happened to her on the night when she received at once the blow that Edward wished her to go to her father in India and the blow of the letter from her mother was this. She called first upon her sweet Saviour—and she thought of Our Lord as her sweet Saviour!—that He might make it impossible that she should go to India. Then she realized from Edward's demeanour that he was determined that she should go to India. It must then be right that she should go. Edward was always right in his determinations. He was the Cid; he was Lohengrin; he was the Chevalier Bayard.

Nevertheless her mind mutinied and revolted. She could not leave that house. She imagined that he wished her gone that she

---

[1] Deborah was an Old Testament judge—rather than a handmaiden, as Dowell suggests—who led the children of Israel to victory over the Canaanites.

[2] Literature devoted to the lives of the saints.

might not witness his amours with another girl. Well, she was prepared to tell him that she was ready to witness his amours with another young girl. She would stay there—to comfort Leonora.

Then came the desperate shock of the letter from her mother. Her mother said, I believe, something like: "You have no right to go on living your life of prosperity and respect. You ought to be on the streets with me. How do you know that you are even Colonel Rufford's daughter?" She did not know what these words meant. She thought of her mother as sleeping beneath the arches whilst the snow fell. That was the impression conveyed to her mind by the words "on the streets." A Platonic[1] sense of duty gave her the idea that she ought to go to comfort her mother—the mother that bore her, though she hardly knew what the words meant. At the same time she knew that her mother had left her father with another man—therefore she pitied her father, and thought it terrible in herself that she trembled at the sound of her father's voice. If her mother was that sort of woman it was natural that her father should have had accesses[2] of madness in which he had struck herself to the ground. And the voice of her conscience said to her that her first duty was to her parents. It was in accord with this awakened sense of duty that she undressed with great care and meticulously folded the clothes that she took off. Sometimes, but not very often, she threw them helter-skelter about the room.

And that sense of duty was her prevailing mood when Leonora, tall, clean-run, golden-haired, all in black, appeared in her doorway, and told her that Edward was dying of love for her. She knew then with her conscious mind what she had known within herself for months—that Edward was dying[3]—actually and physically dying—of love for her. It seemed to her that for one short moment her spirit could say: "*Domine, nunc dimittis....* Lord, now lettest thou thy servant depart in peace."[4] She imag-

---

[1] Purely spiritual.

[2] Fits.

[3] Ford has toned down his depiction of Nancy's passion for Edward in *The Good Soldier*. In the Cornell manuscript of the novel, the text reads: "I knew then [what] she had known for months—that for months she had longed, craved, and prayed within herself."

[4] See Luke 2.29, a common evening prayer.

ined that she could cheerfully go away to Glasgow and rescue her fallen mother.

IV

And it seemed to her to be in tune with the mood, with the hour, and with the woman in front of her to say that she knew Edward was dying of love for her and that she was dying of love for Edward. For that fact had suddenly slipped into place and become real for her as the niched marker on a whist tablet slips round with the pressure of your thumb. That rubber[1] at least was made.

And suddenly Leonora seemed to have become different and she seemed to have become different in her attitude towards Leonora. It was as if she, in her frail, white, silken kimono, sat beside her fire, but upon a throne. It was as if Leonora, in her close dress of black lace, with the gleaming white shoulders and the coiled yellow hair that the girl had always considered the most beautiful thing in the world—it was as if Leonora had become pinched, shrivelled, blue with cold, shivering, suppliant. Yet Leonora was commanding her. It was no good commanding her. She was going on the morrow to her mother who was in Glasgow.

Leonora went on saying that she must stay there to save Edward, who was dying of love for her. And, proud and happy in the thought that Edward loved her, and that she loved him, she did not even listen to what Leonora said. It appeared to her that it was Leonora's business to save her husband's body; she, Nancy, possessed his soul—a precious thing that she would shield and bear away up in her arms—as if Leonora were a hungry dog, trying to spring up at a lamb that she was carrying. Yes, she felt as if Edward's love were a precious lamb that she were bearing away from a cruel and predatory beast. For, at that time, Leonora appeared to her as a cruel and predatory beast. Leonora, Leonora with her hunger, with her cruelty had driven Edward to madness. He must be shel-

---

[1]   The winning set of games in cards, especially in Bridge.

tered by his love for her and by her love—her love from a great distance and unspoken, enveloping him, surrounding him, upholding him; by her voice speaking from Glasgow, saying that she loved, that she adored, that she passed no moment without longing, loving, quivering at the thought of him.

Leonora said loudly, insistently, with a bitterly imperative tone:

"You must stay here; you must belong to Edward. I will divorce him."

The girl answered:

"The Church does not allow of divorce. I cannot belong to your husband. I am going to Glasgow to rescue my mother."

The half-opened door opened noiselessly to the full. Edward was there. His devouring, doomed eyes were fixed on the girl's face; his shoulders slouched forward; he was undoubtedly half drunk and he had the whisky decanter in one hand, a slanting candlestick in the other. He said, with a heavy ferocity, to Nancy:

"I forbid you to talk about these things. You are to stay here until I hear from your father. Then you will go to your father."

The two women, looking at each other, like beasts about to spring, hardly gave a glance to him. He leaned against the doorpost. He said again:

"Nancy, I forbid you to talk about these things. I am the master of this house." And, at the sound of his voice, heavy, male, coming from a deep chest, in the night, with the blackness behind him, Nancy felt as if her spirit bowed before him, with folded hands. She felt that she would go to India, and that she desired never again to talk of these things.

Leonora said:

"You see that it is your duty to belong to him. He must not be allowed to go on drinking."

Nancy did not answer. Edward was gone; they heard him slipping and shambling on the polished oak of the stairs. Nancy screamed when there came the sound of a heavy fall. Leonora said again:

"You see!"

The sounds went on from the hall below; the light of the candle Edward held flickered up between the hand rails of the gallery. Then they heard his voice:

"Give me Glasgow ... Glasgow, in Scotland ... I want the number of a man called White, of Simrock Park, Glasgow ... Edward White, Simrock Park, Glasgow ... ten minutes ... at this time of night ..." His voice was quite level, normal, and patient. Alcohol took him in the legs, not the speech. "I can wait," his voice came again. "Yes, I know they have a number. I have been in communication with them before."

"He is going to telephone to your mother," Leonora said. "He will make it all right for her." She got up and closed the door. She came back to the fire, and added bitterly: "He can always make it all right for everybody, except me—excepting me!"

The girl said nothing. She sat there in a blissful dream. She seemed to see her lover, sitting as he always sat, in a round-backed chair, in the dark hall—sitting low, with the receiver at his ear, talking in a gentle, slow voice, that he reserved for the telephone—and saving the world and her, in the black darkness. She moved her hand over the bareness of the base of her throat, to have the warmth of flesh upon it and upon her bosom.

She said nothing; Leonora went on talking....

God knows what Leonora said. She repeated that the girl must belong to her husband. She said that she used that phrase because, though she might have a divorce, or even a dissolution of the marriage by the Church, it would still be adultery that the girl and Edward would be committing. But she said that that was necessary; it was the price that the girl must pay for the sin of having made Edward love her, for the sin of loving her husband. She talked on and on, beside the fire. The girl must become an adulteress; she had wronged Edward by being so beautiful, so gracious, so good. It was sinful to be so good. She must pay the price so as to save the man she had wronged.

In between her pauses the girl could hear the voice of Edward, droning on, indistinguishably, with jerky pauses for replies. It made her glow with pride; the man she loved was working for her. He at least was resolved; was malely determined; knew the right thing. Leonora talked on with her eyes boring into Nancy's. The girl hardly looked at her and hardly heard her. After a long time Nancy said—after hours and hours:

"I shall go to India as soon as Edward hears from my father. I cannot talk about these things, because Edward does not wish it."

At that Leonora screamed out and wavered swiftly towards the closed door. And Nancy found that she was springing out of her chair with her white arms stretched wide. She was clasping the other woman to her breast; she was saying:

"Oh, my poor dear; oh, my poor dear." And they sat, crouching together in each other's arms, and crying and crying; and they lay down in the same bed, talking and talking, all through the night. And all through the night Edward could hear their voices through the wall. That was how it went....

Next morning they were all three as if nothing had happened. Towards eleven Edward came to Nancy, who was arranging some Christmas roses in a silver bowl. He put a telegram beside her on the table. "You can uncode it for yourself," he said. Then, as he went out of the door, he said:

"You can tell your aunt I have cabled to Mr. Dowell to come over. He will make things easier till you leave."

The telegram, when it was uncoded, read, as far as I can remember:

"Will take Mrs. Rufford to Italy. Undertake to do this for certain. Am devotedly attached to Mrs. Rufford. Have no need of financial assistance. Did not know there was a daughter, and am much obliged to you for pointing out my duty. White." It was something like that.

Then that household resumed its wonted course of days until my arrival.

V

It is this part of the story that makes me saddest of all. For I ask myself unceasingly, my mind going round and round in a weary, baffled space of pain—what should these people have done? What, in the name of God, should they have done?

The end was perfectly plain to each of them—it was perfectly manifest at this stage that, if the girl did not, in Leonora's phrase, "belong to Edward," Edward must die, the girl must lose her reason because Edward died—and, that after a time, Leonora, who was the coldest and the strongest of the three, would console herself by marrying Rodney Bayham and have a quiet, comfortable, good time. That end, on that night, whilst Leonora sat in the girl's bedroom and Edward telephoned down below—that end was plainly manifest. The girl, plainly, was half-mad already; Edward was half dead; only Leonora, active, persistent, instinct with her cold passion of energy, was "doing things." What then, should they have done? It worked out in the extinction of two very splendid personalities—for Edward and the girl *were* splendid personalities, in order that a third personality, more normal, should have, after a long period of trouble, a quiet, comfortable, good time.

I am writing this, now, I should say, a full eighteen months after the words that end my last chapter. Since writing the words "until my arrival," which I see end that paragraph, I have seen again, for a glimpse, from a swift train, Beaucaire with the beautiful white tower, Tarascon with the square castle, the great Rhone, the immense stretches of the Crau.[1] I have rushed through all Provence—and all Provence no longer matters. It is no longer in the olive hills that I shall find my heaven; because there is only Hell....

Edward is dead; the girl is gone—oh, utterly gone; Leonora is having a good time with Rodney Bayham, and I sit alone in Branshaw Teleragh. I have been through Provence; I have seen Africa; I have visited Asia to see, in Ceylon, in a darkened room, my poor girl, sitting motionless, with her wonderful hair about her, looking at me with eyes that did not see me, and saying distinctly: "*Credo in unum Deum Omnipotentem.... Credo in unum Deum Omnipotentem.*"[2] Those are the only reasonable words she uttered; those are the only words, it appears, that she ever will

---

[1] Very dry plain of the Rhône River in the south of France between Tarascon and Marseilles.

[2] From the Nicene (Apostles') Creed: "I believe in one omnipotent God." Nancy omits the word *Patrem* ["the father"] after *Deum*.

utter. I suppose that they are reasonable words; it must be extraordinarily reasonable for her, if she can say that she believes in an Omnipotent Deity. Well, there it is. I am very tired of it all....

For, I daresay, all this may sound romantic, but it is tiring, tiring, tiring to have been in the midst of it; to have taken the tickets; to have caught the trains; to have chosen the cabins; to have consulted the purser and the stewards as to diet for the quiescent patient who did nothing but announce her belief in an Omnipotent Deity. That may sound romantic—but it is just a record of fatigue.

I don't know why I should always be selected to be serviceable. I don't resent it—but I have never been the least good. Florence selected me for her own purposes, and I was no good to her; Edward called me to come and have a chat with him and I couldn't stop him cutting his throat.

And then, one day eighteen months ago, I was quietly writing in my room at Branshaw when Leonora came to me with a letter. It was a very pathetic letter from Colonel Rufford about Nancy. Colonel Rufford had left the army and had taken up an appointment at a tea-planting estate in Ceylon. His letter was pathetic because it was so brief, so inarticulate, and so business-like. He had gone down to the boat to meet his daughter and had found his daughter quite mad. It appears that at Aden[1] Nancy had seen in a local paper the news of Edward's suicide. In the Red Sea she had gone mad. She had remarked to Mrs. Colonel Luton, who was chaperoning her, that she believed in an Omnipotent Deity. She hadn't made any fuss; her eyes were quite dry and glassy. Even when she was mad Nancy could behave herself.

Colonel Rufford said the doctor did not anticipate that there was any chance of his child's recovery. It was, nevertheless, possible that if she could see someone from Branshaw it might soothe her and it might have a good effect. And he just simply wrote to Leonora: "Please come and see if you can do it."

I seem to have lost all sense of the pathetic; but still, that simple, enormous request of the old colonel strikes me as pathetic. He was cursed by his atrocious temper; he had been

---

[1] Former British protectorate located in the coastal region between Yemen and Oman.

cursed by a half-mad wife, who drank and went on the streets. His daughter was totally mad—and yet he believed in the goodness of human nature. He believed that Leonora would take the trouble to go all the way to Ceylon in order to soothe his daughter. Leonora wouldn't. Leonora didn't ever want to see Nancy again. I daresay that that, in the circumstances, was natural enough. At the same time she agreed, as it were, on public grounds, that someone soothing ought to go from Branshaw to Ceylon. She sent me and her old nurse, who had looked after Nancy from the time when the girl, a child of thirteen, had first come to Branshaw. So off I go, rushing through Provence, to catch the steamer at Marseilles. And I wasn't the least good when I got to Ceylon; and the nurse wasn't the least good. Nothing has been the least good.

The doctors said, at Kandy,[1] that if Nancy could be brought to England, the sea air, the change of climate, the voyage, and all the usual sort of things, might restore her reason. Of course, they haven't restored her reason. She is, I am aware, sitting in the hall, forty paces from where I am now writing. I don't want to be in the least romantic about it. She is very well dressed; she is quite quiet; she is very beautiful. The old nurse looks after her very efficiently.

Of course you have the makings of a situation here, but it is all very humdrum, as far as I am concerned. I should marry Nancy if her reason were ever sufficiently restored to let her appreciate the meaning of the Anglican marriage service. But it is probable that her reason will never be sufficiently restored to let her appreciate the meaning of the Anglican marriage service. Therefore I cannot marry her, according to the law of the land.

So here I am very much where I started thirteen years ago. I am the attendant, not the husband, of a beautiful girl, who pays no attention to me. I am estranged from Leonora, who married Rodney Bayham in my absence and went to live at Bayham. Leonora rather dislikes me, because she has got it into her head that I disapprove of her marriage with Rodney Bayham. Well, I disapprove of her marriage. Possibly I am jealous.

---

[1] The chief city of Ceylon, a British colony off the southeast coast of India. Ceylon is now the independent state of Sri Lanka.

Yes, no doubt I am jealous. In my fainter sort of way I seem to perceive myself following the lines of Edward Ashburnham. I suppose that I should really like to be a polygamist; with Nancy, and with Leonora, and with Maisie Maidan and possibly even with Florence. I am no doubt like every other man; only, probably because of my American origin I am fainter. At the same time I am able to assure you that I am a strictly respectable person. I have never done anything that the most anxious mother of a daughter or the most careful dean of a cathedral would object to. I have only followed, faintly, and in my unconscious desires, Edward Ashburnham. Well, it is all over. Not one of us has got what he really wanted. Leonora wanted Edward, and she has got Rodney Bayham, a pleasant enough sort of sheep. Florence wanted Branshaw, and it is I who have bought it from Leonora. I didn't really want it; what I wanted mostly was to cease being a nurse-attendant. Well, I am a nurse-attendant. Edward wanted Nancy Rufford and I have got her. Only she is mad. It is a queer and fantastic world. Why can't people have what they want? The things were all there to content everybody; yet everybody has the wrong thing. Perhaps you can make head or tail of it; it is beyond me.

Is there any terrestrial paradise where, amidst the whispering of the olive-leaves, people can be with whom they like and have what they like and take their ease in shadows and in coolness? Or are all men's lives like the lives of us good people—like the lives of the Ashburnhams, of the Dowells, of the Ruffords—broken, tumultuous, agonized, and unromantic, lives, periods punctuated by screams, by imbecilities, by deaths, by agonies? Who the devil knows?

For there was a great deal of imbecility about the closing scenes of the Ashburnham tragedy. Neither of those two women knew what they wanted. It was only Edward who took a perfectly clear line and he was drunk most of the time. But, drunk or sober, he stuck to what was demanded by convention and by the traditions of his house. Nancy Rufford had to be exported to India and Nancy Rufford hadn't to hear a word of love from him. She was exported to India and she never heard a word from Edward Ashburnham.

It was the conventional line; it was in tune with the tradition of Edward's house. I daresay it worked out for the greatest good of the body politic. Conventions and traditions I suppose work blindly but surely for the preservation of the normal type; for the extinction of proud, resolute and unusual individuals.

Edward was the normal man, but there was too much of the sentimentalist about him and society does not need too many sentimentalists. Nancy was a splendid creature, but she had about her a touch of madness. Society does not need individuals with touches of madness about them. So Edward and Nancy found themselves steam-rollered out and Leonora survives, the perfectly normal type, married to a man who is rather like a rabbit. For Rodney Bayham is rather like a rabbit, and I hear that Leonora is expected to have a baby in three months' time.

So those splendid and tumultuous creatures with their magnetism and their passions—those two that I really loved—have gone from this earth. It is no doubt best for them. What would Nancy have made of Edward if she had succeeded in living with him; what would Edward have made of her? For there was about Nancy a touch of cruelty—a touch of definite actual cruelty that made her desire to see people suffer. Yes, she desired to see Edward suffer. And, by God, she gave him hell.

She gave him an unimaginable hell. Those two women pursued that poor devil and flayed the skin off him as if they had done it with whips. I tell you his mind bled almost visibly. I seem to see him stand, naked to the waist, his forearms shielding his eyes, and flesh hanging from him in rags. I tell you that is no exaggeration of what I feel. It was as if Leonora and Nancy banded themselves together to do execution, for the sake of humanity, upon the body of a man who was at their disposal. They were like a couple of Sioux who had got hold of an Apache and had him well tied to a stake. I tell you there was no end to the tortures they inflicted upon him.

Night after night he would hear them talking; talking; maddened, sweating, seeking oblivion in drink, he would lie there and hear the voices going on and on. And day after day Leonora would come to him and would announce the results of their deliberations.

*They were like judges debating over the sentence upon a criminal; they were like ghouls with an immobile corpse in a tomb beside them.

I don't think that Leonora was any more to blame than the girl—though Leonora was the more active of the two. Leonora, as I have said, was the perfectly normal woman. I mean to say that in normal circumstances her desires were those of the woman who is needed by society. She desired children, decorum, an establishment; she desired to avoid waste, she desired to keep up appearances. She was utterly and entirely normal even in her utterly undeniable beauty. But I don't mean to say that she acted perfectly normally in this perfectly abnormal situation. All the world was mad around her and she herself, agonized, took on the complexion of a mad woman; of a woman very wicked; of the villain of the piece. What would you have? Steel is a normal, hard, polished substance. But, if you put it in a hot fire it will become red, soft, and not to be handled. If you put it in a fire still more hot it will drip away. It was like that with Leonora. She was made for normal circumstances—for Mr. Rodney Bayham, who will keep a separate establishment, secretly, in Portsmouth, and make occasional trips to Paris and to Buda-Pesth.[1]

In the case of Edward and the girl Leonora broke and simply went all over the place. She adopted unfamiliar and therefore extraordinary and ungraceful attitudes of mind. At one moment she was all for revenge. After haranguing the girl for hours through the night she harangued for hours of the day the silent Edward. And Edward just once tripped up and that was his undoing. Perhaps he had had too much whisky that afternoon.

She asked him perpetually what he wanted. What did he want? What did he want? And all he ever answered was: "I have told you." He meant that he wanted the girl to go to her father in India as soon as her father should cable that he was ready to receive her. But just once he tripped up. To Leonora's eternal question he answered that all he desired in life was that—that he

---

[1]   Budapest, a city on the Danube River in the Austro-Hungarian empire. Now the capital of Hungary, Budapest had a somewhat "roguish" reputation for seedy activities. Portsmouth, the chief port of the British navy on the southern coast of England, was also known for its "night life."

could pick himself together again and go on with his daily occupations if—the girl, being five thousand miles away, would
continue to love him. He wanted nothing more. He prayed his
God for nothing more. Well, he was a sentimentalist.

And the moment that she heard that, Leonora determined that
the girl should not go five thousand miles away and that she should
not continue to love Edward. The way she worked it was this:

She continued to tell the girl that she must belong to Edward;
she was going to get a divorce; she was going to get a dissolution of marriage from Rome. But she considered it to be her
duty to warn the girl of the sort of monster that Edward was.
She told the girl of La Dolciquita, of Mrs. Basil, of Maisie
Maidan, of Florence. She spoke of the agonies that she had
endured during her life with the man, who was violent, overbearing, vain, drunken, arrogant, and monstrously a prey to his
sexual necessities. And, at hearing of the miseries her aunt had
suffered—for Leonora once more had the aspect of an aunt to
the girl—with the swift cruelty of youth and, with the swift solidarity that attaches woman to woman, the girl made her resolves.
Her aunt said incessantly: "You must save Edward's life; you must
save his life. All that he needs is a little period of satisfaction from
you. Then he will tire of you as he has of the others. But you
must save his life."

And, all the while, that wretched fellow knew, by a curious
instinct that runs between human beings living together—
exactly what was going on. And he remained dumb; he stretched
out no finger to help himself. All that he required to keep himself
a decent member of society was, that the girl, five thousand miles
away, should continue to love him. They were putting a stopper
upon that.

I have told you that the girl came one night to his room. And
that was the real hell for him. That was the picture that never left
his imagination—the girl, in the dim light, rising up at the foot
of his bed. He said that it seemed to have a greenish sort of effect
as if there were a greenish tinge in the shadows of the tall
bedposts that framed her body. And she looked at him with her
straight eyes of an unflinching cruelty and she said: "I am ready
to belong to you—to save your life."

He answered: "I don't want it; I don't want it; I don't want it." And he says that he didn't want it; that he would have hated himself; that it was unthinkable. And all the while he had the immense temptation to do the unthinkable thing, not from the physical desire but because of a mental certitude. He was certain that if she had once submitted to him she would remain his for ever. He knew that.

She was thinking that her aunt had said he had desired her to love him from a distance of five thousand miles. She said: "I can never love you now I know the kind of man you are. I will belong to you to save your life. But I can never love you."

It was a fantastic display of cruelty. She didn't in the least know what it meant—to belong to a man. But, at that, Edward pulled himself together. He spoke in his normal tones; gruff, husky, overbearing, as he would have done to a servant or to a horse.

"Go back to your room," he said. "Go back to your room and go to sleep. This is all nonsense."

They were baffled, those two women.

And then I came on the scene.

VI

My coming on the scene certainly calmed things down—for the whole fortnight that intervened between my arrival and the girl's departure. I don't mean to say that the endless talking did not go on at night or that Leonora did not send me out with the girl and, in the interval, give Edward a hell of a time. Having discovered what he wanted—that the girl should go five thousand miles away and love him steadfastly as people do in sentimental novels, she was determined to smash that aspiration. And she repeated to Edward in every possible tone that the girl did not love him; that the girl detested him for his brutality, his over-bearingness, his drinking habits. She pointed out that Edward, in the girl's eyes, was already pledged three or four deep. He was pledged to Leonora herself, to Mrs. Basil, and to the memories of Maisie Maidan and to Florence. Edward never said anything.

Did the girl love Edward, or didn't she? I don't know. At that time I daresay she didn't, though she certainly had done so before Leonora had got to work upon his reputation. She certainly had loved him for what I call the public side of his record—for his good soldiering, for his saving lives at sea, for the excellent land-lord that he was and the good sportsman. But it is quite possible that all those things came to appear as nothing in her eyes when she discovered that he wasn't a good husband. For, though women, as I see them, have little or no feeling of responsibility towards a county or a country or a career—although they may be entirely lacking in any kind of communal solidarity—they have an immense and automatically working instinct that attaches them to the interest of womanhood. It is, of course, possible for any woman to cut out and to carry off any other woman's husband or lover. But I rather think that a woman will only do this if she has reason to believe that the other woman has given her husband a bad time. I am certain that if she thinks the man has been a brute to his wife she will, with her instinc-tive feeling for suffering femininity, "put him back," as the saying is. I don't attach any particular importance to these generaliza-tions of mine. They may be right, they may be wrong; I am only an ageing American with very little knowledge of life. You may take my generalizations or leave them. But I am pretty certain that I am right in the case of Nancy Rufford—that she had loved Edward Ashburnham very deeply and tenderly.

It is nothing to the point that she let him have it good and strong as soon as she discovered that he had been unfaithful to Leonora and that his public services had cost more than Leonora thought they ought to have cost. Nancy would be bound to let him have it good and strong then. She would owe that to femi-nine public opinion; she would be driven to it by the instinct for self-preservation, since she might well imagine that if Edward had been unfaithful to Leonora, to Mrs. Basil and to the memories of the other two he might be unfaithful to herself. And, no doubt, she had her share of the sex instinct that makes women be intol-erably cruel to the beloved person. Anyhow, I don't know whether, at this point, Nancy Rufford loved Edward Ashburnham. I don't know whether she even loved him when, on getting, at Aden, the news of his suicide she went mad. Because that may just as well have been for the sake of Leonora as for the sake of Edward. Or it may have been for the sake of both of them. I don't know. I know nothing. I am very tired.

Leonora held passionately the doctrine that the girl didn't love Edward. She wanted desperately to believe that. It was a doctrine as necessary to her existence as a belief in the personal immortality of the soul. She said that it was impossible that Nancy could have loved Edward after she had given the girl her view of Edward's career and character. Edward, on the other hand, believed maunderingly that some essential attractiveness in himself must have made the girl continue to go on loving him—to go on loving him, as it were, in underneath her official aspect of hatred. He thought she only pretended to hate him in order to save her face and he thought that her quite atrocious telegram from Brindisi was only another attempt to do that—to prove that she had feelings creditable to a member of the feminine commonweal. I don't know. I leave it to you.

There is another point that worries me a good deal in the aspects of this sad affair. Leonora says that, in desiring that the girl should go five thousand miles away and yet continue to love him, Edward was a monster of selfishness. He was desiring the ruin of a young life. Edward on the other hand put it to me that, supposing that the girl's love was a necessity to his existence, and, if he did nothing by word or by action to keep Nancy's love alive, he couldn't be called selfish. Leonora replied that showed he had an abominably selfish nature even though his actions might be perfectly correct. I can't make out which of them was right. I leave it to you.

It is, at any rate, certain that Edward's actions were perfectly—were monstrously, were cruelly—correct. He sat still and let Leonora take away his character, and let Leonora damn him to deepest hell, without stirring a finger. I daresay he was a fool; I don't see what object there was in letting the girl think worse of him than was necessary. Still there it is. And there it is also that all those three presented to the world the spectacle of being the best of good people. I assure you that during my stay for that fortnight in that fine old house, I never so much as noticed a single thing that could have affected that good opinion. And even when I look back, knowing the circumstances, I can't remember a single thing any of them said that could have betrayed them. I can't remember, right up to the dinner, when Leonora read out that telegram—not the tremor of an eyelash, not the shaking of a hand. It was just a pleasant country house-party.

And Leonora kept it up jolly well, for even longer than that—she kept it up as far as I was concerned until eight days after Edward's funeral. Immediately after that particular dinner—the dinner at which I received the announcement that Nancy was going to leave for India on the following day—I asked Leonora to let me have a word with her. She took me into her little sitting-room and I then said—I spare you the record of my emotions—that she was aware that I wished to marry Nancy; that she had seemed to favour my suit and that it appeared to be rather a waste of money upon tickets and rather a waste of time upon travel to let the girl go to India if Leonora thought that there was any chance of her marrying me.

And Leonora, I assure you, was the absolutely perfect British matron. She said that she quite favoured my suit; that she could not desire for the girl a better husband; but that she considered that the girl ought to see a little more of life before taking such an important step. Yes, Leonora used the words "taking such an important step." She was perfect. Actually, I think she would have liked the girl to marry me well enough but my programme included the buying of the Kershaw's house, about a mile and a half away upon the Fordingbridge road, and settling down there with the girl. That didn't at all suit Leonora. She didn't want to have the girl within a mile and a half of Edward for the rest of their lives. Still, I think she might have managed to let me know, in some periphrasis or other, that I might have the girl if I would take her to Philadelphia or Timbuctoo. I loved Nancy very much—and Leonora knew it.

However, I left it at that. I left it with the understanding that Nancy was going away to India on probation. It seemed to me a perfectly reasonable arrangement and I am a reasonable sort of man. I simply said that I should follow Nancy out to India after six months' time or so. Or, perhaps, after a year. Well, you see, I did follow Nancy out to India after a year....

I must confess to having felt a little angry with Leonora for not having warned me earlier that the girl would be going. I took it as one of the queer, not very straight methods that Roman Catholics seem to adopt in dealing with matters of this world. I took it that Leonora had been afraid I should propose to the girl or, at any rate, have made considerably greater advances to her than I did, if I had known earlier that she was going away so soon. Perhaps Leonora was right; perhaps Roman Catholics, with their queer, shifty ways, are always right. They are dealing with the queer, shifty thing that is human nature. For it is quite possible that, if I had known Nancy was going away so soon, I should have tried making love to her. And that would have produced another complication. It may have been just as well.

It is queer the fantastic things that quite good people will do in order to keep up their appearance of calm pococurantism.[1] For Edward Ashburnham and his wife called me half the world over in order to sit on the back seat of a dog-cart whilst Edward drove the girl to the railway station from which she was to take her departure to India. They wanted, I suppose, to have a witness of the calmness of that function. The girl's luggage had been already packed and sent off before. Her berth on the steamer had been taken. They had timed it all so exactly that it went like clockwork. They had known the date upon which Colonel Rufford would get Edward's letter and they had known almost exactly the hour at which they would receive his telegram asking his daughter to come to him. It had all been quite beautifully and quite mercilessly arranged, by Edward himself. They gave Colonel Rufford, as a reason for telegraphing, the fact that Mrs. Colonel Somebody or other would be travelling by that ship and that she would serve as an efficient chaperon for the girl. It was a most amazing business, and I think that it would have been better in the eyes of God if they had all attempted to gouge out each other's eyes with carving knives. But they were "good people."

---

[1]   Indifference.

After my interview with Leonora I went desultorily into Edward's gun-room. I didn't know where the girl was and I thought I might find her there. I suppose I had a vague idea of proposing to her in spite of Leonora. So, I presume, I don't come of quite such good people as the Ashburnhams. Edward was lounging in his chair smoking a cigar and he said nothing for quite five minutes. The candles glowed in the green shades; the reflections were green in the glasses of the book-cases that held guns and fishing-rods. Over the mantelpiece was the brownish picture of the white horse. Those were the quietest moments that I have ever known. Then, suddenly, Edward looked me straight in the eyes and said:

"Look here, old man, I wish you would drive with Nancy and me to the station to-morrow."

I said that of course I would drive with him and Nancy to the station on the morrow. He lay there for a long time, looking along the line of his knees at the fluttering fire, and then suddenly, in a perfectly calm voice, and without lifting his eyes, he said:

"I am so desperately in love with Nancy Rufford that I am dying of it."

Poor devil—he hadn't meant to speak of it. But I guess he just had to speak to somebody and I appeared to be like a woman or a solicitor. He talked all night.

Well, he carried out the programme to the last breath.

It was a very clear winter morning, with a good deal of frost in it. The sun was quite bright, the winding road between the heather and the bracken was very hard. I sat on the back-seat of the dog-cart; Nancy was beside Edward. They talked about the way the cob[1] went; Edward pointed out with the whip a cluster of deer upon a coombe[2] three-quarters of a mile away. We passed the hounds in the level bit of road beside the high trees going into Fordingbridge and Edward pulled up the dog-cart so that Nancy might say good-bye to the huntsman and cap[3] him a last sovereign. She had ridden with those hounds ever since she had been thirteen.

· The train was five minutes late and they imagined that that

---

[1] A stocky, short-legged riding horse.
[2] Hillside.
[3] Tip.

was because it was market-day at Swindon or wherever the train came from. That was the sort of thing they talked about. The train came in; Edward found her a first-class carriage with an elderly woman in it. The girl entered the carriage, Edward closed the door and then she put out her hand to shake mine. There was upon those people's faces no expression of any kind whatever. The signal for the train's departure was a very bright red; that is about as passionate a statement as I can get into that scene. She was not looking her best; she had on a cap of brown fur that did not very well match her hair. She said:

"So long," to Edward.

Edward answered: "So long."

He swung round on his heel and, large, slouching, and walking with a heavy deliberate pace, he went out of the station. I followed him and got up beside him in the high dog-cart. It was the most horrible performance I have ever seen.

And, after that, a holy peace, like the peace of God which passes all understanding,[1] descended upon Branshaw Teleragh. Leonora went about her daily duties with a sort of triumphant smile—a very faint smile, but quite triumphant. I guess she had so long since given up any idea of getting her man back that it was enough for her to have got the girl out of the house and well cured of her infatuation. Once, in the hall, when Leonora was going out, Edward said, beneath his breath—but I just caught the words:

"Thou hast conquered, O pale Galilean."[2]

It was like his sentimentality to quote Swinburne.

But he was perfectly quiet and he had given up drinking. The only thing that he ever said to me after that drive to the station was:

"It's very odd. I think I ought to tell you, Dowell, that I haven't any feelings at all about the girl now it's all over. Don't you worry about me. I'm all right." A long time afterwards he said: "I guess it was only a flash in the pan." He began to look after the estates

---

[1] See Philippians 4.7: "And the peace of God, which passeth all understanding, shall keep your hearts and minds through Christ Jesus."

[2] From "Hymn to Proserpine," by Algernon Charles Swinburne (1837–1909), a Pre-Raphaelite poet and friend of Ford's grandfather, Victorian artist Ford Madox Brown (1821–93).

again; he took all that trouble over getting off the gardener's daughter who had murdered her baby. He shook hands smilingly with every farmer in the market-place. He addressed two political meetings; he hunted twice. Leonora made him a frightful scene about spending the two hundred pounds on getting the gardener's daughter acquitted. Everything went on as if the girl had never existed. It was very still weather.

Well, that is the end of the story. And, when I come to look at it I see that it is a happy ending with wedding bells and all. The villains—for obviously Edward and the girl were villains—have been punished by suicide and madness. The heroine—the perfectly normal, virtuous and slightly deceitful heroine—has become the happy wife of a perfectly normal, virtuous and slightly deceitful husband. She will shortly become a mother of a perfectly normal, virtuous, slightly deceitful son or daughter. A happy ending, that is what it works out at.

I cannot conceal from myself the fact that I now dislike Leonora. Without doubt I am jealous of Rodney Bayham. But I don't know whether it is merely a jealousy arising from the fact that I desired myself to possess Leonora or whether it is because to her were sacrificed the only two persons that I have ever really loved— Edward Ashburnham and Nancy Rufford. In order to set her up in a modern mansion, replete with every convenience and dominated by a quite respectable and eminently economical master of the house, it was necessary that Edward and Nancy Rufford should become, for me at least, no more than tragic shades.

I seem to see poor Edward, naked and reclining amidst darkness, upon cold rocks, like one of the ancient Greek damned, in Tartarus[1] or wherever it was.

And as for Nancy ... Well, yesterday at lunch she said suddenly: "Shuttlecocks!"[2]

---

[1] In Greek mythology, Tartarus is the deepest part of Hades where sexual wrongdoers are punished.

[2] The feathered object hit back and forth in the game of Badminton. In this instance, it refers to people who are bandied about or manipulated by external forces. In *Henry James* (1914), Ford addresses James's metaphorical use of the term as a descriptor for his young heroine in *What Maisie Knew* (1897).

And she repeated the word "shuttlecocks" three times. I know what was passing in her mind, if she can be said to have a mind, for Leonora has told me that, once, the poor girl said she felt like a shuttlecock being tossed backwards and forwards between the violent personalities of Edward and his wife. Leonora, she said, was always trying to deliver her over to Edward, and Edward tacitly and silently forced her back again. And the odd thing was that Edward himself considered that those two women used *him* like a shuttlecock. Or, rather, he said that they sent him backwards and forwards like a blooming parcel that someone didn't want to pay the postage on. And Leonora also imagined that Edward and Nancy picked her up and threw her down as suited their purely vagrant moods. So there you have the pretty picture. Mind, I am not preaching anything contrary to accepted morality. I am not advocating free love in this or any other case. Society must go on, I suppose, and society can only exist if the normal, if the virtuous, and the slightly deceitful flourish, and if the passionate, the headstrong, and the too-truthful are condemned to suicide and to madness. But I guess that I myself, in my fainter way, come into the category of the passionate, of the headstrong, and the too-truthful. For I can't conceal from myself the fact that I loved Edward Ashburnham—and that I love him because he was just myself. If I had had the courage and virility and possibly also the physique of Edward Ashburnham I should, I fancy, have done much what he did. He seems to me like a large elder brother who took me out on several excursions and did many dashing things whilst I just watched him robbing the orchards, from a distance. And, you see, I am just as much of a sentimentalist as he was....

Yes, society must go on; it must breed, like rabbits. That is what we are here for. But then, I don't like society—much. I am that absurd figure, an American millionaire, who has bought one of the ancient haunts of English peace. I sit here, in Edward's gun-room, all day and all day in a house that is absolutely quiet. No one visits me, for I visit no one. No one is interested in me, for I have no interests. In twenty minutes or so I shall walk down to the village, beneath my own oaks, alongside my own clumps of gorse, to get the American mail. My tenants, the village boys and the tradesmen will touch their hats to me. So life peters out. I shall return to dine and Nancy will sit opposite me with the old nurse standing behind her. Enigmatic, silent, utterly well-behaved as far as her knife and fork go, Nancy will stare in front of her with the blue eyes that have over them strained, stretched brows. Once, or perhaps twice, during the meal her knife and fork will be suspended in mid-air as if she were trying to think of something that she had forgotten. Then she will say that she believes in an Omnipotent Deity or she will utter the one word "shuttlecocks," perhaps. It is very extraordinary to see the perfect flush of health on her cheeks, to see the lustre of her coiled black hair, the poise of the head upon the neck, the grace of the white hands—and to think that it all means nothing—that it is a picture without a meaning. Yes, it is queer.

But, at any rate, there is always Leonora to cheer you up; I don't want to sadden you. Her husband is quite an economical person of so normal a figure that he can get quite a large proportion of his clothes ready-made. That is the great desideratum[1] of life, and that is the end of my story. The child is to be brought up as a Romanist.

It suddenly occurs to me that I have forgotten to say how Edward met his death. You remember that peace had descended upon the house; that Leonora was quietly triumphant and that Edward said his love for the girl had been merely a passing phase. Well, one afternoon we were in the stables together, looking at a new kind of flooring that Edward was trying in a loose-box.[2] Edward was talking with a good deal of animation about the necessity of getting the numbers of the Hampshire territorials[3] up to the proper standard. He was quite sober, quite quiet, his skin was clear-coloured; his hair was golden and perfectly brushed; the level brick-dust red of his complexion went clean up to the rims of his eyelids; his eyes were porcelain blue and they regarded me frankly and directly. His face was perfectly expressionless; his voice was deep and rough. He stood well back upon his legs and said:

---

[1] Object, desire.
[2] A stable that allows a horse to move about freely.
[3] In 1908, the British Home Defense volunteer army, the territorials, were organized on a local basis.

"We ought to get them up to two thousand three hundred and fifty."

A stable-boy brought him a telegram and went away. He opened it negligently, regarded it without emotion, and, in complete silence, handed it to me. On the pinkish paper in a sprawled handwriting I read: "Safe Brindisi. Having rattling good time. Nancy."

Well, Edward was the English gentleman; but he was also, to the last, a sentimentalist, whose mind was compounded of indifferent poems and novels. He just looked up to the roof of the stable, as if he were looking to Heaven, and whispered something that I did not catch.[1]

Then he put two fingers into the waistcoat pocket of his grey, frieze suit;[2] they came out with a little neat pen-knife—quite a small pen-knife. He said to me:

"You might just take that wire to Leonora." And he looked at me with a direct, challenging, brow-beating glare. I guess he could see in my eyes that I didn't intend to hinder him. Why should I hinder him?

I didn't think he was wanted in the world, let his confounded tenants, his rifle-associations, his drunkards, reclaimed and unreclaimed, get on as they liked. Not all the hundreds and hundreds of them deserved that that poor devil should go on suffering for their sakes.

When he saw that I did not intend to interfere with him his eyes became soft and almost affectionate. He remarked:

"So long, old man, I must have a bit of a rest, you know."

I didn't know what to say. I wanted to say, "God bless you," for I also am a sentimentalist. But I thought that perhaps that would not be quite English good form, so I trotted off with the telegram to Leonora. She was quite pleased with it.

---

[1]   In the Cornell manuscript of the novel, the text reads: "He just looked up to the roof of the stable, as if he were looking to Heaven, and he remarked 'Girl, I will wait for you there.'"

[2]   A coarse, woolen-cloth suit.

Appendix A: Ford Madox Ford, "On Heaven"

[Written for Violet Hunt in 1913 and later published in Ford's *On Heaven and Poems Written on Active Service* (1918), "On Heaven" resulted from Hunt's comments about Ford's "tempestuous" religious beliefs. "You say you believe in a heaven," she reportedly told him. "I wish you'd write one for me. I want no beauty, I want no damned optimism; I want just a plain, workaday heaven that I can go to some day and enjoy it when I'm there." In the poem, Ford offers an imaginative vision of Provence in which God improves Ford's earthly condition, sending Violet to him in a "swift red car" and allowing the beleaguered couple to leave their worldly cares behind in England.]

On Heaven
To V. H., who asked for a working Heaven

I

That day the sunlight lay on the farms;
On that morrow the bitter frost that there was!
That night my young love lay in my arms,
    The morrow how bitter it was!

And because she is very tall and quaint
And golden, like a *quattrocento*[1] saint,
I desire to write about Heaven;
To tell you the shape and the ways of it,
And the joys and the toil in the maze of it,
For these there must be in Heaven,
Even in Heaven!

For God is a good man, God is a kind man,
And God's a good brother, and God is no blind man,
And God is our father.

---

[1] The fifteenth-century Italian Renaissance.

I will tell you how this thing began:
How I waited in a little town near Lyons[1] many years,
And yet knew nothing of passing time, or of her tears,
But, for nine slow years, lounged away at my table in the shadowy
        sunlit square
Where the small cafés are.

The *Place*[2] is small and shaded by great planes,
Over a rather human monument
Set up to *Louis Dixhuit*[3] in the year
Eighteen fourteen; a funny thing with dolphins
About a pyramid of green-dripped, sordid stone.
But the enormous, monumental planes
Shade it all in, and the flecks of sun
Sit market women. There's a paper shop
Painted all blue, a shipping agency,
Three or four cafés; dank, dark colonnades
Of eighteen-forty *Maîrie*.[4] I'd no wish
To wait for her where it was picturesque,
Or ancient or historic, or to love
Over well any place in the land before she came
And loved it all too. I didn't even go
To Lyons for the opera; Arles for the bulls,
Or Avignon[5] for glimpses of the Rhone.[6]
Not even to Beaucaire![7] I sat about
And played long games of dominoes with *maîre*,[8]
Or passing *commis-voyageurs*.[9] And so
I sat and watched the trams come in, and read
The *Libre Parole*[10] and sipped thin, fresh wine

---

[1] City in east-central France.
[2] City square.
[3] Louis XVIII (1755–1825) ascended the French throne after the restoration of the monarchy in the wake of the overthrow of Napoleon Bonaparte (1769–1821).
[4] City hall.
[5] Arles and Avignon, cities in the south of France.
[6] River in southeastern France.
[7] City in the south of France.
[8] Mayor.
[9] Traveling salesmen.
[10] Notoriously anti-Semitic French newspaper (translated as "The Free Word") established in July 1893.

They call Piquette,[1] and got to know the people,
The kindly, southern people ...

Until, when the years were over, she came in her swift red car,
Shooting out past a tram; and she slowed and stopped and lighted
          Absently down,
A little dazed, in the heart of the town;
And nodded imperceptibly.
With a sideways look at me.

So our days here began.

And the wrinkled old woman who keeps the café,
And the man
Who sells the *Libre Parole*,
And the sleepy gendarme,[2]
And the fat *facteur*[3] who delivers letters only in the shady,
Pleasanter kind of streets;
And the boy I often gave a penny,
And the *maîre* himself, and the little girl who loves toffee
And me because I have given her many sweets;
And the one-eyed, droll
Bookseller of the *rue Grand de Provence*,—[4]
Chancing to be going home to bed,
Smiled with their kindly, fresh benevolence,
Because they knew I had waited for a lady
Who should come in a swift, red, English car,
To the square where the little cafés are.
And the old, old woman touched me on the wrist
With a wrinkled finger,
And said: "Why do you linger?—
Too many kisses can never be kissed!
And comfort her—nobody here will think harm—
Take her instantly to your arm!

---

[1]   Wine created by adding water to the pulp of grapes and proceeding with fermenta-
    tion.
[2]   Police officer.
[3]   Mail carrier.
[4]   Greater Provence Street.

It is a little strange, you know, to your dear,
To be dead!"

But one is English,
Though one be never so much of a ghost;
And if most of your life has been spent in the craze to relinquish
What you want most,
You will go on relinquishing,
You will go on vanquishing
Human longings, even
In Heaven.

God! You will have forgotten what the rest of the world
        Is on fire for—
The madness of desire for the long and quiet embrace,
The coming nearer of a tear-wet face;
Forgotten the desire to slake
The thirst, and the long, slow ache,
And to interlace
Lash with lash, lip with lip, limb with limb, and the fingers of the
        hand with the hand
And ...

You will have forgotten ...
        But they will all awake;
Aye, all of them shall awaken
In this dear place.

And all that then we took
Of all that we might have taken,
Was that one embracing look,
Coursing over features, over limbs, between eyes, a making sure,
        and a long sigh,
Having the tranquility
Of trees unshaken,
And the softness of sweet tears,
And the clearness of the clear brook
To wash away past years.
(For that too is the quality of Heaven,
That you are conscious always of great pain

Only when it is over
And shall not come again.
Thank God, thank God, it shall not come again,
Though your eyes be never so wet with the tears
Of many years!)

II

And so she stood a moment by the door
Of the long, red car. Royally she stepped down,
Settling on one long foot and leaning back
Amongst her russet furs. And she looked round ...
Of course it must be strange to come from England
Straight into Heaven. You must take it in,
Slowly, for a long instant, with some fear ...
Now that *affiche*,[1] in orange, on the kiosque:
"Six Spanish bulls will fight on Sunday next
At Arles, in the arena" ... Well, it's strange
Till you get used to our ways. And, on the *Maîrie*,
The untidy poster telling of the *concours*
De vers de soie,[2] of silkworms. The cocoons
Pile, yellow, all across the little Places
Of ninety townships in the environs
Of Lyons, the city famous for her silks.
What if she's pale? It must be more than strange,
After these years, to come out here from England
To a strange place, to the stretched-out arms of me,
A man never fully known, only divined,
Loved, guessed at, pledged to, in your Sussex[3] mud,
Amongst the frost-bound farms by the yeasty sea.
Oh, the long look; the long, long searching look!
And how my heart beat!

      Well, you see, in England
She had a husband, and four families—
His, hers, mine, and another woman's too—

---

1   Poster, playbill.
2   A competition of silkworms.
3   County alongside the southern coast of England.

Would have gone crazy. And, with all the rest,
Eight parents, and the children, seven aunts
And sixteen uncles and a grandmother.
There were, besides, our names, a few real friends,
And the decencies of life. A monstrous heap!
They made a monstrous heap. I've lain awake
Whole aching nights to tot the figures up!
Heap after heap, of complications, griefs,
Worries, tongue-clackings, nonsenses and shame
For not making good. You see the coil there was!
And the poor strained fibres of our tortured brains,
And the voice that called from the depth in her to depth
In me ... my God, in the dreadful nights,
Through the roar of the great black winds, through the sound
        Of the sea!
 Oh agony! Agony! From out my breast
It called whilst the dark house slept, and stairheads creaked;
From within my breast it screamed and made no sound;
And wailed ... And made no sound.
And howled like the damned ... No sound! No sound!
Only the roar of the wind, the sound of the sea,
The tick of the clock ...
And our two voices, noiseless through the dark.
O God! O God!

(That night my young love lay in my arms ...

There was a bitter frost lay on the farms
In England, by the shiver
And the crawling of the tide;
By the broken silver of the English Channel,
Beneath the aged moon that watched alone—
Poor, dreary, lonely old moon to have to watch alone,
Over the dreary beaches mantled with ancient foam
Like shrunken flannel;
The moon, an intent, pale face, looking down
Over the English Channel.

But soft and warm she lay in the crook of my arm,
And came to no harm since we had come quietly home

Even to Heaven;
Which is situated in a little old town
Not very far from the side of the Rhone,
That mighty river
That is, just there by the Crau,[1] in the lower reaches,
Far wider than the Channel.)

But, in the market place of the other little town,
Where the Rhone is a narrower, greener affair,
When she had looked at me, she beckoned with her long
        white hand,
A little languidly, since it is a strain, if a blessed strain, to have just
        died.
And going back again,
Into the wine of the hurrying air.
And very soon even the tall grey steeple
Of Lyons cathedral behind us grew little and far
And then was no more there ...
And, thank God, we had nothing any more to think of,
And, thank God, we had nothing any more to talk of;
Unless, as it chanced. The flashing silver stalk of the pampas
Growing down to the brink of the Rhone,
On the lawn of a little château, giving onto the river.
And we were alone, alone, alone ...
At last alone ...

The poplars on the hill-crests go marching rank on rank,
And far away to the left, like a pyramid, marches the ghost of Mont
        Blanc.[2]
There are vines and vines, all down to the river bank.
There will be a castle here,
And an abbey there;
And huge quarries and a long white farm,
With long thatched barns and a long wine shed,
As we ran alone, all down the Rhone.

---

[1]   Vast marshy expanse in the south of France.
[2]   Mountain range in the western Alps on the French-Italian border.

And that day there was no puncturing of the tyres of fear;
And no trouble at all with the engine and gear;
Smoothly and softly we ran between the great poplar alley
All down the valley of the Rhone.
For the dear, good God knew how we needed rest and to be
        alone.
But, on the other days, just as you must have perfect shadows
        to make Perfect Rembrandts,[1]
He shall afflict us with little lets and hindrances of His own
Devising—just to let us be glad that we are dead ...
Just for remembrance.

III

Hard by the castle of God in the Alpilles,[2]
In the eternal stone of Alpilles,
There's this little old town, walled round by the old, grey gardens ...
There were never such olives as grow in the gardens of God,
The green-grey trees, the wardens of agony
And failure of gods.
Of hatred and faith, of truth, of treachery
They whisper; they whisper that none of the living prevail;
They whirl in the great mistral over the white, dry sods,
Like hair blown back from white foreheads in the enormous gale
Up to the castle walls of God ...

But, in the town that's our home,
Once you are past the wall,
Amongst the trunks of the planes,[3]
Though they soar never so mightily overhead in the day,
All this tumult is quieted down, and all
The windows stand open because of the heat of the night
That shall come.
And, from each little window, shines in the twilight a light,
And, beneath the eternal planes

---

[1]   Chiaroscuro paintings by Dutch baroque artist Rembrandt van Rijn (1606–1669). A
    technique for pictorial representation, chiaroscuro alternates light and dark shades.
[2]   The Alpine hills.
[3]   Flowering trees with large leaves.

With the huge, gnarled trunks that were aged and grey
At the creation of Time,
The Chinese lanthorns, hung out at the doors of hotels,
Shimmering in the dusk, here on an orange tree, there on a sweet-
       scented lime.
There on a golden inscription: "Hotel of the Three Holy Bells."
Or "Hotel Sublime," or "Inn of the Real Good Will."
And, yes, it is very warm still,
And all the world is afoot after the heat of the day.
In the cool of the evening in Heaven ...
And it is here that I have brought my dear to pay her all that I
       owed her,
Amidst this crowd, with the soft voices, the soft footfalls, the
       rejoicing laughter.
And after the twilight there falls such a warm, soft darkness,
And there will come stealing under the planes a drowsy odour,
Compounded all of cyclamen, of oranges, or rosemary and bay,
To take the remembrance of the toil of the day away.

So we sat at a little table, under an immense plane,
And we remembered again
The blisters and foments
And terrible harassments of the tired brain,
The cold and the frost and the pain,
As if we were looking at a picture and saying: "This is true!
Why this is a truly painted
Rendering of that street where—you remember?—I fainted."
And we remembered again
Tranquilly, our poor few tranquil moments,
The falling of the sunlight through the panes,
The flutter for ever in the chimney of the quiet flame,
The mutter of our two poor tortured voices, always a-whisper
And the endless nights when I would cry out, running through all
       the gamut of misery, even to a lisp, her name;
And we remembered our kisses, nine, maybe, or eleven—
If you count two that I gave and she did not give again.

And always the crowd drifted by in the cool of the even,
And we saw the faces of friends,
And the faces of those to whom one day we must make amends,

Smiling in welcome.

And I said: "On another day—

And such a day may well come soon—

We will play dominoes with Dick and Evelyn and Frances

For a whole afternoon.

And, in the time to come, Genée

Shall dance for us, fluttering over the ground as the sunlight
      dances."

And *Arlésiennes*[1] with the beautiful faces went by us,

And gipsies and Spanish shepherds, noiseless in sandals of straw,
      Sauntered nigh us,

Wearing slouch hats and old sheep-skins, and casting admiring
      Glances

From dark, foreign eyes at my dear ...

(And ah, it is Heaven alone, to have her alone and so near!)

So all this world rejoices

In the cool of the even

In Heaven ...

And, when the cool of the even was fully there,

Came a great ha-ha of voices.

Many children run together, and all laugh and rejoice and call,

Hurrying with little arms flying, and little feet flying, and little
      Hurrying haunches,

From the door of the stable,

Where, in an *olla podrida*,[2] they had been playing at the *corrida*[3]

With the black Spanish bull, whose nature

Is patience with children. And so, through the gaps of the branches

Of jasmine on our screen beneath the planes,

We saw, coming down from the road that leads to the olives and
      Alpilles,

A man of great stature,

In a great cloak,

And a little joke

For all and sundry, coming down with a hound at his side.

And he stood at the cross-roads, passing the time of day

In a great, kind voice, the voice of a man-and-a-half!—

---

[1] Costumed dancers from Arles.

[2] Assorted mixture.

[3] Bullfight.

With a great laugh, and a great clap on the back,
For a fellow in black—a priest I should say,
Or may be a lover,
Wearing black for his mistress's mood.
"A little toothache," we could hear him say; "but that's so good
When it gives over."[1] So he passed from sight
In the soft twilight, into the soft night,
In the soft riot and tumult of the crowd.

And a magpie flew down, laughing, holding up his beak to us.
And I said: "That was God! Presently, when he has walked through
       The town
And the night has settled down,
So that you may not be afraid,
In the darkness, he will come to our table and speak to us."
And past us many saints went walking in a company—
The kindly, thoughtful saints, devising and laughing and talking,
And smiling at us with their pleasant solicitude.
And because the thick of the crowd followed to the one side God,
Or to the other saints, we sat in solitude.
In the distance the saints went singing all in chorus,
And out Lord went on the other side of the street,
Holding a little boy.
Taking him to pick the musk-roses that open at dusk,
For wreathing the statue of Jove,[2]
Left on the Alpilles above
By the Romans; since Jove,
Even Jove,
Must not want for his quota of honour and love;
But round about him there must be,
With all its tender jollity,
The laughter of children in Heaven,
Making merry with roses in Heaven.

Yet never he looked at us, knowing that that would be such joy
As must be over-great for hearts that needed quiet;

---

[1]   When the toothache ceases to be painful.
[2]   In Roman mythology, the ruler of the gods.

Such a riot and tumult of joy as quiet hearts are not able
To taste to the full ...
...And my dear one sat in the shadows; very softly she wept:—
Such joy is in Heaven,
In the cool of the even,
After the burden and toil of the days,
After the heat and haze
In the vine-hills; or in the shady
Whispering groves in high passes up in the Alpilles,
Guarding the castle of God.

And I went on talking towards her unseen face:
"So it is, so it goes, in this beloved place,
There shall be never a grief but passes; no, not any;
There shall be such bright light and no blindness;
There shall be so little awe and so much loving-kindness;
There shall be a little longing and enough care,
There shall be a little labour and enough of toil
To bring back the lost flavour of our human coil;
Not enough to taint it;
And all that we desire shall prove as fair as we can paint it."
For, though that may be the very hardest trick of all
God set Himself, who fashioned his godly hall.
Thus He has made Heaven;
Even Heaven.

For God is a very clever mechanician;
And if He made this proud and goodly ship of the world,
From the maintop to the hull,
Do you think He could not finish it to the full,
With a flag and all,
And make it sail, tall and brave,
On the waters, beyond the grave?
It should cost but very little rhetoric
To explain for you that last, fine, conjuring trick;
Nor does God need to be a very great magician
To give to each man after his heart,
Who knows very well what each man has in his heart:
To let you pass your life in a night-club where they dance,
If that is your idea of heaven; if you will, in the South of France;

If you will, on the turbulent sea; if you will, in the peace of the
    night;
Where you will; how you will;
Or in the long death of a kiss, that may never pall:
He would be a very little God if He could not do all this,
And He is still
The great God of all.

For God is a good man; God is a kind man;
In the darkness He came walking to our table beneath the planes,
And spoke
So kindly to my dear,
With a little joke,
Giving Himself some pains
To take away her fear
Of His stature,
So as not to abash her,
In no way at all to dash her new pleasure beneath the planes,
In the cool of the even
In Heaven.

That, that is God's nature.
For God's a good brother, and God is no blind man,
And God's a good mother and loves sons who're rovers,
And God is our father and loves all good lovers.
He has a kindly smile for many a poor sinner;
He takes note to make it up to poor wayfarers on sodden roads;
Such as bear heavy loads
He takes note of a poor old cook,
Cooking your dinner;
And much he loves sweet joys in such as ever took
Sweet joy on earth. He has a kindly smile for a kiss
Given in a shady nook.
And in the golden book
Where accounts of His estate are kept,
All the round, golden sovereigns of bliss,
Known by poor lovers, married or never yet married,
Whilst the green world waked, or the black world quietly slept;
All joy, all sweetness, each sweet sigh that's sighed—
Their accounts are kept,

And carried
By the love of God to His own credit's side.
So that is why He came to our table to welcome my dear, dear
        bride,
In the cool of even
In front of a café in Heaven.

Appendix B: Ford Madox Ford, excerpts from Henry James: A Critical Study

[Published in 1913, Ford's *Henry James: A Critical Study* explores James's considerable contributions—both fictional and nonfictional—to the emergence and development of the English novel as a literary form. Ford first met James (1843–1916), the celebrated author of such volumes as *Daisy Miller* (1878), *The Portrait of a Lady* (1881), and *The Golden Bowl* (1904), in London in the late 1890s. James would later use Ford as physical model for Merton Densher in *The Wings of the Dove* (1902).]

I have said elsewhere that, considering that our contacts with humanity are nowadays so much a matter of acquaintanceship and so little a matter of friendship, considering that for ourselves, moving about as men do today, we may know so many men and so little of the lives of any one man, the greatest service that any one man can render to the Republic, the greatest service that any novelist can render to the State, is to draw an unbiased picture of the world we live in. To beguile by pretty fancies, to lead armies, to invent new means of transport, to devise systems of irrigation—all these things are mere steps in the dark; and it is very much to be doubted whether any lawgiver can, in the present state of things, be anything but a curse to society. It seems at least to be the property of almost every law that today we frame to be infinitely more of a flail to a large number of people than of a service to any living soul. Regarding the matter historically, we may safely say that the feudal system in its perfection has died out of the world except in the islands of Jersey, Guernsey, Alderney, and Sark.[1] The Middle Ages with their empirical and tricky enactments against regrating and the like; the constitutional theories, such as they were, of the Commonwealth and the Stuart age, have disappeared; the Whigism[2] of Cobden and Bright,[3] the bourgeois democracy of the first and third Republics and the oppressive, cruel, ignorant and

---

[1]   Islands in the English Channel near the French coast.
[2]   Political movement that limits the monarchy in favor of parliamentary power.
[3]   Richard Cobden (1804–1865), British politician; John Bright (1811–1889), British statesman and orator.

blind theorising of later Fabianism[1] have all died away. We stand today, in the matter of political theories, naked to the wind and blind to sunlight. We have a sort of vague uneasy feeling that the old feudalism and the old union of Christendom beneath a spiritual headship may in the end be infinitely better than anything that was ever devised by the Mother of Parliaments in England, the Constitution of the United States.[2] And, just at this moment when by the nature of things we know so many men and so little of the lives of men, we are faced also by a sort of beggardom of political theories. It remains therefore for the novelist—and particularly for the realist among novelists—to give us the very matter upon which we shall build the theories of the new body politic. And, assuredly, the man who can do this for us, is conferring upon us a greater benefit than the man who can make two blades of grass grow where one grew before; since what is the good of substituting two blades for one—what is the benefit to society at large if the only individual to benefit by it is some company promoter?

That is the reason for my saying that I consider Mr. James to be the greatest man now living. He, more than anybody, has observed human society as it is, and more than anybody has faithfully rendered his observations for us. It is perfectly true that his hunting grounds have been almost exclusively "up town" ones—that he has frequented the West End[3] and the country house, practically never going once in his literary life east of Temple Bar or lower than Fourteenth Street. But a scientist has a perfect right—nay more, it is the absolute duty of the scientist—to limit his observations to the habits of lepidoptera, or to the bacilli of cancer if he does not feel himself adapted for enquiry into the habits of bulls, bears, elephants or foxes. Mr. James, to put the matter shortly, has preferred to enquire with an unbiased mind into the habits and necessities of any other class or race of the habitable globe as it is. That is why Mr. James deserves so well the Republic.

I am aware that my penultimate statement is what is called a large proposition, but I think I am justified in making it. The English novel

---

[1] Based upon the political activities of Roman general Quintus Fabius Maximus (d. c.291 B.C.), Fabianism refers to a belief in cautious rather than revolutionary change in government.

[2] The Constitution established the system of federal government in the United States that began to function in 1789.

[3] London's theatre district.

has hitherto occupied a very lowly position, whether in the world of art or in the world where sermons are preached, political speeches listened to, railway trains run, or ships plough the sea; and, in both these worlds, its lowly position has upon the whole been justified. The critic has been forced to say that the English novelist has hardly ever regarded his art as an art; the man of affairs has said that to read English novels was a waste of time. And both the critic and man of affairs have hitherto been right. The worlds of art and affairs are widely different spheres, but that is not to say that they are spheres that should not interact one upon the other. Indeed, my grand-aunt Eliza amply summed the matter up, busy woman as she was, when she exclaimed that sooner than be idle she would take a book and read. But this attitude is only justifiable in a world of affairs that can't get hold of books worth reading. For, when books are worth reading the world of affairs that omits to read them is lost both commercially and spiritually. You cannot have a business community of any honesty unless you have a literature to set a high standard....

If Mr. James, then, has given us a truthful picture of the leisured life that is founded upon the labours of all this stuff that fills graveyards, then he, more than any other person now living, has afforded matter upon which the sociologist of the future may build—or may commence his destructions.

For, given that he has achieved this, the problem which will then present itself to the sociologist is no more and no less than this—are the prizes of life, is the leisured life which our author has depicted for us, worth the striving for? If, in short, this life is not worth having— this life of the West End, of the country house, of the drawing-room, possibly of the studio, and of the garden party—if this life, which is the best that our civilisation has to show, is not worth the living; if it is not pleasant, cultivated, civilized, cleanly and instinct with reasonably high ideals, then, indeed, Western civilisation is not worth going on with, and we had better scrap the whole of it so as to begin again. For, you may by legislation increase the earnings of the labourer; you may by organizing or by inventing increase the wealth of our particular Western communities, but what is the use of this wealth if the only things that it can buy are no better than are to be had in any city store—unless, along with material objects that it does buy, it gets "thrown in," as the phrase is, some of the things that were never yet bought by mortal's money. For it is no use saying anything else than that the manual labourer, if you give him four hundred a year and an excellent education, will have no ambition to live any otherwise, things being as they are, than as the dwellers in any suburb. And, supposing that you gave him a thousand a year he would, as things at present stand, have no other ambition than to live like one of the less wealthy characters of any one of Mr. James's books. There is no getting away from these facts in any Anglo-Saxon community, and even in France and Germany the tendency is much the same; though, of course, in both of those countries you happen upon such phenomena as farmers of very large income who continue to live and to wear the dress of farmers, without any thought of snobbishly imitating the lives and habits of suburban clerks or of hunting gentry.

So that the problem remaining to the sociologist, the politicoeconomist or the mere voter, after reading Mr. James's work is simply this; is the game worth the candle; is the prize worth the life? If they are not, then political economists must entirely change their views of what is meant by supply and demand, introducing a new factor which I will call the "worth whileness" of having one's demands supplied; the sociologist must shut up all the books that he has ever read until he, too, has evolved some theory of what is worth while; and the voter must insist upon the closing of all the legislatures known to this universe—until some reasonable plan of what they are all striving for shall have been arrived at. For the fact is that our present systems of polity and laws, being entirely based upon theories of economics, we have paid—none of us who are interested in public questions—any heed at all to the purchasing power of that money which by our activities we produce and which by our legislation we seek as equally as possible to distribute.

It is because Mr. James has so wonderfully paid attention to this question that I have advanced for him—and heaven knows he won't thank me for it—the claim to be the greatest servant of the State now living. Heaven knows too, that, things being as they are, it isn't much of a claim....

But it has been necessary for Mr. James's immense process of refining himself, that he should keep away from the manifestations of the uncontrollable, and so very high-voiced, West. I have said earlier in this little study, that Mr. James has had no public mission in life. But that is only a half truth, if it is not an absolute lie. For, during the whole seventy years of his life which began in New England in 1843, Mr. James has had just one immense mission—the civilizing of America. New England presented our subject with glimpses of what a civilisation might be. But you have only got to go to New England today to realize all that New England hadn't got, in those days, in the way of civilisation. You have only got to go to Concord,[1] Massachusetts with its dust, its heat, its hard climate, its squalid frame houses, its mosquitoes, to realize how little, on the luxurious and leisured side of existence, New England had to offer to a searcher after a refined, a sybaritic civilisation.

I am not saying that there wasn't, between Salem and Boston, enough intellectual development to provide a non-materialistic state with fifty civilisations. It is obvious that you could not have produced an Emerson, a Holmes, a Thoreau or a Hawthorne—or for the matter of that a Washington Irving[2]—without having a morally, an intellectually and even a socially refined atmosphere. Hampstead[3] itself could not more carefully weigh its words or analyse its actions. But it would be fairly safe to say that, except for some few specimens of "Colonial" ware and architecture you wouldn't in the 60s have found in the whole world of New England a single article of what is called *vertu*.[4] If you will look at the photograph which forms that frontispiece of *The Spoils of Poynton*,[5] in Mr. James's collected edition, you will see the sort of civilisation for which Mr. James must obviously have craved and which New England certainly couldn't have produced.

I must confess that I myself should be appalled at having to live before such a mantelpiece and such a *décor*[6]—all this French gilding of the Louis Quinze period;[7] all these cupids surmounting florid clocks; these vases with intaglios; these huge and floridly patterned walls; these tapestried fire-screens; these gilt chairs with backs and seats of Gobelins, of Aubusson, or of *petit point*.[8] But there

---

1   Suburb of Boston in eastern Massachusetts.
2   Ralph Waldo Emerson (1803–1882), American essayist and poet; Oliver Wendell Holmes (1809–1894), American physician and author; Henry David Thoreau (1817–1862), American writer and naturalist; Nathaniel Hawthorne (1804–1864), American author; Washington Irving (1783–1859), American author, essayist, and historian.
3   Northern heights of Camden, one of London's inner boroughs.
4   Love of the fine arts; virtuosity.
5   A novel by James published in 1897.
6   Furnishings.
7   Era denoted by the monarchy of Louis XV (1710–1774), who was king of France from 1715 to 1774.
8   Three different interior styles associated with the Louis Quinze period.

is no denying the value, the rarity and the suggestion of these articles which are described as "some of the spoils"—the suggestions of tranquillity, of an aged civilisation, of wealth, of leisure, of opulent refinement. And there is no denying that not by any conceivable imagination could such a mantelpiece with such furnishings have been found at Brook Farm.[1]

It was in search of these things that Mr. James traveled, as he so frequently did, to Florence where palazzi,[2] and all that palazzi may hold, were so ready of access, so easy of conquest for the refined Transatlantic. In various flashes, in various obscurities, hints, concealments, reservations and reported speeches, Mr. James has set us the task of piecing together a history of his temperament. The materials for this history are contained in various volumes. There is, for instance, his very last production, *A Small Boy*;[3] there are the prefaces to the volumes of his collected editions; there are his comparatively scanty collections of criticisms, the most important of which are contained in the volume called *French Poets and Novelists*;[4] there is the life of Hawthorne;[5] there are the books about places such as *A Little Tour in France, English Hours,* and *The American Scene.*[6] It is therefore to these works that I shall devote my consideration for the space of this section.

A Small Boy, which is a touching tribute to the memory of our subject's brother, adumbrates the existence, mostly in the state of New York, of a young male child—of two young male children in a household of the most eminent and the most cultivated. As far as one can make the matter out—as far, that is to say, as it is necessary to make it out for a work which is in no sense biographical—Mr. James's father, Henry James senior,[7] was a person of great cultural position in what is now called the Empire State. He was not so much a representative citizen as a public adornment. He was occupied in something like the reconciling of reveled religion with science, which was then beginning to adopt the semblance of a destroyer of Christianity. His published works were numerous; his

---

[1] During the 1840s, Brook Farm was an experimental farm at West Roxbury, Massachusetts, based on cooperative living.

[2] Large Italian museums or places of residence.

[3] An autobiographical work by James published in 1913.

[4] A work of criticism published by James in 1878.

[5] *Hawthorne*, a work of criticism published by James in 1879.

[6] Works of travel writing published by James in 1884, 1905, and 1907, respectively.

[7] Henry James, Sr. (1811–1882), American philosopher.

eloquence renowned; his refinement undoubted. For the matter of that it was demonstrable, so that we have the image of two small boys, whether in the clean, white-porticoed streets of Buffalo or of Albany,[1] or in the comparative rough-and-tumble and noise of a yellow-painted New York that contained nevertheless at that date gardens and pleasaunces. We have the impression of these two small boys of the '50s pursuing a perhaps not very strenuous, but certainly a very selected, educational path towards that stage in which William James[2] displayed all the faculty of analysis of a novelist, and Mr. Henry James all the faculties of analysis of a pragmatic philosopher.

And there is no doubt that there were afforded to the quite young James—the small boy—a quite unusual number of contacts with quite the best people. Figuratively speaking, not only did this particular small boy live amongst the placid eccentrics of New England but, in his father's house, he was exposed to the full tide that, running counter to the Gulf stream, from quite early days of the Victorian age, bathed the shores of the Western World—the tide, I mean, of European celebrities. I am not, of course, writing a history of American culture—though indeed a history of Mr. James's mind might well be nothing more nor less than that; but a very interesting subject lies open for some analyst in recording the impressions and adventures of the early tourists who entered on the formidable task of visiting, lecturing in, or, in whatever other intellectual way, exploiting the States of before the War. You will find traces of them in the Mississippi Pilot of Mark Twain[3] where the formidable author tomahawks Mrs. Trollope,[4] and several French and English writers who, having visited that gigantic but uninteresting and desolate stream, failed of seeing its snags and bluffs and streamer saloons eye to eye with the Clemens. You will read the actual impressions of such a visit in *Martin Chuzzlewit*[5] and in *American Notes*;[6] or, in later, American Memoirs you will read of the disappointment caused to distinguished hearers by Matthew Arnold's

---

1 Cities in western and northeastern New York, respectively.
2 Henry James, Jr.'s brother, William James (1842–1910), American psychologist and philosopher.
3 Pseudonym of Samuel Langhorne Clemens (1835–1910), American writer.
4 Frances Trollope (1780–1863), English novelist and travel writer, as well as the mother of English novelist Anthony Trollope (1815–1882).
5 Novel published in 1843–1844 by Charles Dickens (1812–1870), English novelist and journalist.
6 *American Notes* (1842), Dickens's controversial travelogue about his American tour.

faulty delivery of his lectures—his mumbling voice, his frigid, English mannerisms (How alas, one sympathizes with the unfortunate author of the "Forsaken Merman"!).[1]

At any rate, lecturing and acclaimed, or lecturing and appalled, and in either case overwhelmed by that immense and blinding thing, the world-famed American Hospitality—they came, those pilgrims, in a steady trickle. And it passed, that trickle, through the house of Mr. Henry James, Sr., under the no doubt observant eyes of Henry James, Jr. It is not my business to particularise who they exactly were—those great figures. In order to catalogue them, I should have to fall back on the record of conversation with our subject; and although I should unscrupulously resort to this, if it suited my turn, it simply does not. It suffices to say that, whatever may have been our subject's personal contacts with Dickens, Thackeray, Arnold[2] or any other English celebrity to whom Henry James, Sr., offered his fine hospitality, nothing of their personalities "rubbed off," as you might say, on to the by then adolescent James—or, if anything came at all it was only from the restrained way, was as "New England" as was ever that of Emerson, of James Russell Lowell[3]....

Balzac[4] we may take to have been our subject's first serious literary model—or at any rate his first conscious one; and it is interesting to consider how, at any rate on the surface, in their late flowering and in their determination to produce contemporary history, the voluminous author of the series of fairy tales called the *Comédie Humaine*[5] and the author of the series of stories about worries and perturbations resembled each other....

As regards the second of the golden spoons that Mr. James had in his mouth—I mean when he was born an American ...There can be no doubt that this in itself is very largely responsible for his knowledge—apart from his mere surmises as to the human heart and as to human manners. The position of the American of some resources and of leisure was, in European society of the nineteenth century, one of a single felicity. Without, or almost without, letters of introduction or

---

[1]   Arnold's poem, "The Forsaken Merman," was published in 1849.
[2]   William Makepeace Thackeray (1811–1863), English novelist and humorist; Matthew Arnold (1822–1888), English poet.
[3]   James Russell Lowell (1819–1891), American poet, essayist, editor, diplomat, and critic.
[4]   Honoré de Balzac (1799–1850), French novelist.
[5]   Multivolume novel by Balzac, published between 1842 and 1848; translated literally as *The Human Comedy*.

social passports of any kind, the American "went anywhere." Anywhere in the world—into the courts of the Emperors of Austria as into the bosom of English county families! To know, or to admit an American into your family circle, appeared to commit you to nothing. There was the whole immense Herring Pond[1] between yourself and their homes and you just accepted the strange and generally quiet creatures on their face values, without any question as to their origins, and taking their comfortable wealths for granted. Thus Mr. James could really get to "know" people in a way that would be absolutely sealed to any European young writer whether he were Honoré de Balzac or Charles Dickens. You can figure him (I am not in any way attempting to do more than draw a fancy portrait)—a quiet, extremely well-mannered and unassuming young gentleman, reputed to be very wealthy and in command of an entire leisure, without indeed even so much tax on his time as an occasional professional call in at the Legation[2] or ministry of his country. Still he would be— he was—taken on the footing of a young diplomat and, if he proved, on nearer acquaintance, to be thought more "intellectual" than one is accustomed to find in the young men that one meets in good houses that was only part of a transatlantic oddness. Some oddnesses the amiable creatures must be allowed to possess, considering their distant and hazy origins; you could be thankful if they did not sleep with derringers under their pillows—which they sometimes did— or pick their teeth with Bowie knives.

Thus we may consider that Mr. James, starting upon his European career, came in, at once, upon the very top. If he had been an English writer he would have been at it twenty years before he knew an English countess; he would die without having exchanged ten words with the wife of a duke, just as Balzac died without having had a glimpse of an interior of the Faubourg St. Germain.[3] But that street of high walls had no terrors for Mr. James, and if his Madame de Bellegarde[4] in some ways resembles a Balzac Marchioness,[5] that is much more owing to the hold that Balzac and his methods had over our subject's imagination than to any want of social knowledge.... A critic may like a class of subject or may dislike

---

[1] Humorous term for the North Atlantic Ocean.
[2] Diplomatic mission.
[3] Affluent area of Paris noteworthy for its mansions and antique shops.
[4] Character in James's novel, *The American* (1877).
[5] Wife or widow of a marquess.

them—for myself I like books about fox-hunting better than any other book to have a good read in. I would rather read *Tilbury Nogo*[1] than *Daniel Deronda*,[2] and any book of Surtees[3] than any book of George Meredith—excepting perhaps *Evan Harrington*,[4] which is a jolly thing with a good description of country house cricket. But that is merely a statement of preferences, like any other English writing about books. This latter leads the reader, as a rule, no further than to tell him that Messrs. Lang, Collins, or who you will, like reading about golf, Charlotte Corday,[5] the *Murder in the Red Barn*[6] and, what you will—facts which may be interesting in themselves but which have nothing to do with how a book should be, or is not, written.

Similarly with disquisitions upon the temperament of a writer—since temperament is a thing like sunshine or the growing of grass, a gift of the good God. Or may write about it if one likes, if one has nothing better to do; it is a sort of gossip like any other sort of gossip and, if it does no good in particular, it breaks no bones. Twenty of us, confined in a country house by a south-westerly gale, may well set to work to discuss the temperaments of our friends. "I like so and so," one of us will say, "he is so considerate"; "I prefer Mrs. Dash," another replies, "she is so forceful." But all the talk will not make the friend of So-and-so, with a taste for the milder virtues, like Mrs. Dash whose attractions are of a more vigorous type. That is as much as to say that any penny-a-liner might call your attention to the temperament of Mr. W. H. Hudson,[7] which is the most beautiful thing that God ever made, though twenty thousand first-class critics thundering together could not make Mr. James like Flaubert.[8] Still, disquisitions upon temperament may do this amount of good: Supposing that the only work of Mr. James that you had happened to glance at had been "The Great Good Place,"[9]

---

1 Novel published in 1880 by George John Whyte-Melville (1821–1878).
2 Novel published in 1876 by George Eliot [Mary Ann Evans] (1819–1880).
3 Robert Smith Surtees (1803–1864), English novelist.
4 Novel published in 1860 by English writer George Meredith (1828–1909).
5 Charlotte Corday (1768–1793), guillotined for the assassination of Jean Paul Marat (1743–1793), a French revolutionary.
6 John Latimer's (1804–1904) *Maria Marten; or, The Murder in the Red Barn: A Victorian Melodrama* (1828).
7 William Henry Hudson (1841–1922), English author, naturalist, and ornithologist.
8 Gustave Flaubert (1821–1880), French novelist.
9 Short story published by James in 1900.

and supposing that you had no taste for mysticism, preferring the eerily horrible or the suavely social! You would have put Mr. James's volume down and would have sworn never to take another up. Then—coming in some newspaper quotation upon some passage about *The Turn of the Screw*,[1] which is the most eerie and harrowing story that was ever written—you might discover that here was a temperament, after all, infinitely to your taste. So that some profit might come from that form of writing.

But criticism concerns itself with methods and with methods and again with methods—and with nothing else. So that, having waded wearily through a considerable amount of writing that I can only compare to duty-calls, I was rejoicing at the thought of letting myself go. I felt as a horse does when, after a tiring day between the shafts, it is let loose into a goodly grass field. There seemed to be such reams that one might, all joyfully, write about the methods of this supremely great master of method. I had promised myself the real treat of my life....

But alas, there is nothing to write! I do not mean to say that nothing could have been written—but it has all been done. Mr. James has done it himself. In the matchless—and certainly bewildering series of Prefaces to the collected edition,[2] there is no single story that has not been annotated, critically written about and (again critically) sucked as dry as an orange. There is nothing left for the poor critic but the merest of quotations.

I desired to say that the supreme discovery in the literary art of our day is that of Impressionism, that the supreme function of Impressionism is selection, and that Mr. James has carried the power of selection so far that he can create an impression with nothing at all. And, indeed, that had been what for many years I have been desiring to say about our master! He can convey an impression, an atmosphere of what you will with literally nothing. Embarrassment, chastened happiness—for his happiness is always tinged with regret—greed, horror, social vacuity—he can give you it all with a purely blank page. His characters will talk about rain, about the opera, about the moral aspects of the selling of Old Masters to the New Republic, and those conversations will convey to your mind that the quiet talkers

---

[1]   Novel published by James in 1898.

[2]   Ford is referring to James's "New York" editions of his novels, stories, criticism, and prefaces, which the author revised and assembled between 1906 and 1910.

are living in an atmosphere of horror, of bankruptcy, of passion hopeless as the *Dies Irae*![1] That is the supreme trick of art today, since that is how we really talk about the musical glasses whilst our lives crumble around us. Shakespeare did that once or twice—as when Desdemona[2] gossips about her mother's maid called Barbara whilst she is under the very shadow of death; but there is hardly any other novelist that has done it. Our subject does it, however, all the time, and that is one reason for the impression that his books give us of vibrating reality. I think the word "vibrating" exactly expresses it; the sensation is due to the fact that the mind passes, as it does in real life, perpetually backwards and forwards between the apparent aspect of things and the essentials of life. If you have ever, I mean, been ruined, it will have been a succession of pictures like the following. Things have been going to the devil with you for some time; you have been worried and worn and badgered and beaten. The thing will be at its climax tomorrow. You cannot stand the strain in town and you ask your best friend—who won't be a friend any more tomorrow, human nature being what it is!—to take a day off at golf with you. In the afternoon, whilst the Courts or the Stock Exchange or some woman up in town are sending you to the devil, you play a foursome, with two other friends. The sky is blue; you joke about the hardness of the greens; your partner makes an extraordinary stroke at the ninth hole; you put in some gossip about a woman in a green jersey who is playing at the fourteenth. From what one of the other men replies you become aware that all those three men know that tomorrow there will be an end of you; the sense of that immense catastrophe broods all over the green and sunlit landscape. You take your mashie and make the approach shot of your life whilst you are joking about the other fellow's necktie, and he says that if you play like that on the second of next month you will certainly take the club medal, though he knows, and you know, and they all know you know, that by the second of the next month not a soul there will talk to you or play with you. So you finish the match three up and you walk into the club house and pick up an illustrated paper....

That, you know, is what life really is—a series of such meaningless episodes beneath the shadow of doom—or of impending bliss, if you

---

[1] Latin hymn for the Day of Judgment sung in requiem masses.

[2] Character in *Othello* (c.1604), one of the tragedies written by English dramatist and poet William Shakespeare (1564–1616).

prefer it. And that is what Henry James gives you—an immense body
of work all dominated with that vibration—with that balancing of
the mind between the great outlines and the petty details. And, at
times, as I have said, he does this so consummately that all mention
of the major motive is left out altogether. But it is superfluous for me
to say this because it is already said—in a Preface. Consider this:—

> Only make the reader's general vision of evil intense
> enough, I said to myself—

Mr. James is considering how to make *The Turn of the Screw*
sufficiently horrible—

> —and that already is a charming job—and his own experi-
> ence, his own imagination, his own sympathy (with the chil-
> dren) and horror (of their false friends) will supply him quite
> sufficiently with all the particulars. Make him *think* the evil,
> make him think it for himself, and you are released from weak
> specifications. This ingenuity I took pains—as indeed great
> pains were required—to apply; and with a success apparently
> beyond my liveliest hope.... How can I feel my calculation to
> have failed ... on my being assailed, as has befallen me, with
> the charge of a monstrous emphasis, the charge of indecently
> expatiating [upon the corruption of soul of two haunted chil-
> dren]? There is ... not an inch of expatiation ... my values are
> positively all blanks save so far as an excited horror ... proceeds
> to read into them more or less fantastic figures ...

Here again is one passage which exactly gives you the measure
of how the horror is suggested. You are dealing with a little boy who
has been expelled from school on a vague charge. This little boy and
his sister have been corrupted—in ways that are never shown—by
a governess and a groom in whose society they had been once left
and who now, being dead, haunt, as *revenants*, the doomed children.
The new governess is asking him why he was expelled from school,
and the little boy answers that he did not open letters, did not steal.

> "What then did you do?"
> He looked in a vague pain all around the top of the room
> and drew his breath two or three times as if with difficulty. He

might have been standing at the bottom of the sea and raising his eyes to some green twilight. "Well—I said things."

"Only that?"

"They thought it enough!" ...

"But to whom did you say them? ...Was it to every one?"
I asked.

"No, it was only to—" But he gave a sick little headshake.
"I don't remember their names."

"Were they then so many?"

"No—only a few. Those I liked."

" ...And did they repeat what you said," I went on after a
pause ...

"Oh, yes," he nevertheless replied—"they must have
repeated them. To those *they* liked."

"And those things come round—?"

"To the masters? Oh yes!" he answered very simply.

I have stripped this episode of all its descriptive passages save one
in order to reduce it to the barest and most crude of bones, in order
to show just exactly what the skeleton is. And it will be observed
that the whole matter—the whole skeleton or the only bone of it—
is the one word "things"—"I said things."

Appendix C: Ford Madox Ford, "On Impressionism"

[Originally published in two installments in *Poetry and Drama* in June and December of 1914, "On Impressionism" addresses the techniques that Ford had developed for many years—often in collaboration with Joseph Conrad—and would later employ in the construction of *The Good Soldier*. Ford derived the term "Impressionism" from the work of such artists as French painter Claude Monet (1840–1926) and novelist Émile Zola (1840–1902). In the essay, Ford contends that an Impressionistic literary narrative should eschew telling the reader what is occurring in a given work, and instead, show the reader what is taking place via a series of impressions or images.]

I

These are merely some notes towards a working guide to Impressionism as a literary method.

I do not know why I should have been especially asked to write about Impressionism; even as far as literary Impressionism goes I claim no Papacy in the matter. A few years ago, if anybody had called me an Impressionist I should languidly have denied that I was anything of the sort or that I knew anything about the school, if there could be said to be any school. But one person and another in the last ten years has called me an Impressionist with such persistence that I have given up resistance. I don't know; I just write books, and if someone attaches a label to me I do not much mind.

I am not claiming any great importance for my work; I daresay it is alright. At any rate, I am a perfectly self-conscious writer; I know exactly how to get my effects, as far as those effects go. Then, if I am in truth an Impressionist, it must follow that a conscientious and exact account of how I myself work will be an account, from the inside, of how Impressionism is reached, produced, or gets its effects. I can do no more.

This is called egotism; but, to tell the truth, I do not see how Impressionism can be anything else. Probably this school differs from other schools, principally, in that it recognizes, frankly, that all art must be the expression of an ego, and that if Impressionism is to do anything, it must, as the phrase is, go the whole hog. The difference between the description of a grass by the agricultural correspondent of the *Times*[1] newspaper and the description of the same grass by Mr. W. H. Hudson is just the difference—the measure of the difference between the egos of the two gentlemen. The difference between the description of any given book by some English reviewer and the description of the same book by some foreigner attempting Impressionist criticism is again merely a matter of the difference in the ego.

Mind, I am not saying that the non-Impressionist productions may not have their values—their very great values. The Impressionist gives you his own views, expecting you to draw deductions, since presumably you know the sort of chap he is. The agricultural correspondent of the *Times*, on the other hand—and a jolly good writer he is— attempts to give you, not so much his own impression of a new grass as the factual observation of himself and as many as possible other sound authorities. He will tell you how many blades of the new grass will grow upon an acre, what height they will attain, what will be a reasonable tonnage to expect when green, when sun-dried in the form of hay or as ensilage. He will tell you the fattening value of the new fodder in its various forms and the nitrogenous value of the manure dropped by the so-fattened beasts. He will provide you, in short, with reading that is quite interesting to the layman, since all facts are interesting to men of good will; and the agriculturist he will provide with information of real value. Mr. Hudson, on the other hand, will give you nothing but the pleasure of coming in contact with his temperament, and I doubt whether, if you read with the greatest care his description of false sea-buckthorn (*hippophae rhamnoides*)[2] you would very willingly recognize that greenish-gray plant, with the spines and the berries like the reddish amber, if you came across it.

Or again—so at least I was informed by an editor the other day—the business of a sound English reviewer is to make the readers of the paper understand exactly what sort of a book it is that the reviewer is writing about. Said the editor in question: "You have no idea how many readers your paper will lose if you employ one of those brilliant chaps who write readable articles about books. You

---

1   Premier London newspaper, established in January 1785.
2   Thorny tree or shrub.

will get yourself deluged with letter after letter from subscribers saying they bought a book on the strength of articles in your paper; that the book isn't in the least what they expected, and that therefore they withdraw their subscriptions." What the sound English reviewer, therefore, has to do is to identify himself with the point of view of as large a number of readers of the journal for which he may be reviewing, as he can easily do, and then to give them as many facts about the book under consideration as his allotted space will hold. To do this he must sacrifice his personality, and the greater part of his readability. But he will probably very much help his editor, since the great majority of readers do not want to read; and they do not want to come into contact with the personality of the critic, since they have obviously never been introduced to him.

The ideal critic, on the other hand—as opposed to the exemplary reviewer—is a person who can handle words that from the very first three phases any intelligent person—any foreigner, that is to say, and any one of three inhabitants of these islands—any intelligent person will know at once the sort of chap that he is dealing with. Letters of introduction will therefore be unnecessary, and the intelligent reader will know pretty well the sort of fellow the fellow is. I don't mean to say that he would necessarily trust his purse, his wife, or his mistress to the Impressionist critic's acre. But that is not absolutely necessary. The ambition, however, of my friend the editor was to let his journal give the impression of being written by those who could be trusted with the wives and purses—not, of course, the mistresses, for there would be none—of his readers.

You will, perhaps, be beginning to see now what I am aiming at—the fact that Impressionism is a frank expression of personality; the fact that non-Impressionism is an attempt to gather together all the opinions of as many reputable persons as may be and to render them truthfully and without exaggeration. (The Impressionist must always exaggerate.)

II

Let us approach this matter historically—as far as I know anything about the history of Impressionism, though I must warn you that I am a shockingly ill-read man. Here, then, are some examples: do you know, for instance, Hogarth's[1] drawing of the watchman with the

---

[1] William Hogarth (1697–1764), English painter, satirist, engraver, and art theorist.

pike over his shoulder and the dog at his heels going in at a door, the whole being executed in four lines? Here it is:

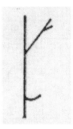

Now, that is the high-watermark of Impressionism; since, if you look at those lines long enough, you will begin to see the watchman with his slouch hat, the handle of the pike coming well down into the cobble-stones, the knee-breeches, the leathern garters strapped round his stocking, and the surly expression of the dog, which is bull-hound with a touch of mastiff in it.

You may ask why, if Hogarth saw all these things, did he not put them down on paper, and all that I can answer is that he made this drawing for a bet. Moreover why, if you can see all these things for yourself, should Hogarth bother to put them down on paper? You might as well contend that Our Lord ought to have delivered a lecture on the state of primary education in the Palestine of the year 32 or thereabouts, together with the statistics of rickets and other infantile diseases caused by neglect and improper feeding—a disquisition in the manner of Mrs. Sidney Webb.[1] He preferred, however, to say: "It were better that a millstone were put about his neck and he were cast into the deep sea." The statement is probably quite incorrect; the statutory punishment either here or in the next world has probably nothing to do with millstones and so on, but Our Lord was, you see, an Impressionist, and knew His job pretty efficiently. It is probable that He did not have access to as many Blue Books[2] or white papers as the leaders of the Fabian Society,[3] but, from His published utterances, one gathers that He had given a good deal of thought to the subject of children.

I am not in the least joking—and God forbid that I should be thought irreverent because I write like this. The point that I really

---

[1]   Beatrice Potter Webb (1858–1943), English socialist economist.
[2]   Books of sociological statistics.
[3]   Followers of Fabianism.

wish to make is, once again, that—that the Impressionist gives you, as a rule, the fruits of his own observations and the fruits of his own observations alone. He should be in this as severe and as solitary as any monk. It is what he is in the world for. It is, for instance, not so much his business to quote as to state his impressions—that the Holy Scriptures are a good book, or a rotten book, or contain passages of good reading interspersed with dulness; or suggest gems in a cavern, the perfumes of aromatic woods burning in the censers, or the rush of the feet of camels crossing the deep sands, or the shrill of long trumpets borne by archangels—clear sounds of brass like those in that funny passage in *Aïda*.[1]

The passage in prose, however, which I always take as a working model—and in writing this article I am doing no more than showing you the broken tools and bits of oily rag which form my brains, since once again I must disclaim writing with any authority on Impressionism—this passage in prose occurs in a story by de Maupassant called "La Reine Hortense."[2] I spent, I suppose, a great part of ten years in grubbing up facts about Henry VIII. I worried about his parentage, his diseases, the size of his shoes, the price he gave for kitchen implements, his relation to his wives, his knowledge of music, his proficiency with the bow. I amassed, in short, a great deal of information about Henry VIII. I wanted to write a long book about him, but Mr. Pollard,[3] of the British Museum, got the commission and wrote the book probably much more soundly. I then wrote three long novels all about that Defender of the Faith. But I really know—so delusive are reported facts—nothing whatever. Not one single thing! Should I have found affable, or terrifying, or seductive, or royal, or courageous? There are so many contradictory facts; there are so many reported interviews, each contradicting the other, so that really all that I *know* about this king could be reported in the words of Maupassant, which, as I say, I always consider as a working model. Maupassant is introducing one of his characters, who is possibly gross, commercial, overbearing, insolent; who eats, possibly, too much greasy food; who wears commonplace clothes—a gentleman about whom you might write volumes if you wanted to give the facts of his existence. But all that

---

[1] *Aïda* (1871), opera by Italian composer Giuseppe Verdi (1813–1901).

[2] Short story published by Guy de Maupassant (1850–93) in 1883.

[3] Albert Frederick Pollard (1869–1948); his biography of Henry VIII was published in 1902.

de Maupassant finds it necessary to say is: "C'était un monsieur à favoris rouges qui entrait toujours le premier."

And that is all that I *know* about Henry VIII.—that he was a gentleman with red whiskers who always went first through a door.

III

Let us now see how things work out in practice. I have a certain number of maxims, gained mostly in conversation with Mr. Conrad, which form my working stock-in-trade. I stick to them pretty generally; sometimes I throw them out of the window and just write whatever comes. But the effect is usually pretty much the same. I guess I must be fairly well drilled by this time and function automatically, as the Americans say. The first two of my maxims are these:

Always consider the impressions that you are making upon the mind of the reader, and always consider that the first impression with which you present him will be so strong that it will be all that you can ever do to efface it, to alter it or even quite slightly to modify it. Maupassant's gentleman with red whiskers, who always pushed in front of people when it was a matter of going through the doorway, will remain, for the mind of the reader, that man and no other. The impression is as hard and as definite as a tin-tack. And I rather doubt whether, supposing Maupassant represented him afterwards as kneeling on the ground to wipe the tears away from a small child who had lost a penny down a drain—I doubt whether such a definite statement of fact would ever efface the first impression from the reader's mind. They would think that the gentleman with the red whiskers was perpetrating that act of benevolence with ulterior motives—to impress the bystanders, perhaps.

Maupassant, however, uses physical details more usually as a method of introduction of his characters than I myself do. I am inclined myself, when engaged in the seductive occupation, rather to strike the keynote with a speech than a description of personality, or even with an action. And, for that purpose, I should set it down, as a rule, that the first speech of a character you are introducing should always be a generalisation—since generalisations are the really strong indications of character. Putting the matter exaggeratedly, you might say that, if a gentleman sitting opposite you in the train remarked to you: "I see the Tories[1] have won Leith

---

[1] Members of one of England's major political parties who support traditional government and the landed gentry interests.

Boroughs,"[1] you would have practically no guide to that gentleman's character. But, if he said: "Them bloody Unionists[2] have crept into Leith because the Labourites,[3] damn them, have taken away 1,100 votes from us," you would know that the gentleman belonged to a certain political party, had a certain social status, a certain degree of education and a certain amount of impatience.

It is possible that such disquisitions on Impressionism in prose fiction may seem out of place in a journal styled *Poetry and Drama*. But I do not think they are. For Impressionism, differing from other schools of art, is founded so entirely on observation of the psychology of the patron—and the psychology of the patron remains constant. Let me, to make things plainer, present you with a quotation. Sings Tennyson:[4]

> And bats went round in fragrant skies,
> And wheeled or lit the filmy shapes
> That haunt the dusk, with ermine capes
> And wooly breasts and beady eyes.[5]

Now that is no doubt very good natural history, but it is certainly not Impressionism, since no one watching a bat at dusk could see ermine, the wool or the beadiness of the eyes. These things you might read about in books, or observe in the museum or at the Zoological Gardens. Or you might pick up a dead bat upon the road. But to import into the record of observations of one moment the observations of a moment altogether different is not Impressionism. For Impressionism is a thing altogether momentary.

I do not wish to be misunderstood. It is perfectly possible that the remembrance of a former observation may colour your impression of the moment, so that if Tennyson had said:

> And we remembered they have ermine capes,

he would have remained within the canons of Impressionism. But that was not his purpose, which, whatever it was, was no doubt praise-

---

1 Area in southeastern England in the county of Surrey.
2 Supporters of the union of the North of Ireland with the mainland.
3 Members of one of England's political parties who support the interests of the labor movement.
4 Alfred Tennyson (1809–1892), English poet.
5 Tennyson, *In Memoriam* (1850) 45.9–12.

worthy in the extreme, because his heart was pure. It is, however, perfectly possible that a piece of Impressionism should give a sense to two, or three, of as many as you will, places, persons, emotions, all going on simultaneously in the emotions of the writer. It is, I mean, perfectly possible for a sensitised person, be he poet or prose writer, to have the sense, when he is in one room, that he is in another, or when he is speaking to one person he may be so intensely haunted by the memory or desire for another person that he may be absent-minded or distraught. And there is nothing in the canons of Impressionism, as I know it, to stop the attempt to render those superimposed emotions. Indeed, I suppose that Impressionism exists to render those queer effects of real life that are like so many views seen through bright glass— through glass so bright that whilst you perceive through it a landscape or a backyard, you are aware that, on its surface, it reflects a face of a person behind you. For the whole of life is really like that; we are almost always in one place with our minds somewhere quite other.

And it is, I think, only Impressionism that can render that peculiar effect; I know, at any rate, of no other method. It has, this school, in consequence, certain quite strong canons, certain quite rigid unities that must be observed. The point it that any piece of Impressionism, whether it be prose, or verse, or painting, or sculpture, is the record of the impression of a moment; it is not a sort of rounded, annotated record of a set of circumstances—it is the record of the recollection in your mind of a set of circumstances that happened ten years ago— or ten minutes. It might even be the impression of the moment—but it is the impression, not the correlated chronicle. I can make what I mean most clear by a concrete instance.

Thus an Impressionist in a novel, or in a poem, will never render a long speech of one of his characters verbatim, because the mind of the reader would at once lose some of the illusion of the good faith of the narrator. The mind of the reader will say: "Hullo, this fellow is faking this. He cannot possibly remember such a long speech word for word." The Impressionist, therefore, will only record his impression of a long speech. If you will try to remember what remains in your mind of long speeches you heard yesterday, this afternoon or five years ago, you will see what I mean. If to-day, at lunch at your club, you heard an irascible member making a long speech about the fish, what you remember will not be his exact words. However much his proceedings will have amused you, you will not remember his exact words. What you will remember is that he said that the sole was not a sole, but a blank, blank, blank plaice;[1] that the cook ought to be shot, by God he ought to be shot. The plaice had been out of the water two years, and it had been caught in a drain: all that there was of Dieppe[2] about this Sole Dieppoise[3] was something that you cannot remember. You will remember this gentleman's starting eyes, his grunts between words, that he was fond of saying "damnable, damnable, damnable." You will also remember that the man at the same table with you was talking about morals, and that your boots were too tight, whilst you were trying, in your under mind, to arrange a meeting with some lady....

So that, if you had to render that scene or those speeches for purposes of fiction, you would not give a word for word re-invention of sustained sentences from the gentleman who was dissatisfied; or if you were going to invent that scene, you would not so invent those speeches and set them down with all panoply of inverted commas, notes of exclamation. No, you would give an impression of the whole thing, of the snorts, of the characteristic exclamation, of your friend's disquisition on morals, a few phrases of which you would intersperse into the monologue of the gentleman dissatisfied with his sole. And you would give a sense that your feet were burning, and that the lady you wanted to meet had very clear and candid eyes. You would give a little description of her hair....

In that way you would attain to the sort of odd vibration that scenes in real life really have; you would give your reader the impression that he was witnessing something real, that he was passing through an experience ... You will observe also that you will have produced something that is very like a Futurist[4] picture—not a Cubist picture, but one of those canvases that show you in one corner a pair of stays, in another a bit of the foyer of a music hall, in another a fragment of early morning landscape, and in the middle a pair of eyes, the whole bearing the title of "A Night Out." And, indeed, those Futurists are only trying to render on canvas what Impressionists *tel que moi*[5] have been trying to render for many years. (You may remember Emma's love scene at the cattle show in *Madame Bovary*.)[6]

---

1   A large European flounder.
2   French town at the mouth of the Arques River on the English Channel.
3   Variety of fish associated with the Normandy region of the English Channel.
4   Futurism, an Italian school of painting, sculpture, and literature that resonated from the early twentieth century through the end of World War I.
5   Such as me.
6   Realist novel published by Flaubert in 1856.

Do not, I beg you, be led away by the English reviewer's cant phrase to the effect that the Futurists are trying to be literary and the plastic arts can never be literary. Les Jeunes[1] of to-day are trying all sorts of experiments, in all sorts of media. And they are perfectly right to be trying them.

IV

I have been trying to think what are the objections to Impressionism as I understand it—or rather what alternative method could be found. It seems to me that one is an Impressionist because one tries to produce an illusion of reality—or rather the business of Impressionism is to produce that illusion. The subject is one enormously complicated and is full of negatives. Thus the Impressionist author is sedulous to avoid letting his personality appear in the course of his book. On the other hand, his whole book, his whole poem is merely an expression of his personality. Let me illustrate exactly what I mean. You set out to write a story, or you set out to write a poem, and immediately your attempt becomes one creating an illusion. You attempt to involve the reader amongst the personages of the story or in the atmosphere of the poem. You do this by presentation and by presentation and again by presentation. The moment you depart from presentation, the moment you allow yourself, as a poet, to introduce the ejaculation:

O Muse Pindarian,[2] aid me to my theme;

Or the moment that, as a story-teller, you permit yourself the luxury of saying:

Now, gentle reader, is my heroine not a very sweet and oppressed lady?—

At that very moment your reader's illusion that he is present at an affair in real life or that he has been transported by your poem into an atmosphere entirely other than that of his arm-chair or his chim-

---

[1] The youth.
[2] The act of summoning the Greek lyric poet Pindar (c.518–c.438 B.C.), as a muse of poetic inspiration.

ney-corner—at that very moment that illusion will depart. Now the point is this:

The other day I was discussing these matters with a young man whose avowed intention is to sweep away Impressionism. And, after I had energetically put before him the views that I have here expressed, he simply remarked: "Why try to produce an illusion?" To which I could only reply: "Why then write?"

I have asked myself frequently since then why one should try to produce an illusion of reality in the mind of one's readers. Is it just an occupation like any other—like postage-stamp collecting, let us say—or is it the sole end and aim of art? I have spent the greater portion of my working life in preaching that particular doctrine: is it possible, then, that I have been entirely wrong?

Of course it is possible for any man to be entirely wrong; but I confess myself to being as yet uncovered. The chief argument of my futurist friend was that producing an illusion causes the writer so much trouble as not to be worth while. That does not seem to me to be an argument worth very much because—and again I must say it seems to me—the business of an artist is surely to take trouble, but this is probably doing my friend's position, if not his actual argument, an injustice. I am aware that there are quite definite aesthetic objections to the business of producing an illusion. In order to produce an illusion you must justify; in order to justify you must introduce a certain amount of matter that may not appear germane to your story or to your poem. Sometimes, that is to say, it would appear as if for the purpose of the proper bringing out of every slight Impressionist sketch the artist would need an altogether disproportionately enormous frame; a frame absolutely monstrous. Let me again illustrate exactly what I mean. It is not sufficient to say: "Mr. Jones was a gentleman who had a strong aversion to rabbit-pie." It is not sufficient, that is to say, if Mr. Jones's dislike for rabbit-pie is an integral part of your story. And it is quite possible that a dislike for one form or other of food might form the integral part of a story. Mr. Jones might be a hard-working coal-miner with a well-meaning wife, whom he disliked because he was developing a passion for a frivolous girl. And it might be quite possible that one evening the well-meaning wife, not knowing her husband's peculiarities, but desiring to give him a special and extra treat, should purchase from a stall a couple of rabbits and spend many hours in preparing for him a pie of great succulence, which should be a solace to him when he returns, tired with his labours and rendered nervous by his growing passion for the other lady. The rabbit-pie would then become a symbol—a symbol of the whole tragedy of life. It would symbolize for Mr. Jones the whole of his wife's want of sympathy for him and the whole of his distaste for her; his reception of it would symbolize for Mrs. Jones the hopelessness of her life, since she had expended upon it inventiveness, sedulous care, sentiment, and a good will. From that position, with the rabbit-pie always in the centre of the discussion, you might work up the murder of Mrs. Jones, to Mr. Jones's elopement with the other lady—to any tragedy that you liked. For indeed the position contains, as you will perceive, the whole tragedy of life.

And the point is this, that if your tragedy is to be absolutely convincing, it is not sufficient to introduce the fact of Mr. Jones's dislike for rabbit-pie by the bare statement. According to your temperament you must sufficiently account of that dislike. You might do it by giving Mr. Jones a German grandmother, since all Germans have a peculiar loathing for the rabbit and regard its flesh as unclean. You might then find it necessary to account for the dislike the Germans have for these creatures; you might have to state that his dislike is a self-preservative race instinct, since in Germany the rabbit is apt to eat certain poisonous fungi, so that one out of every ten will cause the death of its consumer, or you might proceed with your justification of Mr. Jones's dislike for rabbits along different lines. You might say that it was a nervous aversion caused by having been violently thrashed when a boy by his father at a time when a rabbit-pie was upon the table. You might then have to go on to justify the nervous temperament of Mr. Jones by saying that his mother drank or that his father was a man too studious in his position. You might have to pursue almost endless studies in the genealogy of Mr. Jones; because, of course, you might want to account for the studiousness of Mr. Jones's father by making him the bastard son of a clergyman, and then you might want to account for the libidinous habits of the clergyman in question. That will be simply a matter of artistic conscience.

You have to make Mr. Jones's dislike for rabbits convincing. You have to make it in the first place convincing to your reader alone; but the odds are that you will try to make it convincing also to yourself, since you yourself in this solitary world of ours will be the only reader that you really and truly know. Now all these attempts at justification, all these details of parentage and the like, may very well prove uninteresting to your reader. They are, however, necessary if your final effect of murder is to be a convincing impression.

But again, if the final province of art is to convince, its first province is to interest. So that, to the extent that your justification is uninteresting, it is an artistic defect. It may sound paradoxical, but the truth is that your Impressionist can only get his strongest effects by using beforehand a great deal of what one may call non-Impressionism. He will make, that is to say, an enormous impression on his reader's mind by the use of three words. But very likely each one of those three words will be prepared for by ten thousand other words. Now are we to regard those other words as being entirely unnecessary, as being, that is to say, so many artistic defects? That I take to be my futurist friend's ultimate assertion.

Says he: "All these elaborate conventions of Conrad or of Maupassant give the reader the impression that a story is being told—all these meetings of bankers and master-mariners in places like the Ship Inn at Greenwich,[1] and all Maupassant's dinner-parties, always in the politest circles, where a countess and a fashionable doctor or someone relates a passionate or a pathetic or a tragic or a merely grotesque incident—as you have it, for instance, in the 'Contes de la Bécasse'[2]—all this machinery for getting a story told is so much waste of time. A story is a story; why not just tell it any how? You can never tell what sort of an impression you will produce upon a reader. Then why bother about Impressionism? Why not just chance your luck?"

There is a good deal to be said for this point of view. Writing up my own standards is such an intolerable labour and such a thankless job, since it can't give me the one thing in the world that I desire—that for my part I am determined to drop creative writing for good and all. But I, like all writers in my generation, have been so handicapped that there is small wonder that one should be tired out. On the one hand the difficulty of getting hold of any critical guidance was, when I was a boy, insuperable. There was nothing. Criticism was non-existent; self-conscious art was decried; you were supposed to write by inspiration; you were the young generation with the vine-leaves in

---

[1]   Outer borough of London, as well as the origin of Greenwich Mean (or Meridian) Time; it is the home of the Royal Observatory, which is located on the prime meridian.

[2]   Short story by de Maupassant published in 1882.

your hair, knocking furiously at the door. On the other hand, one writes for money, for fame, to excite the passion of love, and one's time continues to be singularly unimpressed.

But young writers to-day have a much better chance, on the aesthetic side at least. Here and there, in nooks and corners, they can find someone to discuss their work, not from the point of view of goodness or badness or of niceness or of nastiness, but from the simple point of view of expediency. The moment you can say: "It is expedient to print *vers libre*[1] in long or short lines, or in the form of prose, or not to print it at all, but to recite it?"—the moment you can find someone to discuss these expediencies calmly, or the moment that you can find someone with whom to discuss the relative values of justifying your character or of abandoning the attempt to produce an illusion of reality—at that moment you are very considerably helped; whereas an admirer of your work might fall down and kiss your feet and it would not be of the very least use to you.

V

This adieu,[2] like Herrick's, to poesy, may seem to be digression. Indeed it is; and indeed it isn't. It is, that is to say, a digression in the sense that it is a statement not immediately germane to the argument that I am carrying on. But it is none the less an insertion fully in accord with the canons of Impressionism as I understand it. For the first business of Impressionism is to produce an impression, and the only way in literature to produce an impression is to awaken interest. And, in a sustained argument, you can only keep interest awakened by keeping alive, by whatever means you may have at your disposal, the surprise of your reader. You must state your argument; you must illustrate it, and then you must stick something that appears to have nothing whatever to do with either subject or illustration, so that the reader will exclaim: "What the devil is the fellow driving at?" And then you must go on in the same way—arguing, illustrating and startling and arguing, startling and illustrating—until at the very end your contentions will appear like a ravelled skein. And then, in the last few lines, you will draw towards you the master-string of that seeming confusion, and the whole pattern of the carpet, the whole design of the net-work will be apparent.

---

[1]   Free verse.
[2]   Farewell.

This method, you will observe, founds itself upon analysis of the human mind. For no human being likes listening to long and sustained arguments. Such listening is an effort, and no artist has the right to call for any effort from his audience. A picture should come out of its frame and seize the spectator.

Let us now consider the audience to which the artist should address himself. Theoretically a writer should be like the Protestant angel, a messenger of peace and goodwill towards men. But, inasmuch as the Wingless Victory[1] appears monstrously hideous to Hottentot,[2] and a beauty of Tunis[3] detestable to the inhabitants of these fortunate islands, it is obvious that each artist must adopt a frame of mind, less Catholic possibly, but certainly more Papist, and address himself, like the angel of the vulgate, only *hominibus bonae voluntatis*.[4] He must address himself to such men as be of goodwill; that is to say, he must typify for himself a human soul in sympathy with his own; a silent listener who will be attentive to him, and whose mind acts very much as his species, so will be the measure of his temporal greatness. That is why a book, to be really popular, must be either extremely good or extremely bad. For Mr. Hall Caine[5] has millions of readers; but then Guy de Maupassant and Flaubert have tens of millions.

I suppose the proposition might be put in another way. Since the great majority of mankind are, on the surface, vulgar and trivial—the stuff to fill graveyards—the great majority of mankind will be easily and quickly affected by art which is vulgar and trivial. But, inasmuch as this world is a very miserable purgatory for most of us sons of men—who remain stuff with which graveyards are filled—inasmuch as horror, despair and incessant striving are the lot of the most trivial humanity, who endure them as a rule with commonsense and cheerfulness—so, if a really great master strike the note of horror, of despair, of striving, and so on, he will stir chords in the hearts of a larger number of people than those who are moved by the merely vulgar and the merely trivial. This is probably why *Madame Bovary* has sold more copies than any book ever published, except, of course, books purely religious. But the appeal of religious books is exactly similar.

---

[1] In Greek mythology, Athena Nike is the Goddess of Victory.
[2] A group of people indigenous to southern Africa.
[3] Capital of Tunisia.
[4] Men of goodwill.
[5] Sir Thomas Henry Hall Caine (1853–1931), English novelist.

It may be said that the appeal of *Madame Bovary* is largely sexual. So it is, but it is only the countries like England and the United States that the abominable tortures of sex—or, if you will, the abominable interests of sex—are not supposed to take rank alongside of the horrors of lost honour, commercial ruin, or death itself. For all these things are the components of life, and each is of equal importance.

So, since Flaubert is read in Russia, in Germany, in France, in the United States, amongst the non-Anglo-Saxon population, and by the immense populations of South America, he may be said to have taken for his audience the whole of the world that could possibly be expected to listen to a man of his race. (I except, of course, the Anglo-Saxons who cannot be confidentially expected to listen to anything other than the words produced by Mr. George Edwardes,[1] and musical comedy in general.)

My futurist friend again visited me yesterday, and we discussed this very question of audiences. Here again he said that I was entirely wrong. He said that an artist should not address himself to *l'homme moyen sensuel*,[2] but to intellectuals, to people who live at Hampstead and wear no hats. (He withdrew his contention later.)

I maintain on my own side that one should address oneself to the cabmen round the corner, but this also is perhaps an exaggeration. My friend's contention on behalf of the intellectuals was not so much due to his respect for their intellects. He said that they knew the A B C of an art, and that it is better to address yourself to an audience entirely untrammelled by such knowledge. In this I think he was wrong, for the intellectuals are persons of very conventional mind, and they acquire as a rule simultaneously with the A B C of any art the knowledge of so many conventions that it is almost impossible to make any impression upon their minds. Hampstead and the hatless generally offer an impervious front to futurism, simply because they have imbibed from Whistler[3] and the Impressionists the contention that painting should not be literary. Now every futurist picture tells a story; so that rules out futurism. Similarly with the cubists. Hampstead has imbibed, from God knows where, the dogma that all art should be based on life, or should at least draw its inspiration and its strength from the representation of nature. So there

---

[1] George Edwardes (1855–1915), British theatre producer.
[2] The average sensual man.
[3] James Abbot McNeill Whistler (1834–1903), American artist and portraitist.

goes cubism, since cubism is non-representational, but has nothing to do with life, and has a quite proper contempt of nature.

When I produced my argument that one should address oneself to the cabmen at the corner, my futurist friend at once flung to me the jeer about Tolstoi[1] and the peasant. Now the one sensible thing in the long drivel of nonsense with which Tolstoi misled this dull world was the remark that art should be addressed to the peasant. My futurist friend said that that was sensible for an artist living in Russia or Roumania, but it was an absurd remark to be let fall by a critic living in Campden Hill.[2] His view was that you cannot address yourself to the peasant unless that peasant has evoked folk-song or folk-lores. I don't know why that was his view, but that was his view.

It seems to me to be nonsensical, even if the inner meaning of his dictum was that art should be addressed to a community of practicing artists. Art, in fact, should be addressed to those who are not preoccupied. It is senseless to address Cervantes[3] to a man who is going mad with love, and an Imagiste poem will produce little effect upon another man who is going through the bankruptcy court.

It is probable that Tolstoi thought that in Russia the non-preoccupied mind was to be found solely amongst the peasant class, and that is why he said that works of art should be addressed to the peasant. I don't know how it may be in Russia, but certainly in Occidental Europe the non-preoccupied mind—which is the same thing as the peasant intelligence—is to be found scattered throughout every grade of society. When I used just now the instances of a man mad for love, or distracted by the prospect of personal ruin, I was purposely misleading. For a man mad as a hatter for love of a worthless creature, or a man maddened by the tortures of bankruptcy, by dishonour or by failure, may yet have, by the sheer necessity of his nature, a mind more receptive than most other minds. The mere craving for relief from his personal thoughts may make him take quite unusual interest in a work of art. So that is not preoccupation in my intended sense, but for a moment the false statement crystallised quite clearly what I was aiming at.

The really impassible mind is not the mind quickened by passion, but the mind rendered slothful by preoccupation purely trivial. The

---

[1]   Count Lev Nikolayevich Tolstoi (1828–1910), Russian novelist and philosopher.

[2]   Area of London where Ford lived before and during World War I.

[3]   Miguel de Cervantes Saavedra (1547–1616), Spanish novelist, dramatist, and poet.

"English gentleman" is, for instance, an absolutely hopeless being from this point of view. His mind is so taken up by considerations of what is good form, of what is good feeling, of what is even good fellowship; he is so concerned to pass unnoticed in the crowd; he is so set upon having his room like everyone else's room, that he will find it impossible to listen to any plea for art which is exceptional, vivid, or startling. The cabman, on the other hand, does not mind being thought a vulgar sort of bloke; in consequence, he will form a more possible sort of audience. On the other hand, amongst the purely idler classes it is perfectly possible to find individuals who are so firmly and titularly gentle folk that they don't have to care a damn what they do. These again are possible audiences for the artist. The point is really, I take it, that the preoccupation that is fatal to art is the moral or the social preoccupation. Actual preoccupations matter very little. Your cabman may drive his taxi through exceedingly difficult streets; he may have half-a-dozen close shaves in a quarter of an hour. But when those things are over they are over; and he has not the necessity of a cabman. His point of view as to what is art, good form, or, let us say, the proper relation of the sexes, is unaffected. He may be a hungry man, a thirsty man, or even a tired man, but he will not hold as aesthetic dogma the idea that no painting must tell a story, or the moral dogma that passion only becomes respectable when you have killed it.

It is these accursed dicta[1] that render an audience hopeless to the artist, that render art a useless pursuit and the artist himself a despised individual.

So that those are the best individuals for an artist's audience who have least listened to accepted ideas—who are acquainted with deaths at street corners, with the marital infidelities of crowded courts, with the goodness of heart of the criminal, with the meanness of the undetected or the sinless, who know the queer old jumble of negatives that forms our miserable and hopeless life. If I had to choose as a reader I would rather have one who had never read anything before but the Newgate Calendar,[2] or the records of crime, starvation and divorce in the Sunday paper—I would rather have him for a reader than a man who had discovered the song that the sirens sang, or had by heart the whole of the *Times Literary Supplement*,[3] from its inception to the

---

[1] Formal pronouncements of principles, propositions, or opinions.

[2] *Newgate Calendar and the Divorce Court Chronicle* (1872).

[3] Established in 1902, the *Times Literary Supplement* reviews contemporary developments in literature, politics, scholarship, and the arts.

present day. Such a peasant intelligence will know that this is such a queer world that anything may be possible. And that is the type of intelligence that we need.

Of course, it is more difficult to find these intelligences in the town than in the rural districts. A man thatching all day long has time for many queer thoughts; so has a man who from sunrise to sunset is trimming a hedge into shape with a bagging hook. I have, I suppose, myself thought more queer thoughts when digging potatoes than at any other time during my existence. It is, for instance, when it has grown cool after a very hot day, to thrust your hand into the earth after a potato and to find that the earth is quite warm—is about flesh-heat. Of course, the clods would be warm because the sun would have been shining on them all day, and the air gives up its heat much quicker than the earth. But it is none the less a queer sensation.

Now, if the person experiencing that sensation has what I call a peasant intelligence, he will just say that it is a queer thing and will store it away in his mind along with his other experiences. It will go along with the remembrance of hard frost, of fantastic icicles, the death of rabbits pursued by stoats, the singularly quick ripening of corn in a certain year, the fact that such and such a man was overlooked by a wise woman and so died because, his wife, being tired of him, had paid the wise woman five sixpences which she had laid upon the table in the form of a crown; or along with the other fact that a certain man murdered his wife by the use of a packet of sheep dip which he had stolen from a field where the farmer was employed at lamb washing. All these remembrances he will have in his mind, not classified under any headings of social reformers, or generalised so as to fulfill a fancied moral law.

But the really dangerous person for the artists will be the gentleman who, chancing to put his hand into the ground and to find it about as warm as the breast of a woman, if you could thrust your hand between her chest and her stays, will not accept the experience as an experience, but will start talking about the breast of mother-nature. This last man is the man whom the artist should avoid since he will regard phenomena not as phenomena, but as happenings, with which he may back up preconceived dogmas—as, in fact, so many sticks with which to beat a dog.

No, what the artist needs is the man with the virgin mind—the man who will not insist that grass must always be painted green, because all the poets, from Chaucer[1] till present day, had insisted on talking about the green grass, or the green leaves, or the green straw.

Such a man, if he comes to your picture and sees you have painted a haycock bright purple will say:

"Well, I have never myself observed a haycock to be purple, but I can understand that if the sky is very blue and the sun is setting very red, the shady side of the haycock might well appear to be purple." That is the kind of peasant intelligence that the artist needs for his audience.

And the whole of Impressionism comes to this: having realized that the audience to which you will address yourself must have this particular peasant intelligence, or, if you prefer it, this particular and virgin openness of mind, you will then figure to yourself and individual, a silent listener, who shall be to yourself the *homo bonae voluntatis*—man of goodwill. To him, then, you will address your picture, your poem, your prose story, or your argument. You will seek to capture his interest; you will seek to hold his interest. You will do this by methods of surprise, of fatigue, by passages of sweetness in your language, by passages suggesting the sudden and brutal shock of suicide. You will give him passages of dullness, so that your bright effects may seem more bright; you will alternate, you will dwell for a long time upon an intimate point; you will seek to exasperate so that you may the better enchant. You will, in short, employ all the devices of the prostitute. If you are too proud for this you may be the better gentleman or the better lady, but you will be the worse artist. For the artist must always be humble and humble and again humble, since before the greatness of his task he himself is nothing. He must again be outrageous, since the greatness of his task calls for enormous excesses by means of which he may recoup his energies. That is why the artist is, quite rightly, regarded with suspicion by people who desire to live in tranquil and ordered society.

But one point is very important. The artist can never write to satisfy himself—to get, as the saying is, something off the chest. He must not write rolling periods, the production of which gives him a soothing feeling in his digestive organs or wherever it is. He must write always so as to satisfy that other fellow—that other fellow who has too clear an intelligence to let his attention be captured or his mind deceived by special pleadings in favour of any given dogma.

---

[1] Geoffrey Chaucer (c.1340–1400), English poet and the author of *The Canterbury Tales*.

You must not write so as to improve him, since he is a much better fellow than yourself, and you must not write so as to influence him, since he is granite rock, a peasant intelligence, the gnarled bole[1] of a sempiternal[2] oak, against which you will dash yourself in vain. It is in short no pleasant kind of job to be a conscious artist. You won't have any vine-leaves in your poor old hair; you won't just dash your quill into an inexhaustible ink-well and pour fine frenzies. No, you will be just the skilled workman doing his job with drill or chisel or mallet. And you will get precious little out of it. Only, just at times, when you come to look again at some work of yours that you have quite forgotten, you will say, "Why, that is rather well done." That is all.

---

[1] Trunk.
[2] Everlasting.

Appendix D: Contemporary Reviews

1. Rebecca West, "Mr. Hueffer's New Novel" (*Daily News and Leader*, 2 April 1915)

Mr. Ford Madox Hueffer is the Scholar Gipsy[1] of English letters: he is the author who is recognised only as he disappears round the corner. It is impossible for anybody with any kind of sense about writing to miss some sort of distant apprehension of the magnificence of his work: but unfortunately this apprehension usually takes the form of enthusiastic but unrelated discoveries of work that he left on the doorstep ten years ago.

The Good Soldier will put an end to any such sequestration of Mr. Hueffer's wealth. For it is as impossible to miss the light of its extreme beauty and wisdom as it would be to miss the full moon on a clear night. Its first claim on the attention is the obvious loveliness of the colour and cadence of its language: and it is also clever as the novels of Mr. Henry James are clever, with all sorts of acute discoveries about human nature, and at times it is radiantly witty. And behind these things there is the delight of a noble and ambitious design, and behind that, again, there is the thing we call inspiration—a force of passion which so sustains the story in its flight that never once does it appear as the work of a man's invention. It is because of that union of inspiration and the finest technique that this story, this close and relentless recital of how the good soldier struggled from the mere clean innocence which was the most his class could expect of him to the knowledge of love, can bear up under the vastness of its subject. For the subject is, one realises when one has come to the end of this saddest story, much vaster than one had imagined that any story about well-bred people, who live in sunny houses; with deer in the park, and play polo, and go to Nauheim for the cure, could possibly contain.

It is the record of the spiritual life of Edward Ashburnham, who was a large, fair person of the governing class, with an entirely deceptive appearance of being just the kind of person he looked. It was his misfortune that he had brought to the business of landowning a fatal touch of imagination which made him believe it his duty to be "an

---

[1] Allusion to "The Scholar-Gipsy" (c.1851), an elegaic poem by Matthew Arnold.

overlord doing his best by his dependents, the dependents meanwhile doing their best by the overlord"; to make life splendid and noble and easier for everybody by his government. And since this ideal meant that he became in his way a creative artist, he began to feel the desire to go to some woman for "moral support, the encouragement, the relief from the sense of loneliness, the assurance of his own worth." And although Leonora, his wife, was fine and proud, a Northern light among women, she simply could not understand that marriage meant anything but an appearance of loyalty before the world and the efficient management of one's husband's estate. She "had a vague sort of idea that, to a man, all women are the same after three weeks of close intercourse. She thought that the kindness should no longer appeal, the soft and mournful voice no longer thrill, the tall darkness no longer give a man the illusion that he was going into the depths of an unexplored wood." And so poor Edward walked the world starved.

His starvation leads him into any number of gentle, innocent, sentimental passions: it delivers him over as the prey of a terrible and wholly credible American, a cold and controlled egoist who reads like the real truth about an Anne Douglas Sedgwick[1] or Edith Wharton[2] heroine. And meanwhile his wife becomes embittered by what she considers as an insane, and possibly rather nasty, obsession, that she loses her pride and her nobility and becomes, in that last hour when Edward has found a real passion, so darkly, subtly treacherous that he and the quite innocent young girl whom he loves are precipitated down into the blackest tragedy. All three are lost: and perhaps Leonora, robbed of her fineness, is most of all.

And when one has come to the end of this beautiful and moving story it is worth while reading the book over again simply to observe the wonders of its technique. Mr. Hueffer has used the device, invented and used successfully by Mr. Henry James, and used not nearly so credibly by Mr. Conrad, of presenting the story not as it appeared to a divine and omnipresent intelligence, but as it was observed by some intervener not too intimately concerned in the plot. It is a device that always breaks down at the great moment, when the revelatory detail must be given; but it has the great advantage of setting the tone of the prose from the beginning to the end. And out of the leisured colloquialism of the gentle American who

---

[1]   Anne Douglas Sedgwick (1873–1935), an expatriate American writer.
[2]   Edith Wharton (1862–1937), American author of *The Age of Innocence* (1920).

tells the story Mr. Hueffer has made a prose that falls on the page like sunlight. It has the supreme triumph of art, that effect of effortlessness and inevitableness, which Mengs[1] described when he said that one of Velazquez's[2] pictures seemed to be painted not by the hand but by pure thought. Indeed, this is a much, much better book than any of us deserve.

2. "Current Literature" (*Daily Telegraph*, 16 April 1915)

This singular novel is a feather of a new sort for Mr. Ford Madox Hueffer's cap. In *The Good Soldier* there is the excellent writing, the play of imagination, the delicate attention to character, that holds the mind in all his best work; and there is a strange, tragic atmosphere, not like the tragic atmosphere he has created in other books. This is a story of two modern married couples, wealthy and unoccupied; "the saddest story I have ever heard" is what one of the husbands, the supposed writer of the book, calls it. He is a gentle-spirited native of Philadelphia, not fond of the country from which he draws his inherited wealth, and he alone retains one's sympathy to the last. The other husband's the "good soldier," Captain Ashburnham, a pattern English gentleman and sportsman, a kind landlord, a brave man, a finished type of British aristocrat, drawn by the loving hand of an American of leisure. The Captain's wife is of his own stamp, the American wife is a brilliant creature with a college degree; and among these four there grows up an intrigue. Only a reader with a considerable experience of the fiction of irregular amours could read this novel to the end without being more than a little nauseated. Mr. Hueffer has set himself to show that a man as perfect in every outward detail of appearance and conduct as his "good soldier" can be the helpless slave of a sentimental, erotic temper. On the other hand, there is an apparently passionless woman, who is a cold sensualist in reality. Mr. Hueffer's way of telling his tale has an attractive quality of discursiveness, which would be novel if Mr. Joseph Conrad had not written his reminiscences. One never knows into what by-path his American first-person-singular is going to wander next; but they all lead somewhere that matters in connection with the story. There is great art in the way in which the reader is gradually brought

---

[1] Anton Raphael Mengs (1728–1779), German neo-classical portraitist.
[2] Diego Velázquez (1599–1660), baroque Spanish painter.

to realise the truth about each of the four "nice people" of the book; one must, however, add that it is an art which would not naturally be practised by the simple-souled Mr. Dowell of Philadelphia, Pa. The whole novel is a frankly and uncompromisingly unpleasant treatment of a tragic subject.

3. "New Novels" (*Illustrated London News*, 24 April 1915)

We doubt if anyone since Mr. Henry James's Maisie[1] has sat on the outside looking as tragically at the inside of things as the man-mouthpiece of Mr. Ford Madox Hueffer's new novel *The Good Soldier* (The Bodley Head). This, of course, is exactly how such things do happen to the puppet of other people's destinies, and exactly how they appear to him when, in the abomination of the after-desolation, he remains gazing, brooding upon a world shattered at his feet. There is the incredible contrast between the outward composure of men and women of breeding and the inner upheaval, the shock of the impossibly obscene made manifest. While it was going on under his eyes he never knew.... Afterwards, it appears, he is never to know anything else. His best friend, the fine fellow, the Good Soldier, must be a libertine scattering havoc in the lives of decent women; his wife, whom his American respect of the sex guards like a queen in her sickroom—his wife is vile, has always been vile, smirches even the stained scutcheon of the unstable Soldier. And they are both such "nice" people! And the Good Soldier is simply a splendid person, who dies of his last and greatest love-affair, dies of its unfulfillment; while the girl who loved him goes mad, and the wife who loved him too, with the fierce, jealous love of her magnificent womanhood, strikes at them both, and, less happy than they, goes on living. The psychological interest of the book is intense. We read it once, and then went back to the beginning to read it again. That is the way it took us. It is a fine piece of work, *The Good Soldier*.

4. C. E. Lawrence, "Passion and People: The Old Story in New Settings" (*Daily Chronicle*, 28 April 1915)

If the fortune of a novel were commensurate with its art, then would Mr. Hueffer's *The Good Soldier* march away with bags of shekels,

---

[1]   Protagonist in Henry James's novel, *What Maisie Knew* (1897).

whereas its very cleverness and subtly will probably undo it, and cause it to be less popular than Sir Gilbert Parker's[1] easier effort.

Both the books tell tales of marriage tangles, and Mr. Hueffer's tangle is so involved that many readers will probably think it not worth the unravelling. Any such decision would, however, be an unfairness and unwise, for, with all its unpleasantness, it is as cleverly told a story as has been printed for months. The effectiveness of the book is in the telling, with its suggestions, its implications, and the light and airy, cold and passionless manner in which a deadly story is unfolded. The design of the book is bold. Two couples stay regularly year after year at a Swiss sanatorium, and the husband of the one happy pair makes free with the wife of the other. It is the cuckold—to use an old, expressive word which false shamefacedness should not be permitted to suppress—who tells the so-called sad story in a cold-blooded manner reminiscent of the ways and works of the Borgias,[2] the Medici,[3] and other such magnificent wrong-doers, who could kiss and slay, smile and at the same time poison. Put down into plain print, the results are preposterous. Of the five persons most concerned, two commit suicide and one goes incurably mad. As horrible as a pre-Shakespearean Elizabethan tragedy; and yet so deftly and artfully is the tale narrated that we read of these deaths and misadventures as if they were the misfortunes of mice and rabbits. *The Good Soldier* is an ill-named, clever book, but we should have admired it more had Mr. Hueffer put a little more force and energy into its smooth passages.

5. R. A. Scott-James, "Men and Books: A Weekly Review" (*Land and Water*, 1 May 1915)

It is to be hoped that Mr. Hueffer's book about Germany, which I reviewed last month, will not divert attention from this novel, the best that he has ever written. Many writers could have produced an equally effective book about Germany, but very few could have written so brilliant a novel. It is not in the least like anything he has written

---

[1]   Sir Gilbert Parker (1862–1932), Canadian novelist. In addition to *The Good Soldier*, Lawrence reviewed *You Never Know Your Luck: Being the Story of a Matrimonial Deserted*.

[2]   Notorious family whose influence—often exerted through a strange combination of murder, greed, and piety—found its way into the upper echelons of power in Italy, Spain, and France from the fourteenth through the fifteenth centuries.

[3]   Powerful Italian family who dominated Florentine politics for two and a half centuries.

before, except in the matter of prose style. It is very far removed from the romantic, historical novels which first brought him into general notice. It also goes far beyond his other, more tentative novels of modern life, in which the satire has sometimes been too much for the situation, the interest flagging from sheer insufficiency of subject-matter. But here he has taken a situation, complex enough, and has completely mastered it. His long admiration for Mr. Henry James has had its effects upon his style and method. But he is never betrayed into obscurity. He has not unfolded his story by recording incident after incident, following in the order of time. It is doubtful if his effect could have been got by that method. It is a "situation" that he is describing, explaining; and a situation in which impulse, training, passion and morality are all at loggerheads, has many aspects; it must be shown from different angles; new incidents will be recalled which throw light on the tangle. Mr. Hueffer begins the tale as if he was sitting down one evening with a friend, to tell him, in the outline, the gist of a perplexing and tragic affair; and he continues it as if he were resuming the conversation, explaining the whole tissue of unhappy errors as this and that occurs to him to clear up the mystery. He has, in fact, arranged the story with consummate art. He has taken a few rather ordinary people, and out of their little emotions and entanglements, and just one real outburst of passion, he has created a tragedy.

It has all been done deftly, with great calm and detachment. The story is supposed to be told by an American, a cold-blooded creature, whose main business is to tell the tale and to have a pretty, nasty, mean, sententious little wife, Florence by name, who allows him to play the part of "nurse" while she keeps up an affair, now with Jimmy, afterwards with Edward Ashburnham.

> She cut out poor dear Edward from sheer vanity; she meddled between him and Leonora from a sheer, imbecile spirit of district visiting. Do you understand that, whilst she was Edward's mistress, she was perpetually trying to reunite him to his wife? She would gabble on to Leonora about forgiveness—treating the subject from the bright, American point of view.

> Leonora, Edward's wife, "desired children, decorum, an establishment; she desired to avoid waste, she desired to keep up appearances." She and her husband were both what this rich and

easy-going American calls "good people." Edward began his married life rather priggishly. He was a personage in his county, a model landlord. "If he played polo and was an excellent dancer he did the one for the sake of keeping himself fit and the other because it was a social duty to show himself at dances, and, when there, to dance well." It is impossible, in the available space, to explain how this instinctively "honourable," clean man, with a "noble" nature was estranged from his economising wife and was led through this love affair and that (including Florence) till everything collapsed in his fatal passion for "the girl"—Nancy Rufford—the strange, quixotic character who flickers in and out of the story till at length she dominates it, as the victim. The conclusion is in this vein:

> Edward was the normal man, but there was too much of the sentimentalist about him and society does not need too many sentimentalists. Nancy was a splendid creature, but she had about her a touch of madness. Society does not need individuals with touches of madness about them. So Edward and Nancy found themselves steam-rollered out and Leonora survives, the perfectly normal type, married to a man who is rather like a rabbit.

A cynical, disagreeable tale, perhaps, but the people stare out from the canvas and caper before us with appalling vitality. Certainly a brilliant achievement.

6. Thomas Seccombe, "*The Good Soldier*" (*New Witness*, 3 June 1915)

This is a novel remarkable alike for its misappropriation of such a title as *The Good Soldier*, its style and its subject-matter or fable. Its style is its most outstanding feature. The story goes along like the wild Whitsun dance of Vianden,[1] four steps forwards and then three back. It is projected along by means of the most curiously colloquial nudges, puffs, shuffles and short rushes. The peculiarity of the style is a studied *negligé*.[2] The author commences rather more consecutive

---

[1] Ceremonial dance held during the Whitsun Catholic holiday week in Vianden, a town in Luxembourg.
[2] Carelessness.

sentences with "and" than has ever been known before. His sentences are dwarfish in length, and sometimes in malignity. He commences again and again with the colloquial "yes" or "well" and ends them with "and all that." Mr. Wells,[1] the George Moore of *Vale* and *Salve*,[2] Henry James, have gone before. Mr. Hueffer combines their manner of hinting and winking with a prodigious nonchalance of his own. But he exaggerates the physical side of life out of all proportion. People have waves of it, but soldiers soon escape the fumes and do not descend so readily to the inferno of caddishness. Florence is cleverly drawn, very. Laura [presumably, Leonora] is a precious fiend. The diablerie[3] might have occurred once, but people could hardly have gone on like that. People in ordinary life manage to forget their disqualifications for a sane existence. To be always harping on them admits a false quantity into a book otherwise penetrating, in many respects original and excessively clever. The dot and dash system justifies itself. Each paragraph ending with a demonstrative. "Well—it was a silly old tune." "Those words were his simple words...." "That was the way it took her." "Poor devil." "I don't know why." "No, she wouldn't have minded." "Of course." "Perhaps she did." "Well, that was a sort of frenzy with me." "Anyhow, Leonora shivered a little as if a goose had walked over her grave. And I was passing her the nickel-silver basket of rolls. Avanti! ...." "And what the devil!" "What a beautiful thing the stone pine is!" "And then...." "No, we never did go back anywhere. Not to Heidelberg, not to Hamelin, not to Verona, not to Mont Majour—not so much as to Carcassonne itself. We talked of it, of course, but I guess Florence got all she wanted out of one look at a place. She had the seeing eye." *Léger de main*;[4] Oscar Wilde![5] But the protagonist of all these eyelash quivers and *demi-sourires*[6] is, of course, Laurence Sterne[7]—creator, too, of *the* good soldier. Perhaps the best ever projected in print. "My Uncle."[8] True, he could not accept the

---

1 Herbert George Wells (1866–1946), English science-fiction author.
2 George Moore (1852–1933), English author; *Salve* and *Vale* are, respectively, the second and third volumes in his fictionalized autobiography, *Hail and Farewell: A Trilogy* (1911–1914).
3 Devilry, sorcery, or black magic.
4 Sleight of hand.
5 Oscar Wilde (1854–1900), Irish author and wit.
6 Half-smiles.
7 Laurence Sterne (1713–1768), English author.
8 Sterne's Uncle Toby relives the trials and tribulations of his youth in Sterne's novel *Tristram Shandy* (1759).

necessity of the Treaty of Utrecht.[1] But a tenderer heart never beat under a British Warm.[2] "When we read over the siege of Troy, brother, which lasted ten years, and eight months—though with such a train of artillery as we had at Namur the town might have been carried in a week—was I not as much concerned for the destruction of the Greeks and Trojans as any boy in the school?" and "What is war? What is it, Yorick, when fought as ours has been, upon principles of *liberty* and upon principles of *honour*—what is it but getting together of quiet and harmless people, with their swords in their hands, to keep the ambitious and the turbulent within bounds?" "'And, for my part,' said my uncle, 'I could have done no more than my duty.' 'Bless your honour!' cried Trim, advancing three steps as he spoke; 'does a man think of his Christian name when he goes to the attack?'—'Or when he's standing in the trench, Trim?' cried my uncle Toby, looking firm— 'Or when he enters a breach?' said Trim, pushing in between two chairs.—'Or forces the lines?' cried my uncle, rising up and pushing his crutch like a pike.—'Or facing a platoon?' cried Trim, presenting his stick like a firelock.—'Or when he marches up the glacis?' cried my uncle Toby, looking warm and setting his foot upon his stool...." Here we have the good soldier. Surely the finest that lives in Fiction, and the usurpation of such a title by Mr. Hueffer's hero is nothing short of profanation. Had we known how to appreciate our soldiers as our best novelists have, Sterne, Meredith and Hardy,[3] to wit, the cant of anti-militarism would never have caught us as it has.

7. Theodore Dreiser, "The Saddest Story" (*New Republic*, 12 June 1915)

I have, I am aware, told this story in a very rambling way, so that it may be difficult for any one to find their path through what may be a sort of maze. I cannot help it. I have stuck to my idea of being in a country cottage with a silent listener, hearing between the gust of the wind and amidst the noises of the distant sea, the story as it comes. And, when one discusses an affair—a long, sad affair—one goes back, one goes forward. One remembers points that one has forgotten, and one

---

[1] Agreement reached in 1713 between England and Spain that ended the War of Spanish Succession.

[2] Overcoat.

[3] Thomas Hardy (1840–1928), English novelist and poet.

explains them all the more minutely since one recognizes that one has forgotten to mention them in their proper places, and that one may have given, by omitting them, a false impression. I console myself with thinking that this is a real story, and that, after all, real stories are best told in the way that a person telling a story would tell them. They will then seem most real.

Thus Mr. Hueffer in explanation of his style; a good explanation of a bad method.

In this story ... the author makes Dowell, Florence's husband, the narrator, and it is he who dubs it the "saddest one." This is rather a large order when one thinks of all the sad stories that have been told of this mad old world. Nevertheless, it is a sad story, and a splendid one from a psychological point of view; but Mr. Hueffer, in spite of the care he has bestowed upon it, has not made it splendid in the telling. In the main he has only suggested its splendor, quite as the paragraph above suggests, and for the reasons it suggests. One half suspects that since Mr. Hueffer shared with Mr. Conrad in the writing of *Romance*, the intricate weavings to and fro of that literary colorist have, to a certain extent, influenced him in the spoiling of this story. For it is spoiled to the extent that you are compelled to say, "Well, this is too bad. This is quite a wonderful thing, but it is not well done." Personally I would have suggested to Mr. Hueffer, if I might have, that he begin at the beginning, which is where Colonel Powys wishes to marry off his daughters—not at the beginning as some tertiary or quadrutiary character in the book sees it, since it really concerns Ashburnham and his wife. This is neither here nor there, however, a mere suggestion. A story may begin in many ways.

Of far more importance is it that, once begun, it should go forward in a more or less direct line, or at least that it should retain one's uninterrupted interest. This is not the case in this book. The interlacings, the cross references, the re-re-references to all sorts of things which subsequently are told somewhere in full, irritate one to the point of one's laying down the book. As a matter of fact, except for the perception that will come to any man, that here is a real statement of fact picked up from somewhere and related by the author as best he could, I doubt whether even the lover of naturalism—entirely free of conventional prejudice—would go on.

As for those dreary minds who find life morally ordered and the universe murmurous of divine law—they would run from it as from the plague. For, with all its faults of telling, it is an honest story, and there is no blinking of the commonplaces of our existence which so many find immoral and make such a valiant effort to conceal. One of the most irritating difficulties of the tale is that Dowell, the American husband who tells the story, is described as, first, that amazingly tame thing, an Englishman's conception of an American husband; second, as a profound psychologist able to follow out to the last detail the morbid minutiae of this tragedy, and to philosophize on them as only a deeply thinking and observing man could; and lastly as one who is as blind as a bat, as dull as a mallet, and as weak as any sentimentalist ever. The combination proves a little trying before one is done with it.

This story has been called immoral. One can predict such a charge to-day in the case of any book, play, or picture which refuses to concern itself with the high-school idea of what life should be. It is immoral apparently to do anything except dress well and talk platitudes. But it is interesting to find this English author (German by extraction, I believe) and presumably, from all accounts, in revolt against these sickening strictures, dotting his book with apologies for this, that, and another condition not in line with this high-school standard (albeit it is the wretched American who speaks) and actually smacking his lips over the stated order that damns his book. And worse yet, Dowell is no American. He is that literary pack-horse or scapegoat on whom the native Englishman loads all his contempt for Americans. And Captain and Mrs. Ashburnham, whom he so soulfully lauds for their love of English pretence and order, are two who would have promptly pitched his book out of doors, I can tell him. Yet he babbles of the fineness of their point of view. As a matter of fact their point of view is that same accursed thing which has been handed on to America as "good form," and which we are now asked to sustain by force of arms as representing civilisation.

After all, I have no real quarrel with the English as such. It is against smug conventionalism wherever found, too dull to perceive the import of anything except money and social precedence, that I uncap my fountain pen. It is this condition which makes difficult— one might almost fear impossible at times—the production of any great work of art, be it picture, play, philosophy, or novel. It is the Leonoras, the Dowells, and the Nancys that make life safe, stale, and impossible. They represent that thickness of wit which prospers impossible religions, and moral codes, and causes the mob to look askance at those finer flowers of fancy which are all the world has to show for its power to think in the drift of circumstance. All the rest is formalism and parade, and "go thou and do likewise." We all, to such a horrible extent, go and do likewise.

But you may well suspect that there is a good story here and that it is well worth your reading. Both suppositions are true. In the hands of a better writer this jointure of events might well have articulated into one of the finest pictures in any language. Its facts are true, in the main. Its theme beautiful. It is tragic in the best sense that the Greeks knew tragedy, that tragedy for which there is no solution. But to achieve a high result in any book its component characters must of necessity stand forth unmistakable in their moods and characteristics. In this one they do not. Every scene of any importance has been blinked or passed over with a few words or cross references. I am not now referring to any moral fact. Every conversation which should have appeared, every storm which should have contained revealing flashes, making clear the minds, the hearts, and the agonies of those concerned, has been avoided. There are no paragraphs or pages of which you can say "This is a truly moving description," or "This is a brilliant vital interpretation." You are never really stirred. You are never hurt. You are merely told and referred. It is all cold narrative, never truly poignant.

This is a pity. This book had the making of a fine story. I half suspect that its failure is due to the author's formal British leanings, whatever his birth—that leaning which Mr. Dowell seems to think so important, which will not let him loosen up and sing. The whole book is indeed fairly representative of that encrusting formalism which, barnacle-wise, is apparently overtaking and destroying all that is best in English life. The arts will surely die unless formalism is destroyed. And when you find a great theme by a sniffy reverence for conventionalism and the glories of a fixed condition it is a thing for tears. I would almost commend Mr. Hueffer to futurists, or to anyone that has the strength to scorn the moldy past, in the hope that he might develop a method entirely different from that which is here employed, if I did not know that at bottom the great artist is never to be commended. Rather from his brain, as Athena from that of Zeus,[1] spring flawless and shining all those art forms which the world adores and preserves.

---

[1]   According to Greek mythology, Athena, the Goddess of Arts and Crafts, sprang from Zeus's head after Hephaestus split the supreme god's skull with an axe.

Appendix E: Ford Madox Ford, "Techniques"

[Originally published in *The Southern Review* in July 1935, "Techniques" illustrates Ford's enduring interest in the function and construction of artistic technique. Drawing upon his beliefs about literary Impressionism, Ford's essay examines the experimental nature of his own literary devices and techniques. *The Southern Review* was founded in 1935 by Robert Penn Warren (1905–1989) and a coterie of other Southern writers. In April of that year, Ford participated in a symposium in Baton Rouge, Louisiana, on the literature of the South.]

I

Technique is perhaps the most odious word in the English language. I hope that by adding the above "s" some of the odium may be dispelled. It is necessary from time to time to emphasise the fact that writing in general and imaginative writing in particular are the products of craftsmanship. In the middle ages a craft was called a mystery. It is a good word, for it is a mystery why we write and a mystery how great writers do it.

They do it by observing certain rules—or after having observed certain rules for a long time, by jumping off from them. You may if you like say that great literatures have only risen when technical rules have been jumped off from—Shakespeare and the Elizabethans having jumped off from the classicisms of *Ferrex and Porrex*;[1] the Cockney School of Poetry[2] from the classical stultifications of an Eighteenth Century in decay; or Flaubert and French, English, and American Impressionists, whose methods I propose here to analyse for you, from the classical slipshodnesses the preceded them. The case of the Impressionist differs from that of the others, however, in that they practiced, and, when they had the time, enjoined, a tightening rather than any slackening of the rules.

---

[1] Thomas Sackville (1536–1608) and Thomas Norton's (1532–1584) *Gorboduc, or Ferrex and Porrex* (1561).

[2] An irreverent name for London romantic poets such as John Keats (1795–1821) and Leigh Hunt (1784–1859) that finds its origins in a scathing review in *Blackwood's Magazine* in October 1817.

Sang Mr. Kipling:[1]

> There are five and forty ways
> Of inditing tribal lays
> And every single one of them is right![2]

That is to say that Mr. Kipling, having proved himself an extraordinarily great master of the most difficult of all crafts—that of the short and short-long story writer—had to hasten to excuse himself by proving that at heart he was, and always meant to be, an English gentleman. For the English gentleman may write ... but before all things he must not be a writer. He may, that is to say, at odd moments sit down and toss off something, but he must not do it earnestly or according to any rules. Or, if he does observe any rules, he must hasten, hasten to assert that he does not. Otherwise he would not be received in really good drawing-rooms.

I do not mean to assert that occasionally a masterpiece may not be tossed off or that the roll of Royal and Noble Authors does not number a master or two. You have Clarendon who wrote the *History of the Rebellion*,[3] Beckford who wrote the *Letters from Portugal*[4] ... But how much more Clarendon might we not have had, had he not been father to a queen, or how much more Beckford, had he not found it necessary to be the nabob-builder of Fonthill? And above all, how much more Cunninghame Graham if Mr. Robert Bontine Cunninghame Graham[5] had not happened to be, in addition to the "incomparable writer of English," Earl of Monteith, King of Scotland if he had his rights, and the very spit and image of his connection, Henri IV of France.[6]

That indeed is the real tragedy of English literature ... is why England has in fact no literature but only some great, isolated peaks. For, to possess a Literature, a country must have a whole cloud—or better still, a whole populace—of writers instinct with a certain skill in, a certain respect for, a certain productivity of, writing. You must

---

1   Rudyard Kipling (1865–1936), English author.
2   Kipling's "In the Neolithic Age" (1895), a satire on literary infighting.
3   Edward Hyde, 1st Earl of Clarendon (1609–1674) published *History of the Rebellion* in 1702–04.
4   William Beckford (1760–1844) published *Letters from Portugal* in 1815.
5   Robert Bontine Cunninghame Graham (1852–1936), English politician and writer.
6   Henry IV (1553–1610), first of the Bourbon kings of France.

in that country be able to go, say to a railway bookstall, and by merely stretching out a random hand, take the first book that comes and find it to be, for certain, well written, well constructed, instinct with a certain knowledge of the values of life—such a work in short, as a proper man may let himself be seen reading without loss of self-respect. You can do that in France, you could do it in Germany before Mr. Hitler[1] began his burnings; you are beginning to be able to do it in the United States. But in the home and cradle of the writings of our race you have not been able to do it since the XVIIth Century—when of course there were no railway bookstalls. It is only a respect for a technique that can ensure this form of civilisation for a country because the writing of books is a difficult matter—the writing of any kind of book.

I am going to write particularly about the writing of works of the imagination—and specifically about the writing of novels. But the factual book is susceptible of, and gains as much by, care of construction, and the poem gains as much by attention to lucidity or verbiage and progression of effect, as does any novel. The convention of the narrative is as important to the historian of the battle of Minden as it is to the novelist trembling lest any slip in his construction should make his reader slacken or altogether lose his interest.

And the real difference between the writers of the Impressionist group, who since the days of Flaubert have dominated the public mind, and their predecessors is that the post-Flaubertians have studied, primarily, to hold just that public mind, whilst their predecessors, though wishing obviously to be read, never gave a thought to how interest may be inevitably—and almost scientifically—aroused. The novelist from, say, Richardson[2] to Meredith thought that he had done his job when he had set down a simple tale beginning with the birth of his hero or his heroine and ending when the ring of marriage bells completed the simple convention. But the curious thing was that he never gave a thought to how stories are actually told or even to how the biographies of one's friends come gradually before one.

The main difference between a novel by the forgotten James Payn[3]—who in his day was a much respected and not too popular

---

1   Adolf Hitler (1889–1945), founder and leader of National Socialism (Nazism) and German dictator.
2   Samuel Richardson (1689–1761), English author of epistolary novels.
3   James Payn (1830–1898), English author and editor.

THE GOOD SOLDIER: A TALE OF PASSION   295

novelist—and a work of the unforgettable author of *The Turn of the Screw*, who also, you will observe was a much respected and certainly not too popular novelist, is that the one recounts whilst the other presents. The one makes statements; the other builds suggestions of happenings on suggestions of happenings.

On the face of it you would say the way to tell a story is to begin at the beginning and go soberly through to the end, making here and there a reflection that shall show that you, the author who is to be forever present in the reader's mind, are a person of orthodox morals and what the French call *bien pensant*.[1]

But already by the age of Flaubert, the novelist had become uneasily aware that if the author is perpetually, with his reflections, distracting his reader's attention from the story, the story must lose interest. Some one noticed that in *Vanity Fair*[2] when Mr. Thackeray had gradually built up a state of breathless interest and Becky Sharp on the eve of Waterloo had seemed almost audibly to breathe and palpitate before your eyes, suddenly the whole illusion went to pieces. You were back in your study before the fire reading a book of made-up stuff though the moment before, you would have sworn you were in Brussels amongst the revellers ... And that disillusionment was occasioned by Mr. Thackeray, broken nose and all, thrusting his moral reflections upon you, in the desperate determination to impress you with the conviction that he was a proper man to be a member of the *Athenæum Club* ... He had, with immense but untrained and unreflecting genius, built up a whole phantasmagoria of realities in which his reader really felt himself walking amongst the actors in the real life of the desperate day that preceded Waterloo ... And then the whole illusion went.

It would be idle to say that it was Flaubert who first observed that the intrusion of the author destroyed the illusion of the reader. Such ideas arise sporadically across the literary landscape though, long before that, they will have been in the air. And Flaubert more than any of his associates clamored unceasingly and passionately that the author must be impersonal, must, like a creating deity, stand neither for nor against any of his characters, must project and never report and must, above all, forever keep himself out of his books. He must write his books as if he were rendering the impressions of a person present at a scene; he must remember that a person pres-

---

[1] A person of good thinking.
[2] Thackeray's *Vanity Fair: A Novel without a Hero* (1848).

ent at a scene does not see everything and is above all not able to remember immensely long passages of dialogue.

These dicta were unceasingly discussed by the members of Flaubert's set who included the Goncourts,[1] Turgenev,[2] Gautier,[3] Maupassant and, in lesser degree, Zola and the young James—this last as disciple of the gentle Russian genius. They met in different cafés and restaurants from the Café Procope which still exists, if fallen from its high estate, to Brébant's which has now disappeared. And their discussions were frenetic and violent. They discussed the *minutiae* of words and their economical employment; the *charpente*,[4] the architecture, of the novel; the handling of dialogue; the renderings of impressions; the impersonality of the author. They discussed these things with the passion of politicians inciting to rebellion. And in those *coenaculae*[5] the modern novel—the immensely powerful engine of our civilisation—was born.

You get an admirable idea of the violence of these discussions from the several accounts that exist of the desperate encounter that took place between the young James and the giant of Croisset[6] over a point of the style of Mérimée.[7] The assembly, it would seem, had been almost unanimous in its contempt for the style of Mérimée and the young James, sitting, a *jeune homme modeste*,[8] as he afterwards used to style me, in the shadow of Turgenev, had ventured to join in the chorus. But that an American should dare to open his mouth in those discussions proved too much for the equanimity of Flaubert. He said so. He said with violence ... To think that an American should dare to have views as to the French of one of the greatest of France's stylists! Only to think it, was enough to make Villon, Ronsard, Racine, Corneille, Chateaubriand[9]—not of course that their styles were anything to write home about—turn in their graves ...

---

[1] Edmund (1822–1896) and Jules de Goncourt (1830–1870), French novelists who collaborated together.
[2] Ivan Sergeyevich Turgenev (1818–1883), Russian novelist and playwright.
[3] Théophile Gautier (1811–1872), French artist, poet, novelist, and critic.
[4] Framework.
[5] Dining rooms.
[6] Flaubert.
[7] Prosper Mérimée (1803–1870), French novelist, critic, translator, and statesman.
[8] A modest young man.
[9] François Villon (1431–c.1463), French poet; Pierre de Ronsard (1524–1585), French poet; Jean Racine (1639–1699), French dramatist; Pierre Corneille (1606–1684), French dramatist; François René de Chateaubriand (1768–1848), French writer.

The pale young James was, it is recorded, led away by the beautiful Russian genius who, nevertheless, induced that brave young trans-Atlantic to call with him next day upon the giant who had inflicted that flagellation. And Flaubert, as I have elsewhere recorded, received Turgenev and his young American friend in his dressing-gown, opening his front door himself, a thing that, till the end of his life, Mr. James regarded as supremely shocking.

I don't mind repeating myself in the effort to emphasise how absolutely international a thing literature is. For Henry James, retiring to England that appeared to be all one large deer park across which the sunlight fell upon ubiquitous haunts of ancient piece—the young James then, like those birds who, carrying the viscous seeds of the mistletoe on their bills and claws, establish always new colonies of the plant of the Druids,[1] planted for a little while in the country of my birth the seeds of the novel as it at present exists.

It is said that James directly influenced Conrad in his incessant search for a new form for the novel. Nothing could be more literally false but nothing would be more impressionistically true. London was at that date—the earlier nineties—a veritable bacteriologist's soup for the culture of modern germs, and the author of *Daisy Miller, Roderick Hudson,* and *The Princess Casamassima,*[2] being enthusiastically received in a city that was weary to death of the novels of James Payn, William Black,[3] and the rest of the more or less respected, sowed around him, like the mistletoe-spreading birds, an infinite number of literary Impressionist germs. And if Conrad, as is literally true, learned nothing directly of James, yet he found prepared for him a medium in which, slowly at first but with an always increasing impetus, his works could spread. It was the London of the *Yellow Book,*[4] of R. L. Stevenson,[5] that sedulous ape, of W. E. Henley,[6] that harsh-mouthed but very beneficent spreader of French influences.

It was a city of infinite curiosity as to new literary methods and of an infinite readiness to assimilate new ideas, whether they came

---

1 Priests of ancient Celtic Britain, Ireland, and Gaul.

2 Novels by Henry James published, respectively, in 1879, 1876, and 1886.

3 William Black (1841–1898), English author.

4 Notorious magazine of the late nineteenth century that served as a catalyst for the Decadent movement.

5 Robert Louis Stevenson (1850–1894), Scottish novelist, poet, essayist, and travel writer.

6 William Ernest Henley (1841–1898), English poet, critic, and editor.

from Paris by way of Ernest Dowson,[1] from Poland by way of Conrad, or from New York or New England by way of Henry James, Stephen Crane,[2] Harold Frederic,[3] or Whistler, Abbey, Sargent, and George Boughton.[4] London had in fact been visited by one of its transitory phases in which nothing seemed good but what came from abroad. We were to see another such phase in '13 and '14 in the flowering days of Ezra Pound, John Gould Fletcher, Robert Frost, Marinetti,[5] the Cubists, the Vorticists, and the bud by the iron shards of war. We may see another tomorrow. At any rate it is overdue....

II

I began by writing the word "techniques" rather than "technique," so as to soften the impact on the ear of that harsh dissyllable. For there is not one only Technique, a chill enemy of mankind known only to and arbitrarily prescribed by a pedantic circle of the high-brow *intelligentsia*. Not only one, but just as many as there are writers, each one differing by a shade, the one from the other, until the difference between the leader of the advancing line and the boy at its end is as great as that that lies between the limpidities of Mérimée and the clouds of virtuosities of *Du Côté de Chez Swann*[6] or of *Ulysses*.[7] Yet we are all going to Heaven and Turgenev shall be of the company.

Mr. Kipling was perfectly right when he wrote that there are five and forty ways for the writer. There are probably five hundred thousand, every single one of them being right. But to tell the whole truth, he must have added that there is only one best way for the treatment of every given subject and only one method best suited for every given writer. And such advocates of the study of technique as Conrad or Dowson or James or Crane or Flaubert are far more

---

[1] Ernest Christopher Dowson (1867–1900), English poet.

[2] Stephen Crane (1871–1900), American writer.

[3] Harold Frederic (1856–1898), American journalist and novelist.

[4] Edwin Austin Abbey (1852–1905), John Singer Sargent (1856–1925), George Henry Boughton (1833–1905)—all of whom, with Whistler—were American expatriate painters and portraitists.

[5] John Gould Fletcher (1886–1950), American expatriate poet; Robert Frost (1874–1963), distinguished American poet; Filippo Tommaso Marinetti (1876–1944), Italian poet, novelist, and critic.

[6] First part of French writer Marcel Proust's (1871–1922) novel cycle *À la recherche du temps perdu* (1913–1927).

[7] Epic novel published in 1922 by Irish writer James Joyce (1882–1941).

interested in the writer's finding himself than in establishing any one rule that shall cover every tribal lay. The young writer, for whom I am principally writing, or the old man setting up as writer, will inevitably—and very properly—go through the stage of expressing himself. He will inevitably desire to get out of his system his reactions to sex, wine, music, homosexuality, parents, puritanism, death, life, immorality, technocracy, communism and existence amongst the infinite flatnesses beneath the suns and tornadoes of the Middle West or the Mississippi Delta. But once all that *Sturm und Drang*[1]—once that milk fever—is inscribed of fair paper, the joys of autobiography are past. The aspirant finds himself faced, if he is to continue [as a] writer, with the drear necessity of rendering one human affair or another. It is then that he will have to go in search of a technique that will suit him as well as the one fishing-cane that will be indispensable to him if he is to cast his fly exactly upstream before the jaws of the waiting trout. For there are innumerable techniques but only one best one for each writer.

What then is a technique? It is a device by which a writer may appeal to his fellows—to so many of his fellows that, in the end, he may claim to have appealed to all humanity from China to the Tierra del Fuego. Nothing less will satisfy the ardent writer—the really ardent and agonizingly passionate renderer of affairs like Flaubert or James. And there are some who attain to that stupendous reward. At any rate I have been informed by a German firm of world-book distributors that the one book that they export all over the world—to Rio de Janeiro as to the Straits Settlements, to Prague as to Berkeley, Cal., and Peking is—*Madame Bovary*.

This does not mean that I am asking the neophyte to pass his life writing *pastiches* of the affair in which poor Emma was involved. But it does mean that, if he is a prudent man, he will read that book and *L'Éducation Sentimentale* and *Bouvard et Pécuchet*[2] a great many times, over and over again, with minute scrutiny, to discover what in Flaubert's methods is eternal and universal in appeal. And having discovered what he thinks that to be, he must experiment for a long time to see whether he can work in that method as easily as he can live in an old and utterly comfortable coat … or dressing gown. And

---

[1]   Literally "storm and stress"; *Sturm und Drang* was a late-eighteenth-century movement in German literature.

[2]   Novels published by Flaubert in 1870 and 1881, respectively.

so he must go on to other writers. For the history of Emma Bovary is not alone amongst world-and-all-time best sellers. Next to that, and circling the globe in flights almost as numerous, come the *Pilgrim's Progress*[1] and the *Pickwick Papers*[2]... And long before them stands the *Imitation of Christ*[3] and a little after that the *Holy Bible*. To each of these works, not excluding the religious masterpieces, the neophyte may well apply his microscopes and his diminishing glasses. At the last he shall come into his own.

He will come into his own when, reading those works a final time in a spirit of forgetfulness, for pleasure and with critical faculties put to sleep, he shall say: "Such and such a passage pleases me," and casting back into his subconsciousness shall add: "This fellow gets that effect by a cadenced paragraph of long, complicated sentences, interspersed with shorter statements, ending with a long, dying fall of words and the final taptaptap of a three monosyllable phrase ... " Just like that.

That was quite the conscious practice of Conrad when seeking to be dramatic as it was the only less conscious practice of Flaubert. And, if you will read again my last paragraph, you will see how dramatic—how even thought vulgar—such a cadence may be.

Or it may be that the devices of Conrad and Flaubert, as you take them to be, do not suit your book after your painful studies. Or you may say that Flaubert in France and Conrad in America lying under temporary clouds of oblivion, you will never attain to the enviable gift of extended popularity if you let them in the slightest degree exercise an influence on you. Try then Hudson.

Hudson, or his Latin-American running mate, Mr. Cunninghame Graham, the most exquisite living of *prosateurs*[4] on English, though of right King of Scotland. Or *The Third Violet*[5] of Stephen Crane who for his own purposes professed to have been born and bred in the Bowery[6] but was actually the son of some one of Episcopal standing. You will discover that Hudson gets his effects by an almost infi-

---

[1]   *The Pilgrim's Progress from This World to That Which Is to Come*, novel published by English author John Bunyan (1628–1688) in 1678.

[2]   Humorous sketches published by Dickens in 1836–1837.

[3]   Devotional work published c.1427 by German monk Thomas à Kempis (c.1380–1471).

[4]   Prose writers.

[5]   Novel published by Crane in 1896.

[6]   Section of lower Manhattan, New York City.

nite and meticulous toning down of language. If you should be fortunate enough to get hold of some of his proofsheets, you will see that he simplifies to the utmost and then beyond. I remember observing—for I went once or twice through his proofs for him—that he had once written: "The buds developed into leaves." He substituted "grew," for "developed." And, finally the passage ran: "They became leaves" ... But of course, behind Huddie's[1] prose there was that infinitely patient temperament of the naturalist, that infinite conscientiousness of observation, that have given the world White's *Natural History of Selborne*,[2] who taught *me* all I know of cadences; as well as the *Sportsman's Sketches*[3] of Turgenev with its matchless *Bielshin Prairie*[4] and, only yesterday, Miss Gordon's *Aleck Maury*,[5] which has a singular spiritual kinship to the *Récits d'un Chasseur*.[6] But that quality is the product of a temperament. You may have it or you may not. If you have it you will write beautifully—but you can never acquire it. The longest study of Hudson or Turgenev will do no more for you than turn you into a writer of *pastiches*.[7] Galsworthy[8] would have been a real major writer if Mr. Edward Garnett[9] had not forced him to read Mrs. Garnett's[10] wonderful translation of *Fathers and Children*.[11]

But by all means read them for the exquisite pleasure they will give you.

Mr. Graham you may read as self-consciously as you will. His prose is always aristocratically unbuttoned; he approaches his subjects with the contemptuous negligence of the Highland Scottish noble or the Southern plantation owner. But that very contempt gives him a power of keying down drama till the result is an economy or resource such as only Stephen Crane, himself aristocratically contemptuous, has otherwise attained. There is a short—a very short—story of Mr.

---

1   Hudson's.
2   Volume published by English naturalist Gilbert White (1720–1793) in 1789.
3   Collection of short stories published by Turgenev in 1852.
4   Short story in Turgenev's *A Sportsman's Sketches*.
5   Novel published by American writer Caroline Gordon (1895–1981) as *Aleck Maury, Sportsman* in 1934.
6   French translation of *A Sportsman's Sketches* published by Turgenev in 1859.
7   Imitations, hodgepodges.
8   John Galsworthy (1867–1933), English novelist.
9   Edward Garnett (1868–1937), English critic and author.
10   Constance Garnett (1862–1946), esteemed English translator.
11   Turgenev's *Fathers and Sons*, published in 1862.

Graham's called "Beattock for Moffatt"[1]—the railway porter's cry meaning: "Beattock, change for Moffatt"—which is one of the great tragedies. It projects nothing more than the railway journey of a dying, homesick Scot of no importance, going home, with a vulgar and uncomprehending but not unkindly Cockney wife, to die of tuberculosis in Moffatt. His whole mind is given to seeing Moffatt again after a long obscuration in London ... And in the keen air after the stuffy railway carriage on Beattock platform he dies, being fated never again to see Moffatt, that Carcassonne[2] of the North ... dies whilst the porters are still calling "Beattock for Moffatt" ... It is told almost as summarily as I have told it ... but with just those differences of touch that make the passing of that obscure Scot as lamentable— nay, more lamentable!—than the death of Hector.[3]

The secret of poor Steevie is very much akin to that of Mr. Graham, be his method of approach to his subject never so different. Mr. Graham—the Don Roberto of a hundred drawing-rooms— with contemptuous negligence does not record; Crane with nervous meticulousness excises and excises. Both having an unerring sense of the essential, the temperamental results arrived at are extraordinarily similar. A Crane drama will end:

> The Girl said:
> "You say ... "
> He answered:
> "Observe that I have never ventured to say ... "
> She threw the third violet at his feet ...

Something like that—for I have no copy of *The Third Violet* from which to quote—but you can observe that, a situation of poignance having been established, such an end may be of an extreme drama.

If you compare it with the famous last sentence of *The Turn of the Screw*, you will see how two writers of the same school and training, using very similar methods in all the essentials of rendering an affair, may give an entirely different temperamental turn to their endings.

"We were alone with the quiet day," wrote Mr. James confidently still. But then you hear him mutter to himself. "This is too direct. This

---

[1] Collected in Graham's *Scottish Stories* (1914).
[2] Medieval fortress in southern France.
[3] Noble mythological figure in the *Iliad* who was killed by Achilles as an act of revenge.

will give the effect of the *coup de canon*[1] at the end of a Maupassant story ... We must delay ... We must give the effect of lingering ... We must let the reader down gently." ... And into the direct statement that was to be completed he inserts the qualificative word "dispossessed." "We were alone with the quiet day and his little heart had stopped," would have been reporting of a high order. But: "We were alone with the quiet day and his little heart, dispossessed, had stopped," is the supreme poetry of a great genius. And yet of an amazing economy.

But it is perhaps Crane of all that school or gang—and not excepting Maupassant—who most observed that canon of Impressionism: "You must render: never report." You must never, that is to say, write: "He saw a man aim a gat at him"; you must put it: "He saw a steel ring directed at him." Later you must get in that, in his subconsciousness, he recognized that the steel ring was the polished muzzle of a revolver. So Crane rendered it in "Three White Mice,"[2] which is one of the major short stories of the world. That is Impressionism!

III

But the great truth that must never be forgotten by you, by me, or by the neophyte at the gate, is that the purpose of a technique is to help the writer to please, and that neither writing nor the technique behind it has any other purpose. In evolving the technique that shall fit your fishing-pole you have to think of nothing but how to please your reader. By pleasing him, you hold his attention, and once you have accomplished that, you may inject into him what you please: for you need not forget, when you write a novel, the gravity of your role as educator: only you must remember that in vain does the fowler set his net in the sight of the bird. The reader wants to be filled with the feeling that you are a clever magician; he never wants to have you intruding and remarking what a good man you are.

I will try to inculcate this most important of all lessons by presenting some instances from the writers best known to myself. With all the others I have mentioned—with the exception of Flaubert who was dead, and of Maupassant who had retired from active life before I entered the bull-ring that is the literary life— with all the others I discussed literary problems and their personal techniques, debating rather strenuously with Crane and Hudson and

---

[1] The climactic moment; literally, a cannon shot or blast.

[2] Short story published as "The Five White Mice" by Crane in the *New York World* in April 1898.

listening with deference to Henry James, Henry Harland,[1] Henley, Miss Ethel Mayne,[2] and others of the *Yellow Book* and the English–American Impressionist group.

With Conrad I descended into the arena and beside him wrestled, rain or shine, through the greater part of a decade. I will therefore now take two or three instances of details of technique and show how we approached them. Conrad, I may say, was more interested in finding a new form for the novel; I, in training myself to write *just* words that would not stick out of a sentence and so distract the reader's attention by their very justness. But we worked ceaselessly, together, on those problems, turning from the problem of the new form to that of the just word as soon as we were mentally exhausted by the one or the other.

That we did succeed eventually in finding a new form I think I may permit myself to claim, Conrad first evolving the convention of a Marlow who should narrate, in presentation, the whole story of a novel just as, without much sequence or pursued chronology, a story will come up into the mind of a narrator, and I eventually dispensing with a narrator but making the story come up in the mind of the unseen author with a similar want of chronological sequence. I must apologize for referring to my own work but, if I did not, this story would become rather incomprehensible and would lack an end, since after Conrad's death I pursued those investigations with a never-ceasing industry and belief in the usefulness of my task—if not to myself, then at least to others. For it is almost as useful to set up an awful example that can be avoided as to erect signposts along a road that should be taken.

We evolved then a convention for the novel and one that I think still stands. The novel must be put into the mouth of a narrator—who must be limited by probability as to what he can know of the affair that he is adumbrating. Or it must be left to the official Author and he, being almost omnipotent, may, so long as he limits himself to presenting without comment or moralization, allow himself to be considered to know almost everything that there is to know. The narration is thus a little more limited in possibilities; the "author's book" is a little more difficult to handle. A narrator, that is to say, being already a fictional character, may indulge in any prejudices or

---

1   Henry Harland (1861–1905), American novelist.
2   Ethel Colburn Mayne (d. 1941), English writer and translator. She was a friend of Ford and Violet Hunt.

wrong-headednesses and any likings or dislikes for the other characters of the book, for he is just a living being like anybody else. But an author-creator, presenting his narration without passion, may not indulge in the expression of any prejudices or like any one of his characters more than any other; for, if he displays either of those weaknesses, he will to that extent weaken the illusion that he has attempted to build up. Marlow, the narrator of *Lord Jim*,[1] may idolize his hero or anathematize his villains with the sole result that we say: "How real Marlow is!" Conrad, however, in *Nostromo*[2] must not let any word or preference for Nostromo or Mrs. Gould or the daughters of the Garibaldino pierce through the surface of his novel or at once we should say: "Here is this tiresome person intruding again," and at once lose the thread of the tale.

You perceive, I trust, how our eyes were forever on the reader—and if, during our fifteenth perusal of *Madame Bovary* we discerned that—as Flaubert himself somewhere confesses—the sage of Croisset was actually in love with poor Emma Bovary, his creation, we hastened to observe the one to the other that *we* must never let ourselves indulge in such mental-carnal weaknesses. A giant like Flaubert might get away with it: but we must avoid temptations ... So you perceive how constantly we considered the interests of You, my Lord, in case You should one day want to glance, for diversion, through the pages we were evolving.

We were, in short, producers who thought forever of the consumer. If Conrad laid it down as a law that, in introducing a character, we must always, after a few vivid words of personal description, apportion to him a speech that *must* be a characteristic generalisation, it was because we were thinking of You. We knew that if we said: "Mr. X was a foul-mouthed reactionary," you would know very little about him. But if his first words, after his introduction were: "God damn it, put all filthy Liberals up against a wall, say I, and shoot their beastly livers ... " that gentlemen will make on you an impression that many following pages shall scarcely efface. Whomever else you may not quite grasp, you won't forget *him*—because that is the way people present themselves in real life. You may converse with a lady for ten minutes about the fineness of the day or the number of lumps of sugar you like in your tea and you will know little about her; but let her

---

[1]   Novel published by Conrad in 1900.
[2]   Novel published by Conrad in 1904.

hazard any personal and general opinion as to the major topics of life and at once you will have her labeled, docketed and put away on the collector's shelf for your curious mind.

Similarly, in evolving a technique for the presenting of conversation, I—and in this it was rather I than Conrad, just as in the evolution of the New Form[1] it was rather Conrad than I, though each countersigned the opinion of the other and thenceforth adopted the device so evolved—I then considered for a long time how conversations presented themselves to the mind. I would find myself in a room with a gentleman who pursued an almost uninterrupted monologue. A week after, I would find that of it I retained, verbally, only his more characteristic expletives—his "God bless my soul's," or his "You don't mean to say so's" and one or two short direct speeches: "If the Government goes to the country, I will bet a hundredweight of China tea to a Maltese orange that they will have a fifty-eight to forty-two majority of the voters against them." But I remember the whole gist of his remarks.

And so, considering that an author-narrator, being supposed to have about the mnemonic powers of a man with a fair memory, will after the elapse of a certain period, be supposed to retain about that much of a conversation that the Reader may suppose him to have heard, I shall, when inventing conversations, give about just that proportion of direct and indirect speech, in which latter I shall present the gist of my character's argument ... For, if I give more direct speech than that, the reader will say: "Confound it, how does this plaguy fellow remember an oration like that, word for word? It's impossible. So I don't believe a word he says about anything else," and he will pitch my book into the wastepaper basket ... Of course I shall lard the indirect speeches with plenty of "God bless my soul's" and "Mr. X paused for a moment before continuing," just to keep my character all the while well in the picture ...

These of course are only two of the technical *trouvailles*[2] that we made in labours that cannot have been exceeded by any two slaves that worked for ten years on the building of the Tower of Babel.[3] We made an infinite number of others, covering an infinite field of

---

[1] Literary impressionism.
[2] Findings, conclusions.
[3] Biblical story in which Noah's descendants attempted to build a tower reaching up to heaven to make a name for themselves.

human activities and reflections. You may find them valid as representing how life comes back to you and in that case they may help you, as writer, a little way along the long road that winds up hill all the way ... All the way! For, so long as you remain a live writer, you will forever be questioning and re-questioning and testing and re-testing the devices that you will have evolved. Or they may not at all fill your bill: in which case you must go forward alone and may a gentle breeze forever temper for you the ardor of the sun's rays!

But you must—there is no other method—pursue your investigation in that spirit of ours. You must have your eyes forever on your Reader. That alone constitutes ... Technique!

Appendix F: F.L. Cross, "Anglo-Catholicism and the Twentieth Century"

[F.L. Cross's (1900–1968) essay—originally published in *The Church and the Twentieth Century* (1936), edited by G.L.H. Harvey—addresses the history and manifestations of Catholicism in the twentieth century. Cross devotes particular attention to the doctrinal and sociological aspects of Catholicism—issues of special significance to Leonora Ashburnham's mindset throughout *The Good Soldier*.]

Permanence and Progress in Religion

Religion surpasses every other form of human activity in that it claims to be concerned with the ultimate facts of life. Its advocates maintain that there is no other pathway towards Reality which brings the enquirer so near his goal. They hold that in so far as it is possible for man to apprehend the nature and content of the Real, it is through religion that such apprehension most readily takes place. In religion, they contend, mankind is confronted with a set of principles and ideals by which, if he is in earnest, he must needs seek to guide his life and to interpret its mysteries. Here he will find principles and ideals which, in the last resort, are beyond the possibility of criticism; for to criticise implies the possession of a criterion which transcends the facts to be criticised and *ex hypothesi*[1] no criterion of measurement can transcend the Absolute. Progress, restatement, reform in religion, therefore, can never be revision in the matter of its first principles. Where revision is demanded or desired, it will be conditioned by the perception that what has hitherto been held to belong to the content of religion has been misconceived as such.

In common with other forms of religion, Christianity also claims to be rooted in a set of absolute principles. These principles, she believes, were revealed in the Person and Work and Teaching of her Divine Lord. All those who should accept the supreme revelation in Christ Incarnate had to take into account new principles, the

---

[1] From this argument.

validity of which was absolute. She claims that the Christ brought with time new categories of interpretation, new ideals of action, new demands for discipleship; and that these new principles were to be the guiding ideals of every philosophy of life which should claim the name of Christian.

But while what may be described, in varying metaphors, as the substance, the essence, the kernel, or the leaven, of the Christian Faith was committed to the Church at the outset, the from which that Faith was to assume in its richness and its universality was to be the work of succeeding generations. Those to whom the Revelation was entrusted were themselves to take a part in interpreting it. By their reception of it, they were to be, in some mysterious way, organically incorporated into it. They became more than purely witnesses to the Christ; they became, in the language of the of the Apostle of the Gentiles, "members of the Christ." In the Mystical Body of Christ there was thus to be continued and developed the content of the revelation. Hence it was to be the function of the Church, guided by the Spirit, to apprehend and set forth the Truth ever more fully. Disciples from far and near were to bring their god and frankincense and myrrh to the feet of their Incarnate Lord to be transmuted and consecrated and synthesised into the fullness of the Christian Life. To use a daring metaphor of St. Paul,[1] they were to "supply the deficiencies" of Christ—those "deficiencies" inherent in the categorical structure of historical events and persons which entail that a man cannot be, e.g., a St. Augustine[2] and a Shakespeare and a Newton[3] simultaneously—so that ultimately in Christ God may be "all in all."

Christianity and Platonism

Since the Christian Revelation claimed to be vastly more than a merely speculative account of the Real, the elucidation and development of that Revelation could never be wholly, or even primarily, the work of theologians. Nevertheless, as far as the *intellectual* content of the Revelation was concerned, it was upon her theologians and philosophers that the task of interpretation necessarily devolved. It was to be their mission to expound its theoretical principles, and to

---

[1]   St. Paul (d. c.A.D. 67), the apostle to the Gentiles.
[2]   Aurelius Augustinus (354–430), one of the four Latin Fathers.
[3]   Sir Isaac Newton (1642–1727), English mathematician and physicist.

relate them to the categories of thought outside the Revelation. Certain facts were soon perceived to belong to the very "deposit" of Revelation. There was the fact that in Christ was to be discovered the inmost nature both of God and man. There was the fact that God judged men's actions not by their conformity to external or ceremonial laws, but by their inward springs. There was the fact, implied by Christ's whole attitude to nature and presupposed by the Old Testament background of his thought, that the relation of our Universe to God is a relation of Creation. Facts such as these were to be the necessary point of departure of every philosophy which sought to give a *rationale* of the Christian Faith. But beyond such basic facts, there was room for a wide range of freedom.

Reflection on the facts soon made it clear to the Church that one of the most characteristic notes of a Christian Philosophy was that it must needs be a "Meditating" one. A Christian philosophy must involve what the late Friedrich von Hugely used to term an element of "tension." The doctrine of Creation, for instance, was perceived to be intermediate between a Pantheism which would equate the whole of Reality with God and a Dualism which, with other forms of Pluralism, would defend the existence of beings other than and totally independent of God. Similarly, the doctrine of the Incarnation[1] insisted that Christ can be understood neither as God alone nor as man alone, but that he is to be conceived somehow as both God and man at once. Christian ethics, again, was neither purely world-accepting nor purely world-renouncing, but in some mysterious way both world-accepting and world-renouncing at the same time. The Christian path was thus to be a *via media*.[2]

It so happened that when Christian speculation set out on its course it found ready to hand a philosophy which exactly suited its needs. The metaphysics underlying the Platonist doctrines was just such a "mediating" philosophy. This philosophy proved to be, in fact, the preparation evangelical in the realm of metaphysics. Patristic theology, as history showed, was the outcome of a long series of attempts to understand the Christian Faith through the eyes of Platonism. The more philosophically minded of the Fathers—St. Clement of

---

[1] Incarnation or incarnationalism involves the belief that Jesus Christ, held by Christians to be God in the flesh, exists simultaneously on divine and human planes of being.

[2] A middle way.

Alexandria,[1] the Cappadocians,[2] St. Dionysius the Areopagite,[3] and St. Augustine—were all Platonists.[4] The result was that the root-principles of Platonist metaphysics were destined to play for two thousand years (and perhaps for all time) an organic and all but inseparable part in every Incarnational interpretation of the Christian Faith.

The essence of this philosophy was its emphasis upon the doctrine of degrees. The Universe was conceived of as a graded structure wherein God alone possessed Absolute Reality while other entities possessed a relative degree of reality depending upon their nearness to the Absolute. The only unconditioned Real was their *Summum Bonum*.[5] Created things were *bona*;[6] and such reality as they possessed, they owed to their participation in this Supreme Good. St. Augustine well summed up the essence of this metaphysic in the formula *In quantum est quidquid est, bonum est*.[7] The only things which were altogether devoid of being were, accordingly, the *mala*.[8] They alone possessed the metaphysical status of "nothing."

This Platonist metaphysic was to be further worked out and refined in the Scholastic era. The important contribution made to the development of it by Mediæval Thought was the introduction of the concept of Analogy. The Scholastics argued that since God's goodness exceeded all human goodness, human language could never be "adequate" to the expression of it. Our use of language in relation to God must therefore be "analogical." For instance, they pointed out that we can never apprehend Divine Justice in its fullness. But though this is so, Divine Justice and human justice cannot be thought of as totally different; recognition of the limitations of language must not lead us to agnosticism. Hence philosophers must strive after a *via media*. They must conceive of Divine and human justice as related *per modum analogiae*.[9]

The doctrine was developed as follows. It was commonly held,

---

1 Titus Flavius Clemens (d. c.215), Greek theologian.
2 Affluent, prosperous people who inhabited the ancient region of Asia Minor.
3 St. Dionysius (c. 1st century A.D.), known as a martyr and the first bishop of Athens.
4 Platonism's philosophy argues that objects find their roots in transcendent ideas, which, in themselves, are the founts of true knowledge as derived through introspection.
5 The supreme good.
6 Good.
7 In whatever quantity exists, is good.
8 Bad.
9 Through a kind of analogy.

for example, that God's justice was indistinguishable from his very essence; but in a just man, his "justice" and his "humanity" were two different things. Here was just one distinction between Divine and human justice. Moreover, when Divine and human justice are compared, they are seen to differ vastly in degree. Such justice as man at his highest can claim is but a shadow of the full and unsurpassable justice of God. Corresponding relations naturally hold true of the other attributes of God, such as his wisdom, his purity, and his love. Perhaps the clearest view of this doctrine is obtained from the image of the ladder, constantly employed by the exponents of it. The top of the ladder represents God, who is absolute Being, absolute Justice, absolute Love, and so on. The bottom of the ladder represents "nothing," which, as has been indicated, was the metaphysical status commonly assigned by theologians to evil. Human existence, human justice, human love, in so far as they derive the being they have from God, who has created them out of nothing, are represented correspondingly by stages up the ladder. "God," wrote St. Thomas,[1] "is not a measure proportionate to any single thing, yet He is said to be the measure of all things on the ground that each individual thing has the more being, according as it the more resembles him."

Nevertheless, however fundamental to Christianity this Platonic (or "mediating," or "Analogical") element has been, it has continuously been in danger of suppression. Theologians and controversialists have been tempted at every turn to abandon it in favour of a method which allowed of greater logical precision. They have tried to substitute for the *per modum analogiae* the *Entweder-Oder*.[2] Words, they have argued, must be capable of exact and univocal usage. Theology must provide formulae which answer with just precision the questions propounded to it. The Christian Faith cannot be content to describe Reality by means of shadow and pointers. It must be possessed of infallibilities and systematic completeness. And this appeal for Absolutes has been a constant threat to Platonism, for it is only in so far as theology abandons the Principle of Analogy that it can reach exactness.

Perhaps the Church of England has fared better than most of her neighbours in this matter. As a number of recent students of Anglicanism have pointed out, Platonism has proved deeply congenial to the English religious mind. Indeed, Anglicanism can fairly claim

---

[1] St. Thomas Aquinas (1225–1274), Italian philosopher and theologian.
[2] Either-or.

that in modern times the Platonist approach to the Christian Faith has been more marked within her limits than anywhere else in Western Christendom. As to how this has come about, opinions may differ. Some may ascribe it mainly to the historic circumstances of the Reformation in this country, others to the peculiarities of the English character, others to an exceptional degree of theological penetration. But of the Platonic temper of Anglican theology there is room for no serious division of opinion. Whether we examine the religious philosophy of Colet[1] or of Hooker,[2] of the Cambridge "Latitudinarians"[3] or of Joseph Butler,[4] of Law[5] or of Wordsworth,[6] of Newman[7] or of F. D. Maurice,[8] the same fact is impressed upon us. It is reflected no less strikingly in the singularly small part which confessional formularies play in the life of Anglicanism. The Church of England has no set of modern dogmatic formulae which occupy a place in her life corresponding to the Decrees of the Tridentine and Vatican Councils on the one hand, nor to the Confessional Formularies of Continental Protestantism on the other.

Catholicism as Incarnational

In our analysis of the nature of Catholic principles, we may take as our point of departure the summary formula of popular theology that "Catholicism is rooted in the doctrine of the incarnation, Protestants in the doctrine of the Atonement." Such is at any rate a rough approximation to the current sense in which the words "Catholicism" and "Protestantism" are used. The Theology of the Protestant Reformation tended to concentrate its attention upon a single element in the plan of Redemption. It believed that the whole faith was contained in the death of Christ on the Cross and its implications for mankind. Here was the one and only fact in the realm of created being which was possessed of merit and goodness in the eyes of God, and of this

---

1   John Colet (c.1467–1519), English humanist and theologian.
2   Richard Hooker (c.1554–1600), English theologian and clergyman.
3   During the eighteenth century, the latitudinarians controlled the church's dogma, liturgy, and ecclesiastical organization.
4   Joseph Butler (1692–1752), English bishop and exponent of natural theology.
5   William Law (1686–1761), English clergyman.
6   William Wordsworth (1770–1850), English poet.
7   John Henry Newman (1801–1890), English churchman, cardinal of the Roman Catholic Church, and one of the founders of the Oxford Movement.
8   Frederick Denison Maurice (1805–1872), English clergyman and social reformer.

goodness even the most faithful Christian disciple could never partake. At most, this goodness could be imputed to him through his acceptance of the Redeemer. For, as the Formula of Concord of 1576 expressed it, "original sin ... is so profound a corruption of human nature as to leave nothing sound, nothing incorrupt in the body or soul of man, or in his mental or bodily powers."

This view of human nature stood in sharp contrast with that characteristic of traditional Catholic theology. The Fathers, as we have seen, had a philosophy which regarded the work of Christ as the culmination of an order in which everything in its degree had its value. Moses, Plato, Seneca had received illumination, each according to his deserts, from the Logaos who was fully revealed in Christ. The Incarnation was thus the culmination of a long process. Wherever in the Universe goodness was to be discovered, it was necessarily related to that of the Incarnate Son. Mediæval theologians came to regard the Christian Moral Law as, in Abelard's[1] phrase, a re-formatio[2] of the law of Natural Morality. It was a view which implied that the virtuous deeds of the heathen were to be regarded not—as some theologians (forgetting their Incarnationalist principles) even in Patristic times occasionally expressed it—as "vices," but rather deeds which through their participation in "the light which lighteneth every man" were good as far as they went. Christianity did not condemn all that had gone before. It raised the best of the past to a new level. *Gratia non tollit naturam, sed perficit*.[3]

Accordingly, every account of the Christian Faith which claims the name of "Catholic" and sets out from Incarnationalist principles must conceive of the Christian Revelation as related to the whole range of human experience. It must consider it to be the end of religion to consecrate every form of experience by raising it from the "natural" to the "supernatural" level. As R.C. Moberly well put it in a famous volume of essays devoted to the subject of Incarnationalism,[4] the Christian Religion "professes to have for its subject-matter, and (in a measure incomplete but relatively adequate) to include, to account for, and to direct the whole range of all man's history, all man's capacities, explored or unexplored, all man's destiny now and for ever.... To the

---

[1] Peter Abelard (1079–1142), French philosopher and teacher.
[2] Reformation.
[3] Grace does not destroy nature but perfects it.
[4] The essay in question is the Reverend Robert Campbell Moberly's (1845–1903) "The Incarnation as the Basis of Dogma," collected in *Lux Mundi: A Series of Studies in the Religion of the Incarnation* (1890), edited by Charles Gore.

religious man ... the fullness of Christian evidence is as many-sided as human life. There is historical evidence—itself of at least a dozen different kinds—literary evidence, metaphysical evidence, moral evidence, evidence of sorrow and joy, of goodness and of evil, of sin and of pardon, of despair and of hope, of life and of death; evidence which defies enumerating. Into this the whole gradual life of the Christian grows; and there is no part nor element of life which does not to him perpetually elucidate and confirm the knowledge which has been given him. Everything that is or has been, every consciousness, every possibility, even every doubt or wavering, becomes to the Christian a part of the certainty, an element in the absorbing reality, of his creed." There can be no fragment of the Real which stands out of relationship to the Christian Faith.

Anglicanism

If we are right in using the word "Catholic" to describe every view of Christianity which holds it to be all-inclusive and Incarnational, then the Church of England, judged by the standard of history, can claim to be a Church whose spirit has been outstandingly Catholic. The Protestant theories of Justification, though zealously advocated in some quarters during the unsettled times of the sixteenth century, soon ceased to exercise any effective influence upon the main stream of Anglican thought. Caroline[1] theology in its characteristic representatives was through and through Incarnational. James I's[2] suspicions of "Arminianism,"[3] imbibed from his Calvinist[4] antecedents, were never a serious rival to the Incarnational theology of such men as Andrewes, Laud, Chillingworth, Forbes, Bramhall, Pearson, and Bull.[5] No less

---

[1] Era associated with Charles I (1600–1649) and Charles II (1630–1685), kings of England.

[2] James I (1566–1625), king of England from 1603 to 1625.

[3] Doctrine established by Jacobus Arminius (1560–1609) opposing the absolute predestination of strict Calvinism and universal salvation.

[4] Calvinism refers to the theological system established by John Calvin (1509–1564) and his followers characterized by a strong belief in the sovereignty of God and the existence of predestination.

[5] Lancelot Andrewes (1555–1626), English theologian; William Laud (1573–1645), Archbishop of Canterbury; William Chillingworth (1602–1644), English theologian; John Forbes (1593–1648), theologian and divinity scholar; John Bramhall (1594–1663), English theologian; John Pearson (1613–1686), English prelate and scholar; John Bull (1562–1628), English scholar.

Incarnational was the thought of the small but influential group of "Latitudinarian" scholars, already referred to, who have since their day become known as the Cambridge Platonists. However much they may have differed in some important respects from the divines whose names we have just cited, they agreed with them (as against the Calvinists) in the way in which they conceived the Universe related to God, while in their emphasis upon the essentially reasonable character of the Christian Religion they were unceasing. The seventeenth century thus saw Incarnationalism permanently established in the National Church.

In 1688 came the Revolution. It brought to its term an era of Anglican theology no less than an epoch of English political history. The theological result of it was that the Anglican ideal was bifurcated. The Caroline divines had recognized that an Incarnational interpretation of religion found its full expression only in a unity which includes thought and life, prayer and cultus, contemplation and action. It understood that Incarnationalism requires that the *Summum Bonum* should be reflected in all these different *bona* in varying degrees; and to a great extent the Anglican ideal, as it had been realized in the seventeenth century, was a comprehensive whole of this nature. But at the Revolution the division of the Church into two parts brought with it the dissolution of this unity. Henceforward the "intellectual" aspects of religion were to be cultivated all but exclusively by the "Jurors," while the "mystical" and the "sacramental" elements of the Faith were to be the peculiar possession of the "Non-Jurors"; and thus at one blow the magnificent unity of Caroline theology was shattered, to remain disunited for nearly two hundred years.

The effects of this bifurcation are brought out clearly in the history of the earlier stagers of both the Tractarian[1] and the Broad Church Movements.[2] On the one hand, the leaders of the Oxford Movement[3] are seen to have been concerned almost solely with the traditional, the mystical, and the Sacramental side of religion, to the

---

[1] Tractarianism refers to the movement that evolved during the 1830s as a reaction against the new liberal theology of that era.

[2] The Broad Church phenomenon refers to the moderate movement that emerged during the mid-nineteenth century as a response to the narrow perceptions of doctrine inherent in the practices of Anglo-Catholics and anti-Roman Evangelicals.

[3] Nineteenth-century movement at the University of Oxford that sought a renewal of Roman Catholic thought and practices within the Church of England in opposition to the church's Protestant tendencies.

neglect of its broader philosophical aspects; while on the other hand, the first phase of the Liberal Movement, though it courageously faced the intellectual problems which discoveries in natural science, in Biblical criticism, in archæology, and in other fields created from religion, only too frequently betrayed little understanding of the Sacramental aspects of the Faith and sometimes ever deeply suspected them. Happily much has happened since the days of the *Tracts for the Times* and of *Essays and Reviews*. The last half-century has seen the growth of an Anglican theology which can find room for the manifold elements of religious experience and life, and yet be in immediate contact with the best "secular" thought of the age. The work of theologians such as those whose names are to be found among the contributors to the collections of essays known as *Lux Mundi, Foundations,* and *Essays Catholic and Critical*, shows how far we have moved from the standpoints both of the eighteenth and of the early nineteenth centuries. It may justly be said that "anyone who comes fresh from reading the Caroline Divines to Gore[1] and the other essayists of *Lux Mundi* will feel that here ... he has picked up again the straight continuity of direction."

Creeds and Formularies

The Christian who believes that human reason is related *per modum analogiae* with the Reason of God will recognize at once the importance of a rational account of his faith. And if he goes on to hold— as surely he certainly must—that in Christ Incarnate was revealed in the most complete form possible under human conditions the nature and being of God, he will turn to this source for the solution of his deepest speculative questionings. This is, of course, what happened in the early history of the Church. As soon as Christians began to mediate upon the implications of the Revelation which had been committed to them, they found themselves face to face with the issues of metaphysics. The Primitive Church could not have understood what was meant by Incarnation, by Divine Sonship, by the conceptions of "Messiah" and of "Son of Man," by the facts of forgiveness, of salvation, of perfection, without bringing them into mutual relatedness in a Christian Philosophy. Believing that to her care had been entrusted the Truth, she was

---

[1]   Charles Gore (1853–1932), English theologian and Anglican bishop.

convinced that the study of the Revelation made in the Incarnate Christ would reveal to her members progressively more about the world, and that what was dim and obscure would be made clearer by the promised guidance of him who was the Spirit of Truth. As time went on she found that, partly under the stress of controversy, partly through more directly constructive influences, the details of the Faith came to receive fuller elucidation and clearer definition. What had hitherto been fluid and undeveloped became crystallized in such forms as the literature of the Bible, the writings of the Fathers, the authoritative pronouncements of Bishops, the formulae of the Creeds, the definitions of Councils, and so on.

The vehicles just named are among those through which the Faith of the Church has come to expression. The use of such created instruments for the embodiment of eternal truth will be seen to be in complete harmony with the Incarnational principle. Man stands at the point of juncture of the temporal and eternal, and hence necessarily perceives the eternal under the language and forms of time. To have recognized the importance of the part played by the empirical factor in human knowing was one of the profoundly Christian elements in St. Thomas's system. As Dr. Kirk[1] remarks with much justice, Aquinas is "perhaps the first Christian philosopher to take the corporeal character of human existence calmly." In modern philosophy, one is reminded of the similar insistence made by Kant[2] upon the relatedness of the temporal and the eternal factors in cognition. We thus see here another instance of a principle in the natural order which is no less applicable—but *per modum analogiae*—to the conditions of the communication of supernatural verity.

A necessary corollary of this consideration would seem to be that no revelation of truth can reach us altogether divorced from an element of contingency. "Infallibilities," that is, are never to be met within religion. The authority which attaches to any particular element of revealed truth will be partly dependent upon the nature of the organ through which it receives expression. There must be, therefore, degrees of dogmatic authority. Some authorities clearly have more inherent claims to be trusted as witnesses to the truth than others. More weight—always *ceteris paribus*,[3] of course—will attach to the solemn

---

[1]   Kenneth E. Kirk (1886–1954), theologian and scholar.
[2]   Immanuel Kant (1724–1804), German philosopher.
[3]   Other things being equal.

decisions of a General Council than to the utterances of the individual Bishops who compose it; to the pronouncements of the Bishop of an important see than to those of an obscure divine; to the utterances of Christians of outstanding saintliness that to those of the worldly or the contentious; to the judgments of the learned than to those of the superficial or ignorant. We have, however, no indication in the teaching of the Gospels that to any of these particular vehicles was to be entrusted the capacity of producing infallible statements; on the contrary, such a presumption would be difficult to reconcile with the conditions under which on the principles of the Incarnation the communication of Divine Truth alone seems possible.

As a concrete illustration of the foregoing, the creeds may be examined in somewhat more detail. To these summaries of dogmatic truth greater importance has probably been attached in the Church of England than in an other Communion in Christendom. Anglicanism, indeed, seems to be unique in considering the "Three Creeds" —the Apostles' Creed, the Nicene Creed, and the Athanasian Creed—as a set of dogmatic formularies *sui generis*. In the Primitive Church there existed a large number of Creeds, but their content and language was fluid, and they differed considerably from place to place. As regards our own familiar Creeds, the origin of all three of them is obscure. The view generally current in the Middle Ages that the Apostles' Creed was compiled by the Twelve Apostles has universally been abandoned by modern scholars. This Creed is now known to be the result of a long growth and believed not to have reached its present form before the eighth century. The origin of what we know as the Nicene Creed is also veiled in darkness. The Creed certainly received Conciliar authority at the Council of Chalcedon in A.D. 451, but it seems probable that the divines of that council were under a misapprehension when they asserted that it had been promulgated at the Council of Constantinople in A.D. 381. At all events it belongs to a much later date than the Council of Nicaea in A.D. 325. Wrapped in still more obscurity are the origins of the so-called Athanansian Creed. It was certainly not written by St. Athanasius,[1] for it is a Latin composition. Such authority then as attaches to the Creeds must belong to them in virtue of other circumstances than the traditional views of their genesis.

Nevertheless, the authority which these Creeds possess is immense. From time immemorial, they have proved invaluable as summaries of

---

[1]   St. Athanasius (c.297–373), patriarch of Alexandria.

the Christian Faith. Through a period of some fifteen centuries they have found a continuous place in the life and worship of the Church and they give expression to the Christian Faith as, in its main outlines, it is still all but universally held. Even in the case of the Athanasian Creed, the objections sometimes raised to it are directed not so much against the positive content of its teaching—which is for the most part admirable—as against the anathemas which are attached to it and the suitability of its form to public worship. Occasionally objection is taken to a very few (hardly more than three) clauses in the Apostles' Creed—namely, "born of the Virgin Mary," "the third day," and "the Resurrection of the Body" (*resurrectio carnis*). But even here, except on a rather rigid literalism, the grounds upon which these clauses are questioned have (so, at least, it may be argued) not sufficient cogency to require the rejection of this Creed from the position which it has come to acquire in historic Christianity.

The Creeds may be taken, then, as instances of dogmatic formularies which, if viewed from the standpoint of broad principle, have stood the test of a long history. The fortunes of the vast majority of such formularies, however, have been less favoured. As an instance of a set of formulae which history has discredited may be taken our Thirty-Nine Articles. Unlike the Creeds, these consist of a number of *theologoumena*,[1] drawn up *ad hoc*[2] by theologians in an epoch singularly ill fitted to legislate for the thought of succeeding generations. They cannot claim the prestige of an extended history, and if they ever possessed any usefulness, they have long since outgrown it. To turn from the Creeds to the Articles is to turn from historic fact and clear principle to narrow partisanship and contentious bickering. Some of the teaching set forth in the Articles implies a view of human nature that is doubtfully Christian, and many of their assertions are quite irreconcilable with an Incarnational view of the Christian Faith. There can be few theologians today, for instance, who could concur with the teaching of the Thirteenth Article that the good deeds of the heathen, so far from being "pleasant to God," "rather, for that they are not done as God hath willed and commanded them to be done, we doubt not but they have the nature of sin." Perhaps there are still fewer who would wish to impose *as an article of religion* the assertion in the Thirty-Seventh Article that "it is lawful for Christian men, at

---

[1] Theological remarks.
[2] For specific needs or purposes.

the commandment of the magistrate, to wear weapons and serve in the wars." Moreover, some of the assertions in the Articles are definite misstatements of fact. The tiro in Church history knows that it is untrue to refer to the Canonical Books of the Old and New Testament as those "of whose authority there was never any doubt in the Church." There was, of course, considerable difference of opinion about the Canonicity of certain of the New Testament books until well into the fourth century.

It may, no doubt, be argued that the specific teachings of the Articles no longer exercise much influence in the Church of England. The present writer has recently had occasion to read the examination papers of some 500 Ordinands[1] on the subject of Christian Morals, and though there has been the fullest occasion for the expression of such views, not a single candidate has indicated that he held the view about Works done before Justification set forth in Article XIII. Perhaps the acquaintance of some Ordinands with the Articles is not vastly greater than that of the seventeenth-century candidate who, when his Bishop confronted him with the searching question, "how many there were of the Articles," boldly replied, "Two and twenty." But it is highly undesirable that a totally antiquated and seemingly useless set of formulae should receive the assent on oath of every candidate for Holy Orders, and that the disproportionately large congregation which comes to church to welcome the newly appointed Incumbent should hear these obsolete theological pronouncements read out as though they epitomized and heralded the teaching which it was his duty to impart. By the retention and use of such formulae, the Church suggests to the uninstructed that she has lost contact with the intellectual, moral, and spiritual needs of the age. In our own view it is much to be wished that at the first opportunity the necessary legislative steps may be taken to abolish the Thirty-Nine Articles to that limbo whither many of the other contemporary formularies have now been consigned.

The Sociological Implications of Catholicism

From the Incarnational character of the Christian Faith, if follows that the Gospel has immediate implications for human society and its ideals. No province of human life can lie without the frontiers

---

[1] Candidates for ordination.

of a faith which claims to be all-inclusive. The Church, therefore, must seek to understand, as far as she can, the individual and corporate strivings of mankind, and endeavor to unify and guide them. It is her sociological vocation to redeem the natural elements in the social order, and to transmute them into a "new creation." The principle again is *Gratia non tollit naturam, sed perficit.*

There are, indeed, some Christians who urge (misguidedly, so the Incarnationalist must believe) that the Church ought to take no part in such matters. They contend that her concern is purely with "personal" religion, and that her one mission is to bring men into the right religious relationship with God—to teach them how to say their prayers, how to repent of their sins, how in a word to "find salvation"; and they argue that beyond this point the Church's function ends. In justification of this view they sometimes maintain that when men have "got right with God," all political, social, and economic issues will look after themselves. But such an attitude is radically at variance with an Incarnational philosophy. *In quantum est quidquid est, bonum est.* Political, economic, and social ideals—the sum-total, that is, of those ends which may be described in a wide sense as "Sociological"—are, for the Catholic, ideals which stand in immediate relationship to God, the *Summum Bonum.* Of several contending sociological doctrines an Incarnational religion must needs hold that only one of them is the "best"; and hence it must seek to discover which one this is and then endeavor to actualize it. The Church, if she is to be true to her vocation, is bound to give guidance to those seeking it on the great issues of contemporary human life.

The demand for the Church to exercise her consecrating and directive influence upon human culture is peculiarly pressing at the present time. Her aim is unity, whereas contemporary civilisation is impeded and threatened on all sides by forces which make for disruption. At every turn we find disunity—a strongly developed class-consciousness, high tariff barriers, and intense nationalism—facts which are the sociological counterparts of over-specialization in thought, in learning, and in science. Even more disconcerting is the absence of unity in personal morality. Clear canons of choice have been abandoned and men are unable to decide between conflicting claims. Probably never before in history have the resources which make for technical efficiency been greater that they are today. Manufactures are pouring out of our industries at so lavish a rate and with so little physical exertion that the labor market is flooded with the unemployed. And yet everywhere the world is crying *Quo tendimus?*[1] It is to this question that the Church believes that she alone can provide the answer. She claims—almost without rivals, be it noted—to be possessed of a principle of unity which can permit of these *bona* being understood in a comprehensive and unified setting.

In relation to the carrying of this takes into effect, two points need emphasis. The first is that the Church should recognize that if her decision is to be of any value, it ought to take the fullest account of the best available "secular" evidence. The pronouncements of some clergy upon sociological questions, it must be feared, suffer only too often from a deplorable "amateurism." Beyond and above all "secular" evidence, the Church has indeed to reckon with evidence belonging to a new Order, facts which have reached her through the Gospel. The possession of such data will enable the Church to arrive at principles and to outline a policy based upon them vastly superior to those which are open to those whose vision is limited by purely "secular" considerations. But when all this is perceived, the Church must not forget that the natural order also has its place in the Divine economy, and that the Christian Sociologist must understand it to the best of his ability.

The other point which needs emphasis concerns the method by which the Church should seek to make her voice heard in a world which has lost the desire for unity. There is no doubt that the Church has not as yet sufficiently adapted to the present age her somewhat stereotyped and now partially antiquated methods of commending her faith. The pulpit is a vehicle which today reaches only a small proportion of our population, and these not always the most critical. We imperatively need a daily newspaper which is definitely and uncompromisingly Christian in outlook. To illustrate what is required, reference may perhaps be made to the treatment week by week of foreign affairs in the opening "Summary paragraphs" of the *Church Times*. The reader finds here Christian principles brought to bear upon matters of international importance by what is widely recognised to be a singularly well-informed and judicious criticism. But presumably the *Church Times* circulates almost exclusively among those who already claim the name of Christian; and like other religious journals is looked upon by its readers as a Friday religious appendage to the secular press which is studied

---

[1]   Where are we going?

exclusively on the other six days of the week. The Church undoubtedly requires a daily newspaper which shall circulate on its own merits, whose outlook from the first page to the last is Christian, and wherein at every turn Christian principles are brought to bear upon the course of events, whether in literature or in politics or in art, or in whatever else may be the subject of the hour.

Christian Asceticism

In virtue of the "tension" to which reference was made at the outset of this essay, Christianity is both world-accepting and world-rejecting. It therefore not only allows a place to "asceticism," but sets a high value upon it. An account of the Universe which was unreservedly Pantheistic could find no scope for renunciation. On purely Immanental[1] premises every action, no matter what its motives or what its consequences, would be an expression of the Divine Nature, and therefore necessarily absolutely good. At the other end of the scale, Dualistic thought, by refusing to allow the possibility of any goodness attaching to things *hic et nunc*,[2] requires the complete renunciation of all that is held in estimations by human standards, and asserts that pleasures as such are evil. Christianity pursues a path between these two philosophies. It holds that whatever is truly human *ipso facto*[3] shares in its degree in the goodness of God. But it also maintains that not all human actions are *equally* good. The fact that goodness has its grades demands that growth towards perfection should go hand in hand with the renunciation of the lower in favour of the higher. "If any one will come after me, let him deny himself, and take up his cross and follow me" (Mark viii.34). Certain pleasures, therefore, are to be renounced by the Christian, not because they are intrinsically evil nor, on the other hand, because renunciation is an end in itself, but because indulgence in them is a hindrance towards the fullest Christian life. Such is the theological justification for the great emphasis which in the history of the Church has been set upon a measure of asceticism. According to a careful definition, asceticism is "the practice of evangelical renunciation which is either demanded by the Christian law or is simply counseled as a means of more

---

[1] Operating within the realm of reality.
[2] Here and now.
[3] By the fact itself.

certainly tending towards Christian perfection and of more effectively contributing to the common good of the Christian Society." There is thus no call to renunciation of pleasures for their own sake. When the call to the sacrifice of pleasure is heard, it comes simply because indulgence in it is an impediment to other and more important claims. Indeed, so far is pleasure from being in itself undesirable that, *ceteris paribus*, a world in which there is more pleasure is "better," and therefore from an Incarnational standpoint more "Christian," than one in which there is less. Yet from the earliest times the Church has sought to encourage *ascesis*[1] among her members, and for this she has made provision in two ways. By the one she has sought to prescribe a minimum amount of mortification upon all her faithful; by the other, she has given opportunity for a much enhanced degree of it to such Christians as receive the call to it.

The former means of discipline is fostered by the place which Days of Fasting and Abstinence occupy in the Liturgical Year. Friday by Friday, the Church bids abstinence in remembrance of the Friday on which the Lord effected the supreme sacrifice for the salvation of the world. In Lent and Passiontide, she recalls the Temptation of the Son of Man and impresses upon her members that only through suffering can they hope to reach the joy of the Resurrection. By her Ember Seasons,[2] with their emphasis upon the close association between prayer and fasting, she reminds her children that the Christian ideal of prayer is not uncontrolled mystical rapture, but a life of disciplined communion. In ways such as these, the Church sets the ideal of *ascesis* before all her members.

But for those to whom the vocation comes to a life of fuller renunciation the Church has sought to make further provision. From the rich young man of the Gospel, there have been those who have heard the call to "perfection"; and it has been the especial function of the Religious Orders and Congregations to train in saintliness and renunciation those who have heard this call. With the varying needs of individuals and the changing circumstances of times, the Religious Life has assumed, as all students of Church history are aware, very different forms; but the record of many of its triumphs and its fruits, both in the spiritual and the temporal orders, belongs to the history

---

[1]   Self-discipline, asceticism.

[2]   Ember seasons refer to the days of fasting to sanctify the season; ember Saturdays were considered especially appropriate for ordinations.

of Western civilisation. It would be difficult, indeed, to overestimate the extent to which the course of European culture has been modified by the work of such religious as St. Anthony and St. Basil, St. Benedict and St. Bernard, St. Francis and St. Dominic, St. Ignatius Loyola and St. Theresa.[1] If Monasticism has here and there had its dark patches, it has been on the whole an enormous influence for good. Moreover, it is of deep significance that the achievements of the Religious Orders, so impressive even when judged by purely "secular"[2] standards, have been brought about by men and women whose ideals were essentially "other-worldly." Whatever be the explanation, it seems to be a fact that a life modeled on the world-denying counsels is found often to lead to more permanent and fruitful results in the temporal order than those which issue from ideals more immediately and consciously philanthropic.

In the Church of England, the last hundred years have seen a remarkable revival of the Religious Life. Such names as Cowley,[3] Mirfield,[4] and Wantage,[5] to mention no others, have become household words throughout the length and breadth of *Ecclesia Anglicana*.[6] But there is still scope for a much fuller growth of the Monastic life amongst us; and as it is possible that the next developments of it will proceed along somewhat less traditional methods than those followed by the existing Orders, we will conclude this section by venturing to suggest lines upon which two possible future Orders might be conceived. Each of these Orders would, we believe, meet an outstanding need of the present time.

The first of these would be an Order whose function it should be to study afresh the bearing of the Christian Faith upon the intel-

---

[1] St. Anthony (c.251–c.350), Egyptian hermit; St. Basil the Great (c.330–379), Greek prelate and bishop of Caesarea in Cappadocia; St. Benedict (d. c.547), Italian monk; St. Bernard of Clairvaux (c.1090–1153), French churchman and mystic; St. Francis of Assisi (c.1182–1226), founder of the Franciscans; St. Dominic (c.1170–1221), Castilian churchman; St. Ignatius Loyola (1491–1556), Spanish churchman and founder of the Jesuits; St. Theresa of Ávila (1515–1582), Spanish nun and mystic.

[2] Beyond the realm of religious considerations.

[3] Cowley was the first Anglican religious community for men. Known as the Society of St. John the Evangelist (the Cowley Fathers), it was founded in 1866 at Oxford.

[4] Mirfield refers to the English Community of the Resurrection (Mirfield Fathers) founded in 1892 at Mirfield, Yorkshire.

[5] Wantage refers to the English Community of St. Mary the Virgin at Wantage, Berkshire (1848).

[6] The Anglican Church.

lectual background of the age. It would set out to do for today what St. Dominic's Order did for the thirteenth century. From the nature of the case, such an Order could not be "enclosed." It would have to keep in immediate contact with the development and progress of contemporary thought; and hence it would be desirable that it should be centered either in a University town or in some other focus of intellectual life. It might be a matter of some difficulty to prescribe what freedom should be allowed to its members; probably this would have to differ more from individual to individual than is the case in most of the now existing Orders. In such an Order, no rule could reasonably require a man to spend so many hours a day at his desk, or to produce so many words for the printer each week. It could not profitably require even that he should devote all his activities to one particular piece of work—to the elucidation, say, of one particular problem or to the writing of one particular book; for doubtless the all but universal experience of scholars is that they derive stimulus from change of work. The freshness which comes from relaxation and diversion of activities would thus have to be fully allowed for. But somehow the community in question would have to insist that each of its members should be willing to subordinate all his other activities to the one particular piece of work which the community assigned to him.

From such a cooperative effort, carried out with determination and purpose by men of tried ability, results of enormous value might be expected. Few theologians living "in the world" today are able to give unfettered attention to their vocation. Their energies are constantly diversified into a vast number of channels—preaching, organizing, tutoring, lecturing, examining, reviewing, controverting, conferring, and so on (to say nothing of such claims as matrimony and their implications). On the other hand, those who are least hindered from study by the interference of such obstacles are apt to suffer seriously from isolation. In a community in which the activities of its members were properly directed such hindrances would be obviated. Great freedom would have to be allowed, of course, for differences of theological opinion. No study can be unfettered if the results at which the student is to arrive are prescribed to him from the outset; and a ludicrous situations would arise if a member of the community were to find that when his studies had reached a certain stage he was liable to suspension or expulsion by reason of his conclusions. Further, it would be imperative that the life of the community should be kept in touch with contemporary culture to the greatest possible extent. The lections at meals might sometimes be the Lives of the Saints—the traditional stand-by of the refectory pulpit—but they might more often be the writings of the Huxleys[1] or Mr. Lloyd George's[2] latest programme for economic reconstruction or the newest set of Gifford Lectures.[3]

The other Order that it is possible to visualise is one which would concern itself with the propagation of International Peace. The masses of the world in revolt against Militarism have as yet no leader, and perhaps under no other leadership except under that of him who is the "Prince of Peace"[4] will they ever make their convictions effective. An Order whose purpose it was to preach in season and out of season the futility and, what is far more important, the immorality of War, and which aimed at uniting men and women throughout the world in groups determined to resist it in all circumstances, might reasonably hope to achieve what other methods have hitherto failed to effect. Indeed, it may be doubted whether anything short of religious motives will ever prove a successful weapon against the potent forces of all kinds and descriptions which make for war.

The members of such an Order would presumably be itinerants. They would be constantly on the move from place to place, preaching in the marketplace and conducting missions in such parish churches as were placed at their disposal. They would attest their sincerity by their selflessness—by accepting no more from the world than was necessary to satisfy their modest needs. They would proclaim incessantly that, however estimable in themselves were the sentiments of "loyalty," such sentiments must be resisted with might and main if exploited by a Government in favour of a war. They would unite those who accepted their principles into an Association pledged religiously to active anti-Militarism.

A comparatively small Order of thoroughly devoted and disciplined men, fired with this sense of vocation, might exercise a determining influence upon the destiny of Western Europe. Through their

---

1   Thomas Henry Huxley (1825–1895), English biologist and educator; Aldous Leonard Huxley (1894–1963), English author of *Brave New World* (1932).
2   David Lloyd George, 1st Earl Lloyd-George of Dwyfor (1863–1945), British statesman.
3   Annual philosophical and theological lectures held at the Universities of Edinburgh, Glasgow, Aberdeen, and St. Andrews.
4   Jesus Christ.

agency there would come into existence a united body of Christian people, definitely bound to do all in their power to hinder a Government when it contemplated entry upon a War. On the occasion of a threatened or an initiated war they would have no hesitation in being "disloyal," knowing that "loyalty" to a Government in such circumstances would be no more justified than "loyalty" to a Government which sought to re-introduce slavery or to stamp out Christianity. The vast majority in every nation are opposed to war and (as circumstances in this country in the last war proved) can be induced to take part in it only by "conscription"; but hitherto they have been effectively silenced on the outbreak of every war, as they have possessed no concerted plan of action. No Government in Europe, however, would venture to embark on a war if it knew that such a course would be resisted within its borders by a large mass of convinced and "Militant Pacificism." At the present time there are multitudes who are awaiting an uncompromising lead from the Church in this direction.

Catholic Sacramentalism

A further principle which is intimately connected with the Incarnation is that of Sacramentalism. The Christian faith is built upon the conviction that the key to human life is to be found in the life and death and resurrection of one born of humble stock and nurtured in comparative obscurity. In this circumstance is discovered the guarantee that the least pretending elements in creation may serve as vehicles for Divine revelation. Popular theology has become accustomed to summarize this conviction in its formula that the Sacraments are "the extension of the Incarnation." Through seemingly unimportant outward instruments, the Godhead makes contact with the human world order.

The emphasis laid by those Christians who value the name of "Catholic" upon the Sacramental elements in religion is too familiar to require elaboration. The particular forms which Sacramentalism assumes in current practice are the outcome of a long development. In this principle in Christianity the outward elements in religion necessarily receive especial prominence—for a Sacrament is, as the Catechism phrases it, "an outward and visible sign of an inward and spiritual grace"—and hence it is natural that Sacramental forms, as external ordinances, should be exceptionally susceptible to the external changes which mark the world of history. Recent Anglo-Catholicism has borrowed much in this field from Rome. For instance, the Tridentine doctrine of the Sacraments, with its insistence upon their sevenfold number, has found increasing favour. But as long as the principle of Sacramentalism is conserved, there is no reason to suppose that any particular form of Sacramentalism will be permanent nor that the differences between the several forms of it are of major importance. Unlike the Tridentine theologians, the Tractarians for the most part followed their Caroline ancestors in restricting the term "Sacrament" to the two "Sacraments of the Gospel"—Baptism and the Eucharist. On the other hand, before the thirteenth century the term was frequently applied to a much larger number of the rites than the seven of Trent. Hugh of St.Victor[1] enumerated no less than thirty *sacramenta*....[2]

In connexion with Sacramental theology, it should also be noticed that the Sacraments are not only channels of Divine communication but are possessed, in addition, of a representative function. Here again their relatedness to the Incarnation becomes evident. Just as Christ was representative of the human race, so correspondingly the Eucharistic Bread and Wine are representative of all bread and wine and, ultimately, of the whole of created nature. The reverence due to the sacred species is thus representative of the reverence due to God's presence throughout the external world. A similar representative function attaches to other religious objects whose character is in essence Sacramental. The Bible is representative of every form of great literature, the Cathedral or the Parish Church of all that is great in the realm of art; and hence the respect paid by the Christian to such things is expressive of his proper attitude to every fraction of crated being. For, on the principle of analogy, the world is through and through Sacramental. Every fragment of creation shares to some degree in the goodness of God and, in so far, can claim our reverence.

Liturgical Worship

Closely connected with Sacramentalism is the subject of Liturgical Worship. The Forms of Liturgy are the outward dress with which Christian devotion is normally clothed, and as such are another

---

[1] Hugh of Saint Victor (1096–1141), European philosopher and theologian.
[2] Sacraments.

expression of the Incarnational principle at the heart of the Christian Faith. For the Incarnationalist the ordering of worship can thus never be a subject of indifference. Indeed, those who have penetrated most deeply not the meaning of interior prayer have usually been among those who have emphasised most the importance of its external forms. What Order of Contemplatives, for instance, would dare to dispense with its Breviary?

In the matter of Liturgy, Incarnationalism makes the same demands as elsewhere for "mediation"; and not without justice many Anglicans hold that the ceremonial ideal of the Church of England is a *via media*. When Simon Patrick[1] approved of "that virtuous mediocrity which our Church observes between the meretricious gaudiness of the Church of Rome and the squalid sluttery of fanatic conventicles," he was uttering no vain boast. The same eulogy of "the mean" is to be discovered in George Herbert's poem, "The British Church,"[2] and the divines of the Savoy Conference summed up over a hundred years of our liturgical history with the assertion that "it hath been the wisdom of the Church of England, ever since the first compiling of her Public Liturgy, to keep the mean between the two extremes of too much stiffness in refusing and of too much easiness in admitting, any variation from it." The *via media* both in the extent to which ceremonies have been prescribed and in the amount of freedom permitted in respect to what has been ordered has marked Anglicanism throughout its history.

But if it is possible for the Church of England to justify the liturgical ideal she has set before herself, she can hardly claim that her present Liturgical forms are altogether satisfactory. Indeed, it is all but universally recognized that the existing Book of Common prayer is no longer fully suited to modern needs. The intellectual, political, social, and economic changes of the three centuries which have now nearly elapsed since 1662 have been so vast that unless we are to believe that Christian worship stands unrelated to these aspects of life, it could scarcely be expected that the devotional forms of the existing Book should be those most adequate to the requirements of the present day. The very fact that our Liturgy uses a "language understanded of the people" makes those who use it the more conscious of the need for change. Consequently the desirability of a

---

[1]   Simon Patrick (1627–1707), English theologian and Bishop of Chichester.
[2]   George Herbert (1593–1633), English metaphysical poet.

revision which should take account of these altered conditions is widely admitted. Certainly few Anglo-Catholics would have any objections to revision in itself, and most Anglo-Catholics would warmly welcome a measure of it.

The reason why the Deposited Book of 1928[1] was distasteful to so many Anglo-Catholics is to be accounted for by the circumstances of its origin. Briefly summarized, they appear to be these. From about the middle of the last century onwards, a certain latitude in interpreting the rubrics of the 1662 Book became widespread, and as time went on some of them came to be universally broken. Dissatisfaction with the letter of the Book was thus felt on almost all sides; and individuals, believing that there was little immediate hope of securing through the legislative channels a revision such as they desired, introduced changes on their own initiative. In one church, for instance, the Athanasian Creed would be omitted from Morning Prayer on the days on which its use was prescribed; in another, Eucharistic prayers and ceremonial would be introduced which the rubrics did not countenance or even forbad; in a third, services for which there was no authority in the Book of Common Prayer—Mission Services, Harvest Thanksgivings, the Three Hours' Service, Compline, Devotions before the Blessed Sacrament—would be used.

It was with this situation that the Royal Commission on Ecclesiastical Discipline sought to deal when in June 1904 it held its first meeting. The natural outcome was that the projected new Prayer Book came to be envisaged by its compilers rather as an instrument to enable the recreation of uniformity than as a manual of worship. As the attempted revision proceeded through its various stages, the disciplinary aspects of the Book were increasingly emphasised while devotional and liturgical considerations receded more and more into the background. When at length those charged with the revision were faced with the practical issue as to how the Book would be received by the legislative courts—the Church Assembly, Convocation, and Parliament—the one motive which seems to have been dominant among its supporters was the determination to secure at any price that the Book should be accepted. Successive changes in the Book thus were made, not because they were demanded by any devotional or liturgical or theological principles, by almost solely (so at least it seemed to many Anglo-Catholics)

---

[1] A controversial new version of the English Book of Common Prayer.

because they were more likely to make the Book commendable to the legislative bodies concerned. A comparison between the 1927 and the 1928 Book makes it abundantly clear that this was so in the final stages of the revision. It is not surprising that a Book produced in this way should have proved from the liturgical point of view a failure. The severe judgment on the 1927 Book of Mr. F.E. Brightman,[1] probably the most outstanding English lituriologist then living, is well known. "As to the Book as a whole I would say ... that on almost every page of it I find something irritating, something inexact or untidy or superfluous or ill-considered or unreal."

Nevertheless a revision in the near future of certain parts, at least, of the Book of Common Prayer is esteemed by many Anglo-Catholics a great *desideratum*.[2] The Occasional Offices are particularly in need of modification and reconstruction. In the Office of Baptism, the Book of 1927 indicated the direction in which alteration is desirable by its excision of the phrase "conceived and born in sin" and its substitution in their place of the words that "we are taught in Holy Scripture that God willeth all men to be saved, for God is love." The references to the Ark and to the Red Sea could also very profitably be removed. In the Marriage Service, the existing introductory exhoration with its assertion about the institution of matrimony urgently demands considerable modification. The services for both the Visitation of the Sick and the Burial of the Dead are likewise in need of reform. In all these cases the Deposited Book supplies many suggestions as to possibilities; for it was in its least controversial parts that the Book naturally achieved most success.

In the matter of Eucharistic worship, most of those who call themselves Anglo-Catholics would like to see not only Reservation of the Sacrament definitely legitimized, but also provision made that the reserved species should be kept in a tabernacle and not in an aumbry or locked chapel. The methods of Reservation countenanced by the promulgators of the Deposited Book were ostentatiously inconvenient. They aimed at erecting obstacles to devotion, and by removing the Sacrament from the altar tended to dissociate it from the idea of Communion. Many Catholics would also wish to see at any rate Devotions to the Blessed Sacrament, if not Benediction, provided for. Some measure of reform in the Eucharisitic Rite would also be

---

[1]   Frank Edward Brightman (1856–1932).
[2]   Something desired as essential.

welcome. In the light of our extended liturgical knowledge and modern needs, our present Canon is evidently susceptible of considerable improvement. The range of Proper Collects, Epistles, and Gospels should be greatly increased to make provision for the now widespread practice of Daily Celebrations and the observance of many Saints and Commemorations. Proper Introits,[1] Graduals,[2] Offertories, and Post-Communions should also be given official recognition. The Ten Commandments could profitably be removed. Not only are their moral precepts not specifically Christian, but their cosmology rings uncouth in modern ears; it is undesirable to convey the impression that the Church holds that "in six days the Lord made heaven and earth."

Perhaps the greatest anomaly in Anglican worship, however, is the place which Matins[3] and Evensong[4] have come to occupy in it. Based upon Offices intended primarily for Monastic Orders, these services have in the majority of Anglican churches come to be the normal form of Sunday worship. The long tradition which lies behind this use of them demands respect, for liturgical forms and customs, somehow, acquire sanctity through usage. But, this consideration apart, it would be hard to conceive of two services more ill fitted for their purpose. By a curious anomaly their contents are predominantly pre-Christian. On an average Sunday, the worshipers at Matins will hear from five to seven passages from the Old Testament, and not more than two (i.e., the "Second Lesson" and perhaps the "Benedictus") from the New. Such a form of worship might be well suited to those who, nurtured in the Christian tradition and familiar with its principles from childhood, as it were grew into it and interpreted it with Christian associations; but it may be seriously doubted whether it is likely to meet the needs of a generation which needs to be instructed almost *ab initio*[5] as to what the Christian Faith is.

In the preceding sections the attempt has been made to expound from a particular standpoint some of the principles of the Christian Faith in their relationship to contemporary conditions. By such readers as have had sufficient patience to proceed this far, several judgments may have been passed. The considerations urged may

---

[1]   Music performed at the beginning of a worship service.
[2]   Verses read after the Epistle during Mass.
[3]   Morning prayers.
[4]   Evening prayers.
[5]   From the beginning.

have been deemed rash or commonplace, individualistic or partisan, antiquated or modernistic, rationalistic or credulous. The writer is fully conscious that they may well have suffered to some extent from all these limitations in different places.

An Incarnationalist interpretation of the Faith, however, cannot be final. It will seek not merely to tolerate but to encourage criticism. It is based upon the conviction that every human exposition of the truth is made by those who are themselves within the time-process. Every historic individual views Reality not *sub specie aeternitiais*,[1] but from a concrete situation *hic et nunc*, and hence every human account of the Faith must reflect the historically conditioned background and prejudices of its author. As long as we are pilgrims, we necessarily approach Reality. The shadows will depart only later. *Ex umbris et imaginibus in veritatem.*[2]

---

[1] From the aspect of eternity.
[2] Out of shadows and imagination into truth.

Appendix G: H.C. Allen, from Great Britain and the United States: A History of Anglo-American Relations, 1783-1952

[Entitled "Emotional Bonds," the following chapter from H. C. Allen's (1917–1998) *Great Britain and the United States: A History of Anglo-American Relations, 1783–1952* (1959) discusses the nature of Anglo-American relations during the Edwardian period. Allen devotes special attention to British and American perspectives of each other, as well as to their cultural and sociological spheres of difference.]

Hard as certain of the other aspects of Anglo-American relations are to assess with accuracy, the emotional is much the most difficult to describe and to evaluate. Not only must the predilections of the writer hinder balanced judgement, but there are immense obstacles in the way of accurate generalizations about human emotions, even in the case of individuals, let alone of whole nations. This is true of a nation like Great Britain, which is homogeneous and unified in a high degree, but it is doubly so of one which, like the United States, is bewildering in the variety of its origins, surroundings and circumstances. J.F. Muirhead[1] in his *Land of Contrasts*, published in 1898, wisely wrote that the object of his book would be "achieved, if it convinces a few Britons of the futility of generalizing on the complex organism of American society from inductions that would not justify an opinion about the habits of a piece of protoplasm." From time to time glaring examples of the disregard of this salutary advice thrust themselves upon attention; Geoffrey Gorer's *The Americans*[2] is a supreme instance of the nemesis which overtakes even observant and perspicuous men who rush into complex social problems and emerge hastily with simple "scientific" solutions. The many notes of interest which he strikes are utterly vitiated by the fact that he raises upon the

---

[1]   James Fullarton Muirhead (1853–1934).
[2]   Geoffrey Gorer (1905–1985) published *The Americans: A Study in National Character* in 1948.

precarious pinpoint apex of a neo-Freudian theory[1] of universal American "father rejection" a vast inverted pyramid of unsubstantiated conclusions. The writer may, therefore, be pardoned if he approaches such questions with the utmost caution.

Yet approached they must be, for human actions are very frequently emotional; this is true of national as well as individual decisions—no one who witnessed the career of Adolf Hitler can have any doubt of that—and we must therefore hazard some generalizations about national emotions for in international affairs we have, to some extent, to live by such conclusions. It is peculiarly necessary to do so in the case of peoples who have advanced to democracy for, as Mahan pointed out in the germinating years of Anglo-American friendship, "in nations of more complex organization ... the wills of the citizens have to be brought not to submission merely, but to accord." It has been a commonplace, at least since 1820 when Castlereagh[2] spoke the words, that "there are no two states whose friendly relations are of more practical value to each other and whose hostility so inevitably and so immediately entails upon both the most serious mischiefs [than] ... the British and American nations." With the development of full-blown democracy and the re-entry of America into world affairs, the feelings of the two peoples towards one another have become of crucial importance to the destiny of mankind, and it behooves us to venture some discussion of them. Nor is the way unlighted nor all the precedents discouraging; whatever the obstacles, men like Bryce[3] and Brogan[4] have brilliantly overcome them, and may help us to do so. But we cannot hope in the space of a brief chapter even to hint at all the important facts in a subject which has filled many books and could fill many more. We shall try merely to indicate in what ways the predominant cast of Anglo-American feeling has altered since 1783, and to show how complex, unstable, and often transient, are the movements lying behind these general changes.

I

The writer is emboldened to generalization by the undoubted fact of common national reactions to the phenomena of other lands.

---

[1]   A theory that finds its origins in the work of renowned Viennese psychoanalyst Sigmund Freud (1856–1939).

[2]   Robert Stewart Castlereagh (1769–1822), 2nd Marquis of Londonderry.

[3]   James Bryce, 1st Viscount (1838–1922), British historian, statesman, and diplomat.

[4]   Denis William Brogan (1900–1974), British historian and political scientist.

Shortly after returning from his first visit to the United States in 1946, he read J.B. Priestley's *Midnight on the Desert*,[1] and was powerfully struck by the identical impressions made upon him and upon Priestley by a multitude of things American both great and small, despite the passage, since the book was published, of a decade which altered much in life on both sides of the Atlantic. These impressions were not merely of things physical—the contrast, for instance, between the overwhelming antiquity of the western deserts and the neoterism of humanity; or the fabulous nature of the Grand Canyon. Nor yet only of the works of men—the ubiquity of the advertisement in American life, the shoddy untidiness of much of the countryside, the superb magnificence of Boulder Dam, or "that long dissonant, mournful cry of American trains, that sound which seems to light up for a second the immense distances and loneliness of that country." They were impressions also of the American people themselves—the combination of individual kindness and mass heartlessness in American life, the lack of a feeling of security, the sense of harsh realities not far beneath the surface of things, the emphasis on individualism and yet the lack of individuality, the extent of anti-Semitism in America, or the bizarre culture of Southern California, where a neon sign "Psychologist," recalled by Priestley, matched one recalled by the writer, "Jesus Saves." Some changes were visible even in ten years—a growth in appreciation of art and music, for example, and a diversification of the economy of Southern California—but a surprising amount remained the same.

Similarly, one can take courage from the correspondence of so many American views of Britain; a multitude of Americans have been impressed by the sort of things that are recorded, for instance, by Margaret Halsey[2] in *With Malice Toward Some*, published in 1938. The smallness of English trains and the diminutive scale of the patchwork countryside (Robert Benchley once said that the British "take pleasure in such tiny, tiny things"); the splendour of English flowers; the Stygian gloom of the English Sunday; the waitress who, when asked by adults for a glass of milk, shakes her head and says, "You Americans!" (the writer once blurted out that Englishmen never drink milk after they have "grown up"); the English "blend

---

[1] John Boynton Priestley (1894–1984), English author. He published *Midnight on the Desert: A Chapter of Autobiography* in 1937.

[2] Margaret Frances Halsey (1910–1997), English author.

of shabbiness and imperturbable good nature" (Emerson noted a century earlier that the English were "good natured," and that an English lord "dresses a little worse than a commoner"); the wonder constituted by polite English children; the courtesy of English railway porters, and the horror of English railway stations (an appalled American of the writer's acquaintance habitually referred to Euston as the Hall of Death); the rural English refusal to recognize the existence of English industrialism; the constant English criticism and jealousy of America: "They have just one big blanket indictment of America. It isn't England"; the masculine dominion in English society; the lack of high pressure salesmanship in British stores; and the placidity of English life compared with American, where there is so much more violence, "a good deal in England makes the blood boil, but there is not nearly so much occasion as there is in America for blood to run cold." Here again, the war has wrought changes—the courtesy of porters is not now so marked and placidity has almost degenerated into inertia—but much remains unaltered.

Nor are such generalizations as these altogether invalid over longer stretches of time. Some English comments upon America run like a recurrent theme through almost the whole history of the two peoples. The wooden houses of Americans have been remarked upon by travellers from Cobbet[1] to the present day; their rocking chairs and their abundant use of ice for almost as long a period; the wonders of the New England fall make a universal impression (Lord Bryce, not a reticent man about American vices, couldn't trust his English reserve to speak properly about its virtues. Lloyd George confessed after his only trip to America that no matter how inconclusive his political mission he would at least go home remembering the overwhelming experience of the fall. A hundred years ago, Mrs. Trollope, who liked very little about these United States, broke down and wrote that at this season of the year "the whole country goes to glory."); the lack of privacy which was bemoaned by Basil Hall[2] on the river steamboats is regretted by J.F. Muirhead in railroad sleeping-cars; the power of the Press and the persistence of its reporters is noted from Dickens to Priestley; the heat of the houses is constantly the subject of comment by Englishmen, so that even Henry James installed central heating in his English home, and

---

[1]   William Cobbet (1763–1835).
[2]   Basil Hall (1788–1844).

could report, "my poor little house is now really warm—even hot"; their headlong hurry is almost universally decried from the earliest times, even before Thackeray wrote: "There is some electric influence in the air and sun here which we don't experience on our side of the globe; people can't sit still, people can't ruminate over their dinners, dawdle in their studies, they must keep moving"; there is even more universal praise for their "crushing hospitality"; the allegedly high rate of dyspepsia among them frequently calls forth amateur diagnoses and no doubt equally erroneous suggestions for cure; but the one persistent trait for which there is never any sympathy is the chewing and spitting of the land dubbed by Rupert Brooke,[1] "El Cuspidorado."

There are also constant strains in the comments of Americans about England during the last century and three-quarters. Gouverneur Morris[2] commented on the stiffness of English manners, and Fenimore Cooper[3] on their proneness to silence, but both found friendship beneath the somewhat forbidding exterior; Morris lamented English cooking, and more than a century later that great Anglophile W.H. Page[4] wrote, "they have only three vegetables and two of them are cabbages"; Cooper's complaints about the English weather found a similar echo in Page: "In this aquarium in which we live … it rains every day"; the London fog comes in for almost as much condemnation as the English rain, although G.H. Putnam[5] spoke of the rush of reminiscence produced by "a whiff of that wonderful compound of soot, fog, and roast mutton that go to the making of the atmosphere of London"; Cooper experienced, upon seeing the White Cliffs of Dover for the first time, a common American feeling of being "home"; Hawthorne also struck a familiar, but more unpleasant, note, when he said: "These people think so loftily of themselves and so contemptuously of everybody else, that it requires more generosity than I possess to keep always in perfectly good humor with them"; he also found the deadweight of English rural tradition, where "Life is … fossilized in its greenest leaf," very distasteful, and declared that it was better to endure the ceaseless changes of the New World than this

---

1   Rupert Brooke (1887–1915), English poet.
2   Gouverneur Morris (1752–1816), American political leader and diplomat.
3   James Fenimore Cooper (1789–1851), American novelist.
4   Walter Hines Page (1855–1918), American journalist and diplomat.
5   George Haven Putnam (1844–1930), American publisher.

"monotony of sluggish ages"; yet, as Emerson admired the orderliness of English life, so Hawthorne loved its scenery, which presented a "perfect balance between man and nature"; almost as many Americans have commented adversely upon the dirt of English barbers' shops, as (from Emerson to Santayana[1]) favourably upon the domesticity of the English; and there has been continuous and universal contempt for the "abject" servility involved in the English social system.

II

Some generalizations about the mutual feelings of the British and American peoples are, then, possible. In the formation of those feelings their attitude to one another's institutions and ideas is clearly of primary importance, and those attitudes have been conditioned by the quantity and quality of the information upon which they were based. Walter Page could still write such works during his ambassadorship as the *Anglo-American Association* (1871), the *Anglo-American League* (1898), and *The Pilgrims* (1901): "The longer I live here the more astonished I become at the fundamental ignorance of the British about us and at our fundamental ignorance about them." The position has improved since then, but to one who has specialized to any extent in Anglo-American history new examples are repeatedly forthcoming. Another Anglo-American Ambassador, Lord Halifax,[2] pointed to one deficiency as late as 1947: "The teaching of American history in British schools too often ends at Yorktown as the teaching of American history in American schools too often begins with Bunker Hill ... It might be said ... that Anglo-American history was for Englishmen to learn and for Americans to rewrite." Nevertheless, it remains true that American knowledge of Britain has always far exceeded her knowledge of any other country, and that British knowledge of America has improved out of all recognition in this century, and is now, perhaps, with the advent of the mass media of information, approaching its counterpart in quantity.

There are two main sources of such knowledge; direct, through travel and reports thereof, and indirect, through culture. In the case of direct knowledge the two peoples have perhaps been on an equal footing; in the case of indirect, the Americans were at first at an unquestionable advantage, though in recent years the English have

---

[1]   George Santayana (1863–1952), American philosopher and poet.
[2]   Edward Frederick Lindley Wood, 1st Earl of Halifax (1881–1959), British statesman.

probably been able to reverse this situation and learn more about the United States. But in any case the common language has always made mutual knowledge far easier than it normally is between different nations. It was no isolated instance when Nathaniel Hawthorne, steeped in English literature, wrote: "Almost always, in visiting such scenes as I have been attempting to describe, I had a singular sense of having been there before"; familiarity with England through the reading of English literature is a factor of the utmost importance in American understanding of Britain. Not that it is always without disadvantages; it often renders information out of date and misleading. To Henry Adams[1] on his first visit to London, "Aristocracy was real. So was the England of Dickens. Oliver Twist and little Nell[2] lurked in every churchyard shadow ... In November, 1858, ... it was the London of the eighteenth century that an American felt and hated." Frequently, too, as we have seen, Americans reacted against this cultural bondage, as witness the oration of an American school-boy heard by Captain Basil Hall in 1827-8: "Gratitude! Gratitude to England! What does America owe to her? ... We owe her nothing! For eighteen hundred years the world had slumbered in ignorance of liberty ... At length, America arose in all her glory, to give the world the long-desired lesson." But in the end the balance of true knowledge outweighed the distortion and the emotional rejections.

Perhaps the most reliable gauge of Anglo-American feeling is to be found among the travellers between the two lands, and here the historian of Anglo-American relations is fortunate enough to find two monographs on the subject ready to his hand. Allan Nevins[3] in his excellent analysis and anthology, *America through British Eyes*, gives a most comprehensive account of American social history seen by British travellers, which throws much light on the emotional relationship between the two peoples. He sees the subject as falling into five main periods, each in its turn broadly reflecting, with one exception, that ripening of friendship over the years, which we know to be one of the main features of Anglo-American relations. The first period, from 1783 to about 1825, he characterises as one of utilitarian enquiry, which marked a distinct improvement after the hatred

---

[1] Henry Adams (1838–1918), American writer and historian.

[2] Characters, respectively, in Dickens's novels *Oliver Twist* (1838) and *The Old Curiosity Shop* (1841).

[3] Allan Nevins (1890–1971) published *America through British Eyes* in 1948.

of the Revolutionary period; the tone of reports was on the whole factual and just. Men like Henry Wansey,[1] interested in American woollen manufacture, Henry B. Fearon,[2] investigating for the settlement of twenty English families, George Glover,[3] who laid out a number of English settlements in Illinois, John Woods,[4] one of those Illinois settlers, and William Cobbet, best known to American readers as *Peter Porcupine*,[5] set the tone of commentary, and drowned out the ill-natured accounts of unreliables, like Thomas Ashe and Isaac Weld,[6] and simpletons, like William Faux.[7]

Unfortunately, in the second period, from about 1825 to 1845, the hyper-critical and malicious voices gained the mastery, and the result was a distinct deterioration in Anglo-American feeling. The outburst of mutual ill-will, which we have seen in the cultural sphere after the War of 1812, was both reflected and caused by the new type of traveller; "instead of seekers after a living, there came seekers after new sights and experiences." Political passions also played their part, for men like Captain Marryat, Captain Thomas Hamilton and Godfrey T. Vigne,[8] while admitting the necessity of democracy in America, bitterly opposed its extension to Britain; their criticisms were made more telling by the fact that, with the advent of Jacksonian Democracy,[9] the tone of American political life had deteriorated in comparison with that of patrician days. Furthermore, the visitors tended to penetrate farther west, where conditions were worst; it was the western experiences of *Martin Chuzzelwit* that were the most unpleasant, and it was Dickens's description of them that Americans found it hardest to forgive, because, although they contained much that was true to life, they were at once the most characteristically American and yet—however unpleasant—the most indispensable for

---

[1]   Henry Wansey (1751–1827).
[2]   Henry Bradshaw Fearon (b. c.1770).
[3]   George Glover (1778–1862).
[4]   John Woods (1785–1861).
[5]   Cobbet employed the pseudonym in two volumes of essays published in the late 1790s.
[6]   Thomas Ashe (1770–1835); Isaac Weld (1774–1856).
[7]   William Faux published *Memorable Days in America* in 1823.
[8]   Captain Frederick Marryat (1792–1848); Captain Thomas Hamilton (1789–1842); Godfrey Thomas Vigne (1801-1863).
[9]   Jacksonian Democracy refers to the movement toward increased popular participation in government during Andrew Jackson's (1767–1845) tenure as President of the United States.

the development of the country. Above all. Because the new travellers included so many authors in search of literary material, American weaknesses were exposed with merciless and often consummate skill. Dickens was not mealy-mouthed at home, and, though his *American Notes* were not so very harsh, they seemed immensely so, because of his popularity in America, and because, with unerring instinct, he put his finger on the tenderest spots in American life, such as slavery. Dickens had, in fact, a number of very appreciative things to say, as did others like Hamilton, Marryat, Thackeray and Charles Augustus Murray,[1] while Harriet Martineau,[2] after careful and searching investigation, was full of praises for many aspects of American society. Unfortunately, men are prone to remember criticism and to forget praise, and Americans in particular, conscious of the newness of their nation, have always been acutely sensitive to criticism—much more so throughout their history than the smug British, long inured to abuse—and never more so than in these formative years of what Tocqueville[3] called "irritable patriotism," when English criticism was most virulent and supercilious.

The tone of it was unhappily set by critics like Basil Hall, and above all, Mrs. Trollope, whom Nevins justly describes as a "censorious harridan."[4] Her son, who made amends for his mother's bitterness in his own account of America later, described her *Domestic Manners of the Americans*[5] as "somewhat unjust ... to our cousins over the water," and as one of those works which have "created laughter on one side of the Atlantic, and soreness on the other." Her pen was veritably dipped in gall: "I do not like their principles, I do not like their manners, I do not like their occupations." Her supercilious assumption of English superiority struck Americans, as always, on the raw; religious "[p]ersecution exists [in America] to a degree unknown, I believe, in our well-ordered land since the days of Cromwell":[6] it would be hard to pack more, calculated to pain Americans, into a single short sentence. Her absolute want of sympathy may be explained by her personal difficulties; it may even be

---

[1] Sir Charles Augustus Murray (1806–1895).
[2] Harriet Martineau (1802–1876), English author and journalist.
[3] Alexis de Tocqueville (1805–1859), French politician and writer.
[4] An ill-tempered old woman.
[5] Trollope published *Domestic Manners of the Americans* in 1832.
[6] Oliver Cromwell (1599–1658), Lord Protector of England during the interregnum of the Commonwealth.

pardoned to her for the gallant struggle she made to support and bring up her family, but it cannot be forgotten. Her ill-humoured comment on American lawlessness contrasts too painfully with the later good humour of, for example, G.K. Chesterton.[1] She wrote: "In England the laws are acted upon, in America they are not"; his words were: "The Americans may go mad when they make laws, but they recover their reason when they disobey them."

But before the tolerance of Chesterton could replace the contumely of Mrs. Trollope a respite was needed. This was provided by the years from approximately 1845 to 1870, a period of narration and description, or what Nevins calls unbiased portraiture. Akin in tone to the first years of the relationship, its accounts are less practical in object and wider in scope, but the "incorrect and caricatured" reports, as William E. Baxter[2] called them, fall into disrepute. There are still some hostile voices, such as Edward Sullivan, Hugh Seymour Tremenheere, and Nassau William Senior,[3] but they are once more drowned out by those of juster critics, such as Sir Charles Lyall, Lord Carlisle, Colonel Arthur Cunynghame, Lady Emmeline Stuart Wortley and Mrs. Houston.[4] Most significant were the serious and encyclopedic works of James Silk Buckingham, and, above all, Alexander Mackay.[5] Despite the difference of opinion in the Civil War between such men as W.H. Russell, who believed the Union could never be restored, and Edward Dicey,[6] who was much more favourable to the North, nearly all Englishmen tended to be well disposed towards the United States as a whole. This was very true of such representatives of the British working class as James D. Burn in his book, *The Working Classes in the United States*.[7] Without doubt this was to a considerable extent due to the growing English realization of the potential power of America. As Eliot Warburton[8] wrote in

---

[1]   Gilbert Keith Chesterton (1874–1936), English author.
[2]   William Edward Baxter (1825–1890).
[3]   Edward Sullivan (1852–1928); Hugh Seymour Tremenheere (1804–1893); Nassau William Senior (1790–1864).
[4]   Sir Charles Lyall (1845–1920); George William Frederick Howard, Earl of Carlisle (1806–1864); Colonel Arthur Cunynghame (1812–1884); Lady Emmeline Stuart Wortley (1806–1855); Matilda Charlotte Houston (c.1815–1892).
[5]   James Silk Buckingham (1786–1855); Alexander Mackay (1808–1852).
[6]   Sir William Howard Russell (1820–1907); Edward Dicey (1832–1911).
[7]   James Drummond Burn (1823–1864) posthumously published *Three Years among the Working-Classes in the United States during the War* in 1865.
[8]   Eliot Warburton (1810–1852).

1846: "Most of the present generation among us have been brought up and lived in the idea that England is supreme in the Congress of Nations ... but ... this giant son will soon tread on his parent's heels." By 1870 Britain was almost overtaken, and there began the first period of serious and comprehensive analysis, of the quality as well as the scale of which the mere list of the leading names gives ample proof: Rudyard Kipling, James Bryce, H.G. Wells, Matthew Arnold, Herbert Spencer,[1] E.A. Freeman, Frederic Harrison,[2] Arnold Bennett,[3] and G.K. Chesterton. In this era a second Mrs. Trollope, Sir Lepel Griffin,[4] was a curious anomaly, whose name is lost to all but the specialist. Not that the British were no longer critical. Bryce himself, the greatest figure of them all in Anglo-American relations, made plain his dislike of corruption in politics. Arnold, as might be expected, found plenty of the same Philistinism[5] that he denounced at home. Spencer and Kipling echo the criticism of political corruption. Wells spoke out against the extreme manifestations of capitalism which were equally his target in Britain. But the criticisms were based on sound information and were much more just and balanced as a result; what is more, almost all the signs of offensive supercilliousness have disappeared, and an increasing warmth of appreciation pervades the whole. Brace's massive work is instinct with admiration for the United States. Bennett's account was acute and friendly, and Chesterton's amiable despite the wildness of his paradoxes—"this land had really been an asylum; even if recent legislation ... had made" some people "think it a lunatic asylum." Some works by lesser figures were important because of their thoroughness, such as James F. Muirhead's *America: The Land of Contrasts*,[6] or their enthusiasm, such as William Archer's *America To-day*[7] and W.T. Stead's *Americanization of the World*,[8] all three published between 1898 and 1902. Even Kipling, who did not mince matters—he characterised the American spittoon as "of infinite and generous gape" and remarked of an American boom town: "The papers tell their

---

[1] Herbert Spencer (1820–1903), English philosopher.
[2] Frederick Harrison (1831–1923), English jurist and sociologist.
[3] Enoch Arnold Bennett (1867–1931), English novelist.
[4] Sir Lepel Henry Griffin (1840–1908).
[5] Crass or materialistic behavior.
[6] Muirhead published *America: The Land of Contrasts* in 1902.
[7] William Archer (1856–1924) published *America To-day* in 1899.
[8] William Thomas Stead (1849–1912) published *The Americanization of the World* in 1901.

readers in language fitted to their comprehension that the snarling together of telegraph wires, the heaving up of houses, and the making of money, is progress"—declared:

> Let there be no misunderstanding about the matter. I love this People, and if any contemptuous criticism has to be done, I will do it myself ... I admit everything. Their Government's provisional; their law's the notion of the moment ... and most of their good luck lives in their woods and mines and rivers and not their brains; but for all that, they be the biggest, finest, and best people on the surface of the globe! Just you wait a hundred years ... There is nothing known to man that he will not be, and his country will sway the world with one foot as a man tilts a see-saw plank!

To such criticism Americans did not find it too hard to reconcile themselves.

The fifth and final period continued this process of amelioration; from World War I onwards, and particularly during World War II, good feeling grew apace under the influence of the increasing likenesses between the two societies. There were still discordant cries, but a new note of respect and admiration for many aspects of American life tends to be dominant. As Priestley, who was by no means unreserved in his praise, put it in 1936: "America is definitely in front. She hardly knows she is leading us, but she is. Russia can turn the old economic and political system upside down, but no sooner has she done so than she takes a long look at America. One country after another follows suit." As the number of travellers increased, so did the flow of books, many of them ephemeral. But there was a residue of works of permanent value, pre-eminent among them *The American Political System*[1] of D.W. Brogan, who worthily continued the work of Bryce. Others were those of J. A. Spender,[2] who almost erred on the side of charity to the Americans in *The America of Today* (1928); of L.P. Jacks,[3] *My American Friends* (1933), who displays that insight which is so characteristic of his other works; and of Graham Hutton,[4] *Midwest at Noon* (1946), who depicts the

---

[1] Published in 1933.
[2] John Alfred Spender (1862–1942).
[3] Lawrence Pearsall Jacks (1860–1955).
[4] Graham Hutton (1904–1988).

Middle West in a fascinating period of change from isolation to something nearer to an active will to participate in international affairs. Most English commentators were impressed by the fact that the New Deal[1] brought the two countries into much closer accord, but the dominant impression, particularly after 1940, is of the growing strength and increasing warmth of Anglo-American friendship.

The picture painted by R.B. Mowat of American traveller's views of Britain, *Americans in England*,[2] is much less comprehensive than that of Nevins. Nevertheless, it makes it obvious that the attitude of American travellers has changed very much less over the years. In the first place, because American travellers to Britain were of wealthier classes, they tended to be sympathetic to the English for cultural reasons; indeed, "background" was what they were usually seeking. Because so much American business was in British hands, there were relatively few American businessmen in England in earlier days, and these might have constituted the most critical section of the well-to-do American public. This meant that there was never a very bad period in American opinion of Britain comparable with British opinion of America in the second quarter of the nineteenth century. The mere list of early American travellers, who left a mark, indicates their sympathetic attitude; Gouverneur Morris, the Federalist, who described the "madness" of war in 1812 as the work of men, "who for more than twenty years have lavished on Britain the bitterest vulgarity of Billingsgate[3] because she impressed her seamen for self-defence"; the cosmopolitan and Anglophile Washington Irving, who painted so romantic a picture of English society; Fenimore Cooper, who, though less sympathetic, seemed to be won over despite himself to something like respect, and even wrote on one occasion that "the English gentlemen stands at the head of his class in Christendom"; Emerson, who retained many close British friendships, such as that with Carlyle,[4] for over forty years: and Nathaniel Hawthorne, who said: "I seldom came into personal relations with an Englishman without beginning to like him, and feeling my favourable impression was stronger with the progress of the acquaintance. I never stood in an

---

[1] Social and political program established by U.S. President Franklin Delano Roosevelt (1933–1945).

[2] Robert Balmain Mowatt (1883–1941) published *Americans in England* in 1935.

[3] A synonym for coarse language, Billingsgate is a wharf and fish market in London on the northern bank of the Thames River.

[4] Thomas Carlyle (1795–1881), English author.

English crowd without being conscious of heredity sympathies." These men found many things in Britain to condemn, and did so freely, but they were altogether more restrained in their criticism or more sympathetic in their approach—showed, not to put too fine a point on it, better manners—than their opposite numbers. Though the correspondent of the *New York Observer* who wrote in 1831, "England to an American is not foreign," exaggerated, Henry Adams spoke for his countrymen who visited England when he wrote later: "Considering that I lose all patience with the English about fifteen times and say ... I get on with them beautifully and love them well." With the great development of friendly contacts which began in the last years of the century, the broadly sympathetic attitude of American travellers did not change materially, but simply fitted in better with the growing warmth of British views of America.

But it is a sign of the unreliability of the views of travellers as a complete guide to Anglo-American feelings, that the nineteenth century appears from them as a period of American goodwill to Britain, when in truth Anglophobia was at it height. The fact is that, though American travellers, who were few, tended to be sympathetic, the mass of the American people at home tended to be hostile; the factors which made for American hatred went deep into her history, and it was only exaggerated by her continued economic and cultural dependence on Britain. It had been in the Revolutionary period, and had waxed under the impact of the War of 1812 and the literary battle which came afterwards; it remained a powerful influence until the middle years of the century, and a significant, though declining one, for nearly a hundred years more. Only after World War II did the slumbering animosity really seem to be sinking into the grave. There is no doubt that it had been kept alive and active by British abuse in the second quarter of the century, but that the advocacy of American travellers and Anglophiles generally had done much to hasten its demise. As Mowat justly remarks: "[T]he American was more generous in his appreciation, and the Englishman less sensitive in his reaction." Mencken[1] puts it in a different way:" There is in the United States.... a formidable sect of Anglomaniacs ... but the corresponding sects of British Americophils is small and feeble though it shows a few respectable names." Though this contains some truth—that Anglophiles in America were vigorous and outspoken, partly

---

[1]   Henry Louis Mencken (1880–1956), American editor, author, and critic.

because of the challenge of widespread and violent Anglophobia—it is not correct to deny the importance of English Americophils, for one of the characteristics of Anglo-America history is that there has always been a group in each country strongly advocating the cause of co-operation with the other. Successors of the English Whigs and the American Tories of the Revolution have never been lacking, although for many decades they tended to be small minorities amongst their own people. The progress of Anglo-American friendship has in fact consisted in turning those minorities into majorities; majorities were achieved somewhere near the end of the nineteenth century, and by the middle of the twentieth, they had become overwhelming.

The course of this development was not the same in England as in America. The pro-American elements had, until the coming of democracy in the last half of the nineteenth century, been a radical and progressive minority, instead of, as in America, a conservative one. Though the American Anglophile group was predominantly wealthy, there were among the pro-American British radicals a number of great Whig aristocrats, like the first Lord Lansdowne, "full of love and kindness for America." Nor was the mass of the British people ever anti-American, in the way that the mass of the American people was anti-British; truth to tell, the impact of America upon Britain was much less than that of Britain upon America until the last quarter of the century. Britons had other interests in plenty, and were never anything like as conscious of American shafts as were Americans of British barbs. The vast majority of Englishmen were indifferent to America until the close of the nineteenth century, all the more so because of their relative political ignorance and immaturity; in America where democracy and literacy were far ahead, the feeling against Britain was genuinely popular. It follows that the anti-American feeling of the British was largely confined to a dominant Tory minority, and that it owed its violence in considerable degree to their consciousness that the great threat to the aristocratic system they represented came from the example of American democracy. In America it was a case of an Anglophile minority and an Anglophobe majority; in Britain of anti-American and pro-American minorities, and an indifferent majority. But as the cause of democracy triumphed, so did popular awareness of America and her increasing power grow, and so did the hold of the anti-American upper classes diminish. It was on the basis of a common democracy that Anglo-American friendship was finally built.

This much is clear. The hurricane of 1776 left the waters of

Anglo-American relations vastly troubled; when it looked like blowing itself out, the turbulence was renewed by the storm of 1812 and its aftermath; after that had, by the middle of the century, died away, a calm began, slowly but steadily, to settle the rough waters; by 1914 only a surface swell remained, while by 1945 there was something approaching stillness; and in 1952, despite the drop in the pressure in 1950, the barometer seemed to be set fair yet. But further than these generalities it is perilous to go. If we try to survey the unruly seas more closely and more accurately, the chart becomes so complex as to diminish rather than increase our understanding. The breezes and eddies, the winds and currents of Anglo-American emotions and attitudes are so disconcerting, variegated and uncertain, that they defy investigation in the short space at our disposal. To examine one only of the main cross currents of Anglo-American feeling is to become convinced that further elaboration of such a study merely adds confusion, but it is salutary to make the examination in order that we may become fully aware of how dangerous it is for Englishmen and Americans to sit in judgement upon one another.

III

Let us take as our example one of the hazards of this subject, the familiar accusation, which buzzes insistently through Anglo-American history, of the "materialism" and "vulgarity" of the United States. The indictment was mostly fully drawn by Henry James: "There is but one word to use in regard to them—vulgar, vulgar, vulgar. Their ignorance—their stingy, defiant, grudging attitude towards everything European—their perpetual references of all things to some American standard or precedent which exists only in their own unscrupulous wind-bags ... these things glare at you hideously." But James is a just man, and, predilections apart, sees the other point of view: "On the other hand we seem a people of *character*, we seem to have energy, capacity and intellectual stuff in ample measure. What I have pointed at as our vices are the elements of the modern man with *culture* quite left out. It's the absolute and incredible lack of *culture* that strikes you in common travelling Americans." Arnold Bennett, interestingly enough, gives him a lesson in tolerance of his countrymen: "But it ought to be remembered by us Europeans (and in sack-cloth!) that the mass of us with money to spend on pleasure are utterly indifferent to history and art ... I imagine that the American horde 'hustling for culture' ... will compare pretty favourably with the European horde in such spots as Lucerne." Nevertheless, James not only saw the other point of view, but the reason for it; in *The American* Newman says, "The fact is I have never had time to 'feel' things so very beautifully. I've had to *do* them, had to make myself felt." More than that, standing as James did on the threshold of American greatness, he was aware of the part America would play, and anxious that it should be a worthy one. His apprehension comes out in the words of Mrs. Tristram to Newman: "You're the great Western Barbarian, stepping forth in his innocence and might, gazing a while at this poor corrupt old world and them swooping down on it." The mutual feeling of discomfort in this period of cultural adjustment is epitomized in Newman's relationship with the Marquis, who "struck his guest as precautionary, as apprehensive; his manner seemed to indicate a fine nervous dread that something disagreeable might happen if the atmosphere were not kept clear of stray currents from windows opened at hazard. 'What under the sun is he afraid of?' Newman asked himself. 'Does he think I'm going to offer to swap jack-knives with him?'" The lingering flavour of aristocracy, often sweet to Englishmen but unpalatable to Americans, is seldom absent from this question; as E. A. Freeman[1] wrote, "the reading class ... of those who ... read enough and know enough to be worth talking to ... from a larger proportion of mankind than they do in England. On the other hand, the class of those who read really deeply ... is certainly much smaller." James's predilections, however, would not be gainsaved; he became, as he said, a "cockney *convaincu*,"[2] and, after moving finally to England in 1876, wrote to his brother William: "I ... am turning English all over. I desire only to feed on English life and the contact of English minds ..." He occasionally felt uneasy about this expatriate urge; as Roderick Hudson said: "It's wretched business ... this viral quarrel of ours with our own country, this everlasting impatience that so many of us feel to get out of it," and it should be noted that Roderick succumbs to the temptations of the Old World, if in a less lurid way than Harry Warrington before him. But James was fundamentally unrepentant; in 1877 he wrote that he felt more at home now in London than anywhere else in the world, and his acceptance, at his life's end, of British citizenship at the height of World War I bore fitting witness to that fact.

---

[1] Edward Augustus Freeman (1823–1892), English historian.
[2] Convinced.

But James was not alone in observing, and being fascinated by, this problem. Some saw it like him very much from the European point of view. Curiously, perhaps, Kipling was one of them, the Kipling of *Puck of Pook's Hill* and not the Kipling of *The Night Mail*,[1] and in no gentry in America, no matter how long you're there. It's against their law. "There's only rich and poor allowed." Others like Mrs. Humphry Ward in *Eleanor*,[2] though seeing all round the subject, laid more emphasis on the contribution which a young, a fresh, even a naïve America might make to the progress of mankind. But even if it be accepted that some distinction of this kind exists between the two societies, to define the American attitude precisely bristles with new and complex difficulties. Supercilious Englishmen may talk of the Almighty Dollar, but the question is not as simple as that. As James makes Newman say, "I cared for money-making, but I never cared so very terribly for the money. There was nothing else to do." Chesterton pointed out that the Englishman's ideal was leisure not labour, the American's labour not dollars, and—acutely—that the American, quite apart from any love of money, has a great love of measurement. It might even be said that the snobbery of Americans is size, and the snobbery of Englishmen antiquity. The cast of mind is in some respects utterly different: as Henry Adams put it:

> The English mind was one-sided, eccentric, systematically unsystematic, and logically illogical ... From the old-world point of view, the American had no mind; he had an economic thinking-machine which could work only on a fixed line. The American mind exasperated the European as a buzz-saw might exasperate a pine forest ... The American mind was ... a mere cutting instrument, practical, economical, sharp and direct ... Americans needed and used their whole energy, and applied it with close economy; but English society was eccentric by law and for the sake of the eccentricity itself ... Often this eccentricity bore all the marks of strength.

This was not the kind of strength that America could afford; the great melting pot had to be strongly and rigidly constructed, and a ruthless

---

[1] Kipling published *Puck of Pook's Hill* in 1906 and "With the Night Mail" in 1905.

[2] Mrs. Humphry Ward [Mary Augusta Arnold] (1851–1920), English novelist who published *Eleanor* in 1900.

pressure of public opinion—"a prairie fire" Chesterton once called it—was needed to create a strong and patriotic American nation. And the advantages were by no means all on the European side.

Rowland might be able to say in *Roderick Hudson*, "But I have the misfortune to be rather an idle man, and in Europe both the burden and the obloquy of idleness are less heavy than here," and reckon it in his heart of hearts a blessing for civilisation that it was so; but Dickens saw another truth when he wrote: "By the way, whenever an Englishman would cry 'All right!' an American cries 'Go ahead!' which is somewhat expressive of the national character of the two countries." If America owes much culturally to Britain, Britain's economic predicament at the present time can only be cured by a vigorous transfusion of the American spirit. America may be obsessed with technical progress, but technical progress is still highly necessary; as L.P. Jacks reminded his English readers as early as 1933, "standardisation is a condition absolutely essential to all forms of human originality." English lethargy and hidebound tradition are as suspect to Americans as American materialism is to Britons. As J.F. Muirhead wrote in 1898, "It is not easy for a European to the manner born to realize the sort of extravagant, nightmare effect that many of our social customs have in the eyes of our untutored American cousins ...The idea of an insignificant boy peer taking precedence of Mr. John Morley![1] [T]he necessity of backing out of the royal presence!" And, as Henry James pointed out, the English did not take to satire against themselves quite as naturally as a duck to water: "It is an entirely new sensation for them ... to be (at all delicately) *ironised* or satirised, from the American point of view, and they don't at all relish it. Their conception of the normal in such a relation is that the satire should all be on their side against the Americans." Finally, be it noted, these differences are always rendered sharper by the fact of American overstatement and English understatement; Chesterton does not exaggerate when he writes, "But the real cross-purposes come from the contrary direction of the two exaggerations, the American making life more wild and impossible than it is, and the Englishman making it more flat and farcical than it is."

Thus the complications, the reservations, the explanations, which are involved in such generalizations as this one concerning American materialism and English culture, become readily apparent. And this

---

[1]   John Morley, 1st Viscount Morley of Blackburn (1838–1923), English statesman and scholar.

is not all. When such generalizations are extended in time, they become even more unreliable, and may prove simply untrue. It is not merely that in the eighteenth century an Englishman might appear overdressed in New York, and in the twentieth an American over-dressed in London, not that Fenimore Cooper in the eighteen-twenties found that his London comforts cost him a third of what they would have done in America, while Nathaniel Hawthorne in the fifties found living more expensive in London than at home. Nor is it only that, with the passage of time, the crude material basis of society becomes encrusted with the delicate evasions of civilisation, so that Margaret Halsey could write with justice in 1938, "The English have refined upon our naïve American way of judging people by how much money they happen to have at the moment. The subtler English criterion is how much expensive, upper-class education they have been able to accord." It is not these things alone: It may be that the whole national character has changed over the years. There are certainly, it is true, remarkable instances of continuity. It is quite fasci-nating, for example, to see Kipling in 1900 forestalling Aldous Huxley and Evelyn Waugh[1] in his comments on the materialism of America's attitude to death. When he was talking to an American mortician on the subject of embalming, the undertaker said: "And I wish I could live a few generations just to see how my people keep. But I'm sure it's all right. Nothing can touch 'em after I've embalmed 'em." Kipling concludes, "Bury me cased in canvas ... in the deep sea; burn me on a back-water of the Hughli ... or whelm me in the sludge of a broken river dam; but may I never go down to the Pit grinning out of a plate-glass window, in a backless dress-coat, and the front half of black stuff dressing-gown; not though I were 'held' against the ravage of the grave for ever and ever." But, apart from the instances of continuity, there are also radical transformations. The America of 1929, the United States of H.L. Mencken and Sinclair Lewis,[2] was in many ways unrecognizable to the visitor of 1946; the development of the cultural maturity of the American people in the intervening years was phenomenal, for nothing chastens like a dose of adversity. There are many such instances, but there is in Anglo-American history one supreme example of this kind of change.

---

[1]   Evelyn Waugh (1903–1966), English satirist and the author of *The Loved One* (1948), a novel that ridicules death rites and enbalming activities at a Hollywood pet cemetery.

[2]   Sinclair Lewis (1885–1951), American novelist.

We have often had occasion to note the similarities between the two peoples, and, in particular, the way in which America has tended to assume the role played earlier by Britain. Before we accept generalizations about the materialism of the United States and our own high culture too freely, we should look at the impact made by Britain upon the rest of the world in the first half of the nineteenth century. It was not for their culture that the British were then primarily admired. George Santayana puts the matter well:

> Admiration for England, of a certain sort, was instilled into me in my youth. My father (who read the language with ease although he did not speak it) had a profound respect for British polity and British power. In this admiration there was no touch of sentiment nor even of sympathy; behind it lay something like an ulterior contempt, such as we felt for the strong exhibiting at a fair. The performance may be astonishing, but the achievement is mean. So in the middle of the nineteenth century an intelligent foreigner, the native of a country materially impoverished, could look on England for a model of that irresistible energy and public discipline which afterwards were even more conspicuous ... in the United States. It was admiration for material progress, for wealth, for the inimitable gift of success.

Even more striking evidence of the dominance of materialism in the Britain of the Industrial Revolution is provided by the comments of Emerson during his visit to England in 1847-8. We have but to shut our inner eyes for a moment, as the remarks follow one after another, to be convinced in extraordinary fashion that they are spoken in judgement not of nineteenth-century England, but of America a century later. "The culture of the day, the thoughts and aims of men, are English thoughts and aims. A nation ... has ... obtained the ascendant, and stamped the knowledge, activity, and power of mankind with its impress. Those who resist it do not feel it or obey it less. The Russian in his snows is aiming to be English. The Turk and Chinese also are making awkward efforts to be English. The practical common-sense of modern society, the utilitarian direction which labour, laws, opinion, religion take, is the genius of the British mind." "Certain circumstances of English life are not less effective; as, personal liberty, plenty of food; ... readiness of combination among themselves for politics or for business strikes; and sense of superiority founded on habit of victory in labour and in war; and the appetite for superiority grows by feeding." "The bias of the nation is a passion for utility ... Now, their toys are steam and galvanism. They are heavy at the fine arts, but adroit at the coarse; ... the best iron-masters, colliers, wool-combers, and tanners, in Europe." "Steam is almost an Englishman." "Machinery has been applied to all work, and carried to such perfection, that little is left for the men but to mind the engines and feed the furnaces. But the machines require punctual service, and, as they never tire, they prove too much for their tenders." "What influence the English have is by brute force of wealth and power."

Even in the broader effects of all this, in everything from the seeing of sights to the smoking of marijuana, the similarity is amazing. "The young men have a rude health which runs into peccant humours. They drink brandy like water ... They chew hasheesh ... they saw a hole into the head of the 'winking Virgin,' to know why she winks; ... measure with an English footrule every cell of the Inquisition, ... every Holy of holies ... There are multitudes of rude young English ... who have made the English traveller a proverb for uncomfortable and offensive manners." "But the English stand for liberty. The conservative, money-loving English are yet liberty-loving; and so freedom is safe ... But the clam, sound ... Briton shrinks from public life, as charlatanism." "There is no country in which so absolute a homage is paid to wealth ... An Englishman ... labours three times as many hours in the course of a year, as any other European ... He works fast. Everything in England is at a quick pace. They have reinforced their own productivity by the creation of that marvelous machinery." It is needless to pursue the analogy any further. The counter to the present-day accusation of American materialism, that in the early nineteenth century England was equally materialist, can, of course, be modified by reference to the contemporary English cultural outburst and explained as the effect of a new and ill-understood industrialism upon a country where the aristocrat cultural tradition was yet able to survive. But we should have proceeded far enough to convince ourselves of the danger of further generalization: any effort here to make our outline chart of the ocean of Anglo-American emotions more detailed must be doomed to failure. We must rest content with the conclusion that, apart from a distinct deterioration in the first half of the last century, there has been a persistent ripening of Anglo-American cordiality. It is indeed the most important theme of our story.

It justly gives ground for confidence in the future of Anglo-American friendship. There may be differences as to how best to promote that future. Many would agree with Hawthorne, that it would not "contribute in the least to our mutual advantage and comfort if we were to besmear one another all over with buttery honey." Some would not, however, agree with Chesterton, that "the very worst way of helping Anglo-American friendship is to be an Anglo-American." Most would agree with Lord Halifax that the friendship which now exists between the two peoples "often demands more ... than a treaty which is negotiated in a few weeks and signed in a day. Matrimony is a more exacting affair for both parties than a commercial contract." Others, advocates of Atlantic union, might not altogether agree with him when he writes that, "there is no magic formula which, when applied to Anglo-American relations, will place and keep them for all time upon a satisfactory footing"; they could point out that part at least of his prophecy, uttered in 1947—"so, as I see it, in the case of the United States, more substantial than any treaty of alliance, *which we are unlikely to achieve,* is an association of friendship and understanding"—had already been falsified by 1949 when N.A.T.O.[1] was born. All would agree that there may be grave Anglo-American differences in the future. But it is certain that greater efforts have never been made by which such differences can be prevented from doing harm. And these positive efforts are supported by the long traditions of Anglo-American history, by the common language, by a kindred democracy, and by the strong emotional bonds of mutual friendship and dependence forged in the one hundred and forty years of Anglo-American peace.

---

[1]   North Atlantic Treaty Organization.

Appendix H: Ezra Pound, Obituary for Ford Madox Ford

[Originally published in *Nineteenth Century and After* in August 1939, Ezra Pound's obituary for Ford Madox Ford underscores Pound's special fondness for Ford, a writer whom Pound (1885–1972) had always believed to be misunderstood and unfairly ignored by the popular and academic press alike.]

There passed from us this June a very gallant combatant for those things of the mind and of letters which have been in our time too little prized.There passed a man who took in his time more punishment of one sort and another than I have seen meted to anyone else. For the ten years before I got to England there would seem to have been no one but Ford who held that French clarity and simplicity in the writing of English verse and prose were of immense importance as in contrast to the use of a stilted traditional dialect, a "language of verse" unused in the actual talk of the people, even of "the best people," for the expression of reality and emotion.

In 1908 London was full of "gargoyles," of poets, that is, with high reputation, most of whose work has gone since into the discard. At that time, and in the few years preceding, there appeared without notice various fasciculae which one can still, surprisingly, read and they were not designed for mouthing, for the "rolling out" of "ohs." They weren't what people were looking for as the prolongation of Victoria's glory.They weren't, that is, "intense" in the then sense of the word.

The justification or programme of such writing was finally (about 1913) set down in one of the best essays (preface) that Ford ever wrote.

It advocated the prose value of verse-writing, and it, along with his verse, had more in it for my generation than all the retchings (most worthily) after "quantity" (i.e., quantitative metric) of the late Laureate Robert Bridges[1] or the useful, but monotonous, in their day unduly neglected, as more recently unduly touted, metrical labours of G. Manley Hopkins.[2]

---

[1] Robert Seymour Bridges (1844–1930), English poet.
[2] Gerard Manley Hopkins (1844–1889), English Jesuit-poet and the author of "The Wreck of the *Deutschland*."

I have put it down as personal debt to my forerunners that I have had five, and only five, useful criticisms of my writing in my lifetime, one from Yeats,[1] one from Bridges, one from Thomas Hardy, a recent one from a Roman Archbishop and one from Ford, and that last the most vital, or at any rate on par with Hardy's.

That Ford was almost an *halluciné*[2] few of his intimates can doubt. He felt until it paralysed his efficient action, he saw quite distinctly the Venus immortal crossing the tram tracks. He inveighed against Yeats's lack of emotion as, for him, proved by Yeats's so great competence in making literary use of emotion.

And he felt the errors of contemporary style to the point of rolling (physically, and if you look at it as mere superficial snob, ridiculously) on the floor of his temporary quarters in Giessen[3] when my third volume displayed me rapped, fly-papered, gummed and strapped down in a jejune provincial effort to learn, mehercule,[4] the stilted language that then passed for "good English" in the arthritic milieu that held control of the respected British critical circles, Newbolt,[5] the backwash of Lionel Johnson,[6] Fred Manning,[7] the Quarterlies and the rest of 'em.

And that roll saved me at least two years, perhaps more. It sent me back to my own proper effort, namely, toward using the living tongue (with younger men after me), though none of us has found a more natural language than Ford did.

This is a dimension of poetry. It is, magari,[8] an Homeric dimension, for of Homer[9] there are at least two dimensions apart from the surge and thunder. Apart from narrative sense and the main constructive, there is this to be said of Homer, that never can you read half a page without finding melodic invention, still fresh, and that you can hear the actual voices, as of the old men speaking in the surge of the phrases.

It is for this latter quality that Ford's poetry is of high importance, both in itself and for its effect on all the best subsequent work of his time. Let no young snob forget this.

---

1   William Butler Yeats (1865–1939), Irish poet and playwright.
2   Hallucinator, lunatic.
3   Central German city.
4   Literally, "by Hercules;" an expletive or oath.
5   Sir Henry John Newbolt (1862–1938), English poet and historian.
6   Lionel Pigot Johnson (1867–1902), British poet and critic.
7   Frederic Manning (1882–1935), English writer and critic.
8   Moreover.
9   Homer, ancient Greek author of the epic poems, *The Iliad* and *The Odyssey*.

I propose to bury him in the order of merits as I think he himself understood them, first for an actual example in the writing of poetry; secondly, for those same merits more fully shown in his prose, and thirdly, for the critical acumen which was implicit in his finding these merits.

As to his prose, you can apply to it a good deal that he wrote in praise of Hudson (rightly) and of Conrad, I think with a bias toward generosity that in parts defeats its critical applicability. It lay so natural on the page that one didn't notice it. I read an historical novel at sea in 1906 without noting the name of the author. A scene at Henry VIIIth's court stayed depicted in my memory and I found years later that Ford had written it.

I wanted for private purposes to make a note on a point raised in *Ancient Lights*; I thought it would go on the back of an envelope, and found to my young surprise that I couldn't make the note in fewer words than those on Ford's actual page. That set me thinking. I did not in those days care about prose. If "prose" meant anything to me, it meant Tacitus[1] (as seen by Mackail),[2] a damned dangerous model for a young man in those days or these days in England, though I don't regret it; one never knows enough about anything. Start with Tacitus and be cured by Flaubert via Ford, or start with Ford or Maupassant and be girt up by Tacitus, after fifty it is kif, kif, all one. But a man is a pig not to be grateful to both sides.

Until the arrival of such "uncomfortables" as Wyndham Lewis, the distressful D.H. Lawrence,[3] D. Goldring,[4] G. Cannan,[5] etc., I think Ford had no one to play with. The elder generation loathed him, or at any rate such cross-section of it as I encountered. He disturbed 'em, he took Dagon[6] by the beard, publicly. And he founded the greatest *Little Review* or pre-*Little Review* of our time. From 1908 to 1910 he gathered into one fasciculus[7] the work of Hardy, H. James, Hudson, Conrad, C. Graham, Anatole France,[8] the great old-stagers, the most competent of that wholly unpleasant

---

1   Cornelius Tacitus (c.A.D. 55–c.A.D. 117), Roman historian.
2   John William Mackail (1859–1945), English translator.
3   David Herbert Lawrence (1885–1930), English novelist.
4   Douglas Goldring (1887–1960), one of Ford's biographers.
5   Gilbert Cannan (1884–1955), English historian.
6   God of fertility, widely worshiped in the Middle East, especially in Canaan.
7   Bundle.
8   Anatole France (1844–1924), French writer.

decade, Bennett, Wells, and I think, even Galsworthy.

And he got all the first-rate and high second-raters of my own decade, W. Lewis, D. H. Lawrence (made by Ford, dug out of a board school in Croydon),[1] Cannan, Walpole,[2] etc. (Eliot was not yet on the scene).

The inner story of that review and the treatment of Ford by its obtainers is a blot on London's history that time will not remove, though, of course, it will become invisible in the perspective of years.

As critic he was perhaps wrecked by his wholly unpolitic generosity. In fact, if he merits an epithet above all others, it would be "The Unpolitic." Despite all his own interests, despite all the hard-boiled and half-baked vanities of all the various lots of us, he kept on discovering merit with monotonous regularity.

His own best prose was probably lost, as isolated chapters in unachieved and too-quickly-issued novels. He persisted in discovering capacities in similar crannies. In one weekly after another he found and indicated the capacities of Mary, Jenny, Willard, Jemimah, Horatio, etc., despite the fact that they all of 'em loathed each other, and could by no stretch of imagination be erected into a compact troop of Fordites supporting each other and moving on the citadels of publication.

And that career I saw him drag through three countries. He took up the fight for free letters in Paris, he took it up again in New York, where I saw him a fortnight before his death, still talking of meritorious novels still pitching the tale of unknown men who had written the *histoire morale contemporaine*[3] truthfully and without trumpets, told this or that phase of American as seen from the farm or the boiler-works, as he had before wanted young England to see young England from London, from Sussex.

And of all the durable pages he wrote (for despite the fluff, despite the apparently aimless meander of many of 'em, he did write durable pages) there is nothing that more registers the fact of our day than the two portraits in the, alas, never-finished *Women and Men*,[4] Meary Walker and "T."[5]

---

[1] Outer borough of greater London.

[2] Sir Hugh Seymour Walpole (1884–1941), English novelist.

[3] Contemporary moral history.

[4] Published in 1923, one of Ford's collections of essays.

[5] Two of the "average people" in Ford's essay-portraits in *Women and Men*. Ford adored Walker, for whom he wrote many moving elegies. "Mr. T.," a barrister who reportedly inherited a fortune, met regularly with Ford at London's National Liberal Club.

Select Bibliography

Primary Texts

The Brown Owl: A Fairy Tale. 1891.
The Shifting of the Fire. 1892.
The Feather. 1892.
The Questions at the Well. 1893.
The Queen Flew. 1894.
Ford Madox Brown: A Record of His Life and Work. 1896.
Poems for Pictures. 1900.
The Cinque Ports. 1900.
The Inheritors: An Extravagant Story (with Joseph Conrad). 1901.
Rossetti: A Critical Essay on His Art. 1902.
Romance (with Joseph Conrad). 1903.
The Face of the Night. 1904.
The Soul of London: A Survey of a Modern City. 1905.
The Benefactor. 1905.
Hans Holbein, The Younger: A Critical Monograph. 1905.
The Fifth Queen. 1906.
The Heart of the Country: A Survey of Modern Land. 1906.
Christina's Fairy Book. 1906.
Privy Seal: His Last Venture. 1907.
From Inland. 1907.
An English Girl. 1907.
The Pre-Raphaelite Brotherhood: A Critical Monograph. 1907.
The Spirit of the People: An Analysis of the English Mind. 1907.
The Fifth Queen Crowned. 1908.
Mr. Apollo: A Just Possible Story. 1908.
The Nature of a Crime (with Joseph Conrad). 1909.
The "Half Moon". 1909.
A Call: The Tale of Two Passions. 1910.
Songs from London. 1910.
The Portrait. 1910.
The Simple Life Limited. 1911.
Ancient Lights and Certain New Reflections: Being the Memories of a Young Man. 1911.
Ladies Whose Bright Eyes: A Romance. 1911.
The Critical Attitude. 1911.

High Germany. 1912.

The Panel. 1912.

This Monstrous Regiment of Women. 1912.

The New Humpty-Dumpty. 1912.

Ring for Nancy: A Sheer Comedy. 1913.

The Desirable Alien (with Violet Hunt). 1913.

Mr. Fleight. 1913.

The Young Lovell. 1913.

Collected Poems. 1913.

Henry James: A Critical Study. 1913.

Antwerp. 1915.

The Good Soldier: A Tale of Passion. 1915.

When Blood Is Their Argument: An Analysis of Prussian Culture. 1915.

Between St. Dennis and St. George. 1915.

Zeppelin Nights: A London Entertainment (with Violet Hunt). 1915.

On Heaven and Poems Written on Active Service. 1918.

A House. 1921.

Thus to Revisit: Some Reminiscences. 1921.

The Marsden Case. 1923.

Mr. Bosphorous and the Muses: Or, A Short History of Poetry in Britain, Variety Entertainment in Four Acts. 1923.

Women and Men. 1923.

Some Do Not. 1924.

Joseph Conrad: A Personal Remembrance. 1924.

No More Parades. 1925.

A Mirror to France. 1926.

A Man Could Stand Up. 1926.

New Poems. 1927.

New York Is Not America: Being a Mirror to the States. 1927.

New York Essays. 1927.

Last Post. 1928.

A Little Less Than Gods: A Romance. 1928.

The English Novel: From the Earliest Days to the Death of Joseph Conrad. 1929.

No Enemy: A Tale of Reconstruction. 1929.

When the Wicked Man. 1931

Return to Yesterday. 1931.

The Rash Act. 1933.

It Was the Nightingale. 1933.

Henry for Hugh. 1934.

Provence: From Minstrels to the Machine. 1935.

Vive Le Roy. 1936.

Collected Poems. 1936.

Great Trade Route. 1937.

Portraits from Life. 1937.

The March of Literature: From Confucius to Modern Times. 1938.

Parade's End. 1950.

The Critical Writings of Ford Madox Ford. Ed. Frank MacShane. 1964.

Letters of Ford Madox Ford. Ed. Richard M. Ludwig. 1965.

Buckshee: Last Poems. 1966.

Selected Poems. Ed. Basil Bunting. 1971.

Your Mirror to My Times: The Selected Autobiographies and Impressions of Ford Madox Ford. Ed. Michael Killigrew. 1971.

Pound/Ford, The Story of a Literary Friendship: The Correspondence between Ezra Pound and Ford Madox Ford and Their Writings about Each Other. Ed. Brita Lindberg-Seyersted. 1982.

The Ford Madox Ford Reader. Ed. Sondra J. Stang. 1986.

A History of Our Own Times. 1988.

The Correspondence of Ford Madox Ford and Stella Bowen. Ed. Sondra J. Stang and Karen Cochran. 1993.

A Literary Friendship: Correspondence between Caroline Gordon and Ford Madox Ford. Ed. Brita Lindberg-Seyersted. 1999.

Bibliographical Studies

Harvey, David Dow. *Ford Madox Ford, 1873–1939: A Bibliography of Works and Criticism.* Princeton: Princeton University Press, 1962.

Saunders, Max. "Ford Madox Ford: Further Bibliographies." *English Literature in Transition, 1880–1920* 43.2 (2000): 131–205.

Biographical Studies

Goldring, Douglas. *The Last Pre-Raphaelite: A Record of the Life and Writings of Ford Madox Ford.* London: Macdonald, 1948.

Hunt, Violet. *The Flurried Years.* London: Hurst and Blackett, 1926.

Judd, Alan. *Ford Madox Ford.* London: Collins, 1990.

Lindberg-Seyersted, Brita. *Ford Madox Ford and His Relationship to Stephen Crane and Henry James.* Atlantic Highlands, NJ: Humanities Press International, 1987.

MacShane, Frank. *The Life and Work of Ford Madox Ford*. New York: Horizon, 1965.

Mizener, Arthur. *The Saddest Story: A Biography of Ford Madox Ford*. New York: World, 1971.

Saunders, Max. *Ford Madox Ford: A Dual Life*. Oxford: Oxford University Press, 1996.

Secor, Robert, and Marie Secor. *The Return of the Good Soldier: Ford Madox Ford and Violet Hunt's 1917 Diary*. Victoria, BC: English Literary Studies, 1983.

Critical Studies

Armstrong, Paul B. *The Challenge of Bewilderment: Understanding and Representation in James, Conrad, and Ford*. Ithaca: Cornell University Press, 1987.

Cassell, Richard A., ed. *Critical Essays on Ford Madox Ford*. Boston: G. K. Hall, 1987.

————. *Ford Madox Ford: A Study of His Novels*. Baltimore: Johns Hopkins University Press, 1961.

Gordon, Ambrose. *The Invisible Tent: The War Novels of Ford Madox Ford*. Austin: University of Texas Press, 1964.

Green, Robert. *Ford Madox Ford: Prose and Politics*. Cambridge: Cambridge University Press, 1981.

Haslam, Sara. *Fragmenting Modernism: Ford Madox Ford, the Novel, the Great War*. Manchester: Manchester University Press, 2002.

Hoffmann, Charles G. *Ford Madox Ford*. New York: Twayne, 1967.

Huntley, H. Robert. *The Alien Protagonist of Ford Madox Ford*. Chapel Hill, NC: University of North Carolina Press, 1970.

Leer, Norman. *The Limited Hero in the Novels of Ford Madox Ford*. East Lansing, MI: Michigan State University Press, 1966.

Lid, Richard Wald. *Ford Madox Ford: The Essence of His Art*. Berkeley: University of California Press, 1964.

MacShane, Frank, ed. *Ford Madox Ford: The Critical Heritage*. London: Routledge and Kegan Paul, 1972.

Meixner, John Albert. *Ford Madox Ford's Novels: A Critical Study*. Minneapolis: University of Minnesota Press, 1962.

Moser, Thomas C. *The Life in the Fiction of Ford Madox Ford*. Princeton: Princeton University Press, 1980.

Ohmann, Carol Burke. *Ford Madox Ford: From Apprentice to Craftsman*. Middleton, CT: Wesleyan University Press, 1964.

Snitow, Ann Barr. *Ford Madox Ford and the Voice of Uncertainty*. Baton Rouge, LA: Louisiana State University Press, 1984.

Stang, Sondra J. *The Presence of Ford Madox Ford*. Philadelphia: University of Pennsylvania Press, 1981.

Weiss, Timothy. *Fairy Tale and Romance in Works of Ford Madox Ford*. Lanham, MD: University Press of America, 1984.

Wiley, Paul L. *Novelist of Three Worlds: Ford Madox Ford*. Syracuse, NY: Syracuse University Press, 1962.